GO, LOVELY ROSE

They find Mrs. Henshaw at the bottom of the cellar stairs with her neck broken. Everyone assumes she has fallen. But when Rose's sister appears on the scene, she immediately begins to cry murder. And she's right! Young Hartley is the obvious suspect. Mrs. Henshaw had been his and his sister Rachel's housekeeper for many years, and there was no love lost between any of them. In fact, no one in town really liked Rose Henshaw. Her ex-husband, Francie, certainly knew how evil she could be—she ruined his life. The rest of them were simply afraid of her: young Dr. Craig, the newcomer in town; and Bix, Hartley's teenage girlfriend; her father, Hugh Bovard, editor of the local paper; and his shattered wife, Althea, still mourning the loss of her son. They all hated Rose Henshaw for one reason or another—but who hated her enough to push her down the stairs?

THE EVIL WISH

Ever since Marcia and Lucy were little girls, they would hide in the basement of their brownstone and listen in on their father's conversations. But now they are in their 30s, still living with their domineering father, and one day they eavesdrop on a very portentous revelation. Their widowed father intends to marry his secretary, give her all his money, and let her kick his daughters out of their house. In their anger and outrage, Marcia and Lucy hatch a plot to murder him. When their father and his secretary are involved in a fatal car crash, their plans prove unnecessary. But what are they to do with their murder scheme and the residual guilt—particularly when the aborted plot develops a life of its own?

Go, Lovely Rose

The Evil Wish

BY JEAN POTTS

Introduction by J. F. Norris

Stark House Press • Eureka California

GO, LOVELY ROSE / THE EVIL WISH

Published by Stark House Press
1315 H Street
Eureka, CA 95501, USA
griffinskye3@sbcglobal.net
www.starkhousepress.com

ISBN-13: 978-1-944520-65-6

Book design by Mark Shepard, SHEPGRAPHICS.COM
Cover Art by James Heimer
Proofreading by Bill Kelly

First Stark House Press Edition: February 2019

FIRST EDITION

CONTENTS

Jean Potts

by J. F. Norris

The seeds of Jean Potts' fascination with uncontrollable imagination and the dire effects of unrestrained dreaming can be seen in one of her auearliest short stories. "The Other Woman" was published in the August 24 issue of *Collier's* in 1946 and tells the story of Roxy who is having an affair with married man Keith and her obsession with his wife Mae. Keith makes the daring move of bringing Roxy to his apartment when Mae is out and that changes everything. Setting foot in the wife's home, seeing how it was decorated, seeing her clothes ("frilly fussy dresses… little high heeled slippers, the foolish hats with veils and feathers, all told their obvious story."), these observations are permanently ingrained in Roxy's mind. Mae, previously merely a name, suddenly becomes a living woman and the images and thoughts won't leave Roxy.

So one day at a local bar not far from Keith's apartment—when Roxy is busy ruminating on what Mae is like, discussing with the bartender her fanciful detective work based on her observations, and then dreaming up what Mae does when Keith is away—in walks a flighty, nervous young woman. She sidles up to Roxy and begins to spout forth her unhappiness and the discovery that her husband is having an affair. Roxy's imagination gets the better of her and she is convinced that she is talking to Mae. The conversation is revealing and confessional. Much of what Keith has said about his wife is echoed in this woman's own story. An immediate intimate friendship is created in this brief encounter as Roxy marvels at coincidences and listens raptly, ironically becoming more and more sympathetic to the troubled wife's story. The woman leaves her calling card with Roxy. She feels that they have bonded and she invites Roxy to visit her or call her in the future. When Roxy finally gets up the nerve to turn over the card and read the words printed there she is convinced she will see Mae's name and address. But of course—it's not there. The name and address are unrecognizable; the woman is a complete stranger.

That one meeting has forever changed the way the Roxy views herself in relationship to Keith and Mae. The adventure of being the other woman is destroyed, all thanks to her wild imagination and her unexpected understanding of how an abandoned wife feels. As Potts so devastatingly states the transformation:

> *"Nothing could restore the flawless portrait of Keith; the plunge that had landed her firmly on her feet, herself again, had shattered it forever."*

So many of Potts' hallmarks in her crime fiction are seen in this early short story: her mastery at everyday conversation, her predilection for ridicule, but most of all her insight into the dark recesses of human imagination and its powerful hold. Thoughts imprison her characters. Take for example the ever grieving mother Althea Bovard in *Go, Lovely Rose,* the first novel in this volume you are holding. Her mind cannot let go of her dead son Ronnie, whose memory haunts the Bovard household like a ghost. His name is never far from his mother's lips. No conversation is free from some memory or wisp of Ronnie's short difficult life. And no wonder she cannot let him go—Ronnie was developmentally delayed and severely disabled. Born with Down's syndrome, a normal life would never be his, in Althea's mind. Althea cannot forgive herself for not allowing him a longer life, for failing to find ways for him to adapt. Her grief—an extension of her inexhaustible imagination, her constant wishing how things might have been—is her punishment.

As an examination of a horrible woman's vindictive lifestyle and its effect on not just two families, but an entire town, *Go, Lovely Rose* is easily one of the most arresting and perceptive crime novels of the 1950s. Potts succeeds in finding the balance between attack and compassion in her critique of the small-minded and malicious Rose and the long lasting wounds she has caused. The murder investigation, as is the case in many of these domestic suspense novels, is both a revelation and healing for all. But the restitution of well-being and equanimity for all families involved always comes at a costly price.

In *The Evil Wish* (1963) as in her magazine short story, Potts explored the theme of powerful imaginative ideas that cannot be dismissed or repressed and must be contended with. As Roxy comes to the realization that her newly formed vision of Keith cannot be replaced with her fantasy lover, so too do sisters Marcia and Lucy learn to confront their failed murder plot. The sisters in *The Evil Wish* not only feel cheated when their father dies in an accident, robbing them of the chance to kill him, they become victims of their own imaginations as well. The murder plot may have been thwarted but the ideas have tainted their minds. They find the plot must be carried through, especially when they are victimized by an opportunistic blackmailer who has evidence of the failed murder plot. "Taint" is a perfect word to describe the way thoughts and ideas alter and poison the mind of her characters. In fact Potts uses a similar word in "The Other Woman" that encapsulates her favorite motif: "...nothing was quite the same that weekend. Her Thoughts didn't *taste* the same; it was as if Mae had somehow tinged her whole mind."

In *The Evil Wish*, perhaps the most original novel of her entire career, Potts' ingenuity lies in the exploration of evil deeds not carried out and the festering remains of criminality that never come to fruition. To say that the novel is merely about the guilty consciences of two sisters is to underestimate its complexity. Look at this scene where Marcia kills a bug:

> *"Absently she scuffed some crumbs of dirt over the caterpillar. One of God's creatures. All right; but so were roses, and you had to make a choice. You had to accept the fact that some of God's creatures were no good. The law of rose-preservation, as basic as the law of self-preservation."*

The ease with which Marcia so callously and brutally severs the bug in two with a garden trowel is mentioned repeatedly after this scene. Potts has created that resounding image as a reminder of how that evil wish has corrupted Marcia, how the ability to perpetrate a violent act has not only become much easier for her, but almost a compelling necessity.

Not surprisingly both of these novels were recognized by the Mystery Writers of America. *Go, Lovely Rose* won Potts an Edgar in 1955 for Best First Mystery Novel (an award reserved for debut novelists) while eight years later *The Evil Wish* was nominated for Best Mystery Novel of the Year.

Time and again Potts will revisit these motifs in her novels: *Lightning Strikes Twice* (1958) features Harriet, a teenage girl, who will not allow the violent death of her Uncle Winthrop to remain labeled a suicide. Her imaginative mind is often her undoing. Like Althea she too clings to memories of loved one long gone—her father whose presence is everywhere in the house ("[the house was] so steeped in Daddy's personality that again she could almost believe there was magic word to bring him back").

The Little Lie (1968) presents us with Dee, who has a habit of telling little lies and truly believing in them, depending on them to construct her own personal reality, to protect her preciously cultivated status in town. One little lie leads to more lies. A fib becomes a grand deceit and soon Dee finds herself desperately trying to reconstruct the truth without ever being found out. She can't admit to the lie, she is incapable of admitting to mistakes. And that's her fatal flaw. Potts shows a warped imagination like Dee's has even more power to change, often to destroy, than one that contains only the faintest of obsessive thoughts.

Potts helped forge the way for more women writers of "domestic suspense"—a sub-genre that focuses on married life and familiar strife, suburban communities rather than urban living—and uncovers the criminality that can arise when the pursuit of the American Dream gives in to darker impulses of greed, jealousy, adultery, and betrayal. Now decades after her novels first appeared, Jean Potts is deservedly being recognized again for her contributions to crime fiction in this fine double volume. Enjoy these two novels that often surpass in originality the work of her writer colleagues who also specialized in "domestic suspense" like Margaret Millar, Charlotte Armstrong and Celia Fremlin. Delve deep into this suburban landscape populated with deceit and grief, where wild imaginations are not as freeing as they are imprisoning, where Jean Potts showed no mercy for her troubled, complex and ultimately fascinating characters.

—November 2018
Chicago, Illinois

J. F. Norris has always been interested in neglected and unappreciated writers of crime, supernatural and adventure fiction. His blog *Pretty Sinister Books* is a seven year long labor of love that celebrates the work of authors whose books have been mostly forgotten yet are well worth reading. His writing has often led to the reissue of long out of print books like *Desert Town* by Ramona Stewart, *The Cook* by Harry Kressing, and the horror novels of John Blackburn. Most recently his essays on crime fiction have appeared in *Girl Gangs, Biker Boys and Real Cool Cats*, Valancourt Books' reissue of *The Other Passenger* by John Keir Cross and *Murder in the Closet*, the Edgar nominated non-fiction anthology on forgotten gay and lesbian mystery writers and LGBTQ motifs in Golden Age detective fiction. He lives in Chicago surrounded by shelves filled with hundreds of books still waiting to be read.

Go, Lovely Rose

BY JEAN POTTS

To My Favorite Sister

I

"Dead as they come," said the old doctor zestfully. "Don't know as I ever saw a deader woman. That's the only kind of patients I get any more, is the dead ones. Now that I'm retired, they don't trust me with anybody's still kicking." He cackled at his own joke.

"Who?" repeated young Dr. Craig. "You haven't told me who yet." He didn't like to push the old man (nearly eighty, and spry as a cricket, though names were apt to slip his mind) but at the same time, he felt, it would be nice to know the essential facts. He had come back from a confinement case in the country to find the old doctor waiting for him, all agog with his news. It had clearly been an exciting afternoon; as the old man said, he was seldom called out any more, except in emergencies.

"I haven't? Why yes, it was—" The quavery voice faltered to a stop. "Oh rats. Right on the tip of my tongue. Know it as well as I know my own. Why, yes, Mrs.—you know, she's been keeping house for the Buckmasters for years—"

"Oh," said Dr. Craig. "Mrs. Henshaw."

They smiled at each other in relief.

"Henshaw. Of course. There she was, at the foot of the cellar stairs, where they'd found her, with her neck broken. When they couldn't get you they called me. Yes sir, the old back number comes in handy once in a while. Plain case of accident, but I told them to get the sheriff up there, and the coroner. Make it official. They agreed with me." The old doctor clasped his hands in front of his round little stomach and nodded with satisfaction.

"It's all settled, then," said Dr. Craig. "Fine." He stretched out his long legs and prepared, good-humoredly, to listen to the story all over again. Tough luck for Mrs. Henshaw. But one thing about it, it had brightened the old doctor's afternoon; it would keep him in conversation for weeks to come.

II

"She's dead, Rachel. Dead as a mackerel. Fell down the cellar steps and broke her neck."

The words seemed to leap at her out of the telephone. Her brother's voice—blurred at first on account of the poor connection; the long-distance operator couldn't understand it—was all at once abnormally loud and clear.

"Dead, Hartley? Dead?" Rachel latched on to the word as if it were a brand-new one, never heard before. It would be a good idea, she decided, to sit down.

She didn't ask who. No need to. Mrs. Henshaw, she thought. Mrs. Henshaw. Dead as a mackerel. How many times, throughout their blighted childhood, had she and Hartley prayed for this? Please, God, make Mrs. Henshaw die. Make Papa get a new housekeeper. Please, God.

It had come true at last. Rachel's mind sped off like an arrow released. She and Hartley could sell the house in Coreyville now; it would pay for Hartley's college; and with her share she could— In split-second vision she saw herself in mink, or maybe sables, in something filmy and impossibly expensive, floating down a staircase on the arm of Greg Larrimore, while an audience composed exclusively of glossy blondes watched and yearned.... Childish. But she couldn't help it; it was so dismal to feel outclassed the way she did at the parties Greg sometimes took her to, and it distorted her judgment about Greg himself, and—

"It was an accident. That's what they decided. An accident," Hartley was saying, and the old taint of frightened stealth in his voice did something queer to Rachel. It jerked her back to another place, another self. For a moment she stopped being the independent young secretary with an apartment of her own in Chicago and became instead that other Rachel, that long-legged, wistful-eyed child who hadn't escaped from Mrs. Henshaw.

Nonsense. There was her own pleasant living room right in front of her, real as anything. Certainly she had escaped. So had Papa, by his own death. Hartley—But even Hartley was free now, with Mrs. Henshaw dead.

"When did it happen, Hartley? How did it happen?"

The line went blurry again. Hartley's voice took on the forlorn quality of a scratchy phonograph record. He was singing: "'Who knows how or when?'"

"Hartley," said Rachel sharply. She remembered what Myra Graves had written in her faithful Christmas letter: You might as well know it. I'm worried about that boy, the way he's been drinking lately. "Hartley, are you drunk?"

"Not me. Never more sober in my life."

"Well, then, tell me what happened."

"I don't know. That's just it, Rachel. I can't remember—" He broke off, and the pause seemed endless. Then he went on quite matter-of-factly. "Myra Graves and I found her. At the bottom of the cellar steps. She'd been there quite a while, I guess. Myra wanted to borrow a cup of sugar. That's why she came over."

"I see," said Rachel. She felt curiously out of breath. "Look, Hartley, why don't I hop on a train and come down tomorrow—"

"Don't be silly. Why should you? Don't be silly. You weren't even here when it happened. You couldn't—" Again the breaking off, the endless pause. "That's not why I called you. There's nothing you can do. It's all been done. No reason for you to get mixed up in it."

"What do you mean, mixed up in it? Hartley—" She couldn't seem to get *hold* of anything. "Hartley, is something wrong?"

"Not a thing. What could be righter? She's dead at last, all's right with the world. Remember how we used to pray? Remember—" There was such a long silence, this time, that Rachel thought the line must have gone completely dead. But Hartley's voice wavered across the miles to her once more. "I can't remember. Isn't that funny? I can't remember." Then came a click and a hum. He had hung up.

She sat still, in obscure alarm. And urgency: she ought to be doing something. Like what? Call Hartley back, insist on extracting some sense out of him? No use. There must be someone (not Greg Larrimore; oh, most definitely not Greg) she could turn to for advice. Nobody in Chicago could be expected to understand. It had to be somebody in Coreyville.

She hesitated between the two possibilities—Hugh Bovard and Myra Graves. Both of them would know what, if anything, was wrong; for that matter, everybody in Coreyville would know. But these were the two she could trust. Hugh had been Papa's best friend; for Rachel the atmosphere of warmth and reassurance that had surrounded Papa still clung to Hugh. He would tell her the truth. If it was something serious he would know what to do. If it wasn't serious (and mightn't it, after all, be just her imagination working overtime?) Hugh would—well, he might laugh at her. Not Myra, who had lived next-door for as far back as Rachel could remember. Myra would say, in her comfortable, cheery voice, I don't blame you a bit, I know exactly how you feel....

Myra's first words, after she had recovered from the fluster of a long-distance call, made Rachel's heart sink. "Rachel honey, I was just debating if I'd ought to call you or not. Hartley told you, I guess? About Mrs. Henshaw?"

"Yes." The question burst out of her. "Myra, what's wrong? Tell me what's wrong."

Immediately Myra's tone became guarded, and Rachel remembered about the party line. "Nothing particular wrong that I know of. It was an accident. Hartley told you that, didn't he? It was an accident."

"But he sounded so—"

"He's a little upset," said Myra quickly. "Only natural, finding her the way we did, and all. You know Hartley. Kind of high-strung."

"He kept saying he can't remember. What did he mean, he can't remember?"

"Oh, that." There was an uneasy silence. "Well. Well, you know how Coreyville is. The least little thing, and people start talking...."

The telephone in Rachel's hand felt slippery. People were talking. It was an accident, but people were talking. "Myra. Tell me straight out. Should I come home?"

Myra's answer came in a rush, and to Rachel nothing could have been a more powerful endorsement of her own rising panic. "Yes. Yes, I think maybe you better come."

III

She had told Myra she would catch the afternoon train. Instead, she made the morning one, so of course no one met her. She was the only passenger for Coreyville, and as she stepped off the train and saw the platform deserted in the failing light of winter afternoon, a wave of lonesomeness washed over her. Already the train was moving off, whistling around the bend in forlorn dignity. Across the tracks Coreyville's Main Street, wider, emptier than she remembered from seven years ago, straggled off up the hill, with the court house at the top.

She picked up her bag, and a voice behind her said, "Was you expecting to be met? There's a phone inside, if you wanted to call."

The depot agent, Mr. Garrett, was standing there, peering at her from under his green eyeshade. His alert, wrinkled little face brightened. "Now wait a minute, I ought to know you, don't tell me.... Why sure. You're Doc Buckmaster's girl. Rachel Buckmaster. Sure. Know you any place." He shook her hand with a triumphant flourish. "Yessir. Why, you was nothing but a kid when you left. Fleshed up a little since then, ain't you? I was just saying to the wife the other day, says, 'Wonder whatever became of Rachel Buckmaster?' What put me in mind of it, was Old Lady Henshaw passing on."

Was there more than just friendly curiosity in his manner? A kind of avid speculation, perhaps? Rachel shifted from one foot to the other.

"A terrible thing, to go like that." Mr. Garrett shook his head with mournful relish. "All alone in the house when it happened, far as anybody knows. Laid there quite a spell, I guess, before they found her. Yes. Well, it comes to us all. Let's see, you ain't been back to Coreyville since your Papa passed away, I guess, and that's been—"

"Three years," said Rachel, "and I didn't come back then." (It had been the summer of her Canadian vacation; the message hadn't reached her in time. Which, perhaps, was just as well. It would have seemed too strange to see Papa no longer in a hurry, minus his big booming laugh and genial doctor's manner.)

"That's right," said Mr. Garrett, "you didn't get back then, did you? Slipped my mind there for a minute." She could see the wheels going round in his head: Seems funny, she couldn't make it for her Papa's funeral, but here she is for Old Lady Henshaw's. Right johnny on the spot. Can't tell me there was any love lost between them, either, even if the old lady was all the mother Rachel can remember. Hated each other like poison. Yet here she is. Seems funny. Seems funny.

"Too bad Hartley ain't here to meet you," Mr. Garrett was beginning; then, as his attention focused on something behind Rachel, his voice rose to a holler. "Hey, Doc! Hey! Hold on a minute! There's Doc Craig," he explained, indicating a rather battered coupe that was bumping its way across the tracks toward Main Street. "He'll give you a ride home. It'll beat walking."

Rachel's protests got lost in the shuffle. Dr. Craig—a stranger to her; he had taken over Papa's practice three years ago—turned out to be youngish and on the homely side. He said he was pleased to meet her, and hop right in, he'd be glad to give her a lift.

He wasn't like Mr. Garrett. He didn't chatter. By the time they were past Main Street Rachel was beginning to develop forebodings about his very lack of conversation. Might Dr. Craig's silence be as significant, in its way, as Mr. Garrett's talkativeness? She stole a glance at him, and found that he was giving her a pretty thorough inspection. He grinned, cool as you please.

"How does the old home town look to you?" He tossed it out with an air of mock-politeness, as though, having sized her up as the prim type, he had no objection to playing along with the small talk she probably expected. During the remaining three blocks they agreed on the weather (raw, even for February) and Chicago (Dr. Craig had taken his training there; he liked it too). Rachel relaxed. He might be a cool customer, this Dr. Craig, but even Rachel's hyper-sensitive imagination could find no cause for alarm in his manner. Then they stopped in front of the house, and his face (he had a long, humorous upper lip) grew suddenly serious.

"Let me know if there's anything I can do for you," he said, and she knew that he felt sorry for her, he thought she was going to need help.

"Thank you very much." She whisked out of the car before he could help her. "Don't bother, please. I can manage. My bag isn't heavy." She slammed the car door shut and faced the house.

It was just the same. Tall and gray, with an angular bay window and two separate front porches, neither of them big enough for the rocking chair comfort of other Coreyville porches. A short distance from it, set back in the yard, and half-hidden by the trees, sat the little square box of a building that had been Papa's office. The name must still be there, in flowery letters on the dust-thick window. G. F. Buckmaster, M.D. And here was the front door, with its frosted glass picture of something like a crane, standing on one reedy leg. And the door bell, which, under her hand, gave off a husky wheeze, like an old man's voice. What if Hartley was too drunk to hear, or not there at all? What if the door was locked and she couldn't get in?

Quick steps in the hall; the red glass chandelier bloomed into light; the something-like-a-crane quaked on his one leg as the door was pulled open.

"Myra!" Rachel reached for the solid comfort of Myra Graves—the round face framed in frizzy graying hair, the plump shoulder, the cheerful voice exclaiming that for goodness' sake, we didn't expect you *yet*, here child, you must be half-froze, come on in out of the cold. Myra was here, just as she had always been, in Rachel's moments of extremity. Everything was going to be all right: Hartley would be sober, the abject child that had been Rachel would dwindle and vanish into the past, Mrs. Henshaw's spell was broken forever....

Myra's lively chatter, as she bustled down the hall, seemed indeed to place a check mark beside each item in Rachel's mind. "Now you mustn't worry about Hartley, it was the shock, finding her the way we did, that's all, just the shock... Rachel honey, you do look elegant! I always knew you'd turn out good looking, once you got past the gawky stage, and all I wish is *she* could see you in that outfit.... Not very nice to say, I guess, but you know I never had much use for her alive, and no sense changing my tune now she's gone. Funeral's all set for tomorrow. Well, no use dragging it out, she hadn't any folks except the one sister, and she's not coming—at least we didn't get any answer to the wire we sent her...."

The reassuring tide of monologue swept Rachel into the library on a wave of confidence.

She didn't see Hartley right away. The library, the room itself, overwhelmed her. Nothing was changed, it seemed, since the days when

Mrs. Henshaw used to shut Hartley and her up here with what she called their traps. The carpet still blossomed with its pattern of unlikely, faded roses; the jolly little fire (that was different; Mrs. Henshaw never would have permitted that) flickered over the heavy chairs and the black leather couch with its green "throw" that was always slipping off. Papa's traps had been consigned to the library too, and here they still were—his medical books jammed into the book cases all along one wall, and on the mantel piece his pipes and the cribbage board inlaid with mother-of-pearl.

All familiar, so familiar that Rachel half-expected Mrs. Henshaw to thrust her ill-tempered fox-face, with its wonderful crown of red hair, in at the door and scold: "How many times do I have to tell you young ones you're not to make such a mess? There, Hartley, you've got those dratted paints all over the rug! I told the Doctor that's what would happen! Rachel—Rachel, you hear me?—you pick up those doll clothes, every scrap, this minute!"

What happened instead was that Hartley—with Queenie, his old brown water spaniel, lumbering along behind—got out of his chair by the fire and crossed the room to meet her. It was three years since they had seen each other, three years since Hartley came to Chicago, right after Papa died, and Rachel had been so sure he was going to make good his escape from Mrs. Henshaw and stay. Why hadn't he listened to her arguments? Why, after that telephone call, had he insisted on coming back here?

How tall he looked! Well, he was nineteen years old, grown up. But he still moved in the uncertain, almost apologetic way that never failed to fill Rachel with a kind of angry sorrow.

"Hey there, Rachel," he said, and it was plain that he was occupied with the embarrassing question of whether or not he was expected to kiss her. They ended by shaking hands awkwardly.

The disconcerting thing about Hartley's face, Rachel found, was that it was a good deal like her own. Here were the large hazel eyes, the high forehead, the cleft chin—and yet all subtly distorted, so that Rachel felt as if she were looking at her own reflection in a pool of not quite still water.

A nightmare reflection, really, for Hartley's eyes held an expression shocking in its intensity. Rachel had no word for it. She saw it. And knew at once that everything was not going to be all right, that the assurance she had drawn from Myra's chatter was hollow, her own confidence fatuous.

To hide her panic, she turned to Queenie, who was thumping her tail in sedate welcome. "Queenie, you fat old frump," she cried—too gaily, perhaps—"What have you got to say for yourself?"

It seemed, indeed, that Queenie might be on the point of speech. Her faithful golden eyes gazed into Rachel's earnestly; the tight brown curls on her sides heaved a little. In a way, Queenie was a symbol, living proof of the fact that on one occasion Papa had defied Mrs. Henshaw. Hartley's going to have a dog, Papa had said; that's all there is to it. No boy of mine is going to be raised without a dog. And who, thought Rachel, would know more about Hartley than Queenie, with her lifetime of pattering at his heels in single-minded devotion? Tell me what's wrong, Rachel wanted to say, tell me....

But Queenie did not talk. She did not quite talk.

Myra did. And Hartley ground out a disconnected assortment of pleasantries in the nervous style of a schoolboy reciting. There was much flurry over hanging up Rachel's coat, settling her beside the fire. Silence, apparently, must not be permitted to fall, not for a moment. Rachel found herself chattering too.

And just when it looked as though, in spite of all their efforts, there was going to be a lull in the conversation, they were saved by Bix Bovard.

Bix didn't bother with the doorbell. She just came bursting in, breathless, as wispy as ever, and looking somehow pathetic in a scuffed leather jacket that Rachel recognized as having once belonged to Hartley. (So teen-agers still did that, thought Rachel, feeling very old indeed. It was still considered the height of something or other to get yourself up in your boy friend's clothes, and the nearer the shoulder seams came to your elbows the more real class.)

"Hey there, Gruesome," said Hartley.

"Hi." For a moment a radiance, almost a blush, suffused Bix's face. It made her nearly pretty. Her eyes were, in fact, beautiful, and always had been. Luminous, gray eyes. But her lipstick was smeared on with a fine disregard for the natural boundaries of her mouth. And her hair! It was straight, light-brown in color, and Bix had apparently cut it herself. In a poor light. With a dull pair of scissors.

"Gee, Rachel, you look stunning!" She thrust out a rather grubby hand. "I'd never have known you. I mean—"

"Oh, brother," said Hartley. "The original good will ambassador!"

Everybody laughed, and Rachel said Bix had changed too, quite grown up.

"Just as skinny, though, isn't she?" Myra Graves ran her hand affectionately over Bix's butchered hair. "I declare, doesn't your mother ever give you a square meal?"

"Of course she doesn't. My mother wouldn't give me the time of day." Bix tossed off this bleak bit of truth nonchalantly, as if she couldn't possibly care less. She lit a cigarette and grinned at Myra. "For God's sake don't look so wounded, Myra. Lots of mothers and daughters are—incompactible. I mean incompatible."

"I guess I'm old-fashioned." Myra sighed as she picked up her coat and started buttoning herself into it. But it was impossible for her to stay gloomy for more than a minute. "Now Rachel, anything I can do, you let me know. I've got the church supper on my hands tonight, or I'd have you over. But I brought Hartley some ham and baked beans, so you won't have to worry about cooking. And I'll run over, first thing in the morning."

Rachel snatched the chance and saw her to the door. "What's it all about, Myra?" she whispered. "What's the matter with Hartley?"

"Well," Myra fiddled with her coat collar. "I don't like to say anything, till you've had a chance to talk to Hartley alone—Oh, pshaw! I'll tell you what I know, and all I hope is you can straighten him out and get him to keep his mouth shut."

"Keep his mouth shut! So far that's all he's done, with me."

"Not with other people," said Myra darkly. "He's been talking foolish all over town—that's what started all the gossip. I vow, I could switch him good, the way he's been acting. Nobody saw a thing out of the way at first. We found her, Hartley and me, plain case of accident, she'd fallen and broken her neck. But then he got this notion. Can't remember, he claims, where he was or what he was doing that afternoon—"

They stared at each other helplessly.

"And the trouble is," Myra went on, "seems like nobody else knows, either. He wasn't at Business College—not that that's anything unusual, he don't go to his classes but about half the time. He wasn't at the pool hall or any of the other places where he hangs out, down town. Nobody saw hide nor hair of him, all that afternoon."

"But that's ridiculous." Rachel grasped at a straw that she would ordinarily have closed her eyes to. "He was just out drinking some place. Got tight and blanked out. It happens all the time."

"He didn't act drunk," said Myra slowly. "When I ran over to borrow a cup of sugar and we found her, I mean. He seemed all right. It was the shock, that's what I think. The shock. Oh Rachel, she was an awful sight! Her neck all out of kilter...." Myra's voice sank to a haunted whisper. Then she took a deep breath and went on. "Well, anyway. He's been asking all over town, trying to figure out where he was, and naturally it's caused a little talk. You know how Coreyville is."

Yes, Rachel knew. She had already had a sample of the talk, from Mr.

Garrett. She recognized it now: "All alone in the house when it happened, *far as anybody knows*."

"Mrs. Lang got ahold of it," Myra was continuing, "and you can imagine what a story *she's* been making of it. Especially after the fuss between Hartley and Mrs. Henshaw last week."

Rachel swallowed. "Fuss? They had a fuss?"

"A humdinger," said Myra with rueful relish. "Seems she burnt up all his pictures. You know what a great hand Hartley's always been for painting and drawing. Still is. More than ever. I've always thought the boy was pretty good at it. Not that I'm any judge of art. Well, what does Mrs. Henshaw do but burn up the whole works, all the sketches and pictures he's been working on for I don't know how long. Claimed it was by mistake, she thought it was trash."

"Trash," echoed Rachel.

"Oh, he was wild when he found it out, just wild. Hartley don't get mad very often, but when he does, watch out. He hotfooted it right down town—Mrs. Henshaw was in at Lang's Store, doing the marketing—and he sailed right into her. Mrs. Lang said she thought he was going to—" Just in time Myra caught herself.

"Everybody heard that too, I suppose," said Rachel hopelessly. "And now everybody knows he can't remember where he was when it happened. Myra, what shall I do?"

For once, Myra's stock of comforting words failed her. She just put her arms around Rachel and held her tight. "If anybody can straighten him out," she said finally, "it's you, Rachel. That's why I thought you'd ought to be here. He'll open up to you. It'll come to him, he'll remember when the shock wears off. It's just the shock." Before she hurried off into the gathering darkness, she added one thing more. "He was always good to her, Hartley was. Real good. Better than she deserved."

A feeling of unreality crept over Rachel; none of this could possibly be happening. Mrs. Henshaw was very likely not dead at all, but still lurking somewhere close at hand, ready to pounce. It was a ghostly feeling, and yet strong enough so that, as she started back to the library, Rachel caught herself moving in the old, self-effacing way, as if she should apologize for taking up space. To snap herself out of it, she shut the door behind her with an unnecessary clatter.

Hartley and Bix—and the pint of whiskey—froze into instant immobility. He had the bottle tilted up to his mouth; Bix stood close to him, waiting her turn. Their heads were turned halfway toward Rachel, and something in their attitudes made her think of derelicts, the bums on Skid Row huddling in gritty doorways, gulping down their joyless drinks. She was suddenly angry, and Bix didn't help a bit.

"Oh, oh," said Bix. Quiet and resigned. The culprit caught red-handed and facing some familiar, tiresome punishment at the hands of the righteous.

You brat, thought Rachel. You insufferable little brat. How dare you make me feel like a social worker!

"If you've going to have a drink," she said evenly, "why not have a civilized one? I could use one myself. Only—I'm sorry to be so stuffy—I think a glass and some ice would be sort of nice. If it's not too much trouble, Hartley."

"Sure. Well, sure," said Hartley, and scurried off to the kitchen, still clutching the bottle.

Rachel sat down in the Morris chair and lit a cigarette. She hoped she looked relaxed.

Bix turned to face her. "I can't help it if you think I'm an indesirable influence," she began belligerently.

"Undersirable," said Rachel. "And I can't help it either. There's just one thing, Bix. I don't see why you had to call him up three years ago, when he came to Chicago after Papa died. It *was* you, wasn't it? I don't see why you had to drag him back here. He should have gotten away from Mrs. Henshaw right then. Then none of this would have happened—"

"What do you mean, none of this?" said Bix very quickly. "I can't see that anything so terrible has happened. Au contrary. So she falls down stairs and breaks her neck. Good for her. That's what I say. Good for her. Everything's fine and dandy now." Tears sprang to her eyes; she blinked disdainfully. "Just fine and dandy."

"Here we are," said Hartley, coming in with the tray. The phrase, for Rachel, carried a wistful echo of Papa's jovial voice. "Here we are, m'boy." That was what Papa used to say, when, after a day's hunting, he and Hugh Bovard—Bix's father—used to settle down in this room for a convivial evening. Occasionally there were other cronies, but more often it was just the two of them. The editor and the doctor. Hughie and Doc. The mellow, masculine rumble of their voices, the aroma of their tobacco, the slap of the cards as they played cribbage, used to give Rachel a wonderful sense of warmth and comfort. Hughie and Doc. They had been lifelong friends, closer than brothers.

"How's your father, Bix?" she asked, and got an aridly polite "Very well, thank you," for a reply.

You couldn't call it, really, a successful social gathering. Bix, balancing herself on the slippery couch, assumed a formidably correct manner that nipped in the bud the feeble conversational shoots Rachel put out.

Hartley just sank back in his chair, withdrawn and silent.

At last the tall old clock in the corner pulled itself together with an alarming series of clicks and whirs and struck six. Hollow and deliberate, the voice of doom.

"I must be going," said Bix, springing up in relief. "Thank you for the drink. It was so nice and civilized."

IV

Now, thought Rachel. I must straighten Hartley out. I must get him to open up. When he came back from seeing Bix to the door, she produced a shaky smile and a shakier attempt at normalcy. "We've got so much to catch up on, Hartley, we won't know where to start."

"Yes," he said. Nothing more.

Silence again. Were they going to sit in this room all night long without uttering a word? At least, when they were children, they had whispered their guilty little secrets to each other, shuddered in unison at the possibility of discovery, reached for each other's hands when all hope of escape was gone.

But now it was as if Hartley and she were no longer inhabitants of the same world. She sat down on the hassock at his feet and put her hand over his, and still the distance stretched between them.

"Tell me," she said. "Tell me what happened."

Beneath her fingers Hartley's strong, nervous hand went suddenly tenser than ever. His nightmare eyes stared past her.

"There's nothing to tell. We found her at the bottom of the cellar stairs. That's all."

"But didn't you hear her fall?"

"I wasn't here. I got here just as Myra did. I was—I don't know where I was."

"Those steps always were treacherous," said Rachel a little breathlessly. "And she was always in such a sweat, to get whatever it was done. Couldn't hurry fast enough."

"I can't remember," Hartley said. "I can't remember where I was."

The fire made a sad puffing sound and flickered briefly on his rapt face. His eyes, though they were still fixed on Rachel were not seeing her. And for a moment Rachel no longer saw him. An ugly, an impossible little picture flashed between his face and hers—a picture of an old woman at the top of a murky, steep flight of stairs, bending forward (what a little push it would take); and there was the hand, crafty and powerful, reaching toward her shoulder....

It couldn't be true. It was a lie, that little picture, a lie twisted out of Rachel's own overwrought nerves. There had been no hand. There had been only Mrs. Henshaw losing her balance and plunging down the stairs, probably with one last bitter squawk against the world and all its exasperations.

Except that Hartley was seeing the picture too.

Her brother; her shy, funny, sensitive little brother. He was always good to her, Myra had said; and in a way it was true. Hartley had been less rebellious than she. He hadn't run away. But he must have wanted to. He must have longed for escape from that annihilating tongue, from those eyes that could at one glance lay waste your confidence, wither the very core of yourself. He had not escaped. Not even now.

When the doorbell wheezed they both stiffened, leaning toward each other beside the dying fire. Queenie began a growl, and stifled it, at Hartley's warning gesture.

"Don't answer it," they whispered to each other, unnecessarily. Whoever it was rang again, waited, rang again.

Rachel's heart sank at the next sound. It was unmistakable. The front door was undoubtedly opening; their caller was walking in, heading of course for the line of light under the library door.

It was the footsteps that transfixed them. Rapid, peremptory, and purposeful, those footsteps touched off in Rachel the old panicky dread; she reached for the thin comfort of Hartley's hand. Together they faced the library door, and as it opened Rachel felt the last barrier between herself and Hartley's nightmare dissolve.

Mrs. Henshaw was standing in the doorway.

V

She wore a black coat, decent rather than fashionable. Her hat had a flashing silver buckle in front, and she carried a shabby suitcase.

"Well," she said, and her edged voice attacked them, her reddish-brown eyes accused them. "It does seem like you'd let a person in."

Her hair, thought Rachel, her beautiful red hair. It's turned all white. She's dead, of course, she's lying down there at the funeral parlor; and yet here she is and we're in for another tongue-lashing.

"I'm sorry, we didn't hear the bell." It was Hartley speaking, and he was getting to his feet, crossing the room with his hand outstretched. He must be in a trance, thought Rachel. "Won't you come in?"

The voice poured on him. "I suppose you're Hartley."

He admitted it. "This is my sister Rachel," he added, and Rachel nodded like a puppet responding to a tug on the strings. Not a trance, she decided. Insanity. They had all suddenly lost their minds.

"We didn't expect you," Hartley said.

"I'm sure I don't know why not. You wired me, didn't you? Well, then. Granted we weren't as close as some sisters, I've still got enough family feeling to come to Rose's funeral, I hope." The piercing glance switched to Rachel. It was unnerving. Even though she understood now that the eyes that were impaling her were not Mrs. Henshaw's, it was still unnerving. "I must say," commented Mrs. Henshaw's sister, "I didn't expect to see *you* here. Didn't think you and Rose got along."

"Let me take your wraps, Mrs. Pierce," said Hartley, and as she whisked out of her coat he added, half to himself, "You look so much like her—"

"I don't know about now. We used to favor each other, as girls. Or so people said. I haven't seen Rose in more than fifteen years. To hear her tell it, she never could get away for a visit. Why not, I'd like to know—I wasn't going to pick up and come visit her. Just as busy as she was. Busier. And with my own family, not somebody else's."

A variation on Mrs. Henshaw's favorite theme: "I don't know why I should be expected to worry my head like this. Over somebody else's young ones. Anybody else would let you go to the orphanage, where you belong. You wouldn't have things all your own way there, I can tell you."

It was like hearing double. All through supper Rachel struggled against sinking back into the old paralyzed silence. But the nervous little stabs at conversation that she made sounded extraordinarily inane to her the moment they were uttered; she felt that they deserved the treatment Mrs. Pierce-Henshaw gave them—terse slaps of answers that disposed of them on the spot. It was no use. The layers of Rachel's poise seemed to fall away, exposing the wretch, the hopeless incompetent that Mrs. Henshaw had always said was there.

But I did run away, she reminded herself. I did scrape up enough courage for that. Courage? Or just a weakling's desperation? When it came to that, Hartley may have found his way of running away, too...

She looked across at her brother's haggard face. It revealed nothing. That careful blankness had always been Hartley's defense. I don't know, Mrs. Henshaw. I don't know anything about anything.

"Well!" Mrs. Pierce's voice cracked at them like a whip. "It's a funny thing to me that I have to bring the subject up, but it doesn't look like you're going to do it, either one of you. A person would think I didn't have the right to know. What happened to Rose?"

"I'm sorry," Rachel stammered. "We—I thought you knew—"

"How, I'd like to know? Mental telepathy?"

"It was an accident," Rachel was beginning, when Hartley spoke.

"She fell down the cellar stairs," he said dreamily, "and broke her neck."

Mrs. Pierce caught her breath. Her round, red-brown eyes, like the eyes of some fierce bird, blinked once or twice. She did not speak.

Her silence seemed to Rachel more ominous than any words could have been. Was the terrible machinery starting up, at this very moment, in Mrs. Pierce's mind? "Something funny about it, from the beginning," Mrs. Pierce might report—tomorrow, next day, maybe even tonight—to the sheriff. "Something funny about both of them. And then the way he came out with it at the supper table...."

To her own astonishment, Rachel rose to the occasion. "It happened while she was alone in the house," she began; and her voice was just right—matter-of-fact, seasoned with sympathy, sure of itself. She could see, from Mrs. Pierce's face, that it was right, it was convincing. As she went on talking she felt almost giddy with her own strength, as if she were telling Mrs. Henshaw herself that she had died in this way and no other. Not only telling her, but convincing her of it. Standing up to Mrs. Henshaw for once.

It was a small, private triumph, and it turned out to be only a stopgap. Hartley soon had them right back where they had started.

Rachel saw the terror flare in his eyes as soon as Mrs. Pierce mentioned, with genteel delicacy, "the remains." Had Rachel viewed them yet? Well then, they could all go down to the funeral parlor this evening; Mrs. Pierce wanted to make sure, anyway, that the arrangements were in order.

"No. No!" With a violent gesture Hartley pushed back his chair and stumbled to his feet. "I can't! Rachel, you know I can't!"

Again the glint appeared in Mrs. Pierce's eyes. Her mouth straightened out, just the way Mrs. Henshaw's used to when she was dealing with a tantrum.

"All right then, don't. But I must say, young man, it seems mighty funny to me, the way you're behaving. Seems to me the least you could do—"

"It's just that Hartley's upset." (I sound too nervous, Rachel thought. I mustn't sound so nervous.) "It's all been a shock to him, and he's upset."

"I guess he is," said Mrs. Pierce drily. She too rose, smoothing down the lap of her black crepe, straightening belt and cameo brooch. "Well. I'm sure it doesn't matter whether anybody goes with me. I wouldn't want to put you to any trouble. I wouldn't want to upset anybody."

"I'll go with you," Rachel hurried to assure her. "Of course I'll go with you. Hartley—"

"All right. I'll drive you down. But I'm not going in there. I won't do it. You can't make me."

The kitchen door slammed behind him, and in a moment they heard the roar of the car backing out of the driveway.

They drove the three blocks to Manning's Funeral Parlor in silence. Rachel could see Hartley's profile, stubbornly turned toward the street light, as she and Mrs. Pierce got out. He would get cold, waiting there without his overcoat. He looked cold already. And very lonely.

Mr. Manning, dealer in Dignified Services At Prices That Are Right, greeted them at the door, his voice so hushed as to be almost soundless, his manner fantastically polite. How good it was to see Rachel again, yes indeed, even under such sad circumstances. And of course this must be Mrs. Henshaw's sister; a remarkable resemblance to the departed, yes indeed, remarkable. Bowing and scraping, he ushered them into a chilly room, arranged them beside the coffin, adjusted the light, and stepped back, poised to receive the praise due him.

Mrs. Henshaw lay still at last, her thin little hands folded, as she would never have folded them, at her waist. Her hair had turned white, almost as white as Mrs. Pierce's, and again Rachel felt a queer pang of sorrow for that wonderful red hair. But even death, even Mr. Manning's art, could not keep Mrs. Henshaw from looking cross. Her brows drew together, flaring in annoyance above the sharp, haughty thrust of nose; she seemed on the point of springing up and giving Mr. Manning—or somebody—a piece of her mind.

From beside Rachel came on indignant-sounding gulp; she was startled to see tears squeezing out of Mrs. Pierce's fierce red-brown eyes.

"I just—Poor Rose, what an awful way to die—"

An awful way to die. Yes. Rachel saw again Hartley's bemused eyes, hearing again his whisper: "I was—I don't know where I was."

Mr. Manning glided forward to take charge of the bereaved sister and was promptly brushed aside. All Mrs. Pierce asked, she said, was that Rose be given a decent, respectable funeral tomorrow. Exactly what Mr. Manning was prepared to provide, yes indeed. Abstractedly Rachel listened to his smooth, hushed preview of the services.

She did not look at Mrs. Henshaw again.

And when they came out Hartley was gone. No sign of him, or of the car. Rachel steadied herself against the porch rail. Bix, of course. Hartley and Bix were no doubt tearing along some country road, or parked somewhere, huddled over another bottle of cheap whisky.

"What's happened to your brother? Gone off and left us, has he?"

Mrs. Pierce's tone implied that she was not in the least surprised; that, in fact, Hartley's disappearance was somehow gratifying to her.

"He may have gone home to get his coat. I expect it was chilly, waiting. Maybe we'll meet him on the way."

They did not meet him on the way, of course. The house was empty except for Queenie, who clicked anxiously down the hall when she heard them and did not bother to hide her disappointment that they were not Hartley.

"I'm sure he'll be along soon," Rachel said several times, and Mrs. Pierce let this feeble statement lie where it fell. Perhaps out of pity. Perhaps it was pity too that prompted her to retire to the spare room as soon as Rachel got the bed made up. Now at least Rachel could suffer without an audience.

She went back to the library; there was more wood in the box, and she took quite a little while building another fire. Then she sat and looked at it. "I don't know what to do," she said to Queenie. "I wonder what I should do."

But Queenie did not know what to do either. She padded around uneasily, ears alerted, eyes questioning.

"There's no cause for alarm," Rachel explained to Queenie. "He and Bix have simply gone off somewhere, he should have told me, but kids are like that, thoughtless, he's upset, only natural, the shock.... I can call Myra if it gets really late. Or Hugh Bovard. There is absolutely no cause for alarm."

Queenie was polite about it. She sat down and put her head on Rachel's knee. She went through all the motions of relaxing. But they were just the motions. Rachel hadn't convinced either of them.

VI

"That does it." Fritz, foreman of the *Coreyville Tribune*, switched off the big press in the back room, pushed back his green eyeshade (leaving a smear of ink on his knobby forehead), and made his standard press-day quip: "One more week's work for Jesus. The *Tribune* rides again." The other members of the *Tribune* staff—Hugh Bovard, who was the boss, and Gloria Johnson, who never missed an opportunity to refer to herself as Mr. Bovard's Girl Friday—obliged with their standard responses. Which, in Hugh's case, was no response at all. He had heard the quip too many times. Gloria, who had heard it a good many times herself, still produced her tireless smile. She just loved her job.

Sometimes Hugh wished she didn't. God knew what he'd do without her, of course. But there was something slightly alarming about all this devotion to duty, this unflagging cooperation, this willingness to serve. In any capacity. This was the thing. Any capacity. Every once in a while the idea—sly, humiliating—flitted across Hugh's mind. He spread a fresh copy of the *Tribune* out on the big table, pretending to study The Stylette display ad, secretly watching Gloria as she cheerfully, nimbly, wrapped the singles into tight gray sticks ready for the mail bags. There was a smear of ink on her forehead, too. Gloria's complexion was inclined to be spotty, and she seemed to have more than her share of teeth. But below the complexion and the teeth was this rich geography of shapely legs, trim little waist, tenderly swelling bosom. Tenderly swelling, eagerly trembling with each of Gloria's movements. The Promised Land. Wrapping the singles was another piece of dog work that had been turned over to Gloria. Would you mind if I left the bill collecting to you this month, Gloria? Would you mind if I asked you to stay overtime and help Fritz with the telephone directories? Would you mind, Gloria, if I ripped off that oh-so-proper blouse of yours, and that skirt that switches around all day long, and...

Good Lord, thought Hugh, at my age. At a time like this. Althea's birthday, and here he was ogling a kid, only half a dozen years older than Bix.

He folded up the paper and reached for his jacket. "Good layout on The Stylette, Fritz. Matter of fact, the whole paper looks pretty good this week. Thank you, ladies and gentlemen, thank you." (That was *his* standard press-day quip, to which Fritz paid no attention. Trust Gloria, though. All the teeth showed in appreciation, the Promised Land swelled and trembled.)

"We're early, too. It's only six o'clock." He had rushed things this week, on account of Althea's birthday. There was plenty of time, now, to pick up the steak he had ordered, plenty of time for the special dinner and the present and the evening at home that this time—oh surely, surely this time—would go right.

"Why shouldn't we be early?" commented Fritz. "Pretty poor pickings on the news this week. If Mrs. Henshaw hadn't busted her neck we'd be running personals on the front page."

There it was, under Hugh's hand. Mrs. Rose Henshaw Killed In Tragic Accident. (Rose, he thought; of all inappropriate names for a woman like Mrs. Henshaw. A rose by any other name. Last rose of summer. Go, lovely rose. It intrigued him, that last one. Go, lovely rose. She had gone, all right. For good and all.) Fifty-six years of age.... For nineteen years housekeeper in the home of the late Dr. G. F. Buckmaster.... Discovered by Hartley Buckmaster and Mrs. Myra Graves....

Survived by....

That had been a problem, that "Survived by." There was the sister, of course, but what about old Francie Henshaw? Should he be mentioned? Technically he was still Mrs. Henshaw's husband, though they hadn't spoken to each other for thirty years, and Francie had been known to go to fantastic lengths to avoid meeting her on the street.

They had never been able to agree on a divorce. Francie frequently declaimed on the subject to Hugh, whom he considered the only person in town worthy of his friendship. "An abomination," Francie would thunder, in revivalist accents, "the woman is an abomination upon the face of the earth."

In the end Francie himself had set the course of etiquette for the *Tribune*. So there it was: "Survived by her sister, Mrs. Viola Pierce of Westburg, and her estranged husband, Francis L. Henshaw."

"You're right, Fritz." Hugh smiled. "May Mrs. Henshaw rest in peace. She picked the right week to break her neck. There's Bix," he added, as the front door slammed and a rush of footsteps sounded through the front office and on, past linotype, cabinets and hand presses.

"Hi! News, Daddy, news. Rachel Buckmaster's back for the funeral. Got here on the four thirty train."

"So what do we do, get out an extra?" said Fritz, grinning. "You've missed the boat, kid. We'll feature it next week."

Bix made a face at him. "She looks like a million dollars, Daddy. A simply stunning black suit, and she's got long hair, done up in a, what-do-you-call-it, a—"

"A chignon?" offered Gloria, who could always supply the word you were groping for.

"Yes. A chignon. She made me feel like an absolute flump."

"So Rachel's back, is she?" Hugh took a thoughtful drag on his cigarette. "Somehow I didn't think she'd come. Though I suppose she and Hartley will want to settle things up. Well. Well, it'll be good to see Rachel again. I always liked her. Plenty of spunk."

Though, to tell the truth, he hadn't been aware of Rachel's spunk until she picked up and ran away. Maybe it had surprised her too, poor, scared-looking little thing that she had been, to find herself escaping from the Henshaw blight. Doc's daughter, he thought, and he felt the familiar pang, like homesickness. Damn, he missed Doc. If it weren't for Althea's birthday, he'd call Rachel right now.

"Okay, Miss Flump," he said, smiling at his own daughter, "do me a favor, will you? Run over to Havelka's and pick up the steak for dinner."

"On condition," said Bix. "For a price. The condition being that you buy me a black suit. Will you, Daddy? Please?"

"We'll see about that." But of course it was settled. He always bought Bix everything she wanted. And it didn't do a bit of good, it didn't make up for Althea at all.

"Oh, Daddy, you've got to! There's something so civilized about a black suit," Bix cried before she dashed off.

"She's so cute," said Gloria. "No wonder you spoil her, Mr. Bovard. She's so cute. I'll help Fritz finish up here, Mr. Bovard. I'll be glad to. Why don't you go on home? You've been looking awfully tired lately."

"Spare me the details of how I look, will you?" he said curtly. "If I'm tired it's my own business." The end of Gloria's nose quivered, as it always did when he snapped at her. Which, he supposed, was far too often. It occurred to him that he probably had a reputation for cussedness to match his father's. The Terrible-Tempered Mr. Bang, they used to call the old man, half-affectionately; maybe they were already doing the same with him.

He felt ashamed of himself. "Here," he said, "I've got another batch of passes to the movies. Why don't you and Fritz blow yourselves to a show tonight?"

Out of the corner of his eye he saw Fritz' face flush up dully, and he thought, ah ha, so Fritz had been peering at the Promised Land too, through his thick glasses. Well, more power to him.

Gloria's thanks trailed after him effusively as he headed for the front office.

He took the present for Althea out of his desk drawer and once more studied the card he had written this morning. "With all my love. Hugh." There it was. All his love, and it wasn't enough, it wasn't what she wanted. Only he couldn't stop hoping. He went on and on. Stubbornly, monotonously hoping, like a bird that knows only the one call.

"What did you get her?" Bix, with the package of meat under her arm, was looking at him with the hostile, contemptuous expression he knew so well. He ignored it. Tonight was going to be a success, come hell or high water. He was going to *make* things go right.

"You'll see. All in good time." But his joviality suddenly cracked. "Bix. Bix, did you get her something?"

"Of course I didn't. Why should I?" Her eyes met his, cruelly honest, and Hugh felt a swift throb of envy. Bix was free, she had long ago stopped hoping for anything from Althea. He envied her.

"Oh *hell*, Daddy. I'll go get her something now, if you feel that way about it."

"Skip it," he said huskily. "Come on, let's go cook the steak."

The Bovard house was on the same street as the Buckmaster's. Brick, another one of Coreyville's old-fashioned houses, set far back from the street. It was a pretty place in summer, with its tapestry of ivy on the north side, its bridal wreath bushes banking the front porch, and the cool, deep shade of its box elders and elms. But winter gave it the sad, ruined look of a decayed gentlewoman dressed in tatters. It didn't seem to Hugh that it had looked that way when he was a boy, even in the bleakest February. Yet actually there had been few changes, either inside or out, since the days when Hugh's mother and father were alive. They were still using quite a lot of the old folks' furniture. From time to time Hugh went on a buying binge, but he was apt to be carried away by grand-scale gadgets, like the electric dishwasher and the glass-enclosed shower for the bathroom. The living room, he felt, probably needed something done to it. He wasn't sure just what, and Althea didn't seem to take much interest. Even when she did, her projects were likely to wind up unfinished, abandoned after the first spurt. It was as though something had been left out of Althea, that happy ingredient that made it possible for other women to busy themselves contentedly with the details of their daily lives. She tried; time after time Hugh had seen her try, and time after time he had seen the desolation sweeping over her face: Oh, what difference does it make? What does it matter, whether the drapes are blue or green, whether there are any drapes at all....

At least there was a light on in the living room, Hugh noted as he and Bix got out of the car and crunched their way across the patches of stale snow in the yard. That was a good omen. On the really bad days Althea did not bother with the light—perhaps she did not even notice when darkness fell—and Hugh would find her sitting there, staring empty-eyed into the shadows.

"Hello, there!" she called, quite gaily, when they came in the door, and Hugh felt the lift of hope, incurable, unreasonable. Althea was curled up in a corner of the couch, a magazine in her lap. She wore a pale blue dress—she seldom wore anything but pale blue or gray—but this dress had a perky, jolly-looking little white collar.

"Happy birthday, darling," he said, and kissed her, neatly. Althea hated long, plastery kisses. "Bix and I are all set to produce the best dinner you ever sat down to." He would save the present until afterwards, he decided. Maybe he could talk Althea into having a drink with him. Maybe tonight she wouldn't draw away from him, aloof and weary, making him feel like some damn animal.

Why yes, Althea said, a drink would be nice. One of those fizzy pink drinks. "Your hands, Beatrix!" she added, in her faint, sweet voice.

"Really!"

"What—" Startled, Bix looked down at her hands. "Oh. You mean the dirt. That's from Gym. I'll wash them. In fact—" Her face flashed into a smile, and it occurred to Hugh that here was Bix's birthday present, the best she could muster up. "—I intend to take an entire, guaranteed anaesthetic shower while you and Daddy get drunk."

She clattered cheerfully up the stairs, and Hugh went out to the kitchen to make the drinks. The sink was full of dirty dishes. (The electric dishwasher hadn't made any difference; it frightened her, Althea said, all that whirring, efficient machinery.) He whistled while he got out the ice and shaker.

"You don't look a day over seventy," he told Althea jovially when he brought in the tray. "Remarkably well preserved, Mrs. Bovard."

There was, to Hugh, something heart-breaking about the remnants of his wife's prettiness. She had been an extremely pretty girl—ash-blonde, fragile as a spun-glass figure. The fragility was still there, and though the ash-blonde hair was turning white it kept its gentle, youthful curl. But grief had cut gullies in Althea's delicate face; only at rare moments—like this one—did her eyes lose their empty look. My poor darling, thought Hugh, my poor ghostly girl.

"I went to club this afternoon," she was saying now, with the bright air of a child reporting her own good conduct. For Hugh was always pleased when she went to club or anywhere else; it wasn't good for her, he said, to spend so much time alone.

"And what was cooking at club?"

"Why, let me see—Oh, Mrs. Henshaw, of course. Nobody talked about anything else. Hugh, have you heard all this gossip about Hartley?" Althea's face took on a look of gentle puzzlement. "You should have heard Mrs. Lang! She all but accused Hartley of murdering Mrs. Henshaw. In fact, she said the sheriff ought to investigate all over again—"

"Oh, my Lord!" Hugh burst out. "Somebody ought to buy that woman a muzzle. Of all the crazy, malicious gossip! It was an accident, I don't care how many quarrels Hartley had with the old witch, or where he was when it happened, it was an accident. The sheriff and everybody else is satisfied, whether Mrs. Bloodhound Lang is or not."

"An accident. Yes. Of course it was an accident." For a moment it seemed to Hugh that Althea's voice throbbed with a queer kind of excitement. It made him feel not quite comfortable; after all, no use dwelling on it. "It couldn't be anything else. She was all alone in the house, so how could it be anything else?"

She saw him watching her, and lifted her glass for another dainty sip.

Her voice got back to normal. "They all seemed to think Hartley and Rachel will sell the house. No reason why they shouldn't, now that she's dead."

That was the way Doc Buckmaster had left things, in his will. The house (which was about all Doc had left) went to Hartley and Rachel. But with the provision that Mrs. Henshaw could live in it as long as she chose to. She had so chosen. Naturally nobody was going to buy the house as long as Mrs. Henshaw went with it.

"No reason at all," said Hugh. There, Althea was all right again. She wasn't going into one of those unhealthy brooding spells of hers, after all. "It's high time Hartley got out of Coreyville. He's just wasting his time, hanging around here, pretending to go to Business College. I don't know why he didn't leave when Doc died." (As a matter of fact, Hugh had a strong suspicion that Bix was the reason. Anyway, part of the reason. They had always stuck to each other, the two lost kids.) "Rachel's back, by the way. Bix said she came on the four thirty train."

"Really? I'll bet she's not going into mourning over Mrs. Henshaw."

"Well, she turned up in a black suit that certainly caught Bix's eye. Simply stunning. End quote. But I doubt if it's out of reverence for the dear departed." A pleasant glow was beginning to spread through Hugh. Here they were, he and Althea, having a sociable drink together, gossiping like any ordinary husband and wife. He moved a little closer to her on the sofa; if only, tonight, he could go slow enough, not try to rush her....

"Let's see, Rachel's—Yes. Twenty-four. Just a month to the day older than Ronnie. Ronnie'd be twenty-four, Hugh, if we hadn't lost him—"

Hugh stiffened. "Now Althea, darling," he began uneasily. Oh God, wasn't she ever going to get over it? How could she go on like this, tearing herself to pieces over a son like Ronnie? Doc Buckmaster had told her bluntly, from the very beginning, that Ronnie wasn't ever going to be right. He had explained to both of them about Mongolism: it was one of those tragedies that happened with perfectly normal parents, nobody was sure why; there was no reason in the world why they shouldn't have other children; Ronnie would probably not live beyond the age of twelve in any case; the most sensible solution was to put him in an institution. Althea had not believed a word of it. Through the eight terrible years of Ronnie's life she had poured out every drop of her strength, every minute of every day and night, in blind, monstrous love. In a way she was still doing it. Hugh knew how she hugged her pillow at night, pretending it was Ronnie; he knew what she saw when she sat staring into the shadows on her bad days.

Ronnie at twenty-four. He shuddered involuntarily.

"That's right, Rachel's twenty-four," he said, snatching forlornly at the coziness of a moment ago. It didn't do any good to try to reason with Althea. He had tried it. He had tried everything. The only hope was to distract her. "Maybe we could drop in and see her, later on, after dinner. Or ask her over here. I'd like to see her again. Wouldn't you?"

Althea pressed her fingers against her temples and closed her eyes. "I'm so tired, Hugh. I don't know why I should be so tired."

"When do we eat?" asked Bix, plunging down the staircase and into the living room. "I'm starved." She had on a terry cloth robe and scuffs, and the wet ends of her hair stuck out in little spikes.

"Those slippers, Beatrix," said Althea. "The eternal slap, slap of those slippers. Can't you do something about them?" Bix raised her eyes heavenward in an elaborate appeal for patience and fortitude. Then she kicked the scuffs viciously. But Hugh drew a relieved sigh as he followed her out to the kitchen. At least they had gotten Althea's mind off Ronnie.

VII

The steak was, as Mr. Havelka had promised Hugh when he ordered it, tender as a virgin's—Well, anyway, tender. Even Althea's portion, which Hugh had been careful to make well done, because she couldn't stand the sight of blood. Bix's salad, too, turned out a success; for once she had exercised reasonable restraint with the hot stuff. Poor kid, she was doing her best. She dug out candles and stuck them in the center of each of the cup cakes they had for dessert, and when she and Hugh carried them in, with the tiny candle flames trembling bravely they both sang Happy Birthday To You.

"How festive!" cried Althea, and she turned her face up gladly for Hugh's kiss.

Now was the moment for the birthday present. With a ceremonial flourish he brought out the package. (Gloria had gift-wrapped it for him; the silver rosettes were her idea.) He kept his eyes fixed, hungry with anticipation, on Althea's face as she slipped off the wrappings and opened the box.

"What—" A second's blank silence—she likes it, she doesn't like it, she does, she—and then, with a shriek of undisguised horror, Althea slammed the lid back on the box and covered her eyes with her hands. The cup cake in front of her toppled over with the violence of her recoil; the candle flame winked and died against the table cloth. "Oh Hugh, how could you! It's simply—"

"What's the matter? What is it?" Bix raced around the table to her mother's place and opened the box again, exposing the handbag which, the salesgirl had assured Hugh, was exquisite, the dream handbag of every woman in the world. Genuine alligator, with a miniature alligator decorating the front, complete down to the last wrinkled leg and crafty eye.

"You don't like it," said Hugh heavily. His face, he felt, was still frozen in the silly half-smile of expectant delight. He tried to rub it away with his hand. "Never mind. I can exchange it. The girl said I could exchange it."

"It's the chickest bag I ever saw," said Bix in a loud voice.

"I just—It looks so *real*," said Althea faintly. "Those awful little fat legs, and the tail. It switched. I swear it switched."

"I wasn't too sure about it myself, but you know how it is. Highly recommended by the salesman." Hugh forced a laugh. "I can exchange it. It doesn't matter."

"It does too matter!" Suddenly Bix's face was fierce red; she crouched over her mother, her shoulders hunched in an angry-cat attitude. "I think you're horrible. You've always got to spoil everything for everybody. You can't stand it to have Daddy feel good, even for a minute. Can you? Can you? I think you're horrible. A horrible, horrible woman—"

"Bix, for God's sake, stop it."

"I do. I hate you." Bix's voice cracked exultantly.

"Bix—" Hugh got out of his chair and took a threatening step toward her. Then he saw Althea's face, and stopped. It was turned up to Bix, and it too was exultant. Her eyes glittered, her whole face was pinched with a cold, bitter triumph.

"You hate me." Althea caught her breath. "How do you think I feel about you? Don't you *know* what you did to me? Don't you know that he'd be alive, Ronnie'd be alive today if it hadn't been for you?"

"Althea, what are you—"

"And you!" She flashed the word at him venomously. "Your doing too. You and Doc Buckmaster. That brilliant family doctor, that true, true friend of yours. I can just hear him telling you, I can just imagine it. Another baby. Oh, my yes indeedy. She'll get interested in another baby.... Couldn't you see that Ronnie was all I ever *wanted?*" Her voice rose, out of control, anguished. Sank again, almost to a whisper. "And while I was having this wonderful, therapeutic other baby, he lay there and died. Died because I couldn't take care of him. Died because—"

"It was flu," said Hugh hoarsely. "You know it was—"

"Flu! I could have saved him! He died because I wasn't there! I was the only one who understood what he wanted, what he needed.... And I wasn't there. I failed him. He knew, he always knew when I wasn't there. He died because—"

It was fantastic. Hugh couldn't have struck her. But his hand seemed to have been busy at something, because here it was out in front of him, tingling slightly and there were the dull red marks on Althea's thin-skinned cheek. Dumbfounded, he stared at his own hand. Except for the shaking, it looked as usual—loose-knuckled, moderately hairy, with the worn gold signet ring. It was shaking like a Model T about to take off.

"My God, Althea." He sat down abruptly.

She was gazing, empty-eyed, at a point beyond his shoulder. After a moment she gave a long, sobbing sigh. Then she got up and walked out of the room. He heard her footsteps whispering, dragging a little, as she went upstairs.

"You're supposed to slap the patient when they get hysterical," said Bix nervously. "Standard treatment. We had it in First Aid."

"I'm glad to hear it. It's always nice to know you've done the right thing." The candle in his cup cake was still burning, and he pinched it out. Bix watched him with big, scared eyes.

"Would you care to join me in a drink?" he asked.

She looked startled, not quite approving. "Well. All right. After I do the dishes. I guess I better do the dishes first."

There was a bottle of Bourbon, half-full, in the kitchen. Hugh carried it and a glass into the living room, sat down, and poured himself a drink. Standard treatment, he thought. Get drunk. The classic reaction; the one more mistake that didn't matter because all the other mistakes had already been made. He was really gifted that way. A genius at making mistakes. They passed before his mind's eye, like a parade of cripples and freaks. The times when he had been clumsy with Althea, or selfish, or just plain unperceptive. (He always saw afterwards, when it was too late.) The things he shouldn't have done, the words he should have said—all the trifling mistakes, right up to the final blundering climax.

He sipped slowly, listening to Bix, still barefooted, paddling from dining room to kitchen, and then the hiss and whir of the dishwasher. Maybe she was crying out there; maybe he should go out and.... What was there to do for Bix? What was there to say? She was better off than he was, at that. She hated Althea, and said so. He loved Althea, and slapped her. And nothing was changed: Althea still loved neither of them, only Ronnie. Business as usual.

Not quite as usual, for Hugh. Because he would surely stop hoping now, wouldn't he? With that slap he had written finis to his flimsy chances; had, in a way, liberated himself. He didn't need to envy Bix anymore. He could be hopeless too.

There was no sound at all from upstairs. How many evenings had he sat here alone, listening to the upstairs silence, knowing that the door to her room was locked? Knowing, too, that in spite of all he could do he was going to try that locked door, very gently, very quietly, when he went upstairs. Then there were the other evenings, when he hadn't sat here alone....

He thought, fleetingly, of Gloria and the Promised Land. He might call her up, invent some forgotten chore at the office. He might just do that. Except that he had given her those movie tickets. She and Fritz and the Promised Land were no doubt installed at this moment in the stale dimness of the Elite Theater. Palpitating, one and all.

Oh, well. Even if he hadn't abdicated in favor of Fritz, it would have been the same old story. Like all the others—not any real good. Why was that? Why did he have to be the original accept-no-substitute boy?

Bix came in. Very matter-of-fact. It was quite possible she hadn't been crying out there, after all. She had a glass in her hand.

"I was just kidding," he said. "I don't really think you're old enough to drink. At least I don't think I should encourage you."

"It's unmaterial to me," said Bix loftily. She sat down on the couch and wiggled her toes. "Indian giver."

"Where's Old Faithful Hartley tonight? Way past time for him to show up, isn't it?"

"He's not coming. I told you, Rachel's here. Naturally he's not going to leave her alone, her first night here."

"That's right. I'd forgotten about Rachel. I ought to call her." But he did not move. His drink stood, neglected, on the table beside him. Inert, sunk in a haphazard reverie, he simply sat. Nothing seemed very real. Nothing except the recurrent thought, sharp as a flash of lightning: I slapped her. I *slapped* her.

The telephone split the silence. He leaped out of his chair, ridiculously alarmed. Evidently he looked ridiculous too: Bix was giggling a little. "It's one of them new-fangled contraptions, Pappy," she said. "You heard tell of it. The telephone, they call it."

"Okay, wise guy." He settled his tie and went out to the telephone in the hall.

"Hello," said the voice, and he got an immediate impression of tension. "Oh, Hugh, is that you? Hugh, this is Rachel."

"Hey there, Rachel!" He put a good deal of effort into the heartiness. "How's the big city girl?"

"Fine, just fine. I was just wondering if you'd like to run over and have a drink, for old times sake...." Again Hugh felt the flicker of panic. "Hartley seems to have absconded with your young daughter for the evening, and I thought—"

"What's that? Hartley's not with Bix. She's right here."

There was a blank silence. "She is? You're sure?" Rachel sounded very far away. "But then—Then where is he?"

Not here. Not at home.... Hugh discovered that he was sweating slightly. He glanced at his watch. Only ten, not really late. No cause for alarm. "Why, I expect he's—Look, Rachel, why don't I hop in the car and take a quick cruise around? He's probably got involved in a red-hot game of pool or something. Did he take the car?"

"Yes. Oh yes, he's got the car. I hate to put you to all this trouble—"

"No trouble at all." Suddenly he had a vivid little picture of her, sitting there alone, waiting, scared out of her wits. Yes; for some reason she was scared out of her wits. But he didn't want to take her with him, in case— Just in case. "And look, Rachel, meantime why don't I drop Bix off at your place to keep you company? Okay? Fine. Don't worry about a thing. We'll be right over."

He didn't have to explain to Bix; she had heard, and was already flying up the stairs to get dressed. Hugh paused in the hallway. There were the stairs, and at the top of them the locked door, and behind it Althea.

Bix could tell her mother where they were going. Bix could explain that they wouldn't be late.

But perhaps.... Perhaps if he apologized (as of course he must, sooner or later), perhaps if he could get her to open door, just for a minute; if he could put his arms around her, kiss her poor ravaged face and tell her....

He couldn't help himself. It was still there, the indestructible humiliating, idiot hope.

Fool, he told himself, you damn fool. But his feet paid no attention. They went right ahead, carrying him up the stairs.

VIII

Rachel couldn't make up her mind. Was she going to burst into tears or—there were moments when it seemed much more likely—into whoops of laughter?

Because there was something about Bix's face (deadpan from the moment she walked in the door) that made Rachel feel exactly like a fractious child consigned to a baby sitter who obviously had no intention of putting up with any nonsense.

"I brought my knitting," said Bix, and unfurled a complicated chunk of needles and yarn. "I'm making Hartley an Argyle sock for his birthday."

"Just one?" quavered Rachel.

"I gave him the other one for Christmas." Bix settled herself, more or less on her shoulder blades, and set the needles to plunging and flashing recklessly. Rachel and Queenie watched, fascinated.

After a while Rachel got up and made another of her excursions to the window. There was nothing to see, nothing but the bare winter trees shivering, and the street light on the corner swinging in the wind, and a crumpled newspaper skittering along the sidewalk.

"Haven't you any idea of where he might have gone?" she asked.

Bix shrugged. "Maybe he's eloped with that fat Lang dame. She's been trying to get her hooks into him all winter."

"Bix, this is serious! Don't you see—"

Bix gave her a long, steady, inscrutable look, and she swallowed the rest of the sentence. Whatever it might have been.

"Excuse me," said Bix. "I have to go to the bathroom."

Okay, Madame Defarge, thought Rachel bitterly, staring at the Argyle sock and listening to the thud of Bix's feet on the stairs. Then, as a freshly alarming idea struck her, she leaped out of her chair and across the room to the little marble topped table. The gun, Papa's gun. It was always kept loaded because, according to Papa, the only safe gun was a loaded one, and if it was gone, if Hartley had taken it— She gave a gasp of relief. It was still there.

She jerked the drawer shut, at the sounds from upstairs. A muted shriek, feet running fast. When she got out into the hall, here was Bix, galloping wild-eyed down the stairs.

"There's somebody *up* there! In the spare room! Thrashing around, kind of muttering. I opened that door by mistake...."

Rachel collapsed against the newel post, laughing feebly. "I'm sorry,

Bix. I forgot to tell you. Mrs. Pierce. She got here just after you left this afternoon. Came down on the bus."

"Mrs. Pierce! Who's she?"

"For the funeral. You know. The sister." They were both whispering. Hissing away like a couple of ham actors cast as spies.

"You might have mentioned it," said Bix. "What's she like? I mean, is she—"

"Like as two peas. I thought it was her, at first."

"No wonder Hartley took a powder. And you forgot to tell anybody. Just a little matter you overlooked. The negligence! The incredulous negligence!"

"Incredible," said Rachel, stung. "And I can't see that it's any dumber than opening the spare room when you're looking for the bathroom." She paused, suddenly struck with the real incredibility, the downright impossibility, of Bix's making such a mistake. She must know this house almost as well as she knew her own. The bathroom was at one end of the hall, and the spare room at the other, next to Mrs. Henshaw's room. Rachel opened her mouth and then closed it again. Next to Mrs. Henshaw's room. Was that what Bix had been doing, at the wrong end of the hall? But what earthly reason could she have for prowling around Mrs. Henshaw's room? Rachel stared into the limpid gray eyes. They stared back unwaveringly.

"Anybody can make a mistake," said Bix haughtily as she turned and started back up the stairs.

This time she really went to the bathroom. Rachel, feeling like a sneak, listened to make sure. Though of course it stood to reason. Bix, knowing that the spare room was occupied, wouldn't be foolhardy enough to make another try. If indeed she had made one to begin with.

It might be pure curiosity, the irresistible lure of forbidden territory. For no one was allowed in Mrs. Henshaw's room. As children, Rachel and Hartley had worked out elaborate plots for getting past that door, simply because it was against the rules. One plot actually worked. Rachel still remembered how disappointed she had been. Because Mrs. Henshaw's room turned out to be just a room, after all. No hair-raising secrets. No witch's paraphernalia, no evil-looking concoctions. Just a room with old-fashioned furniture, like that in the rest of the house—marble tops on chest of drawers and table, candlewick spread on the bed, a fancily-carved desk, a pretty little sewing chair by the window.

Bix was still mostly child, after all. She might easily have been drawn to that room just as Rachel had been, years ago. And, if Mrs. Pierce's thrashings and mutterings hadn't interrupted her, she would have been just as disappointed, for just the same reason.

Rachel scurried back to her chair in the library and arranged, for Bix's benefit, a face of innocence. Bix did the same for her. Queenie looked puzzled by the whole performance. The old clock shuddered and whanged out the time. A quarter of eleven.

"He wouldn't go up to the Business College for any reason, would he?" asked Rachel. Bix didn't even bother to answer that one.

Out of nervousness, Rachel went on, rather tartly. "I can't see why he ever enrolled there, anyway. The Coreyville Business College. It's not even accredited. And if there's anybody in the world more un-fascinated by business than Hartley I don't know who it would be. Does he actually go to classes?"

"Oh yes. I mean, every now and then he does. He thinks the adding machine is a remarkable invention."

"I bet he does."

"Well, so do I," said Bix reasonably. "I guess he figured he might as well be doing something, as long as he was going to stick around here."

"But he didn't have to stick around here! That's just the point. He could have stayed with me and gone on to school. They have adding machines in Chicago, too. Not to mention art schools. That's what Hartley ought to be doing. It's the only thing he's ever been interested in, the only thing he's any good at. No wonder he drinks too much! He must be bored to distraction."

(She was saying too much, too many tactless things. She was jittering herself into alienating her best possible ally. Bix might be misguided, but she was still devoted to Hartley. They were both on Hartley's side, and Rachel was somehow treating Bix as if they weren't.)

But Bix was listening to something else, anyway. The knitting needles stopped flashing. "That's Daddy's car," she said matter-of-factly. She got up and went into the hall with Queenie at her heels.

Rachel sprang up too, and then stopped in the middle of the room, her hands pressed tight together. Were there two sets of footsteps, or only one? Hugh must have found him; he surely wouldn't have given up the search yet. Maybe Hartley had drunk himself into immobility. Or maybe he had—done something rash. No no, he wouldn't do that, it mustn't be that. If the doorbell rang it would mean only that Hartley wasn't sober enough to navigate.

She heard Queenie's tail thumping on the hall floor (Queenie, whose ears were sharper than hers) and she gave a sob of relief. The doorbell did not ring. He was home, then. Home, and navigating. She took a few steps on her trembling legs.

Hugh Bovard came in the library door, holding out his hand and smiling. "The lost is found," he said cheerfully. (How different he looked, thought Rachel. How much older, how terribly tired.) "Safe and sound. I had a hunch he might be out at Louie's. Sure enough, there he was."

"Is he—all right?"

"Why, he's got himself sort of worked up about something. I don't know if he told you or not. Seems he blanked out, the other afternoon—" There was a mixture of caution and casualness in Hugh's voice. He ran his hands through his thick, graying hair—it had been sandy, like Bix's, last time Rachel saw him—and hunched his shoulder, in a gesture that she remembered. "He was talking a good deal, down at Louie's. Sort of wild talk. Not that anybody's going to take that kind of talk seriously."

"I'm sorry, Rachel." Hartley was standing in the doorway, very pale, with Bix behind him. "Don't cry, please don't cry, Rachel."

"I *have* to," she blurted against his shoulder. "You weren't there when we came out of Manning's, and I didn't know where you were, and—"

"I drove around. I thought maybe if I drove around a while I'd remember. I can't. It's just a blank. I asked everybody I could think of that might have seen me, and nobody did."

She must not protest. To protest would be to admit that she too had seen the ugly little picture that obsessed him. She must stop crying and help him.

"It'll come to you, Hartley. Those things always do." (Unfortunately, perhaps.) "Does anybody besides me want a drink?"

"I'll fix them," said Bix promptly. "Come on, Daddy, you can help."

"Where is she?" asked Hartley. "Mrs. Pierce?"

"Gone to bed. Hours ago."

He glanced toward the door. "She's just like her. Remember how Mrs. Henshaw used to look at us, just stand and look at us for a minute, before she pounced?"

Unwillingly, Rachel remembered.

"She makes me feel like that. As if she's going to pounce. 'Don't try to lie to me, young man. I know what you've been up to. I've got eyes in the back of my head.'"

A gust of ghostly laughter swept them. Hartley had always had a gift for mimicking Mrs. Henshaw; he used to send Rachel, and himself too, off into gales of perilous merriment. What a funny, high-spirited creature he might have been! It wasn't fair, thought Rachel. It was wrong that he should have turned into this guilt-haunted wreck.

"She's going to pounce," he repeated. "She's just like Mrs. Henshaw. Maybe she is Mrs. Henshaw, come back to get even."

"Take it easy, Hartley," said Hugh, handing around the drinks. "She'd come back if she could, all right. But she can't. So here's to her. Go, lovely rose. Bon voyage." He lifted his glass, smiling, looking a good deal more like himself than he had at first. Of course he was older. But he still had the high-spirited, confident air that Rachel had always found so reassuring.

Only Hartley was not reassured. "I've got to know for sure," he whispered. "Somehow I've got to remember."

For the first time Rachel faced the truth. Hartley did have to remember. He would never be free of Mrs. Henshaw until he knew for sure. Well, then.... How did you help someone else remember? Did you ask questions, hoping by chance to hit upon the one magic point that would turn the key? Did you talk irrelevancies, tricking the unconscious into doing its work while no one was looking? Or was it best not to talk at all—

"Well," said Mrs. Pierce from the doorway. "So you got back. High time, I must say." She wore felt house slippers—that was the reason she had taken them all by surprise—and a flannel wrapper, the color of dust. Her hair was covered by an incongruously dainty little cap. A boudoir cap. That was what Mrs. Henshaw used to call the ones she wore.

"I'm sorry if we disturbed you, Mrs. Pierce." Rachel, who, along with Hartley, had sprung up in nervous haste, collected her wits enough to introduce the Bovards. "We were just having a nightcap. Won't you come in and have one with us?"

Mrs. Pierce snorted. It appeared that she disapproved of nightcaps and of everybody who drank them. "Where were you?" she shot at Hartley, exactly as if it were her business.

Hugh rose to the occasion smoothly. "Hartley remembered an errand he'd promised to do for me. I'm afraid I'm to blame for the whole thing, and I hereby apologize. Not only for inconveniencing you and Rachel, but for disturbing your sleep."

"Sleep. I can't sleep." Mrs. Pierce sounded indignant about it, but her voice quavered ever so slightly. "I keep thinking. Poor Rose. I don't see how it could have happened."

"We don't know for sure, of course," said Rachel. "The steps are pretty steep and narrow."

"I'd like to take a look at them," said Mrs. Pierce.

Here it was, the pounce they had been waiting for. Rachel waited for someone to protest. But no one did, and as they trooped out to the kitchen a secret excitement began to take hold of her.

How did you help someone remember? If you could lay the scene, the little replica scene that would set the mind on the track that it had followed (perhaps) before.... The pattern would repeat itself, wouldn't it? Automatically the mind, the nerves and muscles, would slip back into grooves that had been worn before.

Why not? Why not? Anything was better than not knowing for sure.

Here indeed was the little replica scene. The door, the musty smell that rose from the cellar, the light bulb, dim with dust, throwing tricky shadows across the steps. And Mrs. Pierce craning her neck like an inquisitive hen. Did she know how familiar that attitude of hers was, how many times Hartley had mimicked it? ("Hartley, what have you got there in that box? Don't tell me you're trying to sneak another puppy in here behind my back!") Did she know what a perfect replica she was?

Rachel stepped back, out of the scene. Beside her Bix was watching round-eyed, her mouth slightly ajar. Hugh leaned against the kitchen table, his drink still in his hand. The murky light fell on Hartley's face: the hollow cheeks, the eyes with their widened pupils fixed, trance-like, on Mrs. Pierce.

"She was cleaning house," he said softly. "I remember that. She was charging around like crazy, cleaning house."

It was beginning. The mind that had to remember had been set on the track; the pattern—if there was one—must repeat itself. Nothing could stop it now.

"Pretty steep you said." Mrs. Pierce threw an accusing glance at Rachel. "Why, they're straight up and down." Her eye fell on Hartley. "What are you muttering about?"

"Nothing. I just—"

"Straight up and down. A public menace." Clutching the splintery hand rail, she leaned farther forward to peer. "And one of them's broken."

"It wasn't before," said Hartley. He took a step forward, and his hand, his long, strong hand, reached toward the defenseless shoulder poised there over the darkness below.

Rachel watched. She could not stop watching. A paralyzing chill crept through her; she could not even close her eyes.

"Be careful," Hartley said. "You might lose your balance." And he drew Mrs. Pierce back, turned the light switch, and shut the cellar door. His movements were quick and sure. Then, just as quickly, just as surely, he turned and went out the back door.

"*Now* where's he going?" Mrs. Pierce wanted to know. "I vow, I never saw the like!"

But Rachel and Bix (who must have caught a glimpse of his eyes too) were already brushing past her, on their way to the back porch. They stopped there. Hartley was a shadow streaking across the bare yard toward Papa's old office. In a minute a light bloomed inside the square little building.

"He pulled her back!" whispered Rachel. "He pulled her back!"

"It worked," said Bix. "He's remembered." They waited, shivering while Hartley's shadow streaked back toward them. He had a sheet of white paper in his hand.

"I remembered!" His voice was breathless but triumphant. "She's just like her, and all at once it hit me—I always high-tailed it for Papa's office when she got to cleaning house, and that's where I was—I was doing a sketch of her—it's even got the date on it—"

He put one arm around Rachel and the other around Bix, pulling them into a tight little circle. United and jubilant they stood, and for the moment Mrs. Pierce's voice was of no more importance than a gnat buzzing in the background.

"I'll thank somebody to tell me what's going on here." Mrs. Pierce was sputtering away like a wet hen. "All at once *what* hit him? That's what I want to know. There's plenty more I want to know, too. Where was he when Rose fell down those stairs? Why's he acting so peculiar? I don't mind telling you the whole thing's struck me as mighty peculiar, from the very beginning.... Where *was* he? What's he got in his hand?"

Eager-eyed, Hartley thrust the sketch toward her. "I know where I was. That's what hit me all at once!" he cried. "I remember it now. I was over in Papa's office the whole afternoon, I've even got this sketch to prove it, and so I couldn't possibly have—I mean—" Too late, he faltered into silence.

"Young man, do you know what you're saying? Have you any idea of what you're admitting? Well, I have, and—"

"He's admitting that he blanked out," said Hugh firmly. "The rest of us already knew that. He blanked out for a while, and now he's remembered where he was. That's no crime, Mrs. Pierce, and you know it as well as I do."

"I don't know anything of the kind! Don't try to tell me what I know! Here, let me see that." She snatched the sketch from Hartley's hand and turned toward the light streaming out from the kitchen door to inspect it.

Rachel's heart sank like a stone. Hartley had a caustic gift for caricature when he chose to use it, and he had chosen to use it on Mrs. Henshaw. There she was, a witch with a wart on her chin, gleefully tending a fire, her face the face of a fanatic, at once ridiculous and terrifying. No one could fail to recognize her. And no one, seeing the sketch, could doubt for a moment that Hartley hated her.

"Good God," said Hugh sorrowfully.

"What's this? What's this?" Mrs. Pierce clamped on to the sketch, eyes and hands.

"It doesn't mean anything," said Hartley. Too fast. "I was just mad at her because she burnt up all my sketches and stuff last week, and this is the way I worked it off. That's all."

Mrs. Pierce let the silence stretch out unbearably. Then she took a long breath. "That's all. Doesn't mean anything. No crime. Well, we'll just see about that. You may be satisfied there's been no crime, but I'm not, and I'm going to call the sheriff and tell him so."

IX

(Lois Dobbs, the night operator at the telephone office, said afterwards that she wasn't the least bit surprised when the call came in for the sheriff. She and her boy friend had been out at Louie's having a beer before she went on duty and with their own ears she'd heard Hartley Buckmaster asking everybody in sight where he was the afternoon Mrs. Henshaw fell down the stairs and broke her neck. If that didn't sound suspicious, then Lois didn't know what did. She'd said to her boy friend at the time, she'd said.... Well, anyway, she wasn't the least bit surprised. The sheriff was, though. Lois thought he never was going to catch on. Of course he'd been wakened up out of a sound sleep. "But Ma'am, the case is closed," he kept saying. "I know they had a quarrel last week, I've heard the talk that's been going round. But the case is closed. Death by accident. The case is closed." "Then you march right over here and re-open it," this Mrs. Pierce, this sister of Mrs. Henshaw's, snapped at him, and before he knew it he'd said "Yes, Ma'am." It gave Lois the creeps, the way the sister sounded like Mrs. Henshaw.)

It was true that Sheriff Charlie Jeffreys had been wakened out of a sound sleep. But he was new at his job—his war record, with the Marines in the Pacific, had won him the election—and therefore extra-alert when it came to performing his duties as officer of the law. It didn't take him long to pull on his pants, grab his badge and gun, jump into his Chevvie and head for the Buckmaster residence.

So little time, in fact, that they were still out on the back porch when they heard him rattling up the street.

"Here he comes," said Hugh. "Now keep your head, Hartley. Charlie's a good guy, and he's going to see how ridiculous this whole thing is. You haven't got a thing to worry about."

"We'll see about that," said Mrs. Pierce with satisfaction. "We'll see what he's got to worry about."

Maybe it was the satisfaction in her voice that did it. She did sound extraordinarily like Mrs. Henshaw, and it may have been a sort of reflex action that hurled Hartley into unreasoning panic. Anyway, he bolted. Just as Sheriff Jeffreys got out of the Chevvie, Hartley lunged down the porch steps, zigzagged for a minute across the yard, and headed finally for Myra Graves' lilac hedge.

Hugh lunged after him, seconds too late. "Don't be a fool, Hartley! Hartley, you damn fool—"

"That's him, Sheriff!" shrieked Mrs. Pierce. "Don't let him get away! There he is!"

Fifteen years ago Sheriff Jeffreys had been the fastest quarterback Coreyville High School ever produced. Thanks perhaps to the Marines, he had not lost his speed. He sprinted for the lilac hedge as if he had been shot out of a cannon.

Scrambling sounds grunts, a thud. "Don't let him shoot him," somebody kept sobbing. "Don't let him shoot him." It turned out that it was Rachel herself.

On the other side of the lilac hedge a car stopped briefly, voices called cheery good nights, footsteps tapped up the sidewalk, and then Myra Graves' voice rang out in open astonishment. "What in the world— Why, Charlie Jeffreys, what are you doing under there? Hartley! Charlie, you've hit him! Why, you ought to be ashamed—Hartley, you come right in with me, I'll fix you up in a jiffy—"

There was a good deal of confused muttering and a little more scrambling, before the three of them emerged from the hedge and crossed to the back porch. Hartley was stumbling, half-dragged, half-supported by Charlie, who was doing his best to look resolute instead of shame-faced. Myra trotted along behind, still exclaiming about band-aids and Well, she never and What in the world!

"Arrest him," screeched Mrs. Pierce. "Sheriff I want him arrested this minute. There's something wrong or he wouldn't have run. It's plain as the nose on your face."

"Yes, Ma'—" Charlie was beginning automatically, when Hugh shouldered Mrs. Pierce aside and interrupted.

"Now look here, Charlie, what are you going to arrest him *for*? There hasn't been any crime. Death by accident—that's what the doctor said and that's what the coroner decided. You've got to prove there was a crime before you go around arresting anybody. And you can't, because there wasn't. This is the craziest damn thing I ever heard of!"

"I know, Mr. Bovard, but—" Charlie's round red face got redder than ever. He remembered to keep a tight, though probably unnecessary, grip on Hartley, whose head was hanging down like a groggy fighter's. With his free hand Charlie scratched his ear. He shifted from one foot to the other. "I know, but—"

"Crazy, is it! I don't care what the doctor said or what the coroner decided. There's something wrong, and if this isn't proof enough to suit you, then I'll get more proof. I'll get to the bottom of this if it's the last—" Mrs. Pierce's red-brown eyes (they looked ready to burst into blaze) switched suddenly to Myra. "You were here. You found Rose, so I gather. Now I want the straight of it. What did you do?"

"Do? What did I do? Why, I—" Myra got a grip on herself by switching her own gaze to Charlie. She squared her shoulders and began bravely enough. "You've heard all this before, Charlie, but if certain people aren't satisfied, why I'm perfectly willing to tell it again. I've got nothing to hide, and neither has Hartley. Like I told you, I ran over to borrow a cup of sugar. Nobody answered when I knocked, so I opened the door and hollered. Still no answer. Well, anybody else, I would have just walked in and helped myself, but you know how she— So I started back home. I'd got to the hedge when I heard Hartley call out my name, so I—"

"Where was he?" demanded Mrs. Pierce. "Where'd he come from?"

Myra kept her eyes fixed desperately on Charlie. "He was there. Right there by the porch steps. I don't know where he came from. I told him how I couldn't raise anybody, so we went in and got the sugar, and then we noticed the cellar door was open, and we—we found her. Well, of course, the first thing we thought of was a doctor. Only Dr. Craig was out in the country, confinement case, so then there wasn't anything to do but call old Doc Fulbright, he don't very often take a case anymore, but—" She made the mistake of pausing, and Mrs. Pierce pounced.

"Why doesn't he? What's the matter with him?"

Myra was jarred. But still game. "Nothing's the matter with him. He's retired, gave up his practice years ago. But he still knows his business, old Doc Fulbright does, and don't let anybody tell you different. He said right off she was dead, and for us to call the sheriff. Gave it as his opinion it was an accident, but said we'd ought to call Charlie anyway."

"That's right. That's the whole story, Mrs. Pierce," Charlie confirmed—being as careful as Myra, however, to avoid getting himself impaled on those red-brown eyes. "I came over, me and Mr. Manning, he's the coroner, and we all agreed it was a clear case of accident. So Doc signed the death certificate, accidental death, due to a broken neck and a what-do-you-call-it where she'd hit the back of her head on the cabinet down at the bottom of the steps. That's it, and I don't see how anybody would have done any different."

"Well, I do," snapped Mrs. Pierce. "In the first place, they got a doctor that isn't even in practice any more. She said so. In the second place, did anybody ask where Hartley popped up from? No. Anybody think it was the least bit out of the way, him not remembering where he was till just a little while ago? Oh my, no. Not for a minute. Not even though they'd had a big quarrel—he's admitted it—just the week before. Third place, why did he run, if he's not guilty? I'd just like to have somebody explain that, if they can." She folded her arms and glared.

"That's so," said Charlie. He scratched his ear again. "You did run, Hartley. You—you resisted me."

Mrs. Pierce saw her advantage, and pressed it. "I'm glad to hear you admit it. If you can't arrest him for murder, you can arrest him for resisting an officer of the law, and after you've done that you can call in a doctor that at least claims to be in practice and find out what really happened to Rose. And I'll tell you this much, young man. If you don't do it, I'll report you to the authorities and see that they do it. I want this case re-opened, and I want something more than a half-baked investigation, and I'm going to get it."

"Well, I guess I—" began Charlie.

Unexpectedly, Hartley lifted his head; he was still swaying slightly and now Rachel could see the lump on the side of his jaw, but he spoke with deadly distinctness. "Go ahead. Arrest me. Arrest me for murder. What's the difference whether I really did it or not? I wish to God I had. That's all. I wish to God I had."

Hugh Bovard threw up his hands in a gesture of surrender, and faithful old Queenie gave a whine of distress.

(Lois Dobbs said afterwards that she wasn't the least bit surprised when the call came through for Dr. Craig, either. But it was funny, what popped into her head. *Murder. Somebody's been murdered.* It wasn't anything that Charlie Jeffreys said. He just told Doc to get over to Buckmaster's right away, so it wasn't anything he said. A premonition, you might call it, woman's intuition. Because that was just exactly what Lois thought. Murder. She remembered the way Hartley had been talking out at Louie's, and she thought, *Murder. Somebody's been murdered.*)

The waiting, it seemed to Rachel, was harder to take than Mrs. Pierce at her most waspish. First, there was the short wait for Dr. Craig. Charlie Jeffreys met him out in the hall and explained what had to be explained, and the doctor left without coming to the library. Then came the long wait, for Dr. Craig's return and his report. (How long did it take, for a doctor to find out whether somebody had been pushed down a flight of steps or had simply, accidentally fallen? How could you tell?)

They sat in the library, though the fire had long since died and it didn't occur to anybody to build a new one. Charlie Jeffreys, looking ill-at-ease but conscientious, sat close to Hartley. The rest of them except, for Mrs. Pierce, huddled together like cattle waiting for a storm, their faces blank with strain. Mrs. Pierce sat bolt upright in a straight chair beside the door, the image of suspicious vigilance. All right, ostracize me, she seemed to be saying. I'm ostracizing you, too. And what's more, I'm right. You'll see. I'm right.

Rachel kept thinking—of all things—of Mr. Manning, and how upset he must be, at having his careful handiwork on Mrs. Henshaw disturbed. Every time she tried to collect her wits and figure out something constructive, her mind played the same irresponsible trick, producing only the crestfallen face of poor Mr. Manning....

"There he is. That's Doc," said Charlie Jeffreys. He sounded scared to death, but he got up and went out to the hall—maybe out of an obscure feeling for the properties, maybe just to get away from the silence. It was twenty minutes of two, and Rachel was suddenly convinced that she could not possibly sit here and listen to the clock whang out another doom-voiced quarter hour. Voices murmured in the hall. At eighteen minutes of two she followed Charlie.

They were standing under the red-glass chandelier, Charlie and Dr. Craig. Rachel had seen him only sitting in the car this afternoon and now, distraught as she was, she caught the sleek tom-cat look of Dr. Craig's back. Her irresponsible mind again. "... administered after death," he was saying. "The fall apparently broke her neck, but her skull was fractured afterwards. And not by anything she hit on the way down, either. Something sharper. It would have killed her, if the fall hadn't. No slur on Dr. Fulbright, you understand. Anybody would have thought what he did, that she got the skull injury in the course of the fall. I would have, myself. Only there's no doubt about it, that's not what happened."

"Holy smoke!" said Charlie. "You mean somebody followed her down the steps and beat in the back of her head after she'd already broke her—" His eye fell on Rachel, and he gulped. "Holy smoke!"

"That's it," said Dr. Craig cheerfully. His back was still turned to Rachel. "If you can prove somebody pushed her in the first place you've got a nice, fat, juicy murder on your hands. All yours, kid."

Rachel gave an unobtrusive little gasp and fainted, neatly enough, against the mahogany hall piece. When she opened her eyes again, Dr. Craig was bending over her. His face simply didn't match the sleek tom-cat back. Such a plain, even homely, face, with that long upper lip and stiff, spiky-looking black hair.

"Excuse me," she said. Then she remembered. A nice, fat, juicy murder. "Hartley didn't do it," she told Dr. Craig earnestly. "He hated her, but so did somebody else. Because Hartley didn't do it. We proved it."

"Good for you," said Dr. Craig.

After that Sheriff Jeffreys took Hartley off to jail.

X

Dr. Craig slept in the back room of his office, which was up above the drug store, and ate all his meals out. This arrangement, which wrung the hearts of Coreyville's female population, suited Dr. Craig fine. Having grown up with seven brothers and sisters, he had never had the luxury of a room all to himself. He ate at odd hours, often hurriedly, and the meals he got out at Louie's or down at the Square Deal Cafe tasted good to him. So did the home-cooked dinners to which the Coreyville ladies sometimes invited him on account of their tender hearts (not to mention their eligible daughters). Food was food, as far as he was concerned. There was a tentative quality about the dinner invitations, because after all, Dr. Craig *did* have a wife when he first came, and though she hadn't stayed in Coreyville more than a couple of weeks, nobody was quite sure of his marital status.

This also suited him fine. For the nonce, anyway. For the nonce.

The morning after Hartley's arrest Dr. Craig woke up late, realized it was Sunday, and lay for a few minutes contentedly surveying his cluttered little back room and his own large feet, which stuck out beyond the end of the studio couch. He had forgotten to pull the shades again, and the winter sunshine lay in lemon-colored wafers on the dusty congoleum rug. Simultaneously the Methodist and Presbyterian church bells began ringing, loud and bossy-sounding, as if they were quarrelling over the souls of Coreyville. They had something to quarrel about all right, thought Dr. Craig affably. A real prize package: the soul of a murderer.

He couldn't quite see Hartley Buckmaster plumping for either the Methodists or the Presbyterians. But when it came to that, he couldn't quite see Hartley murdering anybody, either. Not even Mrs. Henshaw? Why not? Any logical reason?

Well, there was that sister of Hartley's. Rachel. Rachel Buckmaster.

All at once Dr. Craig found that he was no longer feeling so affable and contented. His feet were cold, for one thing. And he wished to God he'd remembered to get somebody in to clean this place up. Squalid, that's what it was. Squalid. With the obscure conviction that he was being persecuted—or anyway heckled—he stalked into the bathroom and stared moodily at his face in the mirror. What a pan. What a personality. What a life.

Daddy, what is logic? Very simple, Junior, it goes like this. Hartley has a sister, and the sister has a cleft chin. Ergo Hartley is not a murderer.

But somebody was. That was the hell of it. Somebody was, and Dr. Craig had lifted up his clarion voice and proclaimed the truth. Well, what else could he have done? Even if he had kept his mouth shut, the Pierce female would have dug up another doctor to prove her point. She might not have. Of course she would have. The woman was a steamroller. Besides, there was the matter of his conscience. A small matter. Granted. And Mrs. Henshaw deserved what she got. Granted. But wouldn't his conscience have given him a slight twinge, if he hadn't told the truth?

Very slight, he decided. Very, very slight.

It was deplorable, what a good-looking babe like Hartley's sister could do to a man's principles. And what she could do to his sense of logic was downright alarming. The realistic approach was needed, and Dr. Craig gave himself the full treatment while he shaved. Good-looking babes were fine. In their place. Which was—well, call it the field of indoor sports. Keep them there. That was the trick. Because the minute you put them on any other plane they stopped being fun and turned into trouble. You got involved, and you got hurt, and nobody knew this better than Dr. Craig.

Well, then. As long as his intentions remained strictly dishonorable, he was safe. He fought his way into his last clean white shirt and went down to the Square Deal for some coffee.

The waitress was a hefty girl named Erma, whose feet were always killing her. She and the only other customer—the kid from the filling station—were avidly discussing just exactly what you would expect. Yak, yak, yak, thought Dr. Craig. With callous lack of consideration for Erma's feet, he settled himself at the other end of the counter and propped the Chicago paper up against the sugar bowl beside him to show how he felt about conversation. Erma and the filling station kid ignored this signal.

"Hey Doc, what's the lowdown? Did Hartley really—"

Dr. Craig gave them a cold, forbidding, professional-ethics stare. "I made my report last night to the authorities, and when they see fit to release it you'll know all I do. In the meantime, Erma, what do I have to do to get a cup of coffee around here? Make it myself?"

Erma, who was accustomed to sociable little chats with Dr. Craig about her feet and last night's movie and her boy friend in the Navy, looked surprised and hurt. Which was just too damn bad, thought Dr. Craig. He fastened his eyes on the Chicago headlines, sipped his coffee, and listened for all he was worth to the conversation at the other end of the counter. Hartley had confessed. No, he hadn't, he just said he was glad she was dead.... Well, why would he say that if he hadn't...? Charlie Jeffreys had called in the state authorities; a detective was coming tomorrow to take everybody's fingerprints. Hugh Bovard was getting a Chicago lawyer for Hartley, and somebody said that proved Bix was mixed up in it too. Somebody else said Rachel Buckmaster was the one that was mixed up in it; she'd planned the whole thing because she and Hartley wanted to sell the house

Dr. Craig slammed some money down on the counter and walked out.

"What's eating on Doc?" asked the filling station kid.

"Nothing except he's tired," said Erma loyally. "You'd be tired too if you'd been up all night, messing around with Mrs. Henshaw."

Main Street was deserted. Hardly a sign of life except for Havelka's calico cat, who was taking a fastidious stroll around the butcher shop window in search of the warmest patch of sunshine. The drug store sign creaked in the raw wind, and some busybody hens a couple of blocks away started cackling. Flawless Sunday peace. It occurred to Dr. Craig that he had nothing whatever to do. He walked up the block to where his coupe was parked and got in.

The chances were that Rachel Buckmaster was not at home. She was probably over at the Bovards', or at Myra Graves'. He thought of what he would say, if by any chance she was at home. Hello, there. I was just driving past, and thought I'd drop in and see if there's anything I can do.... It sounded too officious. Making like the old friend of the family, when he hadn't even seen her until yesterday. Okay, then, too officious. Hello, there. I was just driving past, and thought I'd drop in and see if you're feeling all right this morning. That might pass; after all, she had fainted last night. A semi-professional call, in a way.

There was a long silence after he turned the doorbell. So long that he was about to take his semi-professional call (what a pity, after all that brainwork) and depart. Then the door opened, and there she was, cleft chin and all. She had on an apron, and her hands were dusty.

He wasted his brainwork, after all, by blurting out, "Did you get over your swoon?"

"My what? Oh. Very well, thank you. Look, I don't know what to think, I've found something funny, I mean I haven't found it—" She stopped helplessly. "Won't you come in?"

He was already in. "What's the matter?"

"I can't find the candlestick," she explained. Something in her manner gave him the feeling that they were resuming a conversation instead of beginning one. It was such an oddly pleasant feeling that he got right into the spirit of the thing and followed her down the hall and out into the kitchen as if he knew exactly where she was leading him, and why. The door to the cellar stairs stood open, and they paused there, peering down at the broken step. In the murky light it looked ugly and jagged, like a fresh cut.

"Morbid curiosity, I guess," said Rachel. "That's what Myra said. She stayed overnight with me. She wouldn't even let me open the door. So I waited till after she went to church."

"Naturally," said Dr. Craig wisely. "And the—er—candlestick?"

"It isn't there. Come on down, I'll show you. I was going to open the cellar window because it's always so stuffy down there, so of course I reached for the candlestick to prop it up with, and it wasn't there. It isn't anywhere. I've looked all over."

They were at the foot of the steps now. Gingerly, Dr. Craig raised the dusty little window. It needed something to prop it open, all right; the minute he let go it slammed shut.

"We always kept it right here," said Rachel. "On the floor beside the window."

"What kind of candlestick was it?"

"Brass. Old-fashioned. It had square corners. One of a pair that belonged to Mrs. Henshaw. She once told me somebody gave them to her for a wedding present. She just had the one, though. Francie kept the other one when they separated. Kept it out of spite, according to her. She said one candlestick wasn't any good to anybody. So we always used it to prop up the window. It was just the right size."

Yes. Dr. Craig thought about the back of Mrs. Henshaw's head. From Rachel's description, the candlestick would be just the right size. And the right shape. And the right weight.

"I can't imagine," began Rachel, "why anybody would move it—" Her eyes got big.

The hell you can't, thought Dr. Craig. He cleared his throat. "This is ticklish. If it's been hidden some place where your brother might have put it, it's not going to be anything to cheer about. On the other hand, if it should turn up somewhere else—in somebody else's house—then it might do him plenty of good." They exchanged a thoughtful look. "You said last night that you proved he didn't do it. How come he was arrested? Didn't you let the sheriff in on his proof?"

They leaned against the cabinet (where Mrs. Henshaw might so easily have hit her head; only she hadn't) and smoked a cigarette while Rachel explained.

"I see," he said when she had finished. "He didn't push Mrs. Pierce. Ergo—" Okay; so he was a sucker for a cleft chin. His intentions, however, were strictly dishonorable. "Ergo he didn't push Mrs. Henshaw. Sounds logical to me. A little subtle for the sheriff, maybe. He's going to want something more solid. Which brings us back to the candlestick. You covered the cellar, you said?"

"Every inch. I know all the hiding places, and it's not down here. Whoever did it must have taken the candlestick away with them. No telling where it might be, by now. In the river, maybe. Or buried somewhere."

"Unless the idea was to plant the whole thing on Hartley. In which case they might tuck it away where it would do him the most harm. Let's take a look at your father's office."

It was an easy place to search. There wasn't much in it; Dr. Craig himself had bought most of the equipment when he first came to Coreyville. There was a rolltop desk, cluttered now with Hartley's paints and sketch pads. A couple of empty cabinets. No candlestick. They went back to the house and sat down at the kitchen table to have a cup of coffee and consider their next move.

"I don't suppose you've heard anything from Mrs. Pierce this morning?" said Dr. Craig.

"No, and I don't expect to. She spent the night at the hotel, and all I hope is that they still have bedbugs. I—evicted her, you know."

"I heard you." Dr. Craig grinned. Rachel had minced no words with Mrs. Pierce last night. "You'll have to go some place else," she had said. "I won't have you in the house." Mrs. Pierce snapped out that she wouldn't think of staying; she wouldn't feel safe in this nest of murderers. But the last, soul-satisfying word had been Rachel's. "You're so right," she had said as Mrs. Pierce marched upstairs. "Believe me, Mrs. Pierce, you wouldn't *be* safe."

"Petty of me," she said now. "I ought to be ashamed. But I'm not. She's Mrs. Henshaw all over again, and so I had to tell her off—" All at once she was on the verge of tears, and Dr. Craig treated himself to a split-second daydream in which she dissolved against his manly shoulder, and he patted her—in a fatherly way, of course, at least at first, and—Instead, she stood up and banged the coffee pot on the stove. "Aren't we ever going to get rid of Mrs. Henshaw? Hasn't she done enough to Hartley and me, without this. She might at least have the decency to die a natural death. But no. She's got to get herself murdered, and she's got to have a carbon copy sister to stir everybody up—"

"Me and my choice little report," said Dr. Craig. "I wish to God I'd kept my mouth shut."

"You think that would have stopped her? Ha! Nothing can stop people like Mrs. Henshaw. I ought to know. I grew up under her thumb." She sank back into her chair. All the poise, or whatever it was that made you look twice, seemed to sift out of her, leaving a woebegone, cringing child.

Dr. Craig couldn't stand to have her look like that. The discovery shook him. Danger, signalled his twice-shy brain; Beware of Getting Involved. Proceed At Your own Risk. Remember Your Dishonorable Intentions. He got up and paced the floor. "What I can't understand—" He was surprised himself at what he said next. It was as if his mind, groping around among a lot of baffling irritations, stumbled against this and latched on to it out of sheer frustration. "What I can't understand is your father. Why the hell did he keep the woman around?"

There was a brief silence. Rachel looked down at her hands; she had straight eyelashes, like funny, tiny little brushes. Slowly, painfully, her face turned red. "He had to have somebody keep house for us," she said at last, "after my mother died. What else could he do but hire a housekeeper?"

"But it didn't have to be Mrs. Henshaw. I mean, he didn't have to keep her. He must have seen what she was doing to you and Hartley, unless he was completely blind."

"Oh no," said Rachel, "Papa wasn't blind. He knew what she was doing."

"And still he didn't fire her." It *was* odd when you thought about it—and now that Rachel had stopped cringing, Dr. Craig's mind seemed to be back in reasonably good working order. "It's almost as if—well, as if she had something on him."

"You mean blackmail?" Suddenly Rachel laughed—in relief? The notion crossed his mind.

"Why not? She was certainly the type for it. Just her dish of tea."

"Yes. Of course," said Rachel. "It's funny, I never thought of that before."

"What did you think? That they were—" He paused, and the tell-tale red showed in Rachel's face again. "So, that's the way you had it figured out. Papa and Mrs. Henshaw, romping in the hay."

The words appalled him, the moment they were out of his mouth. Craig, the diplomat, he thought in despair. Craig, weaver of the magic phrase. The Bard of Coreyville....

Rachel blinked and gave a little sigh. "Yes. Why not? It's exactly the way I had it figured out. Only I never said so. Not even to myself. Don't look so scared," she added parenthetically. "Close your mouth, it's more becoming. I'm sure Freud has an explanation for it. Maybe it's the usual thing, with girls whose fathers have housekeepers."

"Maybe," said Dr. Craig rather feebly.

"Because I don't remember anything definite that I based it on. I couldn't understand why he kept her around, either, and I'd never heard of blackmail. She did have beautiful red hair...."

"It must have been either that or blackmail." (She wants it to be blackmail, Dr. Craig was thinking. It must really have eaten on her when she was a kid.) "When it comes to that, I suppose a small town doctor would be pretty good pickings for a blackmailer."

"What do you—oh. Abor— You mean Papa might have—" She let the question dangle.

"Of course he might have," said Dr. Craig brusquely. (Any doctor with a grain of humanity might have, given the right combination of circumstances. The moral being that doctors shouldn't have humane impulses.) "So let's say she did have something on the poor guy. Where does that get us?" He answered the question himself. "It gets us nowhere. Papa might have had a motive for pushing Mrs. Henshaw downstairs. Only he wasn't here to do it. A classic example of lack of opportunity. All we've done is waste time on a dead end street. We're right back where we started."

"We could search the rest of the house for the candlestick," said Rachel. "It wouldn't have to be planted in Papa's office. Any place in the house would do. Hartley's room, or mine, or Mrs. Henshaw's. Mrs. Henshaw's room. I wonder if that's what Bix—" A peculiar expression crossed her face. She did not finish the sentence.

"What about Bix? You think she knows something?"

"Of course not. How could she? She's nothing but a kid. Come on, let's start down here."

They covered the downstairs rooms without result. It wasn't a hard job; while Mrs. Henshaw had obviously been a string-saver, she had been orderly about it. A place for everything, and everything in its place. Her bedroom upstairs, which they left till last, was fanatically tidy. Even the hairpins were sorted according to size and stowed away in little boxes.

"Depressing, isn't it? All this tidiness," said Rachel. She closed the bottom dresser drawer and sat back on her heels. "And no candlestick. Whoever did it took it away. They've had plenty of time to dispose of it."

"I don't suppose Hartley saw anybody coming or going, the day it happened?"

"Not a soul. I asked him this morning, when Hugh Bovard and I went up to the court house to see him. Of course he was over in Papa's office, and he wasn't paying any attention—as usual. You know how Hartley is. Kind of other-worldly. He didn't see anybody and what's worse, nobody saw him, so who's going to believe that he was really in Papa's office and not here in the house, polishing off Mrs. Henshaw?"

"Yeah," sighed Dr. Craig.

"Hugh says not to worry." Rachel's voice quavered. "He says the whole thing's just ridiculous. He called Mr. Whitman in Chicago this morning—he's a lawyer that Hugh's known for years. Papa knew him too, and he's coming down Tuesday. Hugh says—"

"Hey! Anybody home?" called Bix's voice from downstairs.

At the sound Rachel jumped a little, shifting on her heels. She looked down at the floor, an almost comically startled expression on her face. "It moved," she said. "It sort of tilted." She shifted again, experimentally; there was no doubt about it, the wide floor board under her heels lifted slightly at one end. Dr. Craig dropped to his knees beside her and turned back the edge of the hooked rug. He felt a prickle of excitement at the back of his neck.

"Hey!" Bix again. "Where are you?"

There was nothing else to do; she had heard them. "Upstairs!" Rachel called back. Then she whispered, "Do you think we should wait?"

"Hell no. This may be important. Bix is okay." He quoted Rachel herself. "Besides, she's nothing but a kid."

There would hardly have been time to cover up what they were doing, anyway. Bix took the stairs at a good fast clip. "Hi!" Her eyes brightened. "What's up? What you doing? Hey, the boards are loose! Doc, what you doing?"

"Appendectomy. Emergency," said Dr. Craig. "There doesn't happen to be a chisel up there on the dresser, does there?"

"No but there's a nail file."

It was as easy as that. They did it with the nail file and Mrs. Henshaw's hair brush. A section of two of the boards lifted out, simply and neatly, exposing a large, sturdy metal box in the cavity below. The three of them stared at it.

"Ah ha," said Dr. Craig. "Mrs. Henshaw's little secret."

"What's in it?" gasped Rachel. "Is it locked?"

Bix said nothing at all.

Dr. Craig lifted it out and tried the lid. It was securely locked. "The key ought to be somewhere in this room," he said, "unless we're all off and it isn't Mrs. Henshaw's box, but somebody else's."

"Of course it's hers. She wouldn't let anybody else in here. It had to be hers." Rachel scrambled to her feet. "Keys. I saw some keys somewhere. Was it in the desk?"

"I'll look," said Bix quickly. Already she was across the room and at the desk. "Here's some keys," she said over her shoulder. "A whole ring of them."

But none of them fit. It was obvious that none of them would, but Bix and Rachel watched, while Dr. Craig tried them all. "We could force it, I suppose," he said tentatively. "Only I'm not sure it's legal. How do you ladies feel about it?"

"It would seem more legal if we could find the key," said Rachel. "Though I don't see what difference it makes, as long as we've gone this far...."

Bix was sternly disapproving. "I bet it isn't legal at all. I bet we shouldn't even be in here. We ought to put it back and—"

"And forget about it? Bix, are you serious?" Rachel's eyes flashed with temper. "Why there might be something in there that would clear Hartley!"

"Well—" Bix shuffled her feet and looked down at the floor.

Dr. Craig watched her thoughtfully. It occurred to him that there might also be something in Mrs. Henshaw's box that wouldn't clear Hartley.

The silence was broken by the doorbell. Whoever had turned it was impatient; it had hardly stopped wheezing before the door downstairs opened and a heavy tread sounded in the hall.

"Hullo! Hullo there!"

"It's the sheriff," whispered Bix. "Don't—"

But Rachel had already called back to him. Her eyes were still sparkling with anger. "What's the matter with you? Don't you want to get Hartley out of jail? Don't you want to know what's in the box? It'll be legal now, Dr. Craig, we'll get Charlie Jeffreys to open it and—" Her voice dwindled away, and Dr. Craig wondered if it was because of his face. Could he possibly be looking as uneasy as he felt? Probably his face had nothing to do with it; after all, Rachel was as bright as he was, the potentialities of Mrs. Henshaw's box were bound to dawn on her sooner or later. Well, it hadn't been sooner. At least things were going to be legal from here on in.

"Hullo, Doc. Afternoon, Miss Buckmaster, Bix." There was a subtle change in the sheriff's manner. The general effect he had given last night was of a man who, never having heard of a roller coaster, suddenly finds himself riding on one. Today he was still on it, but he had learned something about roller coasters since last night. He was taking it calmer.

"What's that?" His round blue eyes blinked at the metal box and at its tidy hiding place (it must be Mrs. Henshaw's handiwork, thought Dr. Craig; no one else could have managed it so neatly).

"We were just going to call you," said Dr. Craig. He was surprised and pleased at how smoothly this whopper rolled out. Here was a talent he hadn't known he possessed. "Miss Buckmaster and I happened on this while we were—er—"

The sheriff waited, plainly interested while Dr. Craig's newfound talent evaporated.

"We were looking for a candlestick," said Rachel. Evidently she had decided that honesty was the best policy. It was certainly more comfortable, thought Dr. Craig as he listened to her explanation. And—since the candlestick hadn't turned up in any place that might embarrass Hartley—it was safe enough. Good old best-policy honesty.

"You mean you've ransacked everything?" said Sheriff Jeffreys when she had finished. "My gosh. I just talked to State Headquarters, and they said for me to seal up the whole house. They're sending a guy down, he'll be here in the morning. And here you've already—"

"We meant well," said Rachel cheerfully. "And you've got to admit we've turned up something for the State guy to work on."

The sheriff conceded the point, but there was a note of bitterness in his voice as he turned back to the box. "What's in it? Don't tell me you eager beavers haven't opened it."

"There's no key, and we didn't think it was legal to force it," explained Dr. Craig virtuously.

"Good," said the sheriff. "I'll take it along with me." They watched wistfully as he took charge of their find. "Could you make arrangements, Miss Buckmaster, to stay somewhere else? Because that's what I'm supposed to do, seal up the whole house. Keep everybody out."

"We've got plenty of room," said Bix, and Dr. Craig wished he could say the same. "You can stay at our house. Hey, that reminds me. I came over to ask you to have dinner with Daddy and me. My mother isn't feeling good but Daddy said we could drive out to Chicken Inn for dinner."

Rachel opened her mouth, but Craig opened his faster. "It's a small world, isn't it? I've already made the same proposition to Miss Buckmaster. So she's tied up for dinner."

"I—" Rachel turned quite pink. "Why, yes. He already— Thanks anyway, Bix. We'll probably see you out there, at Chicken Inn."

"Probably." On her way to the door, Bix turned, suddenly grinning. "Bless you, my children," she said before she ran downstairs.

XI

Dr. Craig helped the sheriff lock all the doors and windows, while Rachel went to her room to repack her belongings. She also changed her dress in honor of the expedition to Chicken Inn, a circumstance which filled Dr. Craig with secret elation. The dress she changed to was brown, with a couple of intriguing gold tassels, and on her head she wore what appeared to be an omelet, done to a golden turn. On her an omelet was becoming.

"Let's not talk about Mrs. Henshaw at all. Let's ignore her," she said as they got into the coupe and waved goodbye to the sheriff. "I wonder what's in the box."

"More string, maybe. Slightly used paper bags. Apparently she never threw anything away."

Rachel sighed. "Don't try to comfort me. It may be stuffed with anti-Hartley evidence, and if it is I'll never forgive myself. Never. And neither will Bix. She had the right idea. If I'd listened to her the box would be where it belongs, with us instead of the sheriff."

"Women," said Dr. Craig. "No respect for the law. You know very well—"

"I don't care what I know. Except that Hartley didn't do it, and he's in jail."

"Who else hated her? I know nobody liked her. She probably didn't have a friend in the world. But it's got to be more than that. Somebody had to hate her so much, or be so afraid of her, that they couldn't let her go on living. There can't be many people with those qualifications."

"One is all we need," Rachel reminded him. "Wouldn't it be nice if it was Mrs. Pierce? But she wasn't even in town. Neither was I, so that lets me out."

Unwillingly, Dr. Craig remembered the snatch of conversation he had overheard in the Square Deal. And unwillingly he blurted out the question. "How bad did you and Hartley want to sell the house?"

"How bad?" Rachel's voice, as frank as ever, was tinged with surprise. "Well, of course we wanted to sell it. No point in keeping it. And of course nobody was going to buy it as long as Mrs. Henshaw was one of the fixtures. But it wasn't crucial. Papa left us a little money, enough to help Hartley through college, and I make out all right on my salary. Not that it keeps me in sables—" For a minute her face took on a faraway expression. Then, belatedly, she drew herself up. "Though I can't see what business it is of yours, Dr. Craig."

"It isn't. Except that tomorrow the State guy is going to ask you all this, and plenty more. We might as well face it."

"Oh. I—I guess you're right. You mean you're giving me sort of a workout?"

"It doesn't hurt to be prepared," said Dr. Craig. "Even when you're just going to tell the truth. One thing I don't get. You say Hartley's got a little money. Then why the hell is he sticking around here?"

"Bix." Her answer was prompt and positive. "He was all set to stay in Chicago with me, three years ago. We had it all planned, I was going to get a bigger apartment, and he was going to finish high school and— And then Bix called him up. I don't know what she said. All he told me was that he'd decided to come back to Coreyville. He clammed up, and when Hartley clams up there's no use arguing. He came back to Coreyville."

"You don't like Bix, do you?" He stole a glance at her in the mirror. That omelet was one of the most effective contraptions he had ever seen. Under it her eyes seemed shot with flicks of pure sunlight. Her nose was a little bit crooked; this pleased him. So did the sudden curve of her mouth. Then there was the vulnerable, heart-breaking cleft chin....

"That's just the trouble," she burst out. "I do like Bix. I wouldn't get so exasperated with her if I didn't like her. And feel sorry for her. It's a wonder she's not a juvenile delinquent, when you consider her home life."

"It must be tough, having a mother like Mrs. Bovard." She had consulted Dr. Craig once or twice, on account of her headaches. A wan, remote, cold woman. And an incurable one. Dr. Craig had felt the dead weight of hopelessness settle on him while he listened to the familiar symptoms, while he wrote out the futile prescriptions. Pills for the headaches. Pills to make her sleep. But there weren't any pills for what was really wrong with her. "It must be even tougher, having her for a wife."

"I've always thought so," said Rachel. "If Hugh philanders now and then, it's because she drives him to it. She used to be the prettiest thing, though. I remember, when we were kids, how pretty she was. She'd bring Ronnie over once in a while. I was supposed to play with him."

"She told me a little about Ronnie." Very little actually; but enough so that Dr. Craig had known the pills weren't going to help. She had known it too; that was what haunted him. She knew she was incurable. My son, my little boy, she had said—and then stopped, as if aware that talk, which might have helped once, was now as futile as pills.

"Ronnie was pretty awful, I guess, but mostly he just bored me. He could only say a few words, and he had this little whistle that he was always blowing. Once I took it away from him, only she saw me—she never let him out of her sight for a minute—and she slapped me. After that I didn't have to 'play' with him anymore, which was exactly the way I wanted it, of course. I felt as if I'd pulled off something very clever." Rachel paused. "Because he really was awful. He grunted. And his tongue was too long."

My son, my little boy.... Poor woman, thought Dr. Craig. But poor Hugh and Bix, too. Poor everybody, if you put your mind to it.

Only he was in no mood to put his mind to it. The car hummed along the highway, and the sun glittered on the patches of stale snow in the fields, and when his eyes met Rachel's she smiled as if she were glad to be here too. He considered putting his arm around her. Decided against it, for the present. Haste makes waste, and this one showed every sign of being too good to waste. Later, after they had dawdled away the afternoon over drinks and dinner.... You could dance at Chicken Inn, too. There was a juke box, and quite a decent-sized dance floor.

"What are you smirking about?" asked Rachel. She looked half inclined to smirk herself.

"It's my jovial nature. Sunny Jim, they call me."

"I see." She hesitated for half a moment. "And what do I call you? I mean—Dr. Craig sounds kind of formal, and I still associate 'Doc' with Papa—"

"Childish of you. You'll have to get over it."

"Don't you have a first name?'

"I do. But it's not fit for human consumption." (It was Cedric. He had no intention of divulging this ridiculous fact.) "You'll have to settle for Doc."

"All right. Doc. I guess it doesn't sound so—daughterly, after all."

"Not the slightest bit," said Dr. Craig, and resumed his smirking.

XII

Chicken Inn did a brisk business on Sundays. The upper crust of half a dozen neighboring towns gathered here—the lively, cocktail-drinking young crowd to dance and get tight, in a reasonably refined way; the less rollicking oldsters to eat their way through the Sunday Special, which was hearty to the point of stupefaction. The resulting atmosphere was about equal parts sportiness and dignity. After four, when the Sunday Special went off the market, sportiness won out. It was already in the ascendancy when Rachel and Dr. Craig arrived, at three thirty. The jukebox throbbed, ice clattered invitingly in the shakers at the bar; voices rose a couple of degrees above normal.

Hugh Bovard, who was having a brandy with his coffee, and Bix, who was polishing off the last crumb of the Sunday Special apple pie a la mode, saw them as soon as they came in and beckoned them over.

"Have a drink," said Hugh. "You're looking bright-eyed and bushy-tailed, the both of you. What's new? Bix tells me you struck oil, or something, in Mrs. Henshaw's room."

"Did she tell you that the sheriff's got it, on account of me not being very bright?" asked Rachel drily. "Your daughter has a low opinion of my mentality, and I can't say I blame her."

Bix, who was "dressed up" in a sheer, ruffly blouse that showed her shoulder blades in back and her pathetic little incipient bosom in front, looked embarrassed. "I don't think you're so dumb," she explained. "But you sure talk a lot sometimes."

"I'll try to reform," Rachel said. "I'd love a martini," she added to Dr. Craig, who was negotiating with the waitress, "but do you think it's safe? It may loosen my tongue even more."

"Paris the thought," said Bix. "Not that it matters any more. I guess you've already told the sheriff everything you know."

"It wouldn't matter if she hadn't, you brat." Hugh was struggling to look disapproving and parental instead of amused. "The sheriff isn't here. She's among friends. Candid friends, I might add." He sipped his brandy. "There's probably nothing crucial in Mrs. Henshaw's box, anyway."

"I like to think it's love letters," said Dr. Craig. What he was really thinking was that he would have preferred to be sitting beside Rachel in the booth, instead of beside Bix. On the other hand, this way he had a better view of her. "Love letters tied with blue."

"Love letters from Francie. Cherished for all these years." The idea obviously entertained Rachel. "How is Francie, by the way? Still in the second-hand business? Still living on peanut butter and crackers?"

Dr. Craig nodded. "The man's been starving himself for years, out of pure stinginess. At this point the shock of a good meal would probably kill him, with his heart in the shape it's in. He's apt to conk off any minute." He had been called to attend Mrs. Henshaw's estranged husband only once—and that once very much against the patient's will. Francie claimed he couldn't afford doctors. But the Smileys had insisted. The Smileys were the dirtiest people in town; Francie rented from them a room that made Dr. Craig's own quarters seem like a paradise of cleanliness and order. There the old man had lain, huddled in an unspeakably dirty bathrobe, as fiercely opposed to spending money on a doctor as though he were not at the point of death. Which he had certainly been. With a mixture of pity and exasperation, Dr. Craig remembered the bony, ramshackle body; the two cases, one of peanut butter, one of canned beans (cheaper by the case) in the corner; the little path, worn by Francie's feet, beside the sidewalk that led from Smiley's house to the second-hand shop. (Sidewalks wore out shoe leather.)

"He's been apt to conk off any minute for years," said Hugh. "Your father used to say the same thing, Rachel. He's a tough old customer, Francie is." A defensive kind of loyalty crept into his voice. "I know everybody says he's stingy. And he is, with himself. I know everybody makes fun of him and his little path and all the rest of it. But let me tell you one thing, Francie'll give the shirt off his back to anybody he likes."

"Try and find somebody he likes," said Rachel. "You're it, Hugh. You're the only person in town he'll put up with, or that will put up with him."

"He wasn't always like that. I can remember him when I was a kid, before he got married, and believe me, nobody made fun of Francis L. Henshaw then. He was the Young Man Most Likely To Succeed. A good-looking fellow, and smart. He worked for old Mr. Kincaid in the bank, and he was all set to marry one of the Kincaid girls. Then she came along. Rose. Rose Anthony she was, in those days."

"Mrs. Henshaw, you mean?"

"That's who I mean. All at once he married her instead of the Kincaid girl, and she sure as hell ruined him." Suddenly Hugh grinned. "He'll be delighted to hear that somebody murdered her."

"Maybe he did it." Bix gave a little wriggle of excitement. "Why not? He could have. He hated her enough."

"It's an idea," said Dr. Craig. But was it such a hot one? It would get Hartley off the hook, sure enough. And Francie hated her sure enough.

He had also avoided her like the plague, for thirty years. Why would he all at once go to see her, even for the purpose of killing her? "I'm not sure he could manage it. With his heart the way it is, and nothing but crackers and peanut butter to fortify him."

"Of course he couldn't have," said Hugh curtly. "Francie's tough, but not that tough. If he was ever going to kill her, he'd have done it years ago, when it might have done him some good. He's no fool."

Much as he regretted it, Dr. Craig had to agree. Not so Bix and Rachel. Neither of them said anything, but Dr. Craig caught the look they exchanged, somehow an intensely feminine look—of secret determination and hope.

"I told Daddy you're going to stay at our house," said Bix. "Can we go now, Daddy? Because you said I could go see Hartley, if they'll let me. Gee, I wish he was here now. That's a real dreamy piece to dance to."

Dr. Craig stood up with alacrity, and he gave Bix a grateful little pat as she slid out of the booth. A sweet kid, really. "What's this lethal weapon?" he asked, as he discovered, on the hook under her coat, a bright green umbrella with a heavy, carved handle.

Bix ducked her head and blushed. "Hartley gave us that for Christmas," her father explained. "If there's a cloud the size of a dime, we carry it.... Okay, Biscuit, don't be mad. I'm just kidding." He stood up too, with not so much alacrity. He looked, in fact, a little wistful, and Dr. Craig thought of the wan, remote woman he was going home to, stretched out, probably, with a wet cloth pressed against the headache that was never going to go away. "Behave yourselves, you two. See you later, Rachel. You're welcome as the flowers of May. We'll be glad to have you. So long, Doc."

They were alone at last. Dr. Craig slid back into the booth, this time beside Rachel. He had a feeling that he might be smirking again.

If he was, it was wasted on Rachel. "It wouldn't surprise me if Bix snitched the key to that box," she said. "I think she knew all the time there was something in Mrs. Henshaw's room, and for some reason she didn't want us or anybody else to go into the subject—"

"Then let's not. Let's dance instead. We weren't going to talk about Mrs. Henshaw. Remember? We were going to ignore her."

It turned into one of those enchanted stretches of time, when all the martinis were just exhilarating enough, all the music was dreamy to dance to, all the things either of them said were witty or charming or profound. At seven or so they ate an ambrosial dish modestly listed on the menu as Chicken in the Pot. At eight or so they floated out into the windy, wintry night, a night of briefly glimmering stars and scudding clouds.

"Heavenly," murmured Rachel. "A heavenly evening." She lifted her face joyfully to the night and wind and the long, long kiss.

A kiss, Dr. Craig reminded himself, was a kiss, and nothing more. It had no significance, except as the opening round in that fine old indoor sport where good-looking babies belonged and must be kept. Though some kisses were better than others. This one, for instance....

Better. But not more significant. Any extraordinary meaning it might seem to have was coincidental, the direct result of martinis and soft music and whatever the scent was, something spicy, that Rachel used. A simple, chemical reaction, you might say. No magic. As long as he kept that firmly in mind, he was okay, he was safe.

"We'd better go home now," said Rachel faintly.

"I wish we didn't ever have to go home. I wish—" He stopped just in time. "Come on," he said, and opened the car door.

They didn't talk during the drive home. Dr. Craig was silent because he was leery of himself, after the narrow escape of that "I wish—." Rachel was silent because she went to sleep, with her head nestled trustfully against his shoulder. (The trustfulness dashed him a little; hadn't she noticed that his intentions were dishonorable?)

But it seemed a shame to wake her. He pulled up in Bovard's driveway and just sat for a minute, looking down at the slightly crooked nose and the eyelashes that were like tiny little brushes. When he kissed her she stirred and whispered, "Greg."

It froze him in his tracks. He would die, however, die a thousand deaths before he would ask who Greg was. In the first place, she wasn't even aware she had said the name. And anyway, it was nothing to him. So all right, she was used to being kissed by some hound by the name of Greg. So what of it? Nothing. Absolutely nothing.

"What are you looking so grim about?" She had straightened up, and was adjusting the omelet hat.

"I'm not," he snapped. "Here, I'll get your bag for you." He helped her out, and she stood beside him, looking a little puzzled, while he opened the trunk.

"Who's Greg?" he croaked.

"Greg? Did you say Greg?

"You said it first. A minute ago, when I— So who is this Greg character? What's so special about him?"

"Why, nothing. I mean, he's just a—"

"Really? I've always wanted to meet a just a."

She glared at him, and he smiled brilliantly, and the battle would no doubt have been joined except that at that moment they both heard the sound.

It seemed to come from the path that ran back of the three houses in the block—Bovards' at one end, Buckmasters' at the other, Myra Graves' in the middle. It was low, like a moan, except that it had a curious overtone of indignation. More like a bitter protest than a cry for help. It grew weaker, died away, rose again

Dr. Craig took off at a gallop. "Somebody's hurt. Wait for me here," he said.

But it didn't do any good; Rachel stayed right at his heels. "Myra's hedge," she panted. "That's where it's coming from."

She was right. They found her half under the hedge, where the frozen earth was pitted with ice. She was making feeble crawling movements, and her hat with the silver buckle was jammed down over her eyes.

"Mrs. Pierce," whispered Rachel. "Oh my. Mrs. Pierce."

XIII

Mrs. Pierce lay (though she somehow still gave the effect of sitting bolt upright) on the Bovard couch and glared at everybody out of one eye. The other eye was swollen shut, the side of her face was scraped, and there was a sizable lump above her ear. But she was very much alive. In fact, thought Bix, she glared better out of one eye than out of two. More concentrated.

"Nothing serious," said Doc cheerfully. "You're going to have a super shiner, but that's all. You'll be right as rain in a couple of days."

"Nothing serious, he says! I just beg to differ with you, young man. When somebody tries to kill me, it's something serious, to my way of thinking."

It was a laugh, thought Bix, the way they all tried to look shocked. As if it hadn't even crossed their minds for one minute that this was anything but an accident. Rachel was better at it than Daddy or Doc. "You mean you think somebody—" she began.

"I don't think. I know. Certainly somebody tried to kill me. They hit me on the head and left me there to die."

Nobody quite looked at anybody else. But Doc came through with something that took the wind out of Mrs. Pierce's sails for a minute. "What were you doing back there, anyway?"

"I can't see that that's got anything to do with it."

"No?" said Daddy. "Why not? It might have everything to do with it."

"Well, if you must know. I just thought I'd check up on that sheriff.

He claimed he'd locked the Buckmaster house up so nobody could get in, but I don't trust him. Not for a minute. I don't trust anybody around here."

"Very sensible attitude," said Daddy. (Bix loved him when he got that little quirk to his mouth.)

"You were nearer Myra Graves' house than the Buckmaster's when we found you," said Doc. "How did that happen?"

"See here, young man, I don't see why I should be put through the third degree, on top of everything else! You'd think *I'd* been going around hitting people over the head, instead of the other way round!"

"But, Mrs. Pierce, you really were nearer Myra—"

"All right. I was there because I just thought I'd have a word with her as long as I was at it. Anything wrong with that?"

"Did you have your word with her?"

"I never got there. Somebody sneaked up behind me and hit me over the head, and that's the last I remember till you found me."

"You couldn't have been out very long," said Doc. "Honest to God, Mrs. Pierce, you're not seriously hurt."

"Watch your language, please. It was quarter past eight when I left the hotel. It's five minutes of nine now. I was hurt serious enough to lay out there a good fifteen minutes."

"You came in about half an hour ago, Bix," said Daddy. "Did you hear anything? See anybody prowling around the back way?"

Bix hesitated briefly before she shook her head. "But then I didn't come the back way. Peggy took me a ways, as far as Buckmaster's, and then I cut through their front yard, and Myra's, and came on home."

"It's icy back there, and dark," Doc reminded everybody. "Be awfully easy to slip and fall. You sure that isn't what happened, Mrs. Pierce?"

Mrs. Pierce propped herself up on her elbow to give him the full benefit of her one fierce eye. "Young man, when I slip and fall, I know it. And when somebody hits me over the head, I know it. Somebody killed Rose, and somebody tried to kill me, and—"

It was time, Bix decided, to make the important point. "Well, anyway," she said, "whoever it was, it wasn't Hartley. There must be two killers. Unless you're insinuating that Hartley broke out of jail to nip back there and bop you."

They all blinked. Honestly, sometimes Bix wondered about people, the way you had to practically draw a diagram before they could see the nose on their face.

Rachel spoke first. "I love you, Bix. Of course Hartley didn't break out of jail. And of course there can't be two killers. So that proves—"

"Proves that Hartley's innocent," said Bix airily. "Natch."

Their three faces—Daddy's and Rachel's and Doc's—broke into smiles of pure joy. But not Mrs. Pierce's. She snorted. "Proves nothing of the sort. I've got my own notion about who hit me, and all it proves is that Hartley's where he ought to be, in jail. There'd ought to be somebody else up there with him, is all." She turned the withering eye on Rachel, who shrank visibly. "You heard her last night. You heard her threaten me. She came right out and said I wouldn't be safe, over there in that house—not that I had any intention whatsoever of staying. A nest of murderers if I ever saw one. The boy killed Rose, and now she's tried to—"

"That's a damn lie!" Doc looked ready to explode. "I've been with Rachel all afternoon and evening. I can vouch for her myself."

"You can vouch for her! You're a fine one to vouch for anybody. Cursing and swearing. Carrying on with her, like as not. Drinking— Oh, I smelled it on you, the both of you, like to knocked me out all over again—"

"Hugh! What's the matter? What's happened?" It was Mother's voice, sad and frail, floating down from the top of the stairs. There she stood, like a ghost, one hand at her temple, the other clutching the neck of her pale gray robe. The martyr, thought Bix. Oh sure, that's all we need, is her suffering patiently all over the place. She turned her back, so as not to watch Daddy tearing up the stairs like a dog who has been whistled home. For a terrible moment she thought she was going to cry, and she wouldn't allow it, she simply would not....

"Nuts!" She gave the hassock a savage kick. Anything to hold back the tears. "Oh nuts!"

"Amen," said Doc. Then he got a grip on himself. "Look here, Mrs. Pierce, I'll call Mrs. Nelson at the hospital and tell her to come and get you. Under the circumstances, I'm sure you wouldn't trust me to drive you there. She's a good practical nurse, she doesn't drink or swear, and she'll take care of your eye. You can stay at the hospital or at the hotel, wherever you'd rather. And you can leap out bright and early tomorrow morning and tell the sheriff and his pals from the state police just exactly how to run the whole show. There. Does that make you happy?" He stamped out to the telephone, looking anything but happy himself.

"You don't need to think for one minute," Mrs. Pierce shot after him, "that I'm going to wait till morning to tell the sheriff about this. I'll call him just as soon as I've gotten some proper medical attention."

And of course she did. Not long after Mrs. Nelson had come and bundled her energetic patient off to the hospital, Sheriff Jeffreys turned up.

He didn't look happy, either.

By that time Daddy had calmed Mother down and was back downstairs. He answered the door. "Oh Lord, Charlie," he said wearily. "You know as much about it as any of us. What did she tell you?"

"What didn't she tell me! She's a terror, Mr. Bovard. That woman is a holy terror. Lit right into me, all about a nest of murderers and she don't trust me either, and—" Charlie drew a long sigh. Then he straightened his shoulders and pulled down his coat. (Making like a sheriff, thought Bix. He forgot it there for a minute.) "Well. Seems she thinks Miss Buckmaster—"

Doc did his exploding act all over again. After that he took Charlie out to show him where they had found Mrs. Pierce, and Daddy fixed a drink for Rachel and patted her on the shoulder. She just sat and stared at the floor, and once in a while she'd take a little sip of the drink, out of politeness. Bix fidgeted. She wished she could think of something to say. She wished Rachel didn't look so much like Hartley. It was no fair for her to look like Hartley; that's what it was, no fair.

"Nobody's going to believe her," said Daddy. "Even if you didn't have Doc to vouch for you, nobody would believe it. And there's one thing sure— Mrs. Pierce may not think Doc's word is worth much, but she's going to find out that nobody else in Coreyville agrees with her. He's as well liked, and as well respected, as any man in town."

Rachel brightened up at that, Bix noticed. Old Doc must be a fast worker, all right. Personally, Bix didn't go for the animal-magnetism type; but then every woman to her own taste.

He came loping back with an all's-right-with-the-world expression on his face, and without the sheriff. "We're all straight with Charlie," he told them. "He's pretty sore at Mrs. Pierce himself. That crack she made about not trusting him hurt his feelings. Says like as not nobody hit her, she just slipped on the ice and had to blame somebody for it."

Bix sighed. In a way, it was an anti-climax. It didn't get Hartley out of jail, but on the other hand it didn't put Rachel up there with him. Which was something to be thankful for, Bix supposed. Doc seemed to think so. He was looking at Rachel like she was a princess he'd just snatched out from under the dragon's nose or something, and she was looking at him like he was a knight on a white charger. The adult infants at play, thought Bix.

"I'm going to bed," she announced. "Goodnight, all." She got halfway up the stairs before she remembered something, and paused. She knew exactly where she had left it: on one of the dining room chairs. That meant going through the living room; they would all see her marching back with it. So what? It was her property, none of their business if she happened to want it with her. And she did want it. She felt all at once as if she couldn't get through the night without it—to comfort her, to prove that she too had something, somebody of her own....

Let them laugh at her. She turned around and sailed back through the living room, past their questioning eyes. "I forgot my umbrella," she said haughtily.

The silence that fell was peculiar. And another peculiar thing—they weren't laughing at her. Their eyes, all three pairs of them, were riveted on the umbrella in her hand. What did you call moments like this? Clairvoyance, that was it: she knew exactly what they were thinking, she could practically see the wheels going round. "What's this lethal weapon?" Doc had said, out at Chicken Inn, and then Daddy had teased her.... They were remembering that, and they were also remembering that she must have gotten home just about the time Mrs. Pierce fell, or was hit. Lethal weapon. Fell, or was hit.

"Goodnight," she gulped. It was all she could do to keep from breaking into a dead run. Up in the sanctuary of her own room, she leaned against the door, waiting for her heart to stop thumping. Anyway, she had her umbrella, her good old rod and staff they comfort me umbrella. She hugged it against her. It was going to be one of those nights when she needed it.

Some nights were okay. Some nights her room seemed cozy and familiar. The lamp beside her bed was a lamp, and that was all; there was nothing under the chintz petticoat on the dressing table except the dressing table legs; nothing at the foot of the bed except her terry cloth robe and the extra blanket; nothing outside the window except the ivy, stirring harmlessly in the wind.

Then there were other nights, like this one, when all the furniture crouched, ready to spring at some secret, pre-arranged signal. The lamp turned into a fist threatening her, the window into an eye watching her. Whatever it was, hiding under the chintz petticoat, moved now and then, ever so slightly, ever so warily. Whatever it was, huddled at the foot of her bed, crept an inch toward her, stopped, waiting for the signal. And outside the window something—what? Not the ivy. Something old and evil—tapped and tapped, trying to get in.

She pulled the covers closer around her ears, and drew her knees up tighter against her shivering body. Long ago, when she was little, she used to cry on nights like this. She hadn't known why she was crying, any more than she knew now why she was shivering. She had never learned the name of what she feared. The face is familiar, she thought—and in a way it was a laugh, only she couldn't quite manage a laugh at the moment—the face is familiar, but the name eludes me.

She was still awake when Daddy came upstairs. She heard him fumbling with the light switch and then pausing—not at Mother's door, for once, but at Bix's. Oh oh, she thought, and screwed her eyes tight shut.

"Bix," he whispered. "Bix. Are you asleep?" He came over and touched her shoulder. "I want to talk to you a minute."

She made what she hoped were sleepy noises. "What? Whatsamatter?"

"I want to talk to you. About tonight. Mrs. Pierce and— You know you can trust me, Bix. You don't need to be afraid to tell me anything."

There was one weapon, Bix had discovered at an early age, that simply made mincemeat out of Daddy. She used it in cases of extremity only, because she always felt so sorry for him. But this was an extremity, and the weapon had better be in good working order or it was going to be just too bad for Miss Beatrix Bovard.

She pulled away from him, buried her face in the pillow, and uttered a small, desolate sob.

Silence. She could feel him shifting helplessly from one foot to the other, in an attempt to steel himself. Poor Daddy. It was time for another sob, or perhaps a whimper this time. She produced a heart-rending blend of the two.

"Now Bix," he began desperately.

"I'm—I'm sorry. I'm so tired, and I haven't got anything to tell you, and—and it was so awful, going up to see H-H-Hartley—"

"Don't, please don't. I didn't mean anything. Please don't cry, Biscuit." He had given up; he was begging. Mincemeat, pure and simple. She didn't pull away from his hand this time. She let him gather her up against his shoulder and pat her hair, the way he always did....

Only something was happening that she hadn't planned on and that never had happened before. The weapon got away from her; she couldn't stop the crying. It was like some terrible machine shaking her. "Daddy! Oh Daddy!" she whispered, and she clung to him.

He picked her up and sat down on the edge of the bed with her in his lap. "There. There. I know, Biscuit. I know." His arm, rocking her, was warm and solid under the scratchy tweed; he smelled of tobacco and bourbon and, very faintly, of the printing shop. The smell—in a way—of shelter and love. Except that Bix knew from way back how, at any moment, the warm, solid arm and the shelter might be withdrawn. One word from Mother, sometimes no more than a look. That was all it took. Daddy would be long gone. There was that, always to be remembered, always, always.

"Sh, sh. It's going to be all right. You mustn't worry about Hartley.

Hartley's going to be all right."

He sounded so sure. Slowly, slowly, the terrible machine loosened its grip on her. He sounded so sure....

After a while he turned on the light (the lamp was just a lamp, after all) and tucked her back into bed. They smiled feebly at each other. But at the sight of his face, haggard and strained with sorrow, she felt shame rush over her. Ah, poor Daddy. Poor, poor Daddy.

She made a silent vow; never, as long as she lived, to use the mincemeat weapon again. She put her hand up to his cheek, silently promising. Cross her heart. Hope to die. Then, all at once, she went to sleep.

XIV

The detective's name turned out to be Mr. Pigeon, of all things. And he couldn't have looked less like a detective if he had actually had pink feet and a fantail. Bix had expected a hatchet face, gimlet eyes, a machine-gun voice rattling out intimidating questions. But Mr. Pigeon's voice was leisurely and rather high-pitched; he was bald, portly, and snubnosed; and his mild brown eyes looked dreamily off in two different directions, neither of them Bix.

They had their "little talk"—to quote Mr. Pigeon—in the study, a small room crowded with glass-fronted book cases, the rolltop desk where Daddy sometimes worked evenings, and the picture of Grandpa and Grandma Bovard frozen forever in their wedding finery. Mr. Pigeon sat at the desk in the swivel chair; Bix perched on the edge of the couch, wary as a fox. She expected tricks. The preliminary chatter, for instance, about school and how old are you, Beatrix, and what do you want to study in college—all that was supposed to soften her up. Pretty corny, if you asked Bix; she could have done a better job herself. But maybe Mr. Pigeon was tired. He had already had "little talks" with all the others. Bix was the end of the line, or very near it—that was how she rated with Mr. Pigeon. Which was fine, from one angle. Not so fine, from another. It was those two angles that were tearing her apart inside.

The preliminaries were over. Let's see, now, Beatrix, you've known Hartley for—how long? All my life, Mr. Pigeon, and he didn't kill Mrs. Henshaw....

He didn't like her, though, did he? Of course not. Nobody liked her. That's no reason for killing her....

"Maybe he had another reason." Mr. Pigeon kept playing a little game that involved wadding up scraps of paper and trying to balance them on the edge of the cigarette box in front of him. He didn't go at it right; he didn't wad his paper pills up tight enough. They all fell into the box, and he just kept on trying again in the same old inefficient way, following the line of least resistance. "Maybe he knew about that box of Mrs. Henshaw's, and what was in it."

Another paper pill bit the dust before Bix said anything. "What was in it?"

"Money," said Mr. Pigeon pleasantly. "A lot of money, Beatrix. Twenty-three thousand dollars."

Her heart leapt up, it soared with relief. *That's all? Just money?* She bit back the questions just in time, and gave Mr. Pigeon, instead, the big eyes and the gasp of amazement he expected. "Twenty-three thou— Jeepers! That's a nice piece of change."

"So it is, so it is. Lots of people have been murdered for less."

"Sure they have. Lots of people, for lots less." She was stuttering a little, with excitement. "That means— Why, that means anybody might have killed her for the money. Anybody at all."

"Well, not quite anybody," said Mr. Pigeon. "It would have to be somebody who knew she had the money."

"Then that lets Hartley out. Because he didn't know it. He would have told me if he'd known, he always tells me everything."

Mr. Pigeon looked amused. "You're sure about that? You don't think he might have been planning to surprise you?"

"Nope. Because—" Oh well, what was the use of trying to explain? She and Hartley simply didn't have secrets from each other. But of course Mr. Pigeon couldn't see that. All he saw was the cute, boy-meets-girl stuff.

"Something else interesting," he was saying. "Where did Mrs. Henshaw get all that money? Do you have any idea?"

"Who, me?" she said quickly. "Saved it, I suppose. Kept squirreling it away her whole entire life. It would be just like her." She hurried back to safer ground. "If it was Hartley, then why didn't he take the money? If that's what he was after, why did he just leave it there?"

"Why not? He had plenty of time—or so he thought. All the time in the world. Remember, nobody was supposed to suspect that this was a murder. Nobody did suspect it, till Mrs. Pierce came along."

"Okay, so whoever did it thought they had plenty of time. You say it's a good reason for Hartley to leave the money there. I say it's just as good a reason for anybody to leave the money there. Why pick on Hartley?"

"Well," said Mr. Pigeon reasonably, "I'll tell you why." One of his eyes gazed off toward the window; the other seemed fixed on the fresh little wad of paper between his fingers. "Of all the people that didn't like her, it looks like Hartley had the best reason for not liking her. And of all the people that might have known about her money, Hartley had the best chance to know, because he lived in the same house with her. And of all the people that might think it was safe to leave the money where it was, he'd feel the safest, because it's his house. That's how detecting goes, Beatrix. Very little juggling, very little fancy footwork. You just take the facts and put them together in the way that makes the most sense, and—"

"But you're not!" cried Bix. "All you're doing is taking the line of least resistance!" (There. The new little paper pill fell into the cigarette box, just like all the others. She had known it would.) "Hartley's the easiest answer, so you just—" She had to stop, to get her breath. "What about what happened to Mrs. Pierce last night? Hartley sure-God didn't have the best chance to do that!"

"There now, there now." Mr. Pigeon made distressed little shifting motions in his chair. For a moment one of his eyes seemed actually to look straight at her. "We're not picking on your boy friend the way you seem to think. Don't you worry, we're following up all the other leads too. When it comes to Mrs. Pierce—well, people aren't always reliable witnesses, you know. Sometimes they get worked up and make mistakes. With a woman like Mrs. Pierce, you've got to allow for a margin of error."

"You don't think anybody hit her," said Bix wearily. She needn't have worried about what might have come out in his little talks with the others. You could count on Mr. Pigeon, every time. The line of least resistance. The easiest answer. She stood up. "Well. You got any more questions to ask me? Can I go now?"

"No more questions. You can run along to school now." Mr. Pigeon stood up too, and gave her an indulgent, goodwill smile. We will now have a moment of soft-soap, thought Bix. I bet he's got a daughter at home just my age, probably just exactly like me, only she's got two heads and her boy friend isn't in jail. "No more questions, and no hard feelings either, I hope. You've been co-operative, Beatrix, and I appreciate it. Something else I appreciate too, and that's loyalty. You're a loyal little person, my dear, and—"

Loyal. Loyal. Something seemed to wrench, inside her chest. "Oh, stop it," she choked out. And fled.

She found Rachel, looking hollow-eyed and lighting one cigarette from another, in the living room. She practically fell on Bix's neck. "I've been sitting here jittering, and nobody to jitter at. Isn't he ever going to leave?" As if on cue, the study door opened and Mr. Pigeon made his leisurely way down the hall and out the door, pausing to smile goodbye at them.

"I suppose he can't help it. It's his job," said Rachel. "He was nice enough to me. Only—"

"Only he's not going to find out who really did it," Bix finished for her. "Leave us face it. Hartley's it, because he's handiest."

"You felt that way too? So did I." Her next words took Bix by surprise—for no good reason. After all, Rachel had run away to Chicago with nothing more substantial in her purse than twenty-five dollars and her high school diploma. "So I guess it's up to us. Or anyway, to me."

"Us," said Bix. She made an impulsive gesture that got them involved in a solemn, awkward, half-handshake. Sort of embarrassing, really. But sort of comforting, too; for a moment the wrench inside Bix's chest was hardly there at all. "Where do we start?"

"Francie," said Rachel briskly. "Francie just loves money. If he knew about Mrs. Henshaw's box, and if he knew she hadn't made a will—which so far it looks as if she hadn't—well, it seems to me Francie's worthy of attention."

"Let's go see him. Daddy said I could skip school this afternoon. Francie's not mad for me, but I am related to Daddy, so he puts up with me. Only we've got to have some excuse. We can't just walk in and say we've come to find out if he killed Mrs. Henshaw."

"I know," said Rachel. "I thought I'd ask his advice about where to sell the silver, and the clock—it's really an antique—and my mother's jewelry. Some of the furniture ought to be worth something, and we're going to need every penny we can scrape up."

They were getting into their coats when they heard Myra Graves' "yoo-hoo" from the back door. She came trotting in, looking flustered and worried. "He's gone, isn't he, that Mr. Pigeon? Listen, Rachel, I forgot to tell him about the handkerchief, and land knows I didn't do it on purpose, I wasn't trying to keep anything from him, but he got me kind of rattled, the way he said for me to remember everything about when we found her, the minute anybody tells me *that* I forget something, sure as you're born, and—" Her breath gave out. She sank down on the sofa, unbuttoned her sweater, fumbled in her apron pocket, and drew out a crumpled blue bandana handkerchief. "There. There it is, for all it's worth. Likely doesn't amount to a row of pins. Only he said for me to remember everything, and it's going to look funny for me to bring it up now. Like I was holding it back before, or maybe making the whole thing up—"

"Making what up?" asked Rachel. "Get organized, Myra. Stop looking so guilty. What about the handkerchief?"

"Why, she had it on," said Myra impatiently. "Had her head tied up in it, you know, to keep out the dust. Looked a fright. I remember it struck me kind of pitiful. I thought to myself I wouldn't be caught dead in a rig like that—"

Bix snickered. Rachel didn't quite. And Myra's plump face got redder than ever. "So I took it off of her," she finished, with dignity. "Took it off and stuck it in my pocket and forgot all about it. Do you think I'd ought to tell that Mr. Pigeon?"

Bix could never resist teasing her. "Oh, brother, are you in trouble! You're going to get arrested. That's what they do with people that conceal evidence. Sure they do. Arrest them. It's a crime."

"But I didn't mean to—" began Myra earnestly. Then she relaxed. "Fresh. If you aren't the freshest young one I ever met up with. I'd ought to smack you. Rachel. What do you think?"

"Go ahead. Smack her. Oh, you mean the handkerchief. I can't see what difference it makes, what she had on. It doesn't prove anything, except that she was cleaning house, and everybody knows that already. It was her handkerchief, wasn't it? Well, then. I wouldn't worry about it."

"He wouldn't do anything about it, anyway, that Pigeon," said Bix. "Somebody else is going to have to confess before he gets his mind off of Hartley. He's in a rut."

The three of them left together, and before she turned up the sidewalk leading to her own house Myra paused, smiling fondly at Rachel. "What's this I hear about you and Doc Craig sashaying around at Chicken Inn yesterday? You're going to have all the girls in town down on you, beating their time like this."

"Look at her blush," said Bix gleefully.

"It's like I've said all along," Myra went on. "Of course he's not married to that wife of his anymore. There's some that keep on saying he is and that's why he hasn't taken up with anybody here, but I claim there just wasn't anybody caught his eye. Till now. This proves it. He wouldn't be shining around you if he was still married to her, would he?" Struck at last by the expression on Rachel's face, Myra floundered in even deeper. "He's not that kind. He's a fine young fellow, Doc is. A fine young fellow."

"Oh my, yes," Rachel said at last. Her smile was brilliant and bleak as an iceberg. "Yes indeed. Dr. Craig's a very slick operator."

XV

Anything, anything at all, was likely to turn up in the window of Francie's second-hand store, because he used it for storage space, rather than display. But there were three landmarks that had been there ever since Bix could remember—the bearskin rug, the black-boy hitching post, and the stuffed canary perched on his little swing, his bill stroking the cuttlebone stuck in the side of his cage. Bix was fond of the canary, but her real favorite was the bear, his great back flattened out in the dust, his head still unbowed, as formidable as ever. His teeth were bared in an everlasting snarl; one amber eye (the other was lost, an empty black hole) glared ferociously at the world. Yes, the bear was her favorite. She gave him a tiny, secret nod in greeting.

Francie had a bell rigged up over the door that jangled out a warning whenever anybody came in or went out. It made Rachel jump, and Bix found that her nervousness was catching. Once inside, they both stopped dead, locked in a sort of stage fright. For one thing, you couldn't see much of anything; the forty-watt bulb Francie had burning toward the back didn't exactly flood the place with light. Then there was the smell, a cold, musty, old smell mixed with the fumes from the kerosene stove. It seemed to lean on you, and so did the stacks of furniture and junk that crammed the place to the ceiling. Like a jungle, with one narrow path leading back to the forty-watt bulb and the kerosene stove. Bix had the feeling that, once she started on that path, the jungle might close in stealthily behind her, choking off any chance of escape. Which was, of course, so much malarky. Kid stuff. She braced herself and called out Mr. Henshaw's name, louder than she intended to.

A shuffling sound came from the end of the path, and a wheezing. Then Francie's voice, a veiled yet shouting sort of voice that always made Bix think of a preacher prophesying hellfire. "Well, I heard you. I heard the bell. That's what it's there for. What do you want?"

Rachel picked her way down the path first, faltering out an explanation of what they wanted as she went. Bix followed, more out of shame than courage. It was all she could do to keep from peering over her shoulder to see if the furniture jungle was really closing in.

The old man, who had apparently been crouched in a ruined velvet chair beside the stove, reading, stood up as they approached. He wore a frayed, rusty-looking sweater, over what seemed to be several layers of garments even more frayed and grimy. His hair had turned white long ago, but his eyebrows were still black and beetling, like little porches over his glittering eyes. The deep hollows in his cheeks and temples made a startling contrast with his mouth; it was as if all the rest of his face was starved for the sake of that full, flexible mouth. He was smiling. Slyly, at some pleasure known only to himself. Bix shivered.

"So you want to sell the furnishings, Miss Buckmaster. Not wasting any time, are you?"

"I need the money," said Rachel.

"Money," declaimed Francie. "Root of all evil. Who steals my purse steals trash." He chuckled. "That's what they say. That brother of yours still incarcerated?"

"That's why I need the money, Mr. Henshaw. He shouldn't be in jail, and I'm going to get him out. Because he didn't kill your wife."

"Why didn't he? He should have. The woman was an abomination upon the face of the earth. Don't refer to her as my wife." He turned suddenly on Bix. "I suppose you're interested in selling the family jewels too? Does your father know you're here?"

"N-no. I just—I just—" (Stop stammering. What are you, a woman or a worm? Look at Rachel, standing there with her chin stuck out. She's not stammering. She's not scared of a skinny, smelly old man.) "Daddy doesn't think Hartley did it, either. He says it's ridiculous."

Francie began to laugh, silently. He threw back his head, and Bix could see the knot of his Adam's apple sliding up and down. "Ridiculous. Says it's ridiculous. What does he know about it?"

"He knows Hartley," said Bix. "Better than you do, anyway."

The Adam's apple did some more sliding. Then Francie wiped his mouth with the back of one long, dirty hand. "Maybe yes, maybe no. I know Hartley well enough. They're all alike, all this younger generation. Riddled with corruption. No stamina. Undermined by soft living—"

"Oh for heaven's sake," burst out Rachel. "If you think Hartley's had a soft life you're—"

"Crazy?" Francie licked his lips. "Mr. Pigeon thinks I'm crazy. Oh, he didn't say so, mind you. But I can tell, I can tell. He had that look in his eye. They all get it. Lots of people think I'm crazy. I don't mind. It's their privilege."

And their mistake, thought Bix, staring in a kind of fascination at that strange, gaunt face. It was typical of Mr. Pigeon to check Francie off as a harmless crackpot. Typical of Mr. Pigeon; very convenient indeed for Francie.

"I may be crazy," he went on, and he was smiling again, craftily. "But

I'm not incarcerated. Like our friend Hartley. Incarcerated for a crime he didn't commit."

"Then you agree with us," said Rachel quickly. "You know he's innocent, too."

"Nothing of the kind. Don't know a thing about it. Care less. I'm just taking your word for it. If he did it, I'd be the first to congratulate him. If he didn't, more's the pity."

"I suppose Mr. Pigeon told you about the money your—Mrs. Henshaw had stashed away? And I suppose you were surprised to hear about it."

"Stunned," said Francie promptly. "The only commendable thing the woman ever did. Especially if she didn't make a will. Dear, careless Rose!"

"I wonder where she got all that money. It sounds—well, it sounds like blackmail to me."

There was a queer silence. Francie's eyebrows rose, as if in surprise, but the glance he darted at Rachel was one of—What? Suspicion? Anger? Fear? Anyway, not surprise.

"Now, now, Miss Buckmaster, don't let your imagination run away with you," said Francie, and Bix let her breath out again, quietly. "I don't see how even Rose could dig up anybody in Coreyville to blackmail. This isn't Chicago, you know. You've been reading too much of this modern detective trash. Why don't you try Schopenhauer instead? I recommend him highly." He tapped the worn volume on the velvet chair, and then, abruptly, smacked his bony hands together. His eyes were sparkling. "There. So much for sociable gossip. Now we can get down to the real reason for your visit. I understand you want to dispose of some furniture?"

He had them licked, and they knew it as well as he did. Bix couldn't trust herself to speak. She turned away, pretending to peer at a bow-legged table that seemed to stagger under its load of chipped china and dusty gimcracks. She could hear Rachel's unsteady voice: "Yes. The furniture. There's a clock—maybe you remember it—very old—"

Hateful, terrifying old man. *I know Hartley well enough. They're all alike, all this younger generation....* And Bix had just stood there with her teeth in her mouth, too dumb, too scared to fight back. No spine whatever. No brains. Nothing but this awful wrenching feeling in her chest and the disgusting sting of tears in her eyes. She blinked at the load of gimcracks. A pink lamp shade, crusted with beads. A cracked mirror with a dented silver handle. A cut-glass bowl, final resting place of two dead flies. A lot of candlesticks...

Yes, there was a brass one; the mate, no doubt, of Mrs. Henshaw's.

A heavy, square-cornered, brass candlestick. Her hand reached out and closed around it. She turned impulsively.

"Isn't this like the one in your house, Rachel?" She held it out. "It looks familiar, somehow."

"Why, yes. Yes, I believe it is. Just like it." Their eyes met, cautiously, and then moved to Francie's face. Bix felt prickly all over. Because there was no doubt about it, Francie's face had changed, he was no longer smiling. "We always kept ours down in the cellar. Come to think about it, I haven't seen it this time. But it's probably around somewhere."

"About this clock you mentioned—" Francie began.

"It's funny you should have a candlestick just like ours," said Rachel.

"What's funny about it? A piece of junk. I've had that one around for years. Dime a dozen."

"Really? It's quite an unusual pattern. I don't think I've ever seen one—"

"A piece of junk, I said! Do you think I've got nothing better to do than stand around all day arguing with you about candlesticks? If you want to talk business with me, talk it. If you don't, get out." The veiled, shouting voice had turned into something like a snarl. "That's what I said. If you want to talk business—"

"We heard you, Mr. Henshaw," said Rachel sweetly. "Come on, Bix. I'm afraid we've taken too much of your time. Thank you, just the same."

They sailed down the path through the jungle. But at the door, just as the bell jangled out its signal of departure, Bix looked back, and it seemed to her that Francie was smiling again. Slyly, at some pleasure known only to himself.

Mr. Pigeon (they went straight up to the courthouse to see him) was very much interested, he said soothingly. He was working on the candlestick angle; so far nothing had turned up, and, frankly, he wasn't banking too much on it. But Francie's reaction was interesting; it certainly was.

"Eccentric old codger, isn't he?" said Mr. Pigeon genially. "Every town has at least one. Very bad heart, they tell me. Apt to cork off any minute."

It was already getting dark when they walked home. One streak of cold, lemon-colored light was left in the west, but fading fast. The patches of ice that had melted a little during the day were skimming over again, sealing themselves up against another long, cold night.

"I don't care," said Bix. "Francie knows something about that candlestick. He wouldn't have acted that way if he didn't. He knows what it was used for. Maybe he even knows where it is."

Rachel didn't answer. Her feet were dragging as much as Bix's. Once she drew a sharp breath—maybe a sob, maybe just a sigh. It was better, Bix decided, not to know for sure.

Dinner didn't help the situation, either. In the first place, Mother chose tonight to start recuperating; for the first time since Rachel's arrival she showed up downstairs. Very wan in her long gray robe. Very patient and sweet. She kept making lady-like conversation at Rachel, and Rachel kept trying to keep her mind on it. Daddy was so busy fussing over darling Althea—"Are you sure you're warm enough, darling? Shall I get you the afghan?"—that he hardly knew anybody else was around. It was ghastly.

Bix cooked. Elaborately—to relieve the pressure. It didn't turn out the way the book said at all. Daddy took one bite of the Spanish rice, blinked, and said, "Jesus, honey, you sure stubbed your toe when you put in the red pepper." Mother said, "Now, Hugh. It's very tasty, Beatrix dear." Bix said viciously, "Eat it, then. I dare you to," and was rewarded with a look of saintly reproach.

The phone rang, and Rachel said, very fast, "If that's—Dr. Craig, I don't want to talk to him. Tell him I'm asleep, or in the bathtub, or dead drunk, or something." It wasn't Doc, though. It was Gloria, down at the office, calling for Daddy. Old Eager-Beaver Gloria. Daddy's Girl Friday working overtime again, loving every minute of it, and never letting Daddy forget it.

Instead, Doc simply rang the doorbell a few minutes later and waltzed in, all set for the welcoming committee. Daddy's mouth got that little quirk of amusement as he ushered Doc in. "Had your supper, Doc? Here, sit down and eat with us." And one thing about Doc, he sat up and ate the rest of the Spanish rice without a whimper. They all—even Rachel—watched him respectfully.

"Nothing like home cooking," he said when he had finished. He smiled at everybody, especially Rachel, and she gave him the full iceberg treatment. She was the one that could do it, too, thought Bix; Docs smile froze in its tracks. After that, while they were having coffee, he kept casting worried little glances at her, and Daddy had to ask him three times to pass the cream. It was kind of a diversion but after a while it began to seem ghastly too. Bix propped her elbow on the table and stared at the sugar bowl. Why doesn't she just ask him if he's still got a wife? she thought. They think they've got troubles! Hartley—

It wasn't the same, trying to talk to him up there in that gray cement room. They had been scared before, she and Hartley, but one of them had always been able to say something. They couldn't now. Helpless; but no one more helpless than she was. Hartley. He had never failed her, not once in all her life, and she was failing him.

"I move we migrate to the comfortable chairs," said Daddy, getting up. "Wait a minute, Althea darling. Wait till I get the couch fixed for you." He went into the living room and turned on the light beside the couch. It flickered several times before it stayed on. "Looks like we need a new bulb. There. I guess it's all right—"

Right then was when it happened. The splintering crash; Daddy's voice, sharp with alarm: "What in the hell—"; a faint scream from Mother; the rush of all their feet.

Someone had thrown a rock through the living room window. It lay in the middle of the rug, as incredible as a visitor from Mars.

Doc Craig moved first. "Hey, there's a note," he said, "a message—" Wrapped around the rock and held there with a rubber band was a scrap of paper on which were pasted words cut from a newspaper. It was not a long message.

> "Warning R. B. and B. B. Mind your own business.
> You know what I mean. You will be sorry if you
> do not."

Doc read it out word by word.

"What?" said Daddy crossly.

"R. B. and B. B." whispered Rachel. "Bix! That's us. R. B. and B. B." her hand, colder than the rock itself, gripped Bix's.

And Bix tore away from her. She tore away from all of them, standing there like so many wax dummies, and rushed to the broken window. A steam of winter air hit her face; it was like a drink of achingly cold water.

"Listen, you out there!" Her voice screeched into the darkness. "Listen to me! You can't scare me. I'm not going to mind my own business! You hear me? I'm going to—"

"Bix, get away from there! Bix, you crazy kid—"

She turned then, and screeched at them. It seemed to her that the sudden gust of wind which sent the curtain cracking inward struck straight through her too, straight to the wrenching place in her chest. Splinters of glass crunched under her feet; she clenched her hands against her chest, and it was rending her, splitting her, once and for all, in two. "I don't care!" she screamed at the whole world. "I don't care! I love Hartley! Do you understand? I *love* Hartley—"

XVI

And then nothing in the room moved except the curtain. Hugh stood at the bottom of the stairs, with one foot on the first step and his hand clamped on to the bannister. In her headlong flight Bix had flung away from him—even from him. He looked defenseless, thought Doc, like a man dazed by a stroke of lightning. Althea huddled in the corner of the sofa with her hands over her eyes. Not crying; simply shutting out the world, closing up like a touch-me-not against the rude hand of reality. As for Doc himself and Rachel, they seemed rooted here in the middle of the room. He stole a glance at her face. It looked the way his felt: blank. He was still holding the rock in his hand.

And only the curtain moved, twisting in the draft, making a faint whipping sound. It seemed to Doc that the air still throbbed with Bix's voice crying love and defiance, that the space in front of the shattered window still held the imprint of her figure—weedy yet staunch, absurd yet somehow majestic. Yes; majestic....

Althea was the first one to speak. "Hugh. The window, Hugh. It's so cold."

"Yes, darling." He, turned, like a machine jerking back into action. "I'll fix it. We'll put something up." He came over and put his arms around her for a moment. Apparently it steadied him. "First, though, I'm going to call Charlie Jeffreys and Pigeon and tell them what's been going on here. I'd like to know how they can fit this in with keeping Hartley in jail. Because it doesn't fit. That's all." He flashed a reassuring smile at Rachel. "Also, I'd like to know how they're planning to protect you and Bix. Maybe that threatening letter is somebody's idea of a joke, but I'd rather not take a chance on it."

"Lord, no." Doc looked down at the rock in his hand. He still didn't quite believe it. "R. B. and B. B. That's what I don't get, why they picked you two. What have you been up to?"

"We went to see Francie Henshaw this afternoon," said Rachel. (But she wouldn't look directly at him; she was talking as much to Hugh as to him. What is this? he thought, as he had thought a dozen times during dinner. She couldn't still be brooding over the Grey thing. They had both forgotten that in the excitement of finding Mrs. Pierce. What the hell was eating on her?) "And when we mentioned the other candlestick he got all upset and practically threw us out."

"The other candlestick?" Hugh stared at her. Kept on staring, while she explained it all. He hunched his shoulder nervously. "Francie? Of course he's a queer old party, but I can't believe that Francie—"

"Oh, Hugh," said Althea in that tired, sweet voice of hers. "Queer old party! Why don't you admit what everybody else knows? You're always so determined to stick up for these crackpot friends of yours."

He flushed a little, at the weary scorn in her tone. (She really is a bitch, thought Doc, in her own quaint way.) "He did act suspicious, Hugh," said Rachel. "And then, to have this happen right afterwards—it's too much of a coincidence."

"I suppose it is. But he couldn't have killed Mrs. Henshaw. He hasn't got the physical strength. Besides, I dropped in on him that afternoon, the way I do every day or so, and there he was with his nose in a book. Not one bit different from any other day. He couldn't have done it."

"He knows who did, then. Or something. He knows something he's not telling. Bix and I went right to Mr. Pigeon, and he said—Well, he said we were very co-operative. He seems to think Francie's just a harmless eccentric."

"Very convenient," said Doc. "For Francie."

Hugh sighed. Then he went out into the hall to the telephone. Doc shifted from one foot to the other, and Rachel took a tentative step away from him and then decided to stay where she was, after all. The lesser of two evils, no doubt. He was no red-hot favorite—she had made that clear enough tonight—but she would still rather be paired off with him, as it were, than with Althea. Which gave Althea a pretty low rating. The feeling, Doc decided, was mutual. Not that this set Rachel apart; Althea's cold indifference took in the whole world. She had forgotten how to love anybody—assuming that she had ever known how. "My son, my little boy...." She had once known how, all right. Only all her heart had been spent on Ronnie; she had none left, thought Doc, she was bankrupt.

There she sat, pale, genteel, and bankrupt. "I must apologize," she said, "for Beatrix and the way she behaved—"

"No!" The flat, rude contradiction startled Doc, who had produced it, as much as it did Althea. He felt his face getting red. He gulped and went on. "Bix doesn't need anybody to apologize for her. The way she behaved was—was—you ought to be—"

"A fine thing," said Hugh, back from his session at the telephone. "Can't get either one of them. Charlie's wife says Pigeon called him a while back, but she's got no idea where they went. This is great. Just great." He cast a curious glance at Doc's face. But he didn't ask any questions. "Oh well. We'll get them eventually. Come on, Doc, how about we fix up this window some way?"

"Sure." As Doc turned, his eyes met Rachel's at last, in a silent, important question. *You think the way I do about Bix, don't you? She was wonderful, wasn't she?* And her whole face glowed with the fervent answer: *Yes. Of course. Wonderful.* For only a second, though. She remembered whatever it was that was eating on her, and snuffed out the glow.

All the same, Doc felt better.

XVII

Mrs. Smiley shooed the cats off the supper table and made another pass at her bleached, upswept hair, which tottered like a ruined castle on top of her head.

"That's just it," she told Mr. Pigeon and Charlie Jeffreys. "Mr. Henshaw ain't home yet. I don't hardly know what to think. Because he's always back, right on the dot of six. Like Smiley says, we set the clock by him."

They hadn't set the clock lately, apparently. It sat on the back of the stove, a drunken-looking pink alarm clock minus one foot, its hands pointing irresponsibly to half past one. Charlie Jeffreys glanced at his wrist watch. "It's after seven," he said. "And he's not down at the store. We tried there."

"Madonna honey," Mrs. Smiley addressed one of the three young Smileys who sat on the floor, all eating something red and sticky, all absorbed in comic books, "Madonna honey, run up and take another look, there's a good girl. Though I know we'd of heard him, we always do. He uses the outside stairs, you know, but he always taps on the kitchen door, looks in and says Good evening, and that's how I know it's six o'clock." Her face, caked with the remains of some other day's make-up, took on an expression of genuine concern. She fumbled worriedly at the belt of the bedraggled, flowered housecoat which seemed to be all she was wearing. Mrs. Smiley's figure, like her face, was large and amiable. "Smiley ain't back with the truck yet, or I'd of sent him out to look. We've been uneasy about him, ever since he had that bad spell with his heart, back in the fall. Madonna honey, you heard Mama. Run up and—"

"Never mind," said Mr. Pigeon. "We'll take a look ourselves, if it's all right with you."

Of course it was all right with Mrs. Smiley. "I better take you up. There's a bad place in the stairs. I keep at Smiley and at him to fix it, but you know how men are. Now I just wonder where that flashlight got to...." It turned out, after some searching, to have gotten into the bread box. From under the sink Mrs. Smiley plucked a shapeless sweater and threw it around her shoulders. Then she opened the back door and led them up the rickety outside staircase to Francie's room, on the second floor.

"Mr. Henshaw!" she called before she opened the door. "Mr. Henshaw! You in there?"

Her voice trailed away forlorn and unanswered on the chilly wind. Slap-slap went her soiled lavender satin slippers; the door clicked open, and in a moment she had turned on the unshaded bulb that dangled from the center of Francie's room. For such a small room, it held a great many things, among them an unmade bed, a kerosene stove, an ancient electric plate, a dusty shelf crammed with books, and Francie's stock of canned goods—but not Francie himself. There was a strong, stale smell of peanut butter, kerosene, and unwashed wool.

"He don't like for me to make his bed for him," said Mrs. Smiley. "He'd sooner fix everything for himself. 'Just leave me alone,' he always says. 'Just leave me be, I know the way I want things.'" Suddenly her big, blurred face seemed to crumple up; her eyes moved in belated alarm from Charlie to Mr. Pigeon, back again to Charlie. "What do you want with him? What's happened? Sixteen years he's lived with us, and he's never been late before. Six o'clock on the dot. Something's wrong! Something's happened to the poor old soul!"

"Now, now," said Mr. Pigeon soothingly. "Don't worry, Mrs. Smiley. We'll find him."

Maybe so, but Charlie didn't see exactly how, at the moment. Of course the old guy couldn't just vanish. But it wasn't like looking for somebody who might have stopped in at the pool hall for a beer, or gone to the movies, or dropped in on some friends for a visit. Francie never did any of these things. If he wasn't at the store or at Smiley's, you could bet he was loping along that little path of his, on his way from one place to the other.

Only tonight you would have lost your bet. Silently Charlie followed Mr. Pigeon down the shaky staircase and out to the Chevvie. He looked back at Mrs. Smiley; she was standing in the kitchen door, wiping her eyes on her sweater sleeve. Not any too bright, thought Charlie, and pig-sty dirty; but good-hearted. You had to give her that. Or maybe all that worried her was losing out on the rent, in case something had happened to Francie. No. She'd called him Mr. Henshaw, and that clinched it, somehow, for Charlie. She thought enough of him to call him Mr. Henshaw.

"We could have looked for the candlestick while we were up there," he ventured as he started up the Chevvie.

"It'll keep," said Mr. Pigeon. "Let's look for the old man first."

"Okay. Where to?"

"Somebody must have seen him when he left the store. Unless he sneaked out the back way, for some reason. And even then—"

Down town three establishments were still open: the pool hall, the drug store, and the Square Deal Cafe. Mitch, who ran the pool hall, produced a fishy stare when Charlie asked if he had seen Francie. "Who, me? You nuts, Charlie? Francie Henshaw never drank a beer or played a game of pool in his life." No, he hadn't noticed Francie going past; and neither had any of the customers, though the kid from the filling station thought maybe he had. But he wasn't sure.

Same story at the drug store.

But Erma, the Square Deal waitress, perked right up at Charlie's question. "Sure I saw him. He came out of his store a little before six, as usual, but then he didn't go right on up the street, like he always does. That's how I happened to notice him. He stopped in front of the Tribune office, sat down on the bench where people wait for the bus, you know, and I thought don't tell me Francie's going somewhere on the bus, or waiting to meet somebody—"

"Was he?"

Erma shrugged. "The bus don't get in till 6:45, and by that time I was too busy to notice. I just saw him kind of hanging around there, is all. The Tribune office was already closed, I know that, so he wasn't stopping in to see Mr. Bovard the way he sometimes does. So that's why I thought of the bus, even though it seemed awful early for anybody to be waiting for it."

Charlie pounded back out to the Chevvie and passed this on to Mr. Pigeon. For what it was worth. The 6:45 bus went back to Westburg, among other places, and Westburg was where Mrs. Pierce lived and where she and Mrs. Henshaw had grown up. Mr. Pigeon thought it over and decided it might be worth while to follow the bus and see if Francie really had caught it.

"Okay," said Charlie. "Here we go." It was the only lead they had. And something told him it was going to be a wild goose chase.

XVIII

Out in the Bovard woodshed, Doc held the flashlight while Hugh scrabbled around among the odds and ends of lumber until he found what he wanted. "This'll do it," he said, pulling out a strip of beaverboard. "We can tack this up over the window for tonight. Let's take in an armload of wood, too. Maybe a fire in the fireplace will cheer us up." He grinned, rather wanly. "I guess we can use a little cheer."

"Amen," said Doc. "You don't happen to know what's eating on Rachel, do you? I mean, even before all this business with the rock she didn't act—well, the way she did yesterday. Unless it's just my imagination working overtime...." He paused, hopefully.

Hugh snapped off that bit of nonsense without ceremony. "It's not. She's sore at you about something, my boy. Don't ask me what. Women. I can't figure 'em out. Why don't you ask her?"

A good question. One that might have occurred to Doc himself, if he had a lick of sense, which it seemed he hadn't. "Well. All right. Well, I guess I will."

Hugh was busy with the piece of beaverboard, maneuvering it through the woodshed door. "Do my eyes deceive me, or have you gone overboard for Rachel?"

"Good Lord, no!" Doc dredged up a reasonable facsimile of a light laugh. "Thanks a lot, but no thanks. It's against my principles, that sort of thing. She's just a good-looking babe, that's all."

"That she is," said Hugh drily. Doc could see his face now—the deep lines running from nose to mouth, the quirked eyebrow that was ordinarily humorous, but that looked at this moment so mortally sad. "I wish you luck with your principles. And I wish to God I'd been bright enough to play it your way. If I had it to do over again—"

Doc waited.

"Oh hell. Let's face it. There's no reason to believe I'd be any brighter, the second time around."

A good guy, Hugh. About as good as they come, thought Doc, and definitely as unlucky. Let this be a lesson to you, just in case you show any signs of going overboard. And don't kid yourself, you've been showing them. The way you fired up about Bix, for instance. That was partly because ... Okay, so Rachel's different, she isn't Althea. It doesn't change the principle. She's just a good-looking babe. That's all she is, and don't you forget it.

The open fire turned out to be quite a success. They sat around it—

after the window was patched up—with drinks and cigarettes, and even Rachel seemed to relax in the mellow warmth. She held out her hands to it: good big hands, for all her slender wrists, and once or twice she went so far as to smile at Doc. It was almost possible to forget the rock lying there on the coffee table. Hugh made a passable joke of the extra precautions he took, locking up doors and windows, and of his trips out to the telephone in the hall. Mr. Pigeon and Charlie Jeffreys were still among those missing at eleven.

"I give up," said Hugh, yawning. "Let's go to bed, Althea. You young folks can set up as late as you want to. Just be sure you lock the door, Rachel, when Doc leaves."

"I'm sort of sleepy myself," said Rachel. But tentatively.

"You can't go to bed yet," Hugh told her. "You've got to finish your drink. Good night, kiddies."

Mr. Cupid Bovard, thought Doc. Not too subtle, maybe, but you had to give him A for Effort. One thing, the setting was made to order: cozy fire, dim lights, soft music purling out of the radio. He stretched out in his chair and stole a quick look at Rachel, stretched out in hers. The thing to do was to plan this campaign. The surprise attack? The encircling movement? Or the marking-time, it's-your-move routine, designed to wear down her resistance?

She turned her face toward him, and instantly he lost track of his cool plans. One bound, and he was out of his chair, kissing her with all the finesse of a high school kid on his maiden date. He got what he deserved—no co-operation. Not that she resisted. She just sat still, detaching herself from the whole proceedings. He balanced himself on the arm of her chair and (be nonchalant) started to light a cigarette. Which was another error, advertising as it did the unsteadiness of his hands.

"All right," he said. "Let's have it. I'm sorry I asked you who Greg is, if that's what you're sore about. Maybe he's a ball of fire, this Greg. Maybe I ought to be flattered that you got me confused with him. I'm just not used to—"

"No. Greg's not a ball of fire. He's just—somebody I used to know." The words seemed to surprise her a little, but then she nodded, as if they were, after all, what she had meant to say. "That's all. I called Greg, late this afternoon. Because I felt so— But he didn't have time to talk. He was due at a dinner party."

So much for the Great Greg. Him and his dinner parties, Lord love him. But the fact still remained....

"What is it, then? What's wrong? Yesterday things were well, quite a bit different."

"Yesterday." She clasped her hands in her lap and regarded them thoughtfully. "Now that you mention it, I guess things were different yesterday."

"So what's happened? Why the difference? After all, I'm the same sweet kid." There. He was doing better, he was hitting his stride again.

"I'm sure you are," she said pleasantly. "Or should we say the same slick operator?"

"Look here, Rachel, let's stop playing games and—" (But that was all wrong. The point was to keep the whole thing on the game-playing level. Good clean fun, with no chance of getting involved or hurt.)

"And what? I'm just an amateur at these games of yours, you know. You're the expert." She said it bravely enough, but all at once something happened to her face. Her mouth started trembling, her eyes fluttered shut, and—well, this time it was no high school kid kiss. It was like yesterday. Too much so for safety.

"Please," she whispered. "No. Oh, please no." She pulled away from him and sat up straight.

"Don't look like that." Somehow, he discovered, he had wound up on his knees beside her chair. He was past caring. "Darling. Tell me. Tell me what's wrong."

"I'm ashamed to," she said. "Because it makes it look as if I—" She took a breath and finished, very fast. "After all, what possible difference can it make to me, whether you have a wife or not?"

A wife. The same slick operator. These games of yours. A wife.

She was waiting. "Oh," he said feebly, "that."

"Yes. That." The cleft chin tilted up, very proud, very vulnerable.

"Here's how it is. Rachel darling, I owe you an explanation—" He swallowed. Why was it that you never sounded phonier than when you were breaking your neck to tell the truth? "It's very simple, really. Believe me. I never meant to—"

He heard the noise, and stopped talking. She heard it, and stopped listening to him. A stealthy thump from the direction of the kitchen. They leaped to their feet and waited tensely. The thump came again.

"Probably nothing. A loose shutter," explained Doc. "You wait here while I take a look."

"Certainly not. Here. Here's the poker. I'll take the shovel."

They crept through the dining room (and the poker made him feel like a fool, only there was the rock, lying back there on the coffee table, the rock and the unlikely note) and noiselessly pushed open the swinging door that led to the kitchen.

XIX

Wild goose chase was right. Charlie Jeffreys shifted from one foot to the other and tried to figure out whether Mr. Pigeon was looking at him or at the bus driver, a fattish young man whose mouth, at the moment, was full of apple pie. He had had just enough start on them, had gotten all the way to the end of the line before they caught up with him. Westburg. The Westburg Eatery, Open Day & Nite. Charlie leaned against the counter and waited for the bus driver to dispose of his mouthful. He knew right now what the answer was going to be. Already the bus driver was shaking his head.

"Nope. Didn't pick up anybody at Coreyville."

"Any passengers get off here tonight?"

The bus driver swilled down some coffee and thought a minute. "Yep. Two dames with shopping bags. I picked them up in Red Rock; they'd spent the day there shopping. Yackety yackety about bargains, all the way to Coreyville."

"Anybody meet them?"

"Nope. They took off up Main Street and I got out and stretched my legs and smoked a cigarette."

"Anybody hanging around there in front of the Tribune office? Anybody sitting on the bench? An old guy, maybe, kind of a funny-looking skinny old guy?"

"Nope. Nothing doing at all. Had the bus by myself till I got to Red Rock. A bunch of high school kids got on there. No funny-looking skinny old guy." The bus driver went back to work on the apple pie, and Charlie followed Mr. Pigeon out to the car.

So back we go to Coreyville, thought Charlie. He's there some place. Got to be. And it's anybody's guess what the old devil's been up to, while we've been kiting around chasing that so-and-so bus. It'll be well after eleven before we get back. Plenty of time for plenty of things to happen.

He watched Mr. Pigeon settling down comfortably in his corner. "Now, now," said Mr. Pigeon, as he had said to Mrs. Smiley. "Don't worry, Sheriff. We'll find him."

XX

Refrigerator, stove, sink glimmered like massive ghosts in the silent kitchen. Doc took another cautious step forward and tried to decide whether or not to turn on the light. The swinging door behind him, where Rachel still paused, was half-open, letting in a finger of feeble light. It seemed to feel its way across the big kitchen to the opposite wall with its two doors, one opening into Hugh's study, the other in the middle of another step. That stairway door was moving inward, very, very slowly. He tightened his grip on the poker, waited while the door inched open and the shadowy figure slid through. Then he plunged across the linoleum and grabbed. At the same moment Rachel flicked on the light.

"Bix! What in the hell are you up to?"

"None of your business! Let go of me!" She stopped wriggling, and some of the scared look faded from her big eyes. She was wearing that beat-up, over-size leather jacket and a pair of slacks. "Jeepers, you don't have to twist a person's arm off."

He put down the ridiculous poker and glanced at Rachel, who had her hand over her mouth no doubt holding back a laugh. Okay, so he was a figure of fun. After all, the poker and shovel had been her idea, not his. He glared at Bix.

"What's the big idea, prowling around like this? Naturally we took you for a burglar. Where do you think you're going?"

"Out," said Bix. She clamped her mouth shut again.

"Listen, you two," said Rachel, "stop snapping at each other, or you'll have everybody else awake, and that's not going to be any help. Or maybe—" She paused by the table, watching Bix. "Maybe that's what we ought to do. Wake up your Dad and—"

"No," whispered Bix. But she stuck her hands in her pockets and made one more stab at defiance. "I guess I've got a right to go out for a breath of fresh air if I want to."

"Oh, stop it. Breath of fresh air, my eye. We know what you're going out for."

"Do we?" inquired Doc.

Rachel paid no attention to him. "It's not safe, Bix. Stop trying to muscle in on Mr. Pigeon's territory. He may not be a thunderbolt, but he knows how to deal with this better than you do."

"Why doesn't he deal with it, then? He can't even be reached. I heard Daddy trying to get him all evening. He can't even be reached."

"For all you know, he may be down there right now. Probably he is."

"Okay, if he is, I'll help him."

"Help him do what? Down where?" put in Doc. "Will one of you dames kindly explain—"

"Down at Francie's store, you dope," Bix flashed back at him. "Hunting for the candlestick."

"For Lord's sake," said Doc. "You mean to tell me you were planning to—"

"Not was. Am." She looked him in the eye. "Try and stop me."

"But Bix, you can't go down there by yourself!"

"Oh, can't I!" She leaned toward him, and he could see the tear streaks on her thin, tragic child-face. It was like the moment when she had stood in front of the broken window with the curtains whipping out and her hands doubled up against her chest. She was whispering now, not screaming; still, it was like that moment. "You make me sick. All of you. 'Poor, poor Hartley. That poor, dear boy.' Well, why don't you do something about him instead of just standing around talking about your bleeding hearts? And now you're trying to keep me from doing anything. You're scared of a crazy old man! You're scared of a rock and a little busted glass! You make me sick!"

It didn't make any sense at all. And yet Doc felt the crawl of shame; his coward eyes shifted under Bix's gaze; he cleared his throat and ran his fingers through his hair. He couldn't think of anything to say? Nonsense, he assured himself. He could think of all kinds of arguments. He was simply taking his time choosing which to use first.

He didn't get a chance to use any of them. Rachel crossed over to Bix. She didn't touch her; she just stood beside her. "All right then, Bix. I'll go with you."

He opened his mouth to protest, but the look on Rachel's face stopped him. An intense look, aimed exclusively at him, telling him something without words. Telling him he was outvoted, for one thing. But more than that. Appealing to him to play it her way for now, to take her word for it, to trust her. It was all there, in the almost imperceptible tip of her head, the flicker of her eyelid. He looked back at her helplessly.

Women. You couldn't win. Maybe you didn't even want to.

"We'll need our coats," he said at last. "Wait here. I'll get them." While he was closing the door to the hall closet, he thought he heard a rustling from upstairs. He waited for Hugh's voice, meanwhile busily preparing his explanation. Rachel and I decided to run down town for a cup of coffee, or a nightcap, or a bite to eat. Taking Bix with us (in case her absence had been noticed, upstairs). But Hugh didn't call down to him. He might have imagined the rustling. No, there it was again, the kind of sound a woman's robe might make. He thought of Althea and her insomnia and her long gray robe. He tried to peer up the stairway, but could see nothing. After a minute the rustling stopped too, and he went back to the kitchen.

They let themselves out the back door with hardly a sound, and set off down the alley three abreast, with Doc in the middle, firmly gripping Rachel's arm on one side, Bix's on the other. He hoped this was the accepted bodyguard procedure. Crazy, he thought; an absolutely hare-brained expedition....

"The least we can do," Rachel was whispering in his ear. "Humor the poor kid. It's awfully lonesome, sometimes, being sixteen. Pigeon's probably already down there, or if he isn't we won't be able to get in—"

"What?" asked Bix suspiciously. "Why don't you talk so I can hear you?"

"We're figuring how to get in the place. You got any ideas?"

"We'll find some way." Bix gave a confident little skip. There was something contagious about her faith, something satisfactory—Doc admitted it to himself—about the whole project. It beat sitting at home, waiting for somebody to throw another rock.

He still couldn't quite believe the rock, anyway. Just as he couldn't really believe that this alley—dark as it was, dark as a pocket—was bristling with weird and wonderful dangers. Sure it was dark; this was familiar, pokey old Coreyville on a winter night. Quiet; except for the wind which made a faint, sad rattling in Myra Graves' lilac hedge, the sound of a car starting up a couple of blocks away on Main Street, and the ring of their own footsteps on the frozen ground. Ordinary, Coreyville noises. For the life of him Doc couldn't get alarmed about them.

They cut across the vacant lot opposite the Buckmaster house and turned down the back street which brought them, by way of another alley, to the rear entrance of Francie's store. Nobody met them or jumped out at them. A dim night-light burned in the grocery store next door; Francie's place was wedged in between it and the barber shop. Bix took out her flashlight and turned it on the weather-beaten door.

"I don't see any signs of your friend Mr. Pigeon," she was saying smugly. "No doubt he's already been here— Hey! Maybe he has! Because somebody has. The lock's busted." The flashlight beam gave a jump of excitement, then settled again on the padlock, which—no doubt about it—had been forced. They needn't have worried about how they were going to get in.

"Solves problem number one. All we have to do is walk in," said Bix, and prepared to suit the action to the word.

"Now wait a minute." Doc pulled her back, none too gently. "This is funny. What if they're still in there? Whoever broke the lock, I mean. Francie wouldn't bust into his own place. It's got to be somebody else."

"There's only one way to find out," said Bix. "Go in and see. You're scared to, I suppose. Well, it was nice seeing you.... Hey! What's that? Down past the barber shop?"

The world's oldest gag, and Doc fell for it. The flashlight beam swerved for a split second down the alley, he turned wildly and stared—at nothing, of course—and by the time he had a brain cell working, she was through the door. The witch. The damn, obstinate, slippery little eel of a witch. He forgot about Rachel (until she gasped) and said several things out loud. Then he followed Bix through the door. Rachel grabbed at his sleeve. "Wait for me. I'm coming too. Here. I've got a lighter." In the flicker of the little flame her eyes looked enormous. "I'm sorry," she whispered. "I didn't think it would be like this."

"Who's blaming you?" he said. "Come on."

There was a cold, stale, kerosene stink. The lighter didn't really help much. They kept bumping into things—sharp-cornered things, things with knobs and splinters, things that jangled or teetered or clattered. Once or twice there was a scurrying sound up ahead that could have been mice or Bix, take your choice. Wherever she was, she was lying low. Clutching her flashlight and biding her time. Unless somebody had been waiting for her.... His insides gave a lurch. Did he dare call out her name? Supposing whoever it was (if there was anyone) hadn't got to her yet, was just waiting for a sign? He played the lighter over another few feet of clutter and moved forward.

"Like a jungle," whispered Rachel. "Isn't it?"

It was. Hide-and-seek in the jungle. Come out, come out, wherever you are. One thing was for sure: he was It. Whatever happened to Bix or Rachel, he was to blame. They weren't responsible—Bix because she was sixteen and in love, Rachel because she was Hartley's sister—but he had no excuse. A real, aged-in-the-wood, bona fide meathead.

They had groped their way into what seemed to be a comparative clearing. Doc blundered against Francie's chair, just missing the kerosene stove. Up ahead lay more jungle, even vaster than the one they had covered. It was no good; they could stumble around in here all night and get no place. "I've got my bearings now," said Rachel in a low voice. She had stopped too; her hand was pressed tight in his. "There's a light, right about here. I remember. Let's—Let's turn it on and get it over with. If there is anybody in here they've already got us spotted, so—"

"Okay," he said after a minute. "Where is it? Turn it on."

"Oh nuts." It was Bix's voice, close at hand, and sagging with disgust. "I give up. Only will you please kindly not bitch everything up by turning on the light?"

"Bix! Where are you? Are you all right?"

"Why wouldn't I be?" She turned the flashlight on her own face briefly; it loomed up disembodied, dust-streaked, but undamaged. "I'm right here. Where else? If you turn on that light somebody's going to notice it from the street and come busting in and spoil everything. So will you please kindly—"

"Will you please kindly excuse me while I wring your neck?" burst out Doc. "You and your low tricks! Sneaking in here behind our backs, and then playing possum. Why the hell didn't you—"

"Temper, temper," reproved Bix. "I just figured I'd save time and avoid an argument."

"Sure. And maybe get yourself exterminated. God knows who's been prowling around in here. May still be here, for all you know."

"Nobody's showed up yet," said Bix airily. "And they've had plenty of time. Here. This is what we're looking for. Another one like this." The flashlight shone on a heavy brass candlestick. "Come on. Let's get busy."

"Busy nothing. We're getting out of here. I mean it, Bix."

"You promised—" she began, and he could see what was coming up. The routine that had trapped him before: the you-make-me-sick, scared-of-a-crazy-old-man business.

He wasn't having any more. "That was before I knew somebody else was going to have the same idea." He reached up and floundered in a wide circle above his and Rachel's heads, searching for the light. Found it. Francie's forty-watt bulb gave out with a foggy yellow glow; as it swung back and forth the shadows seemed to leap and flee every which way in terror. Doc stopped the swinging. Dusty velvet chair; cheerless stove; bow-legged table loaded with junk; a nightmare clutter of furniture, almost ceiling-high, stretching into the gloom ahead. Was someone lurking there, watching and waiting? There was no sound.

He braced himself and met Bix's eye. She was standing beside the table, grasping the candlestick in one hand and the flashlight in the other. Her face was white with the fury of one betrayed; oh Lord, he thought, she'll never forgive me, poor kid. That was the trouble with being sixteen—everybody was against you. Lonesome, Rachel had said. Awfully lonesome.

"Okay," she said stonily. "So we advertise. I'm still going to look, till somebody stops me."

And Doc, she left no doubt, wasn't the man who could stop her. She turned and set off up the path toward the front of the store, an absurd, exasperating, indomitable figure. He glanced at Rachel. She looked as if she didn't know whether to laugh or cry.

"Look then, damn it," he said, and he took off after her, herding Rachel along with him. "But we stick together. I still insist on that."

(Long Lars, the night watchman, was sure to notice the light in the course of his rounds and investigate. Besides, by this time Doc himself was finding it hard to believe that their friend the lock-breaker was still around. Surely he wouldn't have passed up all these golden opportunities to dispose of Bix, or all three of them, and nip out the back door. What had he been after, anyway? The candlestick? But that didn't make sense. If it was Francie, why would he break his own lock? And if it wasn't Francie, what was wrong with leaving the candlestick here, where it would implicate Francie and no one else?)

"Here," said Bix. "Make yourself useful. Hold the flashlight, will you?"

Doc obeyed meekly enough, while Bix began her search. Rachel helped. They opened drawers, they clambered up on tables and chairs and peered in corners. All they found was plenty of dust. (Ten minutes, and still nobody from the street had spotted them. Where was Long Lars? Drinking coffee, probably; chinning, in his monosyllabic way, with Erma over in the Square Deal, instead of tending to his duties.)

"How about the window?" asked Doc. "Plenty of junk there." He swept the flashlight beam over the incredible array: hitching post, chafing dishes, a child's rocking chair, a moth-eaten bearskin and a stuffed canary in a cage, urns half as tall as Dr. Craig and a set of teacups no bigger than thimbles.

"Why not?" said Rachel. "It might be Francie's idea of a joke, to hide it in the window. Providing he's the one that hid it, of course. Those vases are plenty big enough—"

"Wait a minute!" said Bix. Her voice was hushed, shaky with excitement; her eyes, as far as Doc could make out, were riveted on the head of the bearskin. A mean-looking customer, all right, with its yellow jags of teeth and its two fiercely gleaming little eyes. Still, it was nothing to go into a trance about. He swiped the light once more across the window, and Bix let out another muted yelp.

"His eyes. He's only supposed to have one eye...." She darted past Rachel and Doc, and leaped up into the window, knocking over a chafing dish and throwing the stuffed canary into a fit of delirious swinging. The teacups expired in a series of dainty crashes while she scrabbled under the bearskin.

The candlestick was there, tucked up under the bear's head, where the flashlight had caught its brassy glint through the one empty eye socket. Bix rubbed it against her leather jacket. Then she held it aloft triumphantly, like a warrior displaying a battle trophy. All she could do was squeak. "Oh, boy! Oh, boy! Oh—"

"That's it," Rachel was babbling. "Bix honey. That's it..."

Doc thrust the flashlight into her hands and lifted Bix out of the window bodily. She felt light and brittle as a bird, and inside the leather jacket she was shivering violently. He didn't feel any too steady himself.

"You found it." He forgot that she was never going to forgive him and hugged her, and he forgot that Rachel was mad at him and hugged her too. Everybody forgot and hugged everybody. "You did it, kid."

Their little love fest didn't last long. They were jarred out of it by noises from the back of the store. The tread of feet, cautious but resolute-sounding; voices demanding, "Francie? Hey there, Henshaw!" The figures of Charlie Jeffreys and Mr. Pigeon emerged in the foggy yellow light back there in the clearing. They raced back with their find, all yammering at once.

"Where the hell were you all night? Somebody threw a rock through Bovard's window, and we've been trying to get you...."

"Look! The candlestick! We found the other candlestick!"

"And somebody else has been prowling around down here, because the lock's busted...."

"Sure," put in Charley. "That was us. Trying to find Francie. We figured maybe he'd had a heart attack and was still in here. That was after we got back from Westburg. We been all over looking for him."

"Francie? You've been looking for Francie? Where is he?"

Charley opened his mouth and then shut it again, more in sorrow than in anger.

Even Mr. Pigeon sounded less tranquil than usual. "We haven't found him yet. He's disappeared. Hasn't been here since before six. Now let's get this straight about the rock and the candlestick and the rest of it."

Bix thrust her trophy at him. "I guess this proves it wasn't Hartley. He couldn't have hidden it here because he never came in here. I guess now you'll have to let him out of jail. He couldn't have thrown the rock, either. It has to be Francie."

"We'll see," said Mr. Pigeon cautiously. "We'll see. Maybe there'll be some fingerprints to help us, unless you've smeared them all up."

Bix's eyes got big. "I didn't think. All I did was pull it out from under the bear, and—" (But Doc had a vivid little picture in his mind of her standing in the window, rubbing the candlestick on her jacket before she held it up in triumph. Had that really been a thoughtless gesture? Of course. It must have been.) "Can we go now?" She was practically jumping up and down with excitement. "I want to go home and tell Daddy. And Hartley. I want to tell Hartley—"

"In a minute." Mr. Pigeon took out his handkerchief and wrapped it around the top of the candlestick before he picked it up gingerly. "Let's have the other candlestick, the one that's always been here. And let's see just where this one was found." They moved in a little procession toward the front window. Questions. Answers. Doc listened, with a kind of objective interest, to his own voice explaining. The rock thrown through the window. The three of them setting out on their expedition. The search. He was making it all sound quite likely, he was convincing himself that it had actually happened. Rachel explained, too, and she left her hand where it belonged, pressed tight in his. All in all, things were looking up; life in general seemed a pretty good deal.

And then he noticed that Bix was gone.

"The kid?" said Charley, looking startled. "Why, she was here just a minute ago."

"She's probably raced off home," said Rachel. Very calm and sensible. Except that Doc felt her hand go suddenly tense. "That's what she wanted to do, and you know how she is when she makes up her mind."

He knew, all right. And he was turning into a hysterical old maid, because nothing could have happened to Bix in these few minutes, there was absolutely no cause for alarm....

"Bix!" they called. Their voices sounded curiously muffled in this crowded place. As if they were all being slowly strangled, thought Doc. "Bix! Where are you?"

There was no answer at first. They were halfway to the door when they heard the muffled cry: "Let go! Let me go!" and running footsteps. Doc got out into the alley first. So he saw her first—the pitifully slight figure, like a bundle of old clothes, huddled against the back wall of the grocery store. His hands flashed into action, apparently of their own accord, searching for the pulse (and finding it, oh thank God, finding it), groping gently over the cropped head, afraid of what they might find. They paused at Bix's neck, and the others were here by now, with flashlights, so he could see that childish neck, smaller at the base, like a jointed doll's. No marks there. Nothing but a graze across her mouth, where she had scraped against the wall.

"Which way? Which way did they go?" Charlie Jeffreys was stammering with the strain of getting set to run both directions at once.

Bix's eyelids quivered and opened. Her beautiful gray eyes looked straight up into Doc's, trying to tell him something, and her swollen lips moved stiffly. It was hardly words that came out. Though it might have been, at that. It might have been, "I—fell—"

"We heard you yell. Whoever it was got scared and ran."

"Which *way?*" pleaded Charley, and when Bix pointed, not very positively, toward the barber shop he shot off.

"Who was it, Bix? Who grabbed you? Can you tell us? Did you see them?"

She closed her eyes, and her dirty face twisted grotesquely, trying to hold back the tears. She could not do it. They squeezed out—the terrible, difficult tears—and as she turned her head, once, from side to side, they trickled back across her temples.

Doc gathered her up in his arms. "Never mind. Don't try to talk any more. You're going to be all right, Baby—"

From down the alley came a hoarse yell, a thudding of footsteps. They turned to see the lanky figure of Long Lars the night watchman bearing down on them at full tilt, his fantastically long shadow flying along beside him. Long Lars was by nature a man of few words; these had now deserted him. His scraggly reddish moustache worked up and down; one arm flailed out, gesturing urgently.

At last a scattering of broken words struggled out past the moustache. "Back yonder. The old man. Old Francie. Sheriff found him. Looks dead to me."

Next, thought Doc. The line forms to the right, and no jostling, please. Just another quiet winter night in familiar, pokey old Coreyville.

Still carrying Bix in his arms, he headed down the alley toward his next customer.

XXI

Once in a while they came snooping around, poking at him, and it was an indignity, in a minute he was going to open his eyes and tell them so, he didn't have to put up with it, and he wasn't going to. In a minute. In just a minute.

The skimming was beginning again, though; better wait till it let up. Faster and faster. Higher and higher, with nothing to hold him down. Like the first time he ever rode on a Ferris wheel. And when was that, in the snarl of yesterday and today and tomorrow? Never mind, it had been some time, because the skimming was like it. The same delicious qualms, the perilous rush of wind, the world tilting crazily....

"Go easy on him, will you?" somebody said. (Now? Or some other time? Close at hand? Or way off somewhere?) "He's not up to much. Whatever he was doing last night, it nearly finished that heart of his. It's a miracle he's pulled out of it at all."

"He seems to be resting comfortably now," said another voice. A ridiculous, know-it-all kind of voice. And there was a murmur about all right, then, no hurry....

Resting comfortably. The fool woman. I am dying, thought Francie with a certain relish; that's what the skimming is, I am dying, and the fool woman says resting comfortably.

Why don't you go ahead and die, then? Francie knew who that was, all right: his old acquaintance the commentator (audible only to Francie) had been asking just such impolite questions for years. A crusty old party, the commentator; Francie had a sneaking fondness for him. *Why don't you go ahead and die, then? What's keeping you?*

Something remained to be done. That was what was keeping him. Something important that he had to do first.

You already did it. Don't you remember? Brain like a sieve. You already did it, and you hid the candlestick—that was pretty smart of you, hiding the candlestick the way you did.

Pretty smart? It had been a masterly touch. Of course he remembered. But that wasn't what he meant. Something else—an important, final something that he had to do. It would come to him, as soon as the skimming sensation let up. He couldn't be expected to remember everything while he was sailing through the air at this dizzy pace.

"How are you, Francie?" said someone. This time Francie knew it was now close at hand. His eyes jerked open, and for an appalling moment everything was clear—one of the faces bending over him belonged to that new-fangled young doctor (he'd charge you for breathing if you didn't keep your eye on him) and the other face was Mr. Pigeon's, and the third belonged to Mrs. Know-it-all Nelson, who ran the hospital.... The hospital! So that was what they had done with him behind his back! Horror-struck, he took in the clean, bare room, the antiseptic smell, the smooth sheet over him. They had stuck him in the hospital at God knows how many dollars a minute, just as they had threatened to do last fall. The Smileys—those mental incompetents, those base and treacherous Smileys—were responsible for this, and they would answer for it. But later. All in good time. Just now, it was more than he could bear. He closed his eyes, and off he skimmed.

"How are you, Francie?"

How do you do, Mr. Henshaw. I'm pleased to make your acquaintance....

The hospital, Dr. Craig, the Smileys—already they were out of sight, left far behind; and Francie, pleasantly conscious of his height, the elegance of his recently acquired moustache, and his new straw hat, was standing in the vestry (Wednesday evening choir practice) being introduced to the new choir member. Miss Rose Anthony, formerly of Westburg, who had very kindly consented to lend her voice to the soprano section. I'm pleased to make your acquaintance. She said it with a kind of demure slyness, as if already he and she had some sweet, terrible secret, and in the churchly dimness her face seemed to bloom like an unearthly flower. What was bewitching about that face with its waxy pallor, its sharp features and down-curving mouth? She was not a pretty girl, Miss Rose Anthony; not even if you considered her hair, which was hidden, when he first met her, under a large, ornate hat. And yet, all during choir practice, he was acutely aware of her and of his own uncontrollable impulse to watch her. Time after time he succumbed and let his eyes slide toward the soprano section, and each time Rose caught him at it. No matter how hastily he looked away, he could not escape her subtle, knowing smile, hardly more than a twitch of her mouth. I know, she seemed to be saying, I know, and you will know, before very long. Something shameless about her, from the beginning; shameless and tainted with evil. So that their little game in the choir loft—the guilty, split-second trysts between his eyes and hers—became a travesty of other, wholesome flirtations. The whole thing was like that, and it was played out against a background of sunshiny innocence that made the taint all the more evil. And all the more irresistible. It was as if Rose Anthony awoke in him a perverse taste, unsuspected until now, that spoiled all other pleasures for him forever.

The world that she poisoned was not so much his as Etta Kincaid's. It was Etta's native land—a happy little world of lawn parties and dances and ice cream socials—into which she had drawn him with all the strength of her warm, merry heart. To him it was all new (he had grown up in an orphanage); a miracle of apple-blossom freshness, like Etta herself. "So you're engaged to Etta Kincaid," Rose Anthony said to him. "How nice. And you work down at the bank, for her father. How nice." Thus, with a flick of Rose's tongue, was love reduced to expediency.

The monstrous part of it was that no one else saw Rose as he did—the serpent in this miniature Eden. "She does have a sharp tongue," Etta admitted. "But then she doesn't really mean it. Poor thing, she's getting over an unhappy love affair. That's why she came here and took the job in the millinery store, you know, to get over it." To the pure all things are pure. Etta and the rest of the crowd rallied around, cheerily bent on helping Rose forget her unhappy love affair. He alone knew that it was a myth: Rose had never heard of love. He alone was singled out for those sly, demure glances of hers, the half-derisive, half-inviting little smiles. Could it be because Rose and he were somehow akin? The same breed of cats? The idea revolted him. And yet.... And yet....

"Can you tell us what happened last night?" asked Mr. Pigeon. "What were you doing in the alley?"

"Summerhouse," Francie corrected him. What were you doing in the Kincaid summerhouse? What were you doing there with Rose Anthony, while Etta and the other innocents drank lemonade on the veranda?

She pulled off her hat, and the moonlight spilled down on her breathtaking hair, on the ghostly whiteness of her arms, on her heartless, haunting face. It was like a collision, that first kiss. Violent, and without tenderness. Then he was engulfed: Rose's body seemed to go boneless and plaster itself against him, her arms twined around him mercilessly, her tongue plunged against his, avid as a snake. And he was lost. He was lost.

He did not know this immediately. He believed that he could find his way back to Etta's fresh little paradise and live happily forever after. The long feverish summer was over before he knew that he could not.

"How did you feel about your wife, Francie?" Mr. Pigeon was saying sociably. "You didn't like her much, did you?"

"Despised her," Francie whispered. "An abomination."

Etta had asked him too, on one of those tense, painful evenings spent away from the crowd. Just the two of them, as Etta wistfully put it. She didn't understand, she faltered in a voice so strained that it no longer sounded like hers, and he got a glimpse—dimly, through the haze of his own misery—of what it was costing her in pride and courage to ask. "But you always said you didn't like Rose, Francis. Why, if you don't like her—"

Why, Why? How was it possible to be captivated by what he most despised? Rose's conversation, petty and drenched in spite; her laugh, invariably malicious; her sharp fox-face; her too-white hands that knew so well what they could do to him—everything about her was exquisitely odious. "I don't know why," he told Etta. Looking into her clear, dark-blue eyes, he felt again a surge of hope. Etta was here, she was real, loving him and beloved; Rose was a bad dream, a delirium, a disease—but not an incurable one. Of course not incurable.

"I'm through with her," he said to the face above him, which seemed half the time to be Mr. Pigeon's and half the time Etta's. "I'm through with her for good and all."

"Of course you are," said Mr. Pigeon. Or it may have been Etta. Because she believed him, each time he said it to her. So did he. Neither of them could believe that he was lying, any more than they could believe that he was really lost.

He made one last effort to save himself. For a whole week he managed to stay away from Rose. Then—choir practice evening again—she waylaid him, outside the church. A mournful fall twilight; smoke in the air, and the dead leaves drifting down. "I'm in the family way," said Rose in a hard, triumphant voice. "What are you going to do about it?" She waited a moment, her face lifted in insolent challenge. "Well? Do you want me to tell your darling Etta and her dear old daddy? What a surprise it's going to be to them. Oh mercy me, yes." His hand reached out and closed over her wrist, and she shrank back as if he had struck her. "You do and I'll kill you," he whispered.

"Of course you're through with her," repeated Mr. Pigeon gently. "Whoever killed her saw to that."

He should have killed her, there on the church steps. He wished to God he had. Because of course she was lying. By the time he found it out (or had he known it all the time, in that dark, shameful part of him that was akin to Rose?) the pattern of his life was set forever in ruin and hate. He and Rose were already absorbed in the vicious wrangling of their marriage. Etta's father and mother had whisked her away to Chicago; she wrote him one desolate little letter, and he never answered it because there was nothing to say, he could not even bear to think of her name or go past the Kincaid house where the grass was withered now and the veranda sunless and empty. He knew what people were saying about him: that he was no good, living off Rose the way he did (he had not even tried to get another job after he resigned at the bank); that—they declared!—you wouldn't know he was the same person, they sometimes wondered if he was all there, he acted so queer, not even speaking to you on the street if he could help it.... Let them say it. Let them think he was crazy.

"You think I'm crazy, don't you?" he said to Mr. Pigeon.

"Why no, Francie, not at all," said Mr. Pigeon, ever so heartily. "You gave us quite a time last night, but of course nobody thinks you're crazy. I expect you had a very good reason for throwing that rock through Bovard's window. Didn't you?"

Now he figures he's tricking me into something, thought Francie indulgently. As a matter of fact, he had forgotten about the rock and the note. He remembered now, though. Doc Buckmaster's girl (wanted to dispose of her furniture! Ha!) and the other one, the skinny little one.

"None of their business," he told Mr. Pigeon. "Time somebody taught them a lesson. Snooping around. Asking questions."

Mr. Pigeon nodded. "After you threw the rock, what did you do? Where did you go? Back to the store?"

Francie paused, trying to unsnarl it in his mind, trying to feel his way back through what seemed to be a long, dark, blank stretch. The rock in his hand, and then the crash, and then somebody screaming. "She hollered out the window," he said cautiously. "Hollered that she wasn't scared, she wasn't going to mind her own business—"

"And so you went back to the store, or hung around in the alley, waiting for her. Is that what you did, Francie?"

He had the wit to snap his eyes shut. He needed a minute to get his bearings. A false move, a step missed in the dark.... "Snooping around," he murmured. (That had been safe, before) "Asking questions."

Apparently it was working again "They asked about your wife, I suppose," said Mr. Pigeon. "And the candlestick. And the money your wife had, hidden away. Where did she get that money, Francie? Did you ever give her any, after you separated?"

But Francie was skimming again, he had lost the thread. Only the last word rang in his ears. Separated. Separated. "Get out, then," Rose used to shrill at him. "Go ahead and leave me. Who's going to keep you if I don't? Who'd give a crackpot like you a job? You can't leave me! You'll never leave me, unless I kick you out!" He must really have been crazy in those days, because he believed her. For three whole years he believed her. (The happiest years of Rose's life, no doubt. What bliss it must have been to her, to know that he was so completely, so abjectly, dependent on her.) As for Francie himself, he lived in a trance of inertia, bound to her body and soul, hugging his hateful chains. People began calling him Francie, instead of Francis or Mr. Henshaw. The few people, that is, that got near enough to him to call him anything. He avoided everybody he could. He took long, frenzied, nocturnal walks—but always, always, he went back to her....

It was Hugh Bovard who first jolted him out of his inertia. Unknowingly; to this day Hugh didn't know that the afternoon he fell off his bicycle was a milestone in Francie's life. Hugh and the bicycle came bucketing down the sidewalk, swerved to avoid a kid on roller skates, and shot across the yard where Francie was raking leaves, to wind up in a jumble of spinning wheels and scattered school books at Francie's feet. "Why don't you look where you're going?" snapped Francie. "Fool kid!" But Hugh was too busy picking himself up and trying out his gangly arms and legs to notice. "Gosh, Mr. Henshaw," he said cheerily, "just missed you, didn't I?" He grinned, and Francie became aware of a strange tugging sensation around his own mouth. It was some time since he had smiled at anybody, and the reason he was doing it now was—well, for one thing, it was some time since anybody had called him Mr. Henshaw or treated him in this offhand, uncurious way.

To cover his confusion, he bent down and started collecting some of the papers and books. Caesar's Gallic Wars. A red, ink-stained volume that took him back to his own school days. He flipped the pages; they were battle-scarred, the margins crowded with laboriously pencilled translations, hardly any of them correct. "This isn't right," said Francie—and that was how it began. Hugh stared at him, as at a gold mine. "You mean you can read that stuff right off, just like that? Holy smoke, Mr. Henshaw!"

It was an odd sort of project to get involved in—translating Caesar for a rattle-brained high school kid—but for some reason it was gratifying to Francie. He liked Latin, he kept telling himself; he didn't give a damn about the kid, he just liked Latin. Or maybe it was the flattery. Hugh was as open-hearted as a puppy: He thought Francie was swell, and said so, frequently. Anybody would have felt flattered by that, of course. But for Francie there was a more subtle flattery in Hugh's casual acceptance of him as a fellow human being, extraordinary only because he could read Caesar just like that. It was unselfconscious on Hugh's part, as natural to him as breathing, and it was balm to Francie's blighted soul. Months passed, though, before he admitted, even to himself, that the two of them were fast friends. Occasionally Hugh brought him little offerings—tickets to the basketball games (he never used them, of course), a bird-book (he still had it), memo pads filched from Bayard Senior's printing shop. Then one day he thrust a wad of money into Francie's hand. "Because I owe it to you," he said sternly. "I've been saving, out of my allowance." There were seven one-dollar bills, a fifty-cent piece, a dime, and a nickel. "You don't owe me anything," whispered Francie. "I don't want your money." But Hugh was already half-way down the steps. "Why not?" he said. "You've earned it."

He had earned it. Fascinated, he looked down at the money in his hand. It was his, his very own, and the sight of it seemed to kindle in him a tiny, wavering spark. The spark never went out. Through the rest of Francie's life it grew into a steady, devouring blaze, and as it grew its whole nature was changed. Because they could say what they liked (and he knew, all right: skinflint, stingiest man in town) but that first spark wasn't avarice at all. It was a glimmer of pure hope, such as a prisoner might feel, coming upon a rusty tablespoon in his cell and seeing in it the promise of freedom. So Francie, staring at the first money he had earned in three years, saw not money but a tool, a means of escape. He had earned this; therefore he could earn more, and with money he could buy freedom. Or at least a piece of freedom.

He could, and he did ("It's about time," Rose said, when he got the job down at old man Frederick's second-hand store. But he caught the flash of alarm and secret fury in her eyes. She saw as well as he did, she knew what was coming.) Was it any wonder that he became obsessed with money, that he grew in time to regard this precious tool as the goal itself? He had nothing else....

"Where did your wife get that money, Francie?" repeated Mr. Pigeon. "Have you any idea?"

He kept his eyes closed, though his mind once more set up a weary bustle. This again was shaky ground: he must move cautiously, if he was to accomplish whatever it was that remained to be done. What was it? What was it? He almost had it, only it slipped away, and he was so mortally tired.

"Hey there, old-timer," said a different voice, and it was the one he had been waiting for, the only one that gave any meaning to the whole snarl. His eyes flew open, and there was the face of his boy—not really a boy any more: a man, as luckless in his way as Francis himself—but his, his friend.

He tried to say, "Hey there, Hugh, my boy," the way he always did, but his voice went back on him. A great wave rose inside him and broke in a triumph of recognition and affirmation. He knew what the important thing was now; in one exultant flash he seemed to see the pattern of his own life, cross-grained yet somehow meaningful. A sob burst out of him, and his old acquaintance the commentator had his usual unflattering say: *Making an exhibition of yourself. At your age. Bawling like a baby.* He didn't care.

"What have you been doing to him?" said Hugh roughly. "For God's sake, can't you see he's worn out? You don't need to worry, he's not going to get away from you."

He started to say "Wait," but they were already too far away to hear. Never mind; they would be back, and next time it wouldn't slip away from him. He had it all clear now; it was just a matter of hanging on till he got it done, and after that there would be nothing to keep him at all.

"Don't try to talk any more. Go to sleep now," Hugh told him. "They've tired you out."

Yes. He was tired. He would like to have told Hugh a lot of things, but right now he was too tired. "Don't worry about me," he said before he let his eyelids close. "Don't worry, my boy."

XXII

Doc and Mr. Pigeon paused when they got outside Francie's room and looked thoughtfully at each other. "Funny," said Doc, "his reaction to Hugh. Seemed to break him all up."

"Oh, I don't know. After all, the old guy's human. As far as I can make out, Hugh Bovard's the only person in the world he cares anything about. Wouldn't it break you up, to think you'd tried to choke your only friend's daughter?"

"It wasn't much of a try. Not a mark on her throat, though Bix insists it hurts. I know—" He held up his hand, anticipating Mr. Pigeon's answer to that one. "Francie's old and not very strong, and she yelled before he could get a good grip on her. He didn't really commit himself on the point, just now."

"No, but he was fuzzy about other things too," said Mr. Pigeon comfortably. "Like when he came out with 'Summerhouse.' Did you hear him? It's anybody's guess, what he meant by that. His mind's still wandering a bit, that's all."

"Could be. Could also be he's fuzzy like a fox. Because he was clear enough about the rock. When you come right down to it, that's all you really got out of him—he threw the rock, and he hated his wife."

"Now, now. No use making things hard for ourselves. Not at this stage, anyway. Another session of two with him will probably clear everything—"

"Well." Hugh shut the door to Francie's room behind him and turned a cold, hard eye on Mr. Pigeon. "Proud of yourself? It must be great sport, badgering an old man when he's about to die anyway. It must take real guts."

Mr. Pigeon blinked mildly. "Believe me, Mr. Bovard, I don't do these things for the sport of it. I'm trying to solve a murder. I'm trying to find out who attacked your daughter last night."

"I realized that," snapped Hugh. He flushed slightly.

"Not everybody would be as quick to forgive as you, Mr. Bovard. Or maybe you don't think Francie did it." He waited courteously, while Hugh swallowed a couple of times and hunched his shoulder.

"I suppose—I suppose he did," he said at last miserably.

"It looks like it," agreed Mr. Pigeon. "It looks like, after he threw the rock through your window, he went back to his shop, maybe just to warm up before he went on home. He may have been there when Jeffreys and I came looking for him. He could have hidden easily enough, we didn't really search the place. We didn't know about the rock, but he undoubtedly thought we did know and were after him. He may even have still been hiding there when Bix and the others came along, or he may have just started home, seen them, and hung around in the alley till he got a chance at Bix. Luckily, it wasn't enough of a chance. He heard us coming and beat it, and that's when his heart gave out—naturally enough—and he collapsed."

Hugh was silent a moment. "Did he tell you all this? Did he admit it?"

"It all fits in," said Mr. Pigeon. "Tell me, Dr. Craig, what are Francie's chances? Is he going to pull out of this?"

"Ordinarily, I'd say no. Last night I would certainly have said no." He glanced back, mentally, over the long, precarious night; half a dozen times he had thought to himself this is it, it's all over. "But— Well, he made it. I don't see how he could have, but he did. Plain will power, maybe. Or maybe he's just too mean to die. I'll be honest with you, after last night I don't trust my own judgment."

"I've never seen him as bad as this. He didn't even make a fuss about being in the hospital." Hugh ran his hand over his forehead wearily. "I know you have to do your job, Mr. Pigeon, the same as anybody else. But hell, I've known the old boy most of my life, and I just can't believe he's a—a murderer. He couldn't have done it. He was right there in his shop that afternoon. I dropped in and spent an hour or so with him."

"Nobody knows just when Mrs. Henshaw was killed," Mr. Pigeon reminded him. "Some time before four thirty, but that's all we're sure of. Then there's the candlestick. It's too much of a coincidence, finding that in Francie's shop. Plus the fact that he's admitted the business with the rock last night. Oh, he's in it, all right. He's in it up to his neck. As for motive—well, you never can tell about these eccentric old birds. They get notions. They brood over some little thing, magnify it till it turns into what is, to them, perfectly good grounds for murder. It happens all the time—people that get killed for picking their teeth, or wearing the wrong color necktie. You can pick a motive practically at random, with a character like Francie."

Plausible enough, thought Doc. A very plausible guy, Mr. Pigeon. Look at the tidy little case he had cooked up against Hartley. "Anyway," he said, "It's got Hartley off the hook."

Hugh brightened. "That's right. At least Hartley's cleared. I understand he's already been up here to see Bix. She must be walking on air."

"Just about," said Doc. He was too bone-tired to pursue the vague uneasiness, or doubt, or whatever it was, that flicked its tail across his mind. With an effort he straightened up (if he kept on leaning against the wall he was going to be asleep on his feet) and started down the hall. "Come on, let's take a look at Our Heroine. You haven't seen her yet, have you, Hugh? That's right, she was asleep when you were here earlier this morning."

"Is she really doing all right?" asked Hugh.

"Bouncing back in fine shape. Youth, you know, youth. Actually, it was more a matter of shock than anything else. Though I don't like to think of what might have happened if we hadn't got there when we did."

"Don't," said Hugh. Suddenly he put his hand on Doc's arm. "You know, Doc. you want to forget all that stuff you were saying last night, about it was your fault for letting Bix and Rachel go down there. All that stuff. I know Bix, when she sets her mind on something. I don't blame you, and you mustn't blame yourself, either."

"I still think I acted like a meathead," said Doc. "But I haven't got the strength to argue with you." He opened the door to Bix's room and looked inside. She was perched on the window sill, hugging her knees and staring out at the wan winter morning. "Hey, you. Get back in bed and make like a patient. There's a guy out here wants to see you. Claims he's a relative."

"Daddy?" She scrambled to her feet; her robe, which seemed too big in some spots and too little in others, gave her the scrawny, pathetic look of a half-grown bird. Her eyes flew from Doc's face to a point behind him, where Hugh must be, and she spread her arms in a wide, theatrical gesture. "Daddy, darling! You're here at last."

This is what comes of seeing too many movies, thought Doc. Even Hugh looked a little startled. Then he hurried into her waiting arms. Over his shoulder Doc could see Bix's face, eyes closed apparently in rapture. Aside from the scraped mouth, she looked quite blooming—the result, no doubt, of Hartley's visit.

"How are you, Biscuit? Doc tells me you're doing fine.... "His hands touched her neck tenderly, and she drew back, shuddering. "Poor baby."

Bix mustered a brave smile. "It's not so bad, really."

"She'll be back to normal in no time," Doc assured them both. "The same fresh brat. I just hope you'll always be as lucky as you were last night."

"Who was it?" asked Hugh. "Have you any idea, Bix? Try to think. Was there anything you saw or heard or felt that would identify him?"

Doc had noticed it before: Bix could look blanker than anybody on earth when she wanted to. Her face at this moment was about as expressive as a door knob. "I didn't see anything. They came up behind me, whoever it was, and grabbed me. They threw something over my head so I couldn't see or yell, and then they grabbed me by the neck and—and that's all I know."

"Was it somebody tall?"

"I guess so. I don't know."

"What about what they threw over your head? Was it a coat or a scarf or what?"

"Something dark and heavy. I don't *know*, Daddy." Her eyes suddenly got dark and distressed-looking. "It all happened so quick. I've told you everything I know."

"I'm sorry, honey. I just wanted to check with you. Pigeon's convinced it was Francie, of course."

Her face had gone blank again. "Aren't you? Who else could it have been?"

"Nobody, I guess. I just don't see—" He broke off and gave her a cheerful pat behind. "Let's skip it. Whoever it was, it wasn't Hartley. The well-known silver lining. It clears Hartley, once and for all. Let's forget the rest and be thankful for that. How is the lad, anyway?"

"He's—wonderful," breathed Bix, and Hugh and Doc grinned at each other.

"Utterly, utterly," said Doc. "I just hope he appreciates the chances you took for him, young lady. I just hope he's properly grateful."

"Why should he be grateful?" Bix's eyes flashed. "He'd do the same for me."

"Okay, okay. Watch your temperature."

Hugh picked her up and started tucking her back in bed. "Your mother sent you her love." He was trying, rather clumsily, to make this sound off-hand and natural. "She said she hopes to get over and see you this afternoon."

"I bet," said Bix. Then she bit her lip, and both she and Hugh flushed.

The situation called for something deft in the way of a subject-change, but nothing suitable occurred to Doc. He kept shifting from one foot to the other and clearing his throat. It was Mrs. Nelson, bringing in Bix's lunch tray, who finally came to the rescue. All three of them greeted her with open relief. "Here we are," said Doc. "I've got to make some calls, but you can stay a while longer, Hugh. Eat hearty, Bix. If you behave yourself there's no reason why you can't be out of here tomorrow."

"Tomorrow?" There was an odd note in Bix's voice, and again Doc was aware of that uneasy impression flicking across his mind, just out of reach. In a moment, though, she was gushing away in her best cinema style. "Oh Daddy, did you hear that? I can maybe go home tomorrow!"

He plodded down the stairs, collected his coat and bag, and was just about to go out the door when Hugh came tearing after him. "Doc, Doc! Come back! There's something wrong—she can't swallow!"

He hurried upstairs again, to find Bix sitting bolt upright in bed, rigid with alarm. "I can't," she whimpered. "I just can't swallow."

"It came on all at once," Mrs. Nelson reported. "She'd eaten half her soup, and all at once her throat just seemed to close up...." She let her voice trail away. Behind her rimless glasses her shrewd eyes looked frankly puzzled.

And that was the way Doc felt after he had examined Bix. He could find nothing wrong with her, aside from the superficial scratches on her face, which couldn't possibly account for this dramatic new development. Besides, she had had no trouble whatever in swallowing a hearty breakfast earlier in the day. Was it hysteria, then? A sort of delayed shock reaction?

Mrs. Nelson put it in a slightly different way. "I think she's putting it on," she told Doc matter-of-factly, after he had given Bix a sedative and done his best to reassure Hugh.

"But for Lord's sake, why?"

Mrs. Nelson shrugged. "Maybe she just wants attention."

"She's already got it," said Doc. "And will have, for some time to come. And don't think she doesn't know it. She's no fool."

"No, she isn't. She's a sensible kid. Plenty of backbone. Not like that mother of hers. That's why I don't think she's hysterical."

"One thing's sure, she'll have to stay here till she snaps out of this. I told her so." He paused, recalling Bix's pitiful little sob when he had warned her about having to stay in the hospital. But there hadn't been any tears in her eyes. "You'd think she'd be sitting on top of the world, with Hartley cleared and all."

"Oh, she was," Mrs. Nelson assured him. "Lively as a cricket. Chattering away to Mr. Bovard and me about going home tomorrow, and then all at once she stiffened up and she couldn't swallow. Scared Mr. Bovard out of his wits. I don't know, I had a feeling right from the start she was putting it on."

Doc sighed. "Well, keep an eye on her. She'll probably sleep most of the afternoon, and she's better off not having any company till this evening."

"Nobody at all?"

"Nobody at all. Hartley can wait till after dinner, and her mother—"

"Ha," said Mrs. Nelson. "That's one visitor we don't have to worry about. She wouldn't cross the street to see Bix if her life depended on it."

XXIII

It was a rugged day for Doc. He had a long list of calls, and when at last he got back it was to find an office full of coughs and sniffles and aching joints—all the afflictions of February—waiting for him. Fortified by a container of coffee from the Square Deal, he worked his way patiently through the lot of them. Back to the hospital for another quick look at Francie and his other patients there. He gulped down something or other at the Square Deal and called it dinner, but for all his haste it was quarter to nine before he rang the Buckmaster doorbell. Rachel had moved back home in the afternoon.

"You poor creature," she greeted him—and the words were music to his ears; they made him feel deliciously sorry for himself—"you must be exhausted."

"Oh well. I'll live." He achieved a martyr's smile. It was all he could do to keep from purring. The red glass chandelier cast a tender glow on Rachel's face; it caught the sheen of her smooth hair and lit up her eyes. He forgot that he was a poor exhausted creature and took her in his arms.

Queenie looked out from the library door, and, when she considered that things had gone far enough, uttered a short bark of disapproval.

"Our chaperon." Rachel gave a little laugh. "Come on in by the fire. We'll have a drink and catch up on everything. Oh Doc, I'm so—"

Happy. That was the word she didn't need to say. It occurred to Doc that happiness was very becoming to Rachel. She had lost all her worries—including, for the moment, the one about whether he was married or not—and the effect was pretty dazzling.

Hartley, who was standing in front of the fireplace, looked different too. Still shy and awkward (he apparently couldn't decide whether to treat his stretch in jail as a joke or to ignore it) but it seemed to Doc that his voice had lost some of its old quality of uncertain, apologetic mumbling. It was going to take time, but who knew, Hartley might even get so he'd hold his head up. (It had always annoyed Doc, the way the kid ducked his head, as if he half-expected somebody to swat him.)

"How's Bix? The Nelson dame wouldn't let me see her this afternoon, and Hugh said—"

"I can't find anything wrong with her physically," said Doc, "and I'm not a psychiatrist, so your guess is as good as mine. Better, in fact, because you know her better. What is your guess, Hartley? Could she be scared of something?"

"Scared?" Hartley paused in the act of poking the fire; his face was turned away. "What's she got to be scared of? The whole thing's settled. Francie's It, poor, ornery old boy, and they've got him. He's thrown his last rock and killed his last wife and choked his last Bix."

"And damn near drawn his last breath. He'll never live to be brought to trial."

"I'm glad of it," said Rachel firmly. "Have they found out yet about the money? She must have been blackmailing Francie too."

"What do you mean 'too'?" asked Hartley sharply.

"Just an inkle of mine. About why Papa kept her around all those years. Think nothing of it."

"Think nothing of it! Rachel, have you lost your mind? You're suggesting that she blackmailed Papa? Doc, let's draw the poor woman a diagram, she doesn't know what blackmail is. Look, it's like this. A can't blackmail B unless A's got something *on* B, and—"

"All right, smarty. You're not telling me anything I don't know. It's not so fantastic."

"It is. Completely fantastic. Papa's life was an open book. The reason he kept her around was because he was too busy to find somebody better for the job. It wouldn't have been any cinch, you know. He probably tried, and when he didn't have any luck he just gave up and kept her."

Rachel stuck out her chin. "I don't believe it."

"All right, kids, try to get along," said Doc. "Pigeon spent the afternoon snooping around in Francie's finances. He's got money, all right. No necessity for him to live the way he's been doing all these years. He's just stingy. Oh, he's not rich, but it seems he ran onto a real antique now and then, and cleaned up. All strictly cash, according to a couple of Chicago dealers that Pigeon talked to. They say the cash thing was a peculiarity of Francie's. And he kept hardly any records, so there's no telling how much he's made in the last thirty-odd years. Or how much of it he may have turned over to Mrs. Henshaw."

"I wonder what she had on him," said Rachel. "Because, according to the authorities, A can't blackmail B unless A's got something *on* B—"

Hartley gave her a friendly half-poke. "He was probably paying her to stay away from him. Look, Doc, can I go see Bix now? Don't you think this No Visitors business has gone far enough?"

"Run along. I've already told Mrs. Nelson to throw you out if you stay too late. And if you can figure out what's eating on her, let me know. It beats me."

"He's changed, isn't he?" Rachel asked eagerly, the moment the door shut after Hartley. "Did you notice how he talked back to me? He never used to do that, not even with me. He'd just get stubborn and clam up. It was the only defense he had against Mrs. Henshaw." She sat down on the hassock beside Doc's chair with her hands clasped in her lap; her face was alive with happiness. "We're going to sell the house as soon as we can, and Hartley can use the money for art school. We're free. Free. Both of us. We're rid of her at last."

"I suppose you'll be going back to Chicago," said Doc. He said it against his better judgment. All the danger signals were flashing their little hearts out, and it made no difference, he could not stop. "No reason for you to stick around here, I suppose."

"I haven't decided what to do about my job yet," Rachel chattered on. "I talked to my boss today, he's been awfully decent about it all, and he'll hold the job for me for another week or so if I want him to."

"It'll take a while to get rid of the house, won't it?" asked Doc. "It's big and old-fashioned, and of course Coreyville's an out-of-the-way place."

That was what Joan used to say. Joan. His wife's name could still produce in Doc the familiar pang—the old reflex, remnant of the grief that had once torn him to pieces. This out-of-the-way dump, Joan used to say. This God-forsaken little hole. He should have known better than to bring her here, of course. He should have faced the truth. In Chicago it had been possible to gloss it over. But in Coreyville there were no diversions for Joan, no excitement, no shelter from the merciless glare of truth: Joan did not love him. It had been perhaps more of a shock to her than to him. Not that that made it any easier for him to bear. She had cried when she left. Quite a little storm of tears. He still didn't know how he had summoned the strength to let her go. It hadn't been pride; that was one of the things love did to you—it stripped you of pride. So it must have been the extremity of despair, the knowledge that to follow her would be merely to postpone the final, inevitable parting. Sooner or later; and he had chosen sooner. A form of emotional mercy-killing.

And now here was Rachel.... "Stop making it sound like a white elephant," she was saying. "So all right, it hasn't got picture windows. It's a good comfortable house, and somebody's going to want to buy it. Mr. What's-his-name, the butcher, wanted it before, only of course he changed his mind when he found out Mrs. Henshaw went with it. As far as that goes, Hartley can tend to selling it. I don't have to stay here for that, if I decide I want to keep my job."

Doc nodded bleakly. No reason why she should stay here at all. He felt left out and forlorn, and it didn't help a bit to remind himself that it was, in a way, his own fault. What had he offered her that she couldn't get in Chicago? Fun and games. The bargain offer, available everywhere. Everywhere was right. Especially Chicago.

Still, he had thought that she'd— Well, didn't she even *care* anymore whether he had a wife or not? Here he was, all primed to tell her the God's truth (yes he was; he might as well admit it) and she didn't even pay any attention.

"I'm not a slick operator," he said in a loud, contradictory voice. "You said last night. I'm not a slick operator."

"No?" She tilted her head, smiling a little, waiting.

"No," he said weakly. His mouth felt dry. "And I want it to make a difference to you whether I have a wife or not, because I—"

She was still waiting. This was going to be tough. To begin with, he was breaking a three-year-old habit of silence. "I've never talked about Joan to anybody," he said. "That's her name. Joan. I've never told anybody about her. I don't know why, exactly."

Maybe it had been hope, at first: for most of the first year he had kept himself going with the standard wishful thinking (the letter, special delivery, or the telegram that might come at any moment: "Darling, I can't live without you," the telephone that might ring in the middle of any night, the train or the bus or the car that might bring her back). It would have been bad luck, of course, to talk at that stage; wishes that were not kept secret never came true. And afterwards it was shame, in a way; an unwillingness to confess to his own failure.

He took the plunge. He wanted to. He couldn't bear not to talk about Joan any more. "I was in love," he said, "and she—well, she wasn't. Maybe, if we'd stayed in Chicago, we could have made out. For a while longer, anyway. She liked excitement and parties, and as long as she had them it kind of made up for the other."

(Had it been that way, he wondered, with Rachel and the Greg character? He reached out and took her hands.)

"We didn't get a divorce right away, when she went back to Chicago. No particular point to it. Then, a year or so ago, she decided she wanted to marry somebody else. So she got a divorce. I didn't mean to make a mystery out of it. I just never felt like talking about it to anybody till now, because I—"

"Never mind," whispered Rachel. "The important thing is...."

Yes. The important thing was the way her eyes were lit up. For him. She was not Joan. She was Rachel; that was the important thing. He drew a sigh of relief, and in that moment his canny, safe-and-sane resolutions crumbled away to dust. So all right, if he got hurt he got hurt. He was like Bix, he didn't care if it was dangerous. It was still worth it.

She's got you, he told himself. Brother, are you sunk.

He hadn't felt so good in years.

XXIV

It was quite a while before they changed the subject. Then Rachel asked about Bix, and he told her the whole puzzling business. He even tried, not very successfully, to pin down the vague impression that had flicked across his mind occasionally throughout the day. "Somehow I feel as if she's scared. Not of what happened to her last night. Something else. She seemed all set up at the idea of going home tomorrow, and yet—"

"She's a funny kid. Cagey. Like Hartley. You can't get much out of either one of them. Mrs. Henshaw's box, for instance. I've got a feeling Bix knew there was something in Mrs. Henshaw's room. She didn't want us to open the box, remember? I suppose she was scared there was something in it that would make things even worse for Hartley."

"One thing about her, she's a woman of action," said Doc. "I'm willing to bet that if anybody socked Mrs. Pierce it was Bix and her umbrella. That was to clear Hartley too, of course. But what I don't understand is last night. Maybe she just wasn't thinking when she rubbed the fingerprints off the candlestick, and then again— She couldn't have thought Hartley's prints were on it. And anybody else's would have been good for our side."

"She wasn't thinking, then. She just did it automatically."

There was one other thing. "She said something funny when I first got to her, there in the alley. At least I think she did. It sounded to me like she said 'I fell', as if she had some notion of making out that nobody grabbed her, she just fell. Only why in the hell would she?"

"She wouldn't. You must be mistaken," Rachel said at last. "You heard her yourself, afterwards. She made quite a story about being choked."

They studied each other a moment in silence. All right, then, Doc was thinking, Bix isn't scared of anything because she's got nothing to be scared of. This can't swallow business is just delayed shock.

He wished he was surer of it. He had a special feeling of responsibility for the kid; they had a good deal in common, he and Bix. Tonight had taught him that.

Suddenly Rachel jumped up. "Let's go see her. It's not too late. Come on. Let's just go see how she is."

"Hartley's still here," Mrs. Nelson told them when they got to the hospital. "I told him he could stay till ten. Mr. Bovard's been and gone. She didn't eat her supper, but I did get a little milk down her. You can't tell me. That child's putting it on, and when she gets hungry enough she's going to decide she can swallow as well as ever."

She was so right. Doc and Rachel walked in on an interesting little scene: patient and visitor were polishing off a spread of hamburgers and candy bars. Bix had her mouth full; at sight of them in the doorway she swallowed, guiltily but efficiently. She had the grace to blush.

"Congratulations," said Doc. "You seem to have made a remarkable recovery." He brushed aside Hartley's bumbling, halfhearted explanation and ushered him out before either he or Bix could protest. "Sure, sure. Your visiting time's up, Hartley. You've done your duty. I want to examine my patient."

His patient watched, wary-eyed but silent, while he gathered up crumbs and wrappers and stuffed them in the wastebasket.

"Now." He sat down beside her, mechanically felt her pulse. It was jumping a bit. And why not? "Why did you try to fool us, honey? Don't look at me like that. I'm not going to bully you. I'm just curious."

"I didn't—" began Bix. She trembled her lip piteously and buried her face in the pillow. Almost a flawless performance. Only she couldn't resist peeking at him, out of the corner of her eye, to observe the effect. Rachel, standing at the other side of the bed, made soothing noises. But she raised her eyebrows at Doc and gave a helpless little shrug that expressed his own feelings pretty accurately.

"We want to help you," said Rachel. "But we can't, if you won't tell us what you're scared of."

A muffled gulp from Bix. No other answer.

"You are scared, aren't you?" said Doc. "Why, Bix? Why are you scared to go home?" It was one of the wildest shots in the dark he had ever made, but it hit the mark. He felt the sharp-boned little wrist between his fingers stiffen and jerk away. Bix sat up straight, her telltale eyes hurrying from Doc's face to Rachel's, her fists pressed defensively against her chest. Before she could decide what tack to take, Rachel collected herself (she had looked as startled as Bix for a minute) and pressed the advantage.

"You can't be scared of your Dad, Bix. Is it something about your mother? Is it on account of your mother that you don't want to go home?"

Woman's intuition, thought Doc. Never underestimate it.

"She hates me," whispered Bix. "She's always hated me. She said so."

"But you've never been afraid of her before." Rachel paused. "Or have you? Bix, you've dodged this one long enough. I want you to tell me the truth. Why did you call Hartley when he came to Chicago three years ago? Why did you get him to come back here? Were you afraid of your mother then?"

Bix drew a long, shuddering breath and closed her eyes. "My mother. Yes. Mrs. Henshaw came to see her—"

"Mrs. Henshaw!" Doc gasped it out. "You don't think your mother had anything to do with this Henshaw business!"

"Yes. No. I don't know." Bix wadded up a corner of the sheet, smoothed it out, wadded it up again. Her eyes were fixed—but unseeingly—on her busy hands. She was staring at something quite different, a three-year-old memory that could still daze her with terror. "She came to see my mother, and I saw her, and she looked—terrible...."

"What did she come to see your mother for? They weren't friends, were they?"

"No. Oh, no. She said to me, 'Is your mother home, dearie?' and her eyes kind of slid around all over, like a—like a ferret. And then my mother came, and there was this awful scene—"

"But what about, Bix? What was it all about?"

"I don't know. I keep telling you. They told me to get out. 'Get out of here.' Said to me, 'What are *you* hanging around for? Get out of here and stay out.' So I went and hid, but I could still hear. Only not what they said. Just sort of screeching and so finally it stopped and I couldn't stand it, I called Hartley." She wasn't faking this performance. She was shaking all over, uncontrollably; her teeth clicked against each other.

"There, there." Rachel put her arms around the thin shoulders; her own face was pale and big-eyed.

"But that was Mrs. Henshaw, Baby," said Doc. "No reason to be so frightened of your mother." Though it might not be so far-fetched, at that. Terror could put some pretty fancy twists into a kid's mind.

"It was—both of them. The way she looked at me. Shoved me out. Said to me, 'Get out of here and stay out.'" Again the shuddering gasp. "I felt like I couldn't stand it without Hartley. She hates me. She looked at me that same way last night, after the rock came through the window. I saw her hating me. She's sorry he didn't kill me...."

Oh Lord, thought Doc, like as not it's the truth. "Now look," he said, "you can depend on me. I won't send you home as long as you feel like this. I think you're probably off the track about your mother, but it's still a deal. I promise. You don't need to pull any more phony symptoms on me."

"You can come stay with me," said Rachel. "Or something. We'll figure out something."

If they had to, they could just tell Hugh the truth. It wouldn't be exactly news to him, poor guy. It might even be the best thing for all the Bovards, to get this mother-daughter antagonism out in the open at last. Just as it seemed to have done Bix good to unload. She was still crying a little, but in a relaxed, relieved way.

"Can't Hartley come back just to say goodnight to me?" she quavered.

"Spare us the schmaltz," Doc told her. "Okay. If he's still around—and I suppose he's waiting outside to challenge me at dawn or something—he can come in for five minutes. No more. I'll have Mrs. Nelson time him."

He paused at the door, looking back at her, propped up on her pillows, waiting to say goodnight to Hartley. Something in her expression struck him. It wasn't exactly like the moment when he had caught her peeking at him to see if he was melting. But there was no doubt about it: she was looking damn pleased with herself.

XXV

Myra Graves had the nicest kitchen in the world, Rachel thought contentedly as she slipped out of her coat and settled down in the old splint-backed chair. Nothing was changed since Rachel's childhood; that was what made it so satisfactory. Myra had even kept her old wood range—for company, as she said—and it seemed to purr in unison with the tortoise-shell cat curled up on her little oval rug in front of it. The hand pump for rain water still stood beside the sink; the red geraniums sunned themselves on the window sill; the familiar blue and white dishes looked out like old friends through the glass doors of the cupboard. And Myra herself, in her rick-rack trimmed apron, was bustling around baking a batch of molasses cookies that smelled just the way Rachel remembered. Heavenly.

"I'll sit down and have a cup of coffee with you soon as I get this last pan in," Myra said. "Seems like old times, having you run over of a morning. Doesn't it?"

"Except I always used to have troubles. You must have gotten fed to the teeth, listening to all my woes." Rachel stretched her arms and smiled. "I got no more troubles no more."

Myra's eyes brightened. "You mean he hasn't got a wife, after all?"

"Not at the moment. But he's going to have one, if I have anything to say about it. And I think I have."

Myra tried to look shocked. "Why, Rachel Buckmaster! That's not a very ladylike way to talk."

"I don't feel ladylike. I feel—"

"What about him?" said Myra hastily.

"I don't think he feels ladylike either."

She laughed, and Myra gave up and laughed with her. "Tell you the truth, Rachel, I don't blame you a bit. Doc's a fine young man, and it's high time somebody made up his mind for him. Go to it. That's what I say. Go to it." She thumped her rolling pin enthusiastically. "Not that he's been resisting any to speak of, anyway."

"That's right. He started it. I think." Rachel gazed off into space and let herself wallow. "It doesn't seem possible, Myra. This time last week I'd never even heard of Dr. C. W. Craig. We've only known each other four days. Just think of it! It doesn't seem possible."

"Well," said Myra briskly, "looks like it's happened, possible or not. My land, Rachel, stop looking so moony-eyed. I don't know but you're easier to put up with when you've got troubles. After all, there's been other things going on too. What about Francie? Do they arrest a man when he's about to die anyway?"

"That's what Mr. Pigeon's trying to decide. He keeps talking about loose ends that have to be tied up."

"Loose ends!" echoed Myra. She drew up a chair, planted the coffee pot on the table between them, and settled down for a good gossip. "Where's any loose ends? Francie did it, didn't he? I thought he as good as admitted it."

"He admitted throwing the rock through Bovard's window. He admitted that he hated Mrs. Henshaw. Doc was there when Mr. Pigeon questioned Francie, and he says that's really all it amounted to."

"Seems to me like that's plenty," said Myra. "He threw the rock to scare you and Bix out of looking for the candlestick. So he must have known that's what she was hit with. How would he know that if he hadn't done it himself? Why else would he hide it? And the reason he did it was because he hated her...." Her voice trailed off into uncertainty.

Rachel sighed. "It really is a loose end. He'd hated her for years. What happened to make him kill her right then, after all this time? Even peculiar people don't commit murder without a special reason. It would be different if they ever saw each other, but as far as anybody knows they hadn't exchanged a word for years."

"Maybe they did see each other," said Myra tentatively.

"In Coreyville? Without anybody knowing about it?"

"Not very likely, I guess. Still, secrets have been kept here. Look at Mrs. Henshaw. Hiding all that money away: and nobody knows where she got it."

"Myra." Rachel cleared her throat and tried again. "Myra, you knew Papa as well as anybody in town. Do you think she could have gotten it from him?"

She wasn't sure what she had expected Myra's reaction to be. Indignant protests, probably, like those Hartley had thrown at her. Reproachful reprimands for a daughter who could ask such a question. She got something quite different. Myra didn't say a word. She just blushed. A rich, guilty red.

"You've thought of it too, then?" said Rachel in a low voice.

Myra gave an odd little shake to her head, as if something hurt her. "Of course I thought of it. A long time ago. She—Rachel, she must have had some hold on him. It doesn't make sense otherwise. He loved you and Hartley."

"I know." Conscientiously Rachel trotted out Hartley's arguments. Give them another chance. See how they sounded to Myra. "But he was busy and overworked. Housekeepers don't grow on trees. He probably couldn't find anybody else for the job."

Again Myra's head jerked in that little gesture of pain and something like pride. "After Mr. Graves passed on—" Myra always referred, thus formally, to her husband; it called forth in Rachel's mind an unapproachable figure, not at all like the easy going Mr. Graves she remembered. "After Mr. Graves passed on, he could have had me for a housekeeper any time he wanted. I thought the world and all of your Papa, Rachel."

The mournful, quiet words seemed to tremble in Myra's cozy kitchen, mingling incongruously with the kettle singing on the stove and the spicy smell of cookies. Even Myra, thought Rachel. Even jolly, warmhearted, forthright Myra had not escaped the Henshaw blight. There she sat across from Rachel, staring into her coffee cup like a child about to cry, her worn hands idle, for once, in her lap. "She must have had some hold on him," she repeated.

"Maybe he—had an affair with her," ventured Rachel.

And once more Myra surprised her. "No. I thought of that too. So I asked him."

"You asked him?"

"Yes." Myra gave a rueful little smile. "I guess I haven't always been so ladylike, myself. I asked him, and it wasn't that. I could have told. Your Papa was one of the poorest hands at lying I ever ran across. It was something else."

"But what, Myra? What? Have you any idea at all? It's important to me, somehow...." She didn't know exactly why. If Papa's money, not Francie's, had filled Mrs. Henshaw's box, of course, it meant that Francie had some other motive. But how could she go to Mr. Pigeon with anything as flimsy as this? I just have a hunch she was blackmailing my father.... Preposterous.

Myra was shaking her head in resignation. "It beats me. Always has. Always will. Whatever it was, it's buried with her. And good riddance. Mrs. Pierce took the body back to Westburg for the funeral, so Mr. Manning was telling me. Buried her yesterday."

"Poor Mr. Manning. He had such a nice service all planned for her here."

They tried out rather weak smiles on each other; close as they were, they had never had a conversation quite like this before. It seemed so odd to think of Myra with sorrows of her own, as confused and uncertain beneath her brisk cheeriness as Rachel herself. It seemed so odd to feel as old as Myra.

"There," cried Myra, jumping up and whipping the tin of cookies out of the oven. "All but burned them, sitting here gabbing. I thought I'd take some up to the hospital to Bix. Or is she well enough to go home yet?"

"No, she's not home yet." Rachel paused. "Myra, do you believe everything Bix says?"

"More or less. As much as I do any kid that age. Why?"

"Well, when Doc and I went to see her last night she went on about how she doesn't want to go home, she's scared of her mother, and then she told this tale about Mrs. Henshaw coming to see her mother three years ago...."

Myra listened, open-mouthed. "I never heard of such a thing," she said when Rachel had finished. "What in the world's got into the child?"

"You don't believe it, then?"

"Why, I don't know what to think! Of course she and Althea never have hit it off, but— Scared of her! Scared to go home!"

"She isn't a normal woman, you know," said Rachel. "I never thought much about it when I lived here, but it's different when you come back and see her. It just isn't normal for a woman to waste her whole life grieving over a son like Ronnie. That's what she's done. She's ruined her own life, and Hugh's, and it looks as if she's done plenty of damage to Bix, too."

"Of course she has. She never loved her. Never paid any attention to her, if she could help it. I know for a fact Hugh used to take Bix down to the Tribune office with him, if they didn't have a hired girl at home, just to make sure the poor child would get fed. With Ronnie Althea'd been just the opposite. Wouldn't let him out of her sight. I declare, I used to wonder how she stood it—lugging that great hulking lump of a kid around, and coaxing him to eat, and trying to teach him to walk and talk. She practically watched over him while he slept. It made you sick to see her—"

"I know," said Rachel. "I remember Ronnie."

"What they should have done, of course, was put him in an institution. But she wouldn't hear of it. Your papa suggested it once, and she flew at him with the butcher knife. Yes she did. Threatened to kill him."

"Maybe Bix knows what she's talking about, after all. Maybe she's got a right to be scared of her mother."

"Oh, now, Rachel—" But it was an automatic protest. Violence, after all, had been done. All over again, Rachel felt the impact of it: somebody had murdered Mrs. Henshaw; somebody had tried to murder Bix. (Somebody? Francie, of course. Francie.)

"I never knew Althea and Mrs. Henshaw to have anything to do with each other," said Myra. "Friendly or otherwise. What could Mrs. Henshaw have gone over there for? Unless it's all just one of Bix's made-up stories. She does play-act sometimes."

"Something scared her," Rachel pointed out. "She was scared enough to call up Hartley and get him to come back. She might lie to the rest of us, but I don't think she'd lie to Hartley."

"No, she wouldn't," said Myra decisively. "She'd never lie to Hartley. What does he say about it?"

"Backs her up, of course. Claims it was all just the way she says, and he came back to 'protect' her. Though I don't know just how. Moral support, I suppose. He just keeps saying he couldn't leave her alone, with nobody to depend on. You know how those two are. They've stuck together like fly paper, all their lives."

"How about Hugh? Was he supposed to be in on this business three years ago?"

"Bix didn't mention him." said Rachel. "Just Mrs. Henshaw and her mother...."

XXVI

"Three years ago?" Hugh was saying in a puzzled voice. "Mrs. Henshaw went to see Althea and made a scene three years ago?" He leaned back in his swivel chair and frowned at the ceiling.

Portrait of a man wracking his brains, thought Doc. He felt suddenly irritated with everything—the racket of the linotype back there beyond the front office; the creaking of Hugh's chair; his own foolish, hesitant voice saying, "That's what Bix told us. Hell, Hugh, I don't want to meddle in your business. But she is my patient, and she's got this notion about not wanting to go home on account of her mother. I know Althea isn't very well, so I thought rather than go to her—"

"Good Lord, yes!" Hugh thumped himself upright and stared at Doc in a kind of anguish. "I'd break your neck if you'd bothered Althea with all this nonsense."

"It isn't nonsense," said Doc unhappily. "Not all of it, anyway. You know as well as I do that Bix and her mother—well—"

The door to the back room opened and Gloria Johnson, jiggling and switching in one place and another, came in with a handful of proofs.

"Oh, good morning, Dr. Craig. Excuse me, Mr. Bovard, but I just wanted to ask you—"

"Later," snapped Hugh. "Don't bother me with it now. Do us a favor, will you, Gloria? Go back and discuss Life and Literature with Fritz for half an hour or so. I'll let you know if I need you."

The end of Gloria's nose quivered; her perfect-secretary smile was replaced by an expression at once wounded and forbearing. "I'm terribly sorry, Mr. Bovard. I didn't realize. I'm terribly sorry." She switched out again, and for a moment the air throbbed with tender, womanly understanding.

Hugh cleared his throat. "To get back to Bix—" He stopped, helplessly. "What in the hell do you do, Doc, when the two people you love hate each other?"

"Well—"

"I'll tell you what you do. You do all the wrong things. You keep pretending it isn't so. Hiding your head in the sand. You ignore so many danger signals and smooth out so many crises that you lose track of what's real and what isn't. You keep trying to make up for it somehow—which is quite a trick, considering how busy you are pretending it isn't so. And you keep hoping. That's the biggest mistake of all. You keep hoping."

Doc kept his eyes carefully fixed on his own feet. He needed a shoeshine. "No use blaming yourself. It's natural enough to try to make the best of an unfortunate situation."

"Natural maybe. But it's all wrong. I should have faced the fact years ago. I should have given up and sent Bix away to school or wherever it is you send kids when their mothers don't want them."

"It's not too late now," said Doc. "For Bix."

Hugh's face twisted. "But for Althea—"

"I don't know. I'm no psychiatrist."

"It wouldn't help if you were. I've tried that, too. She didn't—co-operate. What was the use, she said, it wasn't going to bring Ronnie back."

In his mind's eye Doc saw Althea's remote face and heard her voice: My son, my little boy. Beyond help, and aware of it; perhaps willing it, choosing to be lost.

Hugh's eyes—gray, like Bix's—were fixed on him imploringly. "It might work for Althea, too. Even now. Maybe, if Bix were gone—She'll be going away to college next year anyway. If it was just Althea and me, maybe I could—"

Doc sighed. The biggest mistake of all. To keep hoping. "Maybe. Meantime, something's got to be worked out for Bix. I promised her I wouldn't send her home as long as she feels this way, and I won't. She's afraid of her mother, whether there's any real reason for it or not."

"There can't be any real reason," said Hugh. "It's ridiculous. Althea wouldn't hurt a fly. She has a horror of any kind of violence. Bix is simply imagining things."

"I was hoping you'd know something about this Mrs. Henshaw business. Lord knows what Pigeon's going to make of it—"

"Pigeon!" Hugh's voice rang out in genuine surprise. "Why would he make anything of it?"

"He's a great little guy for loose ends. Keeps worrying away at what he calls the loose ends in the case against Francie. There are some, you know. Such as motive. Immediate motive, that is. You said yourself yesterday, that you couldn't believe it. Pigeon does believe it, but at the same time he's got the loose ends on his mind. He's not overlooking any bets. He wants to know about all the quarrels Mrs. Henshaw ever had in her life—and believe me there were plenty of them. The butcher, the baker, and all the rest. Pigeon's been after all of them."

"I don't blame him. I'll be glad to tell him anything I can remember—" Suddenly Hugh's face darkened. "But I won't have him going to Althea. I won't have it!" He brought his hand down flat on his desk, and the photographs of Althea and Bix jumped nervously.

Doc continued to stare at his feet. He certainly did need a shoeshine. After a moment Hugh went on more quietly, "Tell me again what Bix said. When was this? Three years ago?"

"Shortly after Dr. Buckmaster died. Hartley was in Chicago, because that's when Bix called him, at Rachel's, and got him to come back."

"So that's why he came back," said Hugh. "I always wondered."

"So did Rachel. That's how she pried all this out of Bix."

"And it was just between Althea and Mrs. Henshaw? I wasn't there?" Something began to dawn in Hugh's face. "Hey, wait a minute. I was there. That must have been the time I came home and found her— Of course I was there." He leaned forward and gave a short laugh. Embarrassment and relief, equal parts. "Poor Bix. She's got it all mixed up."

"I don't doubt it," said Doc. "She's got a prize mixer-upper when she puts her mind to it." An inherited trait? The notion just brushed through his head. Apparently all three Bovards had done a passable job of bollixing themselves up. "So you were there? You know what she was talking about?"

"Sure I know what she was talking about. Though how she hooked it all on to Althea— Well." Again Hugh gave the short, embarrassed laugh. "You understand I'm not exactly proud of this little episode. It's not something I'd care to see published, if you know what I mean. It was me that made the scene."

"Yes?" said Doc. He waited.

"Okay. Here goes. I came home one night and found we had company. The late lamented Rose. She hadn't come to see me. In fact, she was quite put out when I showed up earlier than usual. I spoiled all the fun, because I knew what she'd come for. Althea didn't, thank God. She still doesn't. Any more than Bix does."

"What had she come for?"

"Gossip," said Hugh promptly. "She'd got hold of a piece of gossip that would have—upset Althea, so there she was, all set to spread the glad tidings. She did things like that, you know. Automatically. She didn't have anything against Althea—or me either, as far as that goes. She was just spiteful in general. Trouble-making was as natural to her as breathing. So when she got hold of this silly piece of gossip—"

"Silly? You mean it wasn't true?"

"No." Hugh swallowed. "Unfortunately, I don't mean that. It was silly, but it was also true. Everybody does silly things, now and then. There was a girl in town that winter, a school teacher. A nice little thing. Very pretty. And— Well, I told you I wasn't proud of this."

And Rachel had told Doc something, too. *If Hugh philanders now and then, it's because she drives him to it.* He remembered it now; it clicked neatly into its place.

"I don't suppose we were very bright about it," Hugh was going on doggedly. "Coreyville isn't the ideal locale. Anyway, here was Mrs. Henshaw with this tasty morsel."

"It's a wonder she didn't blackmail you," said Doc. "It was right up her alley."

"Probably figured it was too small potatoes. Which it was, sure enough—much as I would have hated for Althea to hear about it. She wasn't in good shape at the time, anyway, and I wasn't going to have her bothered with anything extra." He half-smiled, bitterly. "Hell, maybe I'm kidding myself. She might not have turned a hair."

That would be Doc's guess, but he refrained from saying so. "So what did you do?"

"I blew my top. I walked in and she gave me this sly stuff about how sorry she was Althea was feeling so poorly, she'd just dropped in for a little visit—God, the woman was a bitch!—and I don't know, I just blew up. I told her what she could do with her neighborly impulses. Told her to get out and stay out."

The phrase struck a chord in Doe's memory. "Did Bix hear all this?"

"Bix? I don't think—No, of course she didn't. I bundled Althea upstairs first, and then I had sense enough to get Bix out of there too. It was nothing for a kid to hear."

"What did you say to her? Bix, I mean."

"Why, I don't know. Told her to get out, I guess. I don't suppose I minced any words with her. I was too sore for that."

Hugh might not remember exactly what he had said to Bix, but Doc was willing to bet that he himself could quote it, word for word. *Get out of here and stay out. What are you hanging around for?* Bix had simply transferred those cruelly cutting words from the father she loved to the mother she hated. You didn't have to be a psychiatrist to figure that out. She might have done it consciously, with some idea of protecting Hugh; or unconsciously, because it was too painful to remember the other way.

"You mean," said Hugh, "she's been brooding over this for three years? Mixing it all up in her mind, somehow twisting it around so it would be Althea's fault?"

"Looks like it. I suppose you've always meant security to her, and so when you blew up and snapped at her it was too much for her. Like the Rock of Gibraltar turning into cardboard. Nothing left to hang to."

"Except Hartley," said Hugh. "Hartley's never let her down." His face looked empty and defenseless; for a moment it merged, in Doc's mind, with Althea's. Both haunted. Both lost. He couldn't tell which face was which. Then, with a little shake of the head, a straightening of the shoulders, Hugh got his identity back. His reassuring, familiar identity—a guy with maybe more than his share of troubles, but definitely not defeated by them.

"I figure it this way," said Doc in a burst of relief. "She got over the first scare—on the surface at least—because Hartley came back and you got back to normal. But Mrs. Henshaw getting herself killed kicked it all up again. It's been a real rugged week for Bix, you know. Anything that happens to Hartley happens to her too, in a way. On top of that, it's not exactly restful to have somebody grab you and choke you. So she gets scared all over again, and by this time, as you say, she's twisted everything around so as to blame her mother. God knows, she may even suspect her mother of choking her."

Hugh's jaw dropped. "You're not serious!"

"Not really. I just mean she's overwrought and confused and very much aware of the fact that her mother doesn't love her. With that combination, you can't expect logic, in the ordinary sense of the word. Though I suppose to Bix it seems perfectly logical."

"I suppose it does." Hugh hunched his shoulder. "To me it's fantastic. Fantastic. I guess I've been hiding my head in the sand too long to grasp it. The mentality of an ostrich. That's just the way I feel. You got any ideas, Doc? What would you do if Bix was your daughter?"

"Well—" The flush of Doc's little triumph (for it had, he felt, been a pretty shrewd analysis for an amateur) faded abruptly. Here it was, what he had always said about psychiatry: So you find out you're the way you are because you hate your mother. So what do you do about it? He was suddenly aware of the strain in Hugh's waiting face, the deep lines that weren't going to be eased by spouting theories. "Is there any place Bix could go for a visit? Grandparents? Aunts? Uncles? It might help if she got clear away from her mother for a while."

"There's my sister in St. Louis," said Hugh. "Bix likes her, and she's got a couple of kids about the same age. Do you think Bix would leave Hartley? I mean, I can't see myself making her do something she doesn't want to...."

"You nor anybody else," Doc told him. "Believe me, your daughter has a whim of iron. There's nothing to do but sound her out. If she won't go away, then we think of something else. Rachel suggested that she come and stay with her a few days. How would you feel about that?"

He looked away from Hugh's face quickly. Okay, Bright Boy, he said to himself, how would you feel about it? How would you like it if your only child would rather go to the neighbors'—would rather stay in a hospital—than come home?

"Whatever she wants," Hugh said after a minute. "Just so Althea's kept out of it...."

Those two phrases, it occurred to Doc, summed up most of Hugh's life. He must have been saying them, thinking them, feeling them, for years. What other course had been open to him? To give Bix whatever she wanted (only he couldn't give her the important thing) and to shield Althea (only it was too late; the mortal blow had been struck long ago).

Perhaps Hugh was thinking the same thing. He did not get up when Doc rose; slumped at his desk, he raised his hand rather absently in a gesture of goodbye. And when Doc looked back from the street, he was still just sitting there, staring at nothing.

XXVII

It was one of the more peculiar half hours of her life, thought Rachel. For one thing, she was all out of practice on The Social Call. And this was a Call, all right; the atmosphere of gentility—engraved cards, lace-edged handkerchiefs, ladies sipping afternoon tea—spread through the library like a delicate fragrance.

Except that the Caller was Althea Bovard, of all unlikely people. There she sat (she who seldom made a social gesture of any kind) complete with hat and gloves and correctly pleasant expression.

"It was so nice of you to come," said Rachel, and realized that she had already said it at least twice before. Her own costume bothered her; she had been ready to step into the shower when Althea rang the bell, and her good old fuzzy bathrobe and mules struck her as not the accepted attire. The hour bothered her too. Too late for lunch. Too early by a couple of hours for afternoon tea or cocktails.

She was visited by inspiration. "Would you like a glass of sherry?"

"That would be very nice," said Althea politely. Apparently she meant it, too. Drank hers right down without ceremony, and didn't demur when Rachel gave her a refill. It set Rachel to wondering whether a bottle might not figure in Althea's withdrawn way of life.

"I must tell you, Rachel, how much I appreciate your asking Beatrix here for a while." Althea removed one glove and patted her lips daintily with her handkerchief. "I realize, of course, how anxious she is to get out of the hospital, but it's more than I can undertake to have her at home until she's fully recovered."

Rachel blinked. This wasn't exactly the way she heard it, but let it go.

"I'm looking forward to having her. I'm sure she'll be no trouble at all."

"I'm afraid I've had to neglect Beatrix a little this winter," the faint, sweet voice went on. "I haven't been at all well myself, you know. These really splitting headaches."

"I'm so sorry," said Rachel. What she was actually feeling was exasperation. How the women could sit there and talk about her headaches when her own daughter had narrowly escaped being choked.... "Bix seemed to be getting along fine when I saw her last night. It was lucky for her somebody turned up in time."

"Yes, wasn't it? That is, if— Oh, I probably shouldn't even be mentioning it. But Beatrix is inclined to dramatize herself, you know. Such a difficult age, isn't it?"

"You mean you think she just made it up? Nobody really grabbed her?"

"I've never been able to understand people who do such things. But of course you know much more about what happened the other night than I do. After all, you were there, weren't you? I didn't even hear about it till in the morning. I was so upset—you know, when the window got broken—that I took a sleeping tablet and slept right through all the excitement. I really don't think I could manage without Dr. Craig and his sleeping tablets."

"I'm sure Bix didn't make it up," said Rachel. Of course she was sure; she had heard the running footsteps in the alley, after Bix cried out. And yet hadn't she herself suspected Bix of embroidering a few other facts, now and then?

"Hugh hasn't told me many of the details. He's so anxious for me not to be upset. But I gather it was Francie Henshaw. Did Beatrix—or the rest of you—see him?" Althea took another drink of sherry and ran through the handkerchief-patting routine again. Her cold, pale eyes, however, remained fixed on Rachel.

"Nobody saw him," Rachel told her. "Bix says he threw something over her head so she couldn't see, and by the time we got there he was gone. We just heard him running away."

"He's always been—queer. But then aren't we all?" A genuine, engaging smile crossed Althea's face; Rachel remembered how pretty she had been, years ago. "As I said, I probably shouldn't ever have mentioned Bix's habit of romancing. Hugh says she'll outgrow it, and I expect she will.... Thank you, just a drop. Mrs. Henshaw's—death has affected us all. Even me, and I hardly knew the woman."

She paused, with an air of significance that puzzled Rachel. After all, why make such a point of hardly knowing Mrs. Henshaw? Nobody had said otherwise. There was, of course, Bix (who was probably going to outgrow her romancing) and the story of Mrs. Henshaw's visit to her mother....

"I didn't even know her to quarrel with," said Althea, and smiled again. "It's been years since I've been inside this house. Not since I used to bring Ronnie over—"

Oh my, thought Rachel, here we go. I knew she'd get around to Ronnie eventually.

The doorbell saved her. "Excuse me," she said, and hurried out to answer it.

There stood Mrs. Pierce, looking somehow armed to the teeth, primed to fight for her rights, no matter what the odds. She wasted no breath on pleasantries.

"We're here for Rose's belongings," she announced. The car in which she had arrived was parked out in front; the challenging gesture of Mrs. Pierce's head indicated that it was loaded with auxiliary troops and heavy artillery. "My son-in-law drove me up from Westburg, and we're here to get Rose's clothes and whatever else belonged to her. No reason in the world why you should keep—"

"No reason whatever," agreed Rachel. "I've already packed everything up. You're welcome to it. Won't you come in?"

Suspiciously, Mrs. Pierce entered. She followed (alert for possible treachery) as Rachel, intending to make her excuses to Althea, opened the library door.

What happened next was a kind of stifled explosion from Althea. The sherry glass slipped from her fingers and shattered on the floor as her eyes fastened on Mrs. Pierce; her whole face seemed to shudder and go slack.

"No, no," she gasped. "It can't be. You're dead, you're dead. It can't be—"

"Dead, am I!" Mrs. Pierce drew herself up. "Well, we'll just—"

"It's all right," put in Rachel, who by this time had a grip on things. "I'm sorry, Althea. I forgot you've never met Mrs. Pierce. It's Mrs. Henshaw's sister. Mrs. Pierce. I took her for Mrs. Henshaw, too, the first time I saw her."

Althea put her hands up to her eyes and gave a little moan. Hugh ought to be here, thought Rachel uneasily. He knew what to do with Althea when she got into a state; Rachel didn't. She tried a timid pat on Althea's shoulder and launched into an explanation of Mrs. Pierce's presence. It was punctuated by snorts from Mrs. Pierce herself.

"What if I do look a good deal like Rose? I don't see that that's any reason for anybody to take such a fit. Just tell me where Rose's things are, Miss, and I'll leave you and your friend to yourselves."

"They're upstairs in the hall," said Rachel with relief. "Why don't you go on up? I'll be with you in a minute."

Althea waited for the door to close behind Mrs. Pierce before she took her hands away from her eyes. It was awful when she tried to smile. The atmosphere of gentility had been shattered with her sherry glass; her hands shook visibly as she fumbled into her coat. And her murmurs of apology and assurance (she was all right now, just her nerves, so silly of her. Rachel mustn't worry) did not hide the fact that this was flight.

Rachel stood at the door and watched her go down the walk. She looked very fragile in her gray caracul coat and little feather hat, and she swayed slightly—whether from the shock or the sherry or a combination of the two was anybody's guess. Just as it was anybody's guess why she had come in the first place. It was odd, the remnants of The Social Call that stuck in Rachel's mind. Althea's sleeping tablets, that made her sleep right through all the excitement. Bix and her dramatic tendencies. And that neat little phrase, "I didn't even know her to quarrel with."

Had Althea planned those remnants to stick in Rachel's mind?

She hadn't planned on Mrs. Pierce. That was one thing sure. Mrs. Pierce had walked in, like a ghost from the grave, and exploded The Social Call and Althea along with it.

There was an indignant-sounding thump from overhead.

"I'm coming, Mrs. Pierce," called Rachel, and started up the stairs.

XXVIII

It was the same routine, Rachel found, all the way down Main Street. At the post office, where she stopped to pick up the mail; at the butcher shop, where Mr. Havelka cut a steak for her with loving artistry and told her exactly how to cook it; at the grocery and Elaine's Beauty Shoppe and the Square Deal Cafe, where she stopped for a coke and a chat. The same routine. Why, hello, there, Rachel! How are you? You're looking fine (or wonderful, or pretty as a speckled pup, depending on the sex and disposition of the exclaimer). How's it seem to be back? How's the old home town look to you?

It looked pretty good, at the moment. Better than it ever had before. The change was not so much in Coreyville (except for the sign above the drug store: Dr. C. W. Craig) as in Rachel herself. She felt free of Mrs. Henshaw, really free at last. Mrs. Pierce's departure, with her sister's belongings, had cut the last tangible bonds. And the afternoon's tour of Main Street had given her a healthier perspective on Althea's visit.

It seemed not so much peculiar now as pathetic—the fumbling attempt of a neurotic woman to behave, for once, in a normally friendly way.

She paused a moment, outside the cafe. Where to now? Home? She had pretty well made the rounds; but she still felt mildly sociable, and like as not Hartley was up at the hospital with Bix. Her eye fell on the Tribune office with its big front window where three giant ears of squaw corn—largest grown in the county—were on dusty display. She could stop in and bandy a few words with Hugh. If he wasn't too busy he might even like to come home with her for a drink.

She went in, and was effusively greeted by Gloria Johnson —Eager-Beaver Gloria, as Hartley and Bix called her. Rachel could see their point, all right. Gloria positively oscillated with helpfulness, with admiration, with earnest explanations.

"Oh, Miss Buckmaster, Mr. Bovard's going to be terribly sorry he missed you." Gloria quivered all over at the tragedy of this circumstance. "He's gone to the hospital to see poor old Mr. Henshaw. I understand he's very low, and Mr. Bovard's so faithful about visiting him. He's wonderful that way, you know. Such a fine character. Won't you sit down? He may be back any minute, and it would be such a shame if he missed you. Maybe you'd like me to call him? I'll be only too glad—"

Rachel rallied enough strength to put the brake on at this point, but further resistance was beyond her. She said feebly all right, she might sit down for a minute or two—

"Oh, not that chair, Miss Buckmaster!" cried Gloria. "This one's much more comfortable! Here, let me pull it a little closer to the radiator, so you'll be sure to be warm enough. Can't I hang your coat up for you? It's so smart-looking, I've admired it every time I've seen you. Do let me hang it up for you."

Rachel clutched her coat, obscurely determined not to let it out of her hands, and perched on the edge of the chair. "Don't let me keep you from your work," she said, more curtly than she intended. (Sure enough, the end of Gloria's nose twitched in a wounded way, and Rachel felt ashamed. But irritated too: somehow Gloria asked for it.) "You're probably up to your ears in something," she added with a conciliatory smile, "and I don't want to interrupt you."

She was immediately, thoroughly, forgiven. "I'm way behind on my filing," Gloria confided, with a rueful glance at the pile of papers on her desk. "Sometimes it just gets away from me. I feel there's so many other things to do that are more worthwhile. You know what I mean? Naturally I try to take as much of the burden off Mr. Bovard's shoulders as I can, and if I can be useful to him in other ways, why, I just feel that's more important than the filing."

"I'm sure you're right," murmured Rachel, because some comment seemed indicated.

"I just love my job." Gloria's face—spotty, almost painfully sincere—took on a dedicated expression. "Mr. Bovard's the most wonderful man to work for in the world. Oh, I know he's supposed to be quick-tempered. He does get mad sometimes, but when he does it's for a good reason. You know what I mean? It's justified."

Again some comment seemed indicated, and Rachel groped mentally. I'm glad to hear you testify? Amen, Sister Gloria? All the possibilities that occurred to her had a distinct religious flavor.

Her gropings turned out to be unnecessary, anyway. Gloria carried on without encouragement. "Besides, I feel that a person with so much on their mind, it's no wonder he loses his temper once in a while." She let a delicately significant pause fall, while she turned to her desk and began pawing away at the papers. "Poor Mrs. Bovard, I mean. It's a terrible worry to him. Not that he ever says much, of course. But I can tell. I'm funny that way. I can tell."

I bet you can, thought Rachel. She took a speculative look at Gloria's figure—the trim little waist, the lush tempting swell above and below. God had done all right by Gloria in some departments, and it was unlikely that those departments were wasted on Hugh. Gloria asked for it, in more ways than one.

"Like all this past week, he's been so edgy, and Fritz says it's just pure orneriness. But I know better." Gloria nodded wisely. "It's poor Mrs. Bovard. Not feeling well again. I can just sense it. She's been doing so well all winter, too. Up till now."

Rachel felt a flicker of genuine curiosity. All this past week. That would be, roughly, since Mrs. Henshaw was killed. Last night's session with Bix rose again to haunt her, and the puzzling visit from Althea this afternoon. "What got Mrs. Bovard upset this time, I wonder?" she said.

But Gloria's psychic powers apparently didn't extend beyond Hugh. "You never know. A delicate person like that, it could be anything. Sometimes if somebody just mentions Ronnie, it sets her off all over again. And then, right away, it shows on Mr. Bovard, and everything gets on his nerves."

"Maybe he's just worried about Francie. And Bix. He certainly got all upset about what happened to her."

"I know." Gloria's eyes brightened. "Isn't it awful, to think of that old man doing a thing like that? Killing his wife, and then trying to choke Bix, when Mr. Bovard's been such a wonderful friend to him, all these years—Oh, Miss Buckmaster, here's your brother! Hello, Hartley! How are you?"

"Hi, Gloria." Hartley came in, the collar of his windbreaker turned up against the cold, Queenie at his heels. "What's up, Rachel?"

"Nothing. I just stopped in to say hello to Hugh, only he's up at the hospital. Any chance of your giving me a ride home?"

"I might, if you play your cards right." He lounged against the corner of Gloria's desk, watching her busy hands as they sorted and stacked. He ran the tip of his tongue along his upper lip; Rachel recognized his teasing expression. "Some secretary you are! Really, Miss Johnson, just look at that desk! An eyesore. A blot on the Tribune escutcheon."

Gloria bridled happily. "Isn't it a sight? I was just telling Miss Buckmaster, I'm way behind on my fil—" She gave such a sudden gasp that Rachel, who was putting on her coat, turned to see what was wrong. Gloria's face (except for the spots) had turned as white as the envelope she was holding in her hand. It was a long envelope, still sealed, with Hugh's name printed on it in neat letters. "Oh, my! How could I have forgotten? Oh, Mr. Bovard'll never forgive me!"

"What's the matter? What's wrong?" Even Hartley looked concerned.

"I forgot to give it to him." Gloria's voice was hushed and bleak. "It came way last week. It came the day Mrs. Henshaw was killed, I remember because we were all excited and mixed up, and that's how I forgot to give it to him. It must have gotten stuck in with the stuff to be filed and— Oh, my!"

"Oh now, look," said Rachel. "He's not going to blame you for a little thing like that. Maybe it's nothing important, anyway. Why don't you open it and see what it is before you end it all?"

She reached for the envelope, and Gloria gave another gasp of alarm. "Oh, you mustn't *open* it! I never open those letters when they come. Mr. Bovard always wants all the personal ones turned over to him."

"What do you mean 'those letters'?" Hartley asked. "How do you know who they're from if you never open them?"

"I don't know who they're from. I just recognize the printing. And the envelope. They always come in a long envelope like this. There was one a few days before this one. He'll be mad at me," wailed Gloria. "He'll be furious."

"I doubt it," said Rachel. But she felt a little click somewhere in her interior, as if something there were being alerted. "After all, anybody can overlook a little thing like a letter."

Hartley was staring at the envelope, too. He even picked it up, and then flicked it back on the desk with what was meant to be a casual gesture. A long white envelope, neatly printed, fatter than an ordinary letter. As if it might contain another envelope. What was so extraordinary about it? Why should she feel again the little click—of curiosity, or recognition, or whatever it was? Anybody might get such a letter; anybody might write it. Lots of men were fussy about having their personal mail turned over to them, unopened. And poor little Eager-Beaver Gloria was just the type to magnify a trivial oversight into the blunder of the century.

"Don't worry about it, Gloria," she said. "It's probably nothing important, anyway."

"I know, but—" At that moment the phone on Hugh's desk rang, and Gloria leaped like a rabbit. Then she got a grip on herself, switched across to the other side of the office, and intoned, in her best girl-Friday manner, "Tribune office.... I'm sorry, Mr. Bovard isn't in just now. May I take a message?"

Her back was turned to Rachel. Hartley's too; or at least partly. He was at the door, ready to leave. And something peculiar happened to Rachel's hand: it shot out, of its own accord, snatched the long white envelope, thrust it into her purse.

"Okay, Hartley," she said breathlessly. "I'm ready. Let's go." (Had he seen her? His face was suspiciously blank.)

They pantomimed goodbye to Gloria, still busy at the phone. Once in the car and on the way home, Rachel relaxed. She even began to wonder if it had really happened, her hand behaving in that peculiar way. Yes, it had. She could feel the bulge of the envelope through her soft broadcloth purse.

"Doc says it's all right for her to leave the hospital," Hartley was saying, and she realized that she had asked him about Bix and he was telling her. "He says you told Bix last night she could stay at our house for a while, and so I thought—"

"Of course. Why don't you bring her over for dinner tonight? I got a fine big steak, and Doc's coming, and we'll have a party." Their eyes met, startled and pleased at the idea. It would be the first time she and Hartley had ever had a party, company of their own in their own home.

"All right. If you want to," said Hartley, as if it happened every day. But his eyes kept their shine. "All right. Swell."

What a nice, shy creature he was! She felt suddenly giddy with happiness, and close to him, closer than at any moment since her return.

"Remember how we used to pray that Mrs. Henshaw would go away?" she asked. "That she just wouldn't be there in the morning? Now that it's come true I can hardly believe it. But it is, she's gone forever. Somebody killed her, and I don't really care who."

"What do you mean you don't care who? We know who. Francie."

"I know." She hurried on, absorbed in her own feelings, bent on opening her heart. She could do it with no one else, not even Doc. Hartley alone would understand what she meant. She could even tell him about the letter. "It has to be Francie. I know it in a way, and yet in another way I don't know it at all, I don't believe it. Do you, Hartley? Do you believe that Francie—"

"What are you talking about?" Hartley's voice cracked at her; when she turned and saw his face alarm sprang up in her, without warning. "What's the matter with you, anyway? 'You don't know it at all, you don't believe it.' For God's sake, Francie's practically confessed. What more do you want?"

"Hartley—" she whispered, but his face did not change. It remained the face of a stranger, furious and alarming.

"You better cut it out, that's all. I'm telling you. You're going to be damn sorry if you don't. You better keep your mouth shut and stop trying to make trouble. Can't you let well enough alone?"

They were home. He turned sharply into the driveway and jolted to a stop. Neither of them spoke while Rachel collected her packages and purse and got out of the car. How bleak the yard looked—dark already falling, and the trees stiff and naked in the biting wind. Behind her she heard the car door slam and Hartley's feet following her, gaining on her. She became aware of an unreasonable impulse to run. To run some place very fast. Only there was no place to run but the house.

And when Hartley caught up with her it was, after all, only to help her with the packages and to say, in a low, shamefaced voice, that he was sorry.

"It doesn't matter," she said. She kept her eyes on the ground, as if she too were ashamed. She hurried into the kitchen, turned on the lights, went on into the front hall to put her coat away.

When she came back and looked in her purse, which she had left on the kitchen table, the long white envelope was gone.

XXIX

It was Bix who salvaged the party. She was in high spirits when she arrived, and she stayed that way, blissfully oblivious of everybody else's mood. Which was far from festive, though they all tried. Hartley, never very dependable socially, was by spells over-talkative, over-silent. Poor Doc, in fine enough fettle when he arrived, caught the jitters from Rachel. So much so that very soon all he was capable of was long, anxious looks at her and jumpy little smiles when she caught him at it. She couldn't help it, she simply could not focus her mind on anything but Hartley and the letter. What had he done with it? Burnt it? Torn it up? Returned it? Hidden it? Plenty of opportunity, she supposed, for him to have done any of these things. When he built the fire in the library, for instance. Or when he went upstairs to clean up and change his clothes. Or when he went back to the hospital to get Bix....

Hugh, who stopped by with an overnight bag for Bix, was least festive of all. He acted so befuddled, so unlike himself, that for a moment Rachel wondered if he could be drunk. Then it came to her: he was too miserable to make sense. Losing Bix—for that must be the way it seemed to him, as if he had lost her forever—had taken the heart out of everything for him. He still had Althea, though. Poor Hugh, thought Rachel. He still had Althea. As much of her as he had ever had.

Still preoccupied with her own problem, she brought him a drink and sat down beside him. "I suppose Gloria told you I paid you a call this afternoon? See what you miss when you don't tend to business?" (And has she broken down and told you about the letter yet? She must be out of her mind, poor kid. Now that it's disappeared, she won't know what to do.)

"What?" said Hugh. "Who? Oh, Gloria." He seemed to make an effort at concentration. "I haven't seen Gloria. I didn't go back to the office."

(So she hasn't told him yet. She's probably still there, tearing the place apart looking for it. Unless Hartley returned it to her. Only wouldn't he have told me, wouldn't he have asked me what the big idea was, stealing other people's mail? Wouldn't that be the natural thing for him to do?)

"I'm sorry I missed you," said Hugh heavily.

Halfway through his drink, he rose abruptly and said he must be getting home. Bix flew to give him one of her Hollywood-type kisses, and he produced a haggard smile. "So long, Biscuit. See you tomorrow. Good night, all."

Rachel saw him to the door and paused under the red glass chandelier, watching him plod down the steps and across the yard. Like an old man, she thought; and shivered. What a long time it seemed since those mellow, convivial evenings of Papa's and Hugh's, when the sound of their voices had seemed to filter all through her, steeping her in security. They had been, to her child's eyes, so solid and unchanging, and now—

The phone rang, and when she answered Gloria's voice broke over her in a distraught flood. "Oh, Miss Buckmaster, I hate to bother you, but I just don't know what to do. You remember the letter that got me so upset, when you were in this afternoon? It's disappeared, simply vanished, I've turned the whole office inside out and it's simply not here, and I wondered if by any chance you or Hartley might have picked it up, by mistake, you know, and—"

She ran out of breath. It was time Rachel said something, anyway. But what? Never mind, Gloria, I stole it, a slight case of kleptomania, think nothing of it. A family trait. Because guess what, Hartley turned right around and stole it from me....

"Hold on a minute, will you, Gloria? I'll ask Hartley." She had been afraid to ask him before. She was still afraid, she discovered; she was going to have to do it quickly or her courage would fail again.

"Hartley!" she called, and when he came out into the hall she blurted it out. "Gloria's in a sweat about that letter again. Says it's disappeared, and wonders if we picked it up by mistake. Have you got it, Hartley?"

"Who, me?" He was giving her the exasperating blank stare he used to reserve for Mrs. Henshaw, the I-don't-know-anything-about-anything expression. She forgot about being afraid.

"Hartley, I could shake your teeth out—" she began, but he gave a little hiss of warning: Bix had stuck her head out the library door and was saying hurry up, she wanted to dance.

"Tell her you don't know anything about it," he said, very quick and low. "And for God's sake tell her not to tell Hugh about it."

She searched his face; it told her nothing. She felt the obscure alarm creeping back over her. And the helplessness. After all, what else was there to do? "I'm awfully sorry, Gloria," she said into the telephone. "We don't seem to find it anywhere...."

Back in the library, Hartley and Bix were engaged in what they called dancing. It looked more like a do-or-die athletic contest to Rachel. Their faces set in the grim expression of football players hitting the line, they flung each other at arm's-length, banged back against each other, whirled and twisted at violent angles. Queenie had retreated under the couch for shelter; Doc was on it, with his feet drawn up and a strained expression on his face. It seemed like the safest place. Rachel joined him.

"Who's ahead?" she asked, and he grinned feebly.

"You got me. All I know is they're in there pitching. Ever see so many elbows in your life?"

Rachel never had. Something else caught her eye, as Hartley crouched for another assault, his jacket flying out like a sail taking the wind. The envelope was there, in his inside pocket. Not burned or torn up or even hidden. Right there in his pocket. Her breath caught in excitement.

"Let's play the other side," said Bix as soon as the record ended. "It's better, anyway. More zing."

"Look at them," said Doc in wonder. "Not even winded. Let's get out of here, Rachel. I feel like I'm aging rapidly."

"Wait a minute," said Rachel. Because while it was true that they weren't winded, they were warm. Bless their energetic little hearts, they had worked up a sweat, and if there was a God, Hartley was going to take off his jacket and....

Yes. She could hardly believe her luck. Just as the music blared out afresh (more zing, sure enough) Hartley shrugged out of his jacket and flung it across the foot of the couch. His eyes were half-closed, his face rapt. He had forgotten the letter and everything else except the call of the wild.

A moment's fumbling, and Rachel was at the door. "Come on, Doc. Let's make a run for it. You can help me with the steak."

Hartley had opened the letter. She leaned against the kitchen table, the envelope jumping in her hands. She had been right: there was another slightly smaller envelope inside. It was addressed to Mrs. Althea Bovard, and as Rachel stared at the familiar, prudish-looking handwriting, it seemed to her that the solid floor under her feet shifted and shook in a kind of slow-motion disintegration. Hartley had opened the inside envelope too. It took less than a minute to read the short message inside. It took less than a minute for the world to fall apart.

"What's up? What's the matter?" Doc was standing right beside her, but his voice seemed to come from a long way off. Her ears rang with tears; she could feel them streaming down her face while she stuffed message into envelope, envelope into envelope.

"Put it back," she sobbed. "Put it back. I never read it, I never saw it. Oh, please. Put it back...."

XXX

She wouldn't tell him what it was all about. That was what threw him. It wasn't enough for her to dissolve like this—and dissolve was the word, all right; she just leaned against the kitchen table with that letter in her hand, her face ugly with tears, and went to pieces. But that wasn't enough. She had to go secretive on him, too. And how could he help her, how could he fix things for her, if he didn't even know what was wrong? What did she mean, treating him like a kid, not old enough to be told the facts of life?

"Tell me what's the matter. What's happened?" he kept asking, and all she did was shake her head and stuff the envelope into her pocket (she had on kind of a swishy skirt and a black sweater; and that he approved of, that sweater was definitely for Rachel). He had seen her snake the envelope out of Hartley's jacket, and he had caught sight of the name Bovard, and that was apparently all the information she considered him capable of coping with.

"Well, then, stop emoting," he said crossly. "If it's none of my business, spare me the tears."

That jolted her out of it a little. "Oh Doc, I'm so sorry," she said, and she might have gone on from there, except that at that moment the two acrobats came romping out from the library, yammering for food. They would.

Rachel turned around, quick, and began rummaging in the refrigerator, and he covered up for her as well as he could. Not that it took much doing, with Bix. She was so full of girlish glee that she wouldn't have noticed if Doc himself had been crying his heart out. (As a matter of fact, Bix was looking downright pretty tonight. Hadn't had a chance to hack at her hair for some time, apparently; and those great luminous eyes of hers made up for everything else.) He wasn't so sure about Hartley. He never was exactly sure about Hartley. The kid had spent so much of his life in mental hiding from Mrs. Henshaw that he was apt to keep his face closed up for everybody else, from force of habit. A real master of the deadpan. And of course he must be mixed up in this letter business; it had been in his pocket.

He had to hand it to Rachel, the way she got a grip on herself and went through with the party. All during dinner he kept thinking: Later, they would shake the juvenile element later, and he would get the whole story out of her or know the reason why. All he had to do was bide a little time.

But, like they say, the best laid plans. They were having coffee in the library, and he was just getting set to remember an errand he had to do ("Come along, Rachel, keep me company. Let the kids do the dishes.") when who should turn up again but Hugh Bovard. He couldn't remember whether he had put bedroom slippers in Bix's overnight bag or not; so here he was, with a sad-looking pair of scuffs. Bix turned up her nose at them.

"Those old things! Why, Daddy, of course I have my others! I had them with me at the hospital."

"Well, I couldn't remember," said Hugh forlornly. He looked so grateful when Rachel offered him a cup of coffee that Doc decided it wouldn't actually hurt him to bide a little more time.

A queer kind of absent-mindedness seemed to clamp down on everybody except Bix, who chattered away about the pros and cons of visiting her aunt in St. Louis. Luckily, few comments were necessary; Doc had a feeling nobody could manage much beyond an occasional nod or shake of the head. He certainly couldn't. At that, the others were better off than he was: they knew what they were thinking about. All he could do was flounder.

At last Bix ran down. "Oh, I meant to ask you," said Hugh, lighting another cigarette, "What's all this fuss about Gloria and some letter that she found, or didn't find, or whatever? I gathered from what she said to me that she'd called you about it. That's all I did gather, I must say. A hysterical type female, if I ever saw one."

Hartley's face stayed blank. But Rachel's was a dead giveaway; her spoon jittered against her saucer. "She called you?" she stammered. "I told her not to—I mean, why should she bother you when like as not it'll turn up tomorrow and probably isn't important, anyway...." She started to lift her cup for a casual sip. Decided against it.

"She claimed she couldn't sleep with it on her conscience." Hugh's eyebrows quirked in amusement. "That conscience of Gloria's. Definitely over-active. I expect you're right, it's probably nothing important anyway. Did you see the letter?"

Rachel gulped, and before she could do any more damage Hartley spoke up. "Sure we saw it. Down at the office. It turned up in a bunch of other stuff, and you'd have thought it was a million dollar check, the way she went on about it. Said she should have given it to you way last week, that you'll undoubtedly have her shot at dawn—"

"Oh now, look," said Hugh. "I'm not such a terror as all that. I guess I do raise a little hell with her now and then, but I don't know, she kind of asks for it."

"I know what you mean." Rachel was over-eager, too quick to snatch at a diversion. "She affects me the same way. Brings out the bully in me. Isn't it funny how some people can do that to you?"

Hugh nodded, but he didn't pursue the side trail. "I still don't get it, though. So she mislaid a letter and then found it. Why call you up about it? Or me either, when it comes to that? What's all the shouting about?" He looked half-puzzled, half-exasperated.

"It disappeared again," said Rachel desperately. "That is—"

The telephone rang. Saved by the bell, thought Doc, as she hurried out to the hall to answer it. Hartley escaped by the simple method of starting the record-player again; Bix brightened right up, all set for another scrimmage; and Hugh settled back in his chair with a fatherly smile. Maybe he was really worried about the letter, maybe not. If he was, he wasn't telling Doc. God forbid that anybody should tell Doc anything.

"It's for you, Doc," said Rachel from the doorway. "Mrs. Nelson at the hospital."

Francie, of course. It was a miracle he had held on this long. The shots had kept him comfortable, in a half-coma; nothing could mend the broken-down machine that was Francie's heart.

It was still sputtering, though. "He insists on seeing you," said Mrs. Nelson's forthright voice. "Says you've got no business going away and leaving him when he's dying. And he wants Mr. Bovard, too. I haven't called him yet, thought I'd let you decide. He doesn't look a bit good to me, and I can't get him quieted down."

"I'll be right over," said Doc. "Bovard's here, so I'll bring him along. Tell him we'll be right over. Did you give him another shot of—"

"I did not," snapped Mrs. Nelson. "He won't have it. Says he's got a right to die in his right mind if he wants to, and I don't know but I agree with him."

"Okay. Hold everything. We'll be there."

Back in the library he explained briefly. Hugh was already on his feet, prepared for the message. He had forgotten about the letter, but Doc caught a flicker of relief in Rachel's eyes when she heard that Hugh was leaving too.

"You'll call me when you get a chance, won't you?" she asked wistfully. "Please call me, Doc."

"Of course. Don't worry."

A futile bit of advice: she was obviously going to sit here and stew—and somehow it wouldn't seem quite so much as if he were abandoning her, if only he knew what she was going to stew about. He couldn't explain the reluctance he felt at leaving her. After all, she wasn't alone, Hartley and Bix were there too. Hartley...

Halfway down the porch steps he turned; she was standing in the doorway, her hands clenched in the pockets of her skirt. The letter must still be there. He took a step back toward her. "Why don't you call Myra, ask her to come over and keep you company?" He said it fast and low. "The kids probably want to go out somewhere."

"Yes, I will. I'll call Myra. That's a good idea." She latched onto it so eagerly that he felt more uneasy than ever. (Did Hartley know yet that the letter was in Rachel's pocket now, instead of his own? What would he do when he found out?)

"I wish I didn't have to go," he said.

But there was nothing else to do.

XXXI

"Hey there," exclaimed Hugh when they walked into Francie's room. "This is more like it! You're looking like yourself again!"

It was true that at first glance the old man seemed to have rallied. Propped up against the pillows, glittering-eyed, gaunt and unshaven, he had recaptured some of his old air. That arresting, even rather majestic air of a legendary character, like one of the early prophets, or the Ancient Mariner. But his pulse—flickering, now rapid, now almost gone—told a different story. And his voice was hardly more than a husky whisper. Hanging on from sheer stubbornness, by the skin of his teeth; and just as well aware of it as Doc was. His eyes softened when he looked at Hugh, but he didn't waste any strength on pleasantries.

He asked right away for the sheriff and Mr. Pigeon. He'd been asking for them as well as for Doc and Hugh, it seemed, but Mrs. Nelson had put it down to the vagaries of a wandering mind. Francie treated himself to a brief snort.

"Get them," he whispered. "Make it official."

So that was why he was hanging on. A full-dress confession. Hugh wheeled abruptly, crossed to the window, and stood there with his back to the others. He might have been looking out at the view, except that the blinds were drawn, there was nothing to see. No help from him. Doc hesitated by the bedside, held by the fierce urgency in Francie's eyes. He remembered what Mrs. Nelson had said over the phone. Says he's got a right to die in his right mind if he wants to. Why not with a clear conscience, too, if that was what he wanted?

"Go ahead," he said to Mrs. Nelson finally. "Call them."

They waited in silence—Francie with his eyes closed, hoarding his meager store of energy; Hugh at the window, staring at the view that wasn't there; Doc with his fingers on the bony wrist, as if by holding the pulse like this he could keep it from flickering out.

It took Mr. Pigeon and Charlie Jeffreys ten minutes to get there. Mr. Pigeon ambled in; Charlie tiptoed, his face as solemn as a funeral. He jumped slightly when Francie (obviously already a corpse in Charlie's mind) opened his eyes and spoke.

"Write this down." Francie's voice, reduced as it was to a whisper, still had a ghostly ring of authority. They did what he said, all of them. Hugh joined the circle at the bedside because Francie wanted him there. His skinny fingers clamped on to Hugh's hand, holding him, and often as he talked his eyes would turn to Hugh's strained, sorrowful face.

Something between them, thought Doc, a powerful current of sympathy or loyalty or whatever it was that had sparked their incongruous friendship in the first place.

Charlie did the writing. His ball-point pen traveled soberly over the paper, tracing a path that from time to time (much to Charlie's chagrin) faded out almost entirely. An appropriate instrument, it seemed to Doc, to record Francie's wavering, husky story.

"I killed Rose Anthony Henshaw," he began with ceremonious relish, "because I hated her. I'm glad I did it." He watched to make sure Charlie got that down.

"No other reason? Such as money?" One of Mr. Pigeon's mild brown eyes was trained on the foot of the bed, the other on the head. This lent a note of polite detachment to his part in the proceedings.

"Money too." Francie's full lips twisted craftily. "She hid it. Didn't believe in banks. Didn't believe in wills, either. Didn't figure on dying, I guess. But she did."

Nobody was going to argue with him on that score.

"So you went to the Buckmaster house that afternoon," prompted Mr. Pigeon. "Thursday afternoon. And—"

"She wouldn't tell me where it was. So I killed her. Pushed her down the cellar steps. 'Go, lovely Rose'. She went, all right. Let out a squawk on the way down." He smiled, as at a rich, mellow memory.

"Then what did you do?"

"Went down and looked at her. I wasn't sure she was dead. So I hit her with the candlestick.... It was there. By the window."

There was quite a long pause. Charlie's ball-point pen waited, conscientiously poised. Francie closed his eyes. His face grew more mottled, his breath more labored, as if he were once more in actuality making the trip down the steps, reaching for the candlestick, crashing it down in that needless, blundering blow.

"What did you do after that? Look for the money?"

Francie's eyes stayed shut. "Didn't need to. No will. I'd get it anyway." Suddenly he shook all over, swept by a gust of soundless laughter. When it subsided he went on. "I went back to the shop. Candlestick under my coat. I hid it in the shop window, under the bearskin...."

"How did you know about Mrs. Henshaw's money, Francie?" asked Mr. Pigeon gently. "How did you know, if you hadn't talked to her in thirty-five years?"

Francie's eyes flew open at that, glittering and scornful. "'If.' Big word. 'If.'"

"You mean you did see her? You did talk to her? How often?"

"As often as I had to." (It was plain that Charlie didn't know what to make of that. But he wrote it down.)

"Let's get this straight, Francie. Let's go back to the beginning. You say you hated your wife. Why?"

For the first time, Francie's voice rose above a whisper, rose to a whirring echo of its old thunder. Hate seized him and rattled his rickety frame like an engine taking hold in a worn-out machine. "The woman was an abomination. Evil clear through. Serpent in the Garden of Eden...." There was a certain grandeur, thought Doc, in the Biblical phrases; nothing half-hearted about Francie's hymn of hate. "Tricked me into marrying her. Ruined me...." The grandeur drained away; something sick and sly took its place. "Only she had me. She knew it. So did I. Same breed of cats. How did I know about her money? How do you think I knew? It was mine. I paid it to her."

"You paid it to her? What for?" The moment the question was out, Mr. Pigeon looked as if he wished he hadn't asked it. Which was precisely Doc's reaction. Because what happened to Francie's face wasn't nice to watch. It seemed to crawl with slyness. Where was the Ancient Mariner now, the early prophet? He had changed before their eyes into a small boy, gloating over obscenities scrawled on a back fence.

"What for?" Francie licked his lips. Something like a snigger escaped him; his elbow jerked, and for an appalling moment Doc thought he was going to dig Mr. Pigeon in the ribs. "Three guesses what for."

Mr. Pigeon cleared his throat. As for Charlie, he bent his head so far over his pen and paper that only his ears could be seen. They were bright red.

Francie clucked his tongue at them in malicious mock-reproval. "I paid her to keep quiet about it. Naturally. Think I wanted the whole town to know I couldn't leave her alone?"

It was fantastic. But no more fantastic then the rest of Francie's life, the part that the whole town had known about for years. Doc thought of the little path worn along the sidewalk between Francie's shop and his room at Smiley's; of the cases of peanut butter and beans; of the sizable bank account Mr. Pigeon had uncovered, and the profitable transactions with Chicago antique dealers. If you wanted to get technical, it was fantastic that Francie was alive at all. Any reasonable man would have given up and died two nights ago.

"So you'd been paying her all these years," Mr. Pigeon had rallied and was going on, "without anybody knowing you ever saw her. And you killed her to get the money back. Nobody saw you, coming or going?"

Francie shook his head. "Years of practice," he whispered, "sneaking to the Buckmaster's and back."

"What time was it? On Thursday, when this happened?"

"Two, two thirty. Didn't find her till four thirty."

"What did you do, the rest of the afternoon?"

Francie looked slightly bored. "Puttered around the shop. Read. Talked to Hugh."

"That right, Mr. Bovard? You went to see Francie?"

"Yes." Hugh's voice sounded strangled. "He seemed—the same as always."

"Did he tell you any of this? Mention Mrs. Henshaw?"

Both of them shook their heads, and Mr. Pigeon turned back to Francie. "Didn't it bother you when Hartley Buckmaster was arrested?"

Francie made a gesture like a shrug. "His tough luck." So much for Hartley. So much for all of it, in fact. Doc became aware of a slackening in Francie, a kind of mortal indifference. The strength that he had stored up so fiercely was spent, where he had meant to spend it; his mission had been accomplished; he wasn't interested anymore.

But Mr. Pigeon still had questions. "You didn't care about Hartley. But then, when Miss Buckmaster and Mr. Bovard's daughter began asking about the candlestick, you got worried. Didn't you?"

"Snooping around," murmured Francie. But perfunctorily, without rancor. "Scared them off...." He hardly bothered to nod assent to the other questions. Yes, he had thrown the rock through Bovard's window. Yes, after that he had gone back to the shop. He didn't seem to hear when Mr. Pigeon asked about the attack on Bix. His eyes stayed half-open and dull; his head sagged a little to one side.

Silence. Doc could hear the tiny, busy tick of Charlie's wrist watch, a sobbing of wind under the eaves. Nothing else. It was as if they were all holding their breaths.

The knobby wrist between his fingers jerked suddenly in one more spurt of energy. Mission not quite accomplished, after all; there was one last chore.

"Sign," said Francie. "Let me sign." He sounded in a hurry and irritable, like a business man at the end of a trying day. And the spurt of energy still held, incredibly, driving the pen across the paper (which Charlie held for him) in the impatient, proud-looking strokes of Francie's signature. Francis L. Henshaw. It trailed off at the end, and the pen fell from Francie's fingers and wept blue-black tears onto the sheet.

So they had their signed confession. Charlie picked it up and held it uneasily, by one corner.

With a sigh, Francie turned to Hugh. For a moment his face, lit up with gaiety and affection; it occurred to Doc that he might once have been quite a handsome man. "Give me a good write-up," he said. "In the paper. See that I get the credit, boy...."

Another sigh. The spark winked out. That was all.

XXXII

The minute he could manage it, he called Rachel and told her about Francie. "So everything's all right now," he finished anxiously. "The whole thing's settled."

She made a small sound, as if she were catching her breath. But she didn't say any of the relieved things he had hoped for. She didn't say anything at all, and her silence made Doc feel irritated and helpless. What was the matter with her, anyway? Everybody else was satisfied: no loose ends left to bother Mr. Pigeon; poor old Francie granted the kind of death he wanted—in his right mind, and with a clear conscience. So why couldn't she forget about that damn letter, which couldn't possibly have any significance anymore...

"Rachel. Rachel, are you all right?"

"Yes. I'm all right." Her voice still sounded strained and faraway, the way it had when she first answered the phone, and he had another lurid, split-second vision of someone standing over her, threatening her.

"You're not alone, are you? Myra came, didn't she?"

"Yes, she's here." (Not that Myra could do anything, really. But it was a comfort to Doc to think of her sitting there with her crocheting or whatever, and her stock of mild gossip that ran on, whether anybody listened or not.)

"Is Hartley— Did the kids go out?"

"No. They're here too." Did her voice tremble, ever so slightly, on that?

"Listen, Rachel—"

"Doc," she broke in breathlessly. "Are you coming back? Please come back."

She wanted him. He would cling to that. Never mind the ramifications. She wanted him to come back, period. "Of course," he said. "I'll be right there."

Hugh was waiting for him in the hall. Just sitting there on one of the straight-backed chairs, staring at the picture on the opposite wall. Hope, done up in her blindfold and blue dress. The poor guy looked dazed, done in. "Come on, Hugh," said Doc. "Nothing more to be done tonight. We might as well get out of here. I'll give you a lift home."

Neither of them spoke until they had almost reached the Buckmaster house. Then Hugh said, "I'd like to say goodnight to Bix. Okay if

I come in with you for a minute?"

"Sure, come in and have a drink. I know I can use one, and you look like you could too."

He did, indeed. The street light played shadowy tricks with Hugh's face as they went up the walk, accenting the jut of cheekbone and brow, making of the eye socket an empty cavern. It gave Doc the feeling of looking at a desolate landscape. The craters of the moon, something like that.

"I know how you feel about Francie," he said awkwardly. "But maybe it was the best way, after all. I mean, he died happier than most people—"

"Yes." Hugh stopped with his hand on the doorknob. "Two good friends I've had in my life, Doc. Nobody ever had better. Doc Buckmaster, and Francis Henshaw."

Francis, not Francie. It gave Hugh's words a formal ring, like an epitaph. And a fitting one, thought Doc; an epitaph that would have suited the old boy right down to the ground.

Rachel was in the hall, talking on the phone, when they walked in. "Oh, Althea," she was saying, "I meant to call you earlier...."

Something queer happened. Hugh—who had seemed in a kind of slow-motion trance for the past hour—was suddenly swift and purposeful as a cat. He whipped down the hall; Doc caught a glimpse of Rachel's startled face as Hugh bent over her, his hand closing on her wrist.

"What are you doing, calling Althea? What are you telling her?"

All at once Doc was there, too, with no recollection of having moved. "What's the idea? Let go of her. Let go." He shoved, and Hugh half-turned, eyes glaring, face dark and hostile. His right hand stayed clamped on Rachel's wrist. With his left he covered the mouthpiece of the telephone. The old game: keeping Althea out of it.

The incredible little tableau held for a minute more. Then Rachel stuck out her chin. "I'm not telling her anything. She called me, asking for you. Here, talk to her yourself."

Hugh's hand fell away from her wrist as she stood up; he put it up to his face, as if to wipe away the unfamiliar, angry mask that had been there. It was gone now. He was himself again, blinking down at Rachel in a bewilderment that matched hers and Doc's.

"Good Lord, Rachel, I'm sorry. I don't know what in the hell's the matter with me." He sat down heavily, staring at the telephone in his hand, and Doc saw Rachel's eyes soften with compassion.

"You're tired, Hugh," she said. "That's all it is. You're tired and upset about Francie. Doc, why don't you fix us all a drink?"

As he headed for the kitchen, Doc heard Hugh's voice, husky but otherwise the same as always speaking into the phone. "Althea, darling, I didn't mean to worry you, I'm terribly sorry I didn't call you...."

They were all gathered in the library by the time Doc showed up with the tray of drinks. (He had dawdled, hoping that Rachel would join him in the kitchen. After all, she had asked him to come back; you'd think she could spare him a minute or two alone. But it seemed not.)

"Well, anyway, this settles it," Myra was saying. "I don't suppose it'll suit Mrs. Pierce—and if it hadn't been for her snooping around getting Hartley arrested, there'd have been nothing to settle—but I for one consider it a God's mercy Francie's out of reach of the law, where he won't have to pay any penalties. There's been enough justice done, that's what I say, murderer or not." She smoothed out her crocheting and looked around a little defiantly, as if she expected somebody to give her an argument. Nobody did.

"You mean I get a drink too?" asked Bix, bouncing a little on the edge of the couch. "Gee, Hartley, lookit. I've been promoted."

"Just one," Doc told her. "For medicinal purposes. Then off to bed with you. I don't allow my patients to sit up till all hours, carousing."

"All hours! Only eleven thirty."

Hugh gave a start of surprise. "Is that all it is? Really? I had a feeling it was something ungodly, like two thirty or three. Lost track of time, I guess, there at the hospital." He had gulped down his first drink; now he watched thirstily as Doc poured him another.

"My," said Myra, sipping hers genteelly, "It's strong, isn't it?"

"Made according to prescription," said Doc. "Recommended for its powerful relaxing properties." He leaned back in his chair, the picture (he hoped) of repose. Maybe if he set an example, the others would unwind too. God knows they needed to.

But the nervous stillness in his own back refused to melt, and when he looked around he got a curious feeling of tension slowly, relentlessly rising. In spite of the cozy little fire. In spite of the sociable drinks in their hands, and the leisurely cigarettes. Myra had stowed away her crocheting and sat bolt upright, acutely conscious of the fact that she, a member in good standing of the Ladies Aid and a number of other straitlaced organizations, was drinking a highball. (Acutely conscious of something else, too? Yes, Doc was almost sure that just that daring drink couldn't account, all by itself, for Myra's rigid little smile.) The kids sat on the couch, Bix with one foot tucked under her in what should have been a casual attitude, Hartley lounging beside her, his face blank yet watchful. Hugh was hunched in his chair, clutching his glass as if it was all he could do to keep from gulping this drink down like the first. And Rachel—poor desperate Rachel with the color all drained from her face, so that the lipstick on her mouth jolted you like a wrong note, and one hand clenched up tight in the pocket of her skirt.... Still hanging on to that damn letter, thought Doc. If she was trying to hide the fact that she had it, he had never seen a lousier job of hiding. You'd have to be blind to miss it.

What was wrong? What were they all waiting for? Because they were waiting—innocent bystander Doc along with the rest of them. Something was going to happen, that was all he knew: a crisis ahead that kept Rachel's hand frozen onto the letter, that had sent Hugh plunging down the hall in terror of what Rachel might be saying to Althea.

A flock of wild surmises scudded across Doc's mind. He had caught sight of the name Bovard on the letter, and there were three Bovards to choose from. Hugh, Althea, Bix. Supposing Bix had been telling the truth—for once in her tricky young life—about that interview between her mother and Mrs. Henshaw. Supposing she had some real grounds for fearing her mother, and supposing not she, but Hugh, had been the liar, skillfully switching the spotlight to himself. He would do that, wouldn't he, if he thought Althea needed shielding? Doc didn't doubt it for a minute. Hugh would shield Althea no matter what she had done, and no matter who got thrown to the wolves in the process. Bix, along with the rest of the world. He was an indulgent father—possibly even an understanding one—but there was not the slightest question as to who came first with him. All Althea had to do was lift her eyebrow. Again, in his mind's eye, Doc saw that remote, ravaged face of Althea's. A violent woman, he thought suddenly; it takes violence to suffer like that. Supposing, supposing....

But that left Rachel and Hartley, and—no use dodging it—you couldn't leave them out. They were in it, both of them, swiping the letter from each other. Rachel scared. Hartley wary.

It also left Francie and his confession and his clear-conscience, right-mind death.

The silence was getting pretty nerve-wracking. Even Myra, with her plump face set in a parody of a Ladies-Aid smile couldn't seem to dredge up any conversation. There was only one thing to talk about, and nobody dared. Well, damn it, thought Doc, I dare. This had gone on long enough.

"You know," he said, "Francie did just one thing wrong. He made just one little mistake."

"Yeah," said Hartley. "All he did was murder her. Naughty, naughty."

"I don't mean that. I mean from his point of view. It was a perfect crime, almost. If he'd let well enough alone, nobody would ever have known it as a crime at all. But that's where he made his mistake. He had to go down and hit her over the head with the candlestick to make sure, and that did it. That spoiled his perfect crime."

The silence showed signs of setting in again, but Myra headed it off. "They say there's plenty of people do get away with murder. More perfect crimes than you can shake a stick at, they say. Deaths that look natural, and nobody's ever the wiser."

"Who says?" asked Hugh irritably. "If nobody's ever the wiser, how do they know—"

"I read it somewhere," Myra persisted. "According to the authorities."

"I don't believe it," said Hugh.

"I do." Bix spoke up smartly, "Why not? Say somebody's sick anyway, not expected to live. Like—" She warmed up to her subject. "Like Francie. Say somebody'd slipped Francie a shot of arsenic tonight, Doc wouldn't know the difference, he'd call it a natural death. Wouldn't he? Wouldn't you, Doc?"

Doc found it necessary to swallow hard. "I'd know arsenic," he said.

"Well, something else then. Some drug that would just make it look like Francie's heart gave out, the way everybody's been expecting it to. It could happen. I bet it does happen, lots of times. I bet—"

"'You bet, you bet,'" Hugh mimicked, in a surprising flare of anger. "Why don't you pipe down? You don't know what you're talking about. Drugs, perfect crimes, natural deaths. It's time you learned to act like a human being instead of a spoiled brat." He paused, as if suddenly aware of the ring of startled faces, all turned his way. He made a visible effort to get a grip on himself. "What I mean is, it's irresponsible, this kind of busybody talk. Irresponsible and dangerous. You all know it as well as I do. Do you realize, Bix, what harm you could do Doc if somebody like Mrs. Pierce latched on to what you've just been saying."

Bix's big eyes flew to Doc's face in consternation. "I didn't—" she began.

"Of course you didn't," said Doc. "Don't be so touchy, Hugh. You've got yourself all worked up about nothing. Nobody slipped Francie anything. And there aren't any Mrs. Pierces present, thank God. I started this little discussion myself, with my crack about Francie's one mistake."

"I wish he hadn't made it," Myra blurted out. She took a sizable sip and blinked.

"You're inebriated," said Doc. "Obviously headed for the gutter. And you, Bix, you should have been in bed long ago. Beat it. Scram."

She surprised him by getting up obediently. "Okay. It's not so skintillating down here, anyway. Night, Daddy. Night, all."

"Don't be mad, Biscuit." Hugh went over and stood beside her, humbly. "I'm sorry I snapped at you. Don't know what's the matter with me tonight. Please don't be mad."

"I'm not," said Bix coolly.

"Give us a kiss, then."

She lifted her face politely enough, but her eyes reflected none of Hugh's tenderness. Kids could be harder-hearted than anybody, thought Doc; they didn't seem to have heard about the quality of mercy, strained or otherwise.

XXXIII

With Bix out of the way, it seemed reasonable to suppose that Hugh would take himself off for home and Althea. Instead, he mixed himself another drink. Not that he relaxed with it. He didn't even sit down; in an uneasy attempt at casualness he propped one elbow on the mantel and stood there, his face set in a strange, tense expression that perhaps felt to him like a sociable smile. Doc began to wonder if he was afraid of Althea, too. Or maybe she was sore at him for not having called her and had told him over the telephone not to come home at all. She was capable of it. Then he noticed how often Hugh's eyes kept straying to Rachel, who still sat with her hand clutched in her pocket. She might as well be waving the letter under everybody's nose.

"Heaven's sakes, Hugh, sit down," said Myra at last. "Enough to make a person climb the walls, the way you're jittering."

"Jittering? Am I? Sorry." But he remained standing, one hand jingling the coins in his pocket, the other fiddling with his glass. "Thinking about Francie, I guess. Francie and his one mistake."

"What I can't get over," said Myra, "is to think they'd been seeing each other all these years, and not a soul in Coreyville knew it. I wouldn't have thought it was possible. Here I was, living right next door, and I never once suspicioned. Never once."

There, thought Doc in relief, we're getting back to normal, mulling it over the way the whole town will be doing tomorrow. Perfectly natural. He added his bit. "When it comes to that, look at Hartley." (The trouble was that everybody did, literally; Hartley's eyes shifted in alarm.) "What I mean is, there he sat, right there in his father's old office, not noticing a thing, while Francie was busy pushing her down the stairs and beating in her head and sneaking away again."

Hugh gave a sudden, excited laugh. "That's the astonishing thing. The really amazing stroke of luck—that nobody saw him. Broad daylight, and yet nobody saw him come or go." He began to pace back and forth between the mantel and the little marble-topped table against the wall. As if he were on a stage, thought Doc; and indeed Hugh seemed to him a little larger than life, like an actor playing his big scene. His eyes took on a glitter, his gestures grew slower, more controlled.

"Imagine, just imagine," he said, and his audience, willing or not, was with him, seeing what he told them to, carried away—as Hugh seemed to be himself—by the power of his words. "Two o'clock in the afternoon. February. Cold and dismal. Lunchtime over. The housewives through with the dishes, the kids back at school, the business men all back down town at their stores or offices. Only *he's* not where he's supposed to be. He's hurrying along, down the back way, ducking behind the hedge. Maybe he knocks at the back door, maybe he doesn't. Anyway, there she is. Can you see her? Can you see that malicious face of hers, with the mean, turned-down mouth and the sharp nose and those reddish eyes? Francie was right, you know. 'Evil clear through. An abomination on the face of the earth.' She was cleaning house. A mop in her hand, and that ugly dust-colored apron and her hair done up in the blue kerchief, skinned back and tied in rabbit ears in front, and the smell of furniture polish and scrub-water—"

Somebody—Rachel? Myra?—drew a sharp breath. Then silence while Hugh paced to the mantel, back again to the table. Absent-mindedly he slid the little table drawer open and shut, open and shut, before he went on. "Who knows what they said to each other? Who knows what set him off? Maybe it was just one of those oily smiles of hers, or the way her eyes slid around, all over him—She wasn't a big woman, just a little push would do it. A little, quick push. And then down the stairs, and the candlestick, because by that time he couldn't stop himself, and then up again with it under his coat, and out onto the street—" Hugh's voice had sunk almost to a whisper; a rapt, triumphant smile spread over his face. "And nobody saw him. The sheer, fantastic luck of it. Nobody saw him."

Doc waited. Now, surely, would come the sigh from the audience, the slackening of tension as the curtain falls. Instead, he felt a queer ripple along his nerves. No one sighed. No one sank back in relief. No one moved at all.

It was Myra who broke the silence at last, but what she said made no sense to Doc. "How did you know?" She leaned forward a little, her round face dazed. "Her hair tied up in a kerchief, you said. How did you know?"

Out of the corner of his eye Doc caught the violent, quickly suppressed jerk of Rachel's shoulders. He could not see Hugh's face; he was still fiddling absent-mindedly with the drawer of the little table. Open, shut. Open, shut. Open....

"Ah." Hugh's voice had an aimless sound. "So you've still got your father's revolver, I see. I'd forgotten about it. Old Man Schwartz made it for him, you know. His masterpiece, and old Schwartz was no slouch as a gunsmith. A beauty. Your father's pride and joy." He took it out of the drawer, stroked it lovingly.

"Don't," whispered Rachel. "Hugh, don't. It's loaded."

"How did you know?" repeated Myra. Again she was leaning forward; Doc had an impression that the question was being drawn out of her against her will. "About the kerchief. Because I'm the only one that saw it. I found her first, and I took it off of her, slipped it in my pocket even before Hartley got there. So how could you know?"

There was a sharpening in Hugh's eyes as they met Myra's, a kind of intense focusing. But he spoke to Rachel, not to Myra. "Loaded? Nonsense. Nobody's fool enough to leave a loaded gun lying around in a drawer like this."

"Papa did. You know he did," chattered Rachel. "You've heard him say it time and again. The only safe gun's a loaded gun, he always said. It's the 'unloaded' ones that do the damage."

"You couldn't know," Myra explained to Hugh, or perhaps to herself. "Unless you—"

"I'm sure you're mistaken, Rachel," Hugh slipped the revolver back into the drawer, without, however, closing it. His voice was still pleasant and soft. "And now suppose you give me the letter you stole from my desk."

Hugh's movements were quick—the swoop of his hand into the drawer, the three or four strides across the room to Rachel—but Doc's were even quicker. He was aware of an impact, like running into a door, but of nothing more. It was startling to find, seconds later, everything changed around: himself waving the gun at Hugh with one hand, while with the other he clutched the letter that had been in Rachel's pocket. Startling and rather embarrassing: what did he do next? He couldn't think of a thing to say.

"Doc, it is loaded," Rachel warned him earnestly. She was standing up now, rubbing her wrist, where a red welt showed. "Really and truly it is. Be careful, Doc, because it really and truly—"

"Shut up," said Hartley. "Stop saying the same thing over and over. The point is, the important point is—" But his eyes swung back to Hugh, and his voice trailed away.

Hugh stood still, in the middle of the room. He was breathing heavily, and his face and neck were flushed a dusky red. "I don't care about anything else," he said. "Only the letter. Althea mustn't see it."

"Oh, Hugh, why?" Rachel burst out imploringly. "Why—"

"You read it, didn't you?" A joyless smile flitted across Hugh's face. "Okay. That's why."

"What's why?" Doc had found something to say at last. "What the hell is this letter?"

"Read it," said Hugh wearily. "Give Hartley the gun. He can keep me covered. Read it, and you'll know too." He stumbled backward a few steps, found the easy chair and sank into it, with his hands dangling lifelessly down over the chair arms. Anything but a dangerous looking character, thought Doc as he handed the revolver to Hartley.

The outside envelope, the one with the cancelled stamp, was addressed to Mr. Hugh Bovard, c/o *The Coreyville Tribune*. The inside envelope read Mrs. Althea Bovard, and the message itself, written in a remarkably tidy, prim-looking hand, was brief but annihilating. "Ask your husband what he knows about how Ronnie died. Dr. Buckmaster knew it too, and why not? It was their doing. Very truly yours, Rose Anthony Henshaw." Doc stared at it for a long, long time. A kaleidoscope pattern of faces and voices skittered across his mind's eye. Rachel's: "You mean blackmail? Papa? It's funny, I never thought of that before." Althea's: "Ronnie. My son, my little boy." Francie's: "Give me a good write-up in the paper. See that I get the credit, boy." And Hugh's: "Two good friends I've had in my life. Nobody ever had better. Doc Buckmaster, and Francis Henshaw."

Dimly, he heard Myra begin a groping sentence. "Then Francie didn't—" She paused, and there came other sounds—a lightning-swift scuffling, a thud, a smothered cry from Rachel. Doc was too late this time. Too late by a full minute. By the time he got into action Hartley was picking himself up and Hugh was back in his chair. Again he was breathing a little heavily. And again the gun had changed hands.

"That's right, Myra," he said amiably. "Francie didn't. I did."

He's a murderer, Doc told himself. A murderer, and armed, and desperate for this letter. But it didn't seem like that. It still just seemed like Hugh Bovard (a good guy, Hugh, maybe a little quick-tempered, but a prince of a fellow) sitting there calmly, patting the gun that had belonged to his old friend.

"It was my idea," he was telling Rachel and Hartley. "Your father wouldn't listen to me at first. But he knew what Ronnie was doing to Althea and me. He knew she'd never consent to putting him in an institution. And Ronnie was one of the first to get the flu, there was a good chance he wasn't going to pull through anyway. Several people did die of it, that winter. Bix had just been born, and it seemed to me like the one chance, for Althea and me...." He searched their faces anxiously, trying to explain. "It got so I couldn't think of anything else. I begged your father. I kept at him and at him, and after a while it began to seem right to him, too. The way it did to me. So right. So merciful and right. It still does only—"

Only, thought Doc, what seemed so right had gone so wrong. Althea must have been beyond help, even then. And somehow—a drink too many, probably, an unguarded word or two—somehow Mrs. Henshaw had found it out.

"She went to work on your father first," said Hugh. "Then when he died it was my turn. I guess I—misled you a little, Doc, about the time she came to see Althea, three years ago."

"Just a little," said Doc.

"I had to." Again the effort to explain, the somehow pathetic wish to be understood. "I had to keep Althea out of it. That was where Mrs. Henshaw had me, of course. She'd send me the letters, whenever she figured another payment was due. Just to remind me.... About that night, three years ago. I didn't really know how much Bix heard. Enough to scare the bejesus out of her, I guess."

He looked inquiringly toward Hartley, who gulped a little, and, after a moment, spoke. "She wasn't sure. But you yelled at her, and *you* were scared of Mrs. Henshaw. That's what really got her. She couldn't imagine anything terrible enough to scare you. Then, the other night when you grabbed her in the alley—"

"But she thinks it was Francie! She couldn't possibly have seen me, she doesn't know it was me!"

"She—smelled you." Hartley brought it out miserably, and Hugh looked so stricken that for a moment Doc considered making another rush for the gun. The impulse died a-borning. He barely moved, and Hugh was once more alert and unobtrusively threatening. "You've got a special smell, she says," Hartley went on. "So then she was really scared."

But still loyal, thought Doc, after her own fashion. Her own confused, stubborn, forlorn fashion. The candlestick rubbed against her jacket, for instance, in case of tell-tale fingerprints. The almost unintelligible words whispered to him in the alley: "I—fell—." And the final, inspired switching of the spotlight of her fear from Hugh to Althea.

"We got our signals all mixed, Francie and I," said Hugh. "I guess we weren't very expert. I never dreamed he'd keep the candlestick. I went straight to his place that afternoon—afterwards. He said he'd get rid of it for me. He must have had some notion about this phony confession of his, even that far back. We figured the rock through the window would clear Hartley. Only Francie must have collapsed in the alley on his way home—"

"My land," put in Myra, "think of that poor old man laying there all that time."

"I thought he was safely home in bed, of course." Hugh sighed. "Otherwise I never would have grabbed Bix. By that time I was good and worried about the candlestick and wasn't making much sense. I followed the three of you, after I heard Bix creeping down the back stairs, so I knew you'd found it. But I thought, they can't pin this on Francie because he's home in bed, and they won't suspect me, because I'm her father.... I didn't choke her, you know. All I did was throw my muffler over her eyes and give her a little shove."

"I know," said Doc. "She made that up, when we did pin it on Francie, after all."

"And Francie," ventured Myra. "He made it up, didn't he, about going to see Mrs. Henshaw all these years?"

Hugh smiled. "Of course. He'd never have gotten past you and the rest of Coreyville that many times. I was lucky to get away with it once. It's funny—" He shook his head in a bewildered way. "I can't remember, now, what made me push her. I didn't plan it. I knew I was going to have to pay her, the way I always had. It wasn't any different from the other times. But then, all at once—It's just kind of a red blur."

There was a silence before he spoke again.

"That brings us right back to the letter." He looked deathly tired. "Doesn't it?"

The letter. And the gun. "We all know now," said Doc. "You can't—dispose of all four of us."

"I wouldn't want to," said Hugh gently. "No, I wouldn't want to do that. On the other hand, I am not going to have Althea see the letter." His eyes made what seemed like a pilgrimage, a brief, hungry search of each of their faces. Myra's. Rachel's. Doc's. They fastened on Hartley's. "That's assuming, of course, that Rachel's right and the gun is loaded. Really and truly loaded. I still have my doubts. We could check, I suppose, but that seems pretty tame. I'm a betting man, myself." A ghost of the old humorous quirk passed across his face; with a playful air he aimed the gun at his own temple. "Any takers?"

He paid no attention to Rachel's half-choked protest, or the gesture Myra made, stirring around like a flustered hen. His offer, his challenge, whatever it was, was for Hartley alone; the others no longer counted. He had chosen Hartley. The one that Bix loved.

The boy stood with his head slightly lifted, as if he were listening. The deadpan look was still there; no telling what went on behind the high forehead and hazel eyes that were so like Rachel's. He swallowed once or twice, as if his throat were dry.

"You can depend on me." Hugh's voice was low but very clear. "Can I depend on you?"

Suddenly, under the pressure of that intense gaze of Hugh's, Hartley's face came alive, burst into a very blaze of affirmation and decision. "Yes. Yes. I'll bet you—" In a flash of movement that was like lightning he snatched the letter from Doc's hand and thrust it into the fire.

Smiling faintly, Hugh pressed the trigger.

It seemed to Doc that the report rocked the library, filled the whole world with a thunder of sound that, instead of fading, simply changed into other sounds. Queenie's voice, raised in frenzied barking. The drum of bare feet on the stairs, and Bix's screams.

"Daddy! Daddy!"

She stopped dead in the doorway, gawky and trembling. In the abrupt stillness the four of them looked away from her and at each other. It was like a pact. Their eyes met in unanimous, steadfast agreement.

Myra was their spokesman. And what she said held, for all of them, a strange quality of echo-in-reverse: here was what they would be saying from now on, as long as anybody asked.

"Bix honey," said Myra, as she put out her arms and drew the shocked child-face to her shoulder, "Bix, honey, there's been an accident. Your Daddy was fooling with Doc Buckmaster's gun...."

THE END

The Evil Wish

BY JEAN POTTS

The evil wish is most evil to the wisher.
—HESIOD

I

Saturday was the best day. For both of them; just as Lucy looked forward to getting away from the house, so Marcia, after her week at the office, enjoyed a day at home. "You're not just saying that?" Lucy would ask, from time to time. Because she always felt a bit guilty, leaving her sister to cope with what had become to her, by the end of each week, a crushing burden. Small as the house was—four stories, a narrow, old-fashioned brownstone, with the two top floors rented out—even so, it was just one thing after another. The two sets of tenants who, failing all else, complained about each other. The plumbers and electricians and furnace repair men who never came when they said they would, no matter how frantically Lucy explained that it was an emergency, or how faithfully they promised. Hansen, the handy man from across the street, who looked after several other houses in the block, and whose attitude toward Lucy alternated between outright surliness and sly, over-familiar affability, she didn't know which was worse...

And of course the biggest worry of all—that she might not be able to prevent one of these crises from reaching Daddy's attention. Charming as he could be, and often was, he was also an irritable man, subject to explosive changes of mood. So whatever else happened, Daddy must not be annoyed. It was the prime rule of the household, and had been ever since either Lucy or Marcia could remember. Poor dear Mama, even the last year of her life when she was so sick, had still contrived to keep things running smoothly for Daddy. It couldn't have been any easier for her than it was for Lucy; they had the same timid temperament. And then as now, Daddy used the front half of the ground floor for his office. Office hours from two to six every afternoon, which meant precious little time when he wasn't right there in the house, in constant danger of being annoyed.

By Saturday Lucy was worn to a frazzle, no two ways about it. Really, she didn't know what she would do without Marcia. Such a comfort, in her unsentimental way. "Of course I am not just saying it," she would answer, whenever Lucy reproached herself half-heartedly for abandoning her post. "You know me, not an unselfish bone in my body. I *like* Saturdays at home. Run along, now. You'll be late for your date with Pierre."

That was the first thing for Lucy on Saturday: her date with Pierre to have her hair done. A small luxury, but important to her; when Pierre got through with her she felt pretty again, the way she used to as a young girl. Not that she was really so old. Lots of girls waited till past thirty to get married. Yes, and went right on waiting. The rest of their lives. Don't think about it, don't think about Bernie. It had been just one of those things. She knew that. All over. Nothing left but a tiny, mindless, grieving voice that she could not always silence.

Anyway, her date with Pierre was the first thing on Saturday. Then lunch. A leisurely, moderately festive lunch uptown with one of the girls; she still kept in touch with several from the old Art School days, or one of the cousins came in from Long Island. After that it was a matinee, or some special show at a museum, or sometimes just poking around by herself in the shops. She seldom came home empty-handed. It was a family joke, Lucy's bargains. Our little forager, Daddy called her. The joy of coming on some unexpected treasure—a scarf or a piece of junk jewelry for Marcia ("I simply couldn't resist it; it just looked like you."); another miniature cat for Lucy's collection; a vase, perfect for that spot in the downstairs sitting room, and of all places to find it, gathering dust in the back room of a Third Avenue second-hand store...

On this particular Saturday she had gone overboard and bought a coffee mug for Daddy. Out-size, extra-thick—because he was always complaining about these damn worthless thimbles of cups, wouldn't keep anything hot for two seconds—and yet handsome. At least Lucy thought so. Daddy might. Then again he might not. She would show it to Marcia first. Marcia was pretty good at predicting His Nibs' reactions. (That was her name for him. His Nibs.) Not that she herself went in for buying him presents. Too risky, she said, and probably it was. Except that if you did happen to hit it right... Those gloves Lucy had given him one Christmas. His gauntlets, he called them. "Where's my good old gauntlets that Lucy gave me?" Wore them to shreds.

Maybe it would be like that with the coffee mug. She hugged it to her as she got on the bus for the ride downtown. Tired as she was—but happily tired—she didn't mind how crowded it was, or how slow. Saturday had refreshed her soul; she could face the house again, and all that went with it. A lovely time of day; not quite dusk, lights just beginning to twinkle here and there, a skein of amethyst and rose clouds showing in the west at the cross streets, the first hint of spring in the air. In Gramercy Square (Lucy got off at the stop just above; she liked walking around the park) the trees were budding out, faint hazy green. Mothers trundled their toddlers home. Poodles frisked on their leashes. The ice cream man's bell rang out, cheery yet with a wistful fall to it. And when she turned on to her own block, there was a flock of little girls skipping rope.

In this light the house took on a gracious, mellow look. Its spindling little tree was swelling with buds too, and inside the front gate its pocket handkerchief of grass was already thick and green. Marcia's doing. Like the window boxes, planted with geraniums and ivy. But the back yard was her special pride; there she had room enough for a real garden, their own private oasis in the summer, with the ailanthus tree waving above.

E. S. Knapp, M.D., read the plaque beside the front door. Restrained. Dignified. The light was on in what had originally been the parlor but was now Daddy's office. He would be finishing up the afternoon's patients soon, though; it must be after six. And Saturday was one of Daddy's nights out. His bridge club. Or something, as Marcia put it, sardonically. Who knew what she meant when she said things like that? Lucy paid no attention to them. She hurried up the steps and let herself in, eager for the evening ahead—a cozy dinner, just the two of them, and a good gossip. Down the hall, past the door with Daddy's name again and beneath it "Please Ring and Walk In."

"Hi," she called as she opened the sitting room door. The room—charming in its Victorian way; marble fireplace, crystal chandelier, Mama's little oval-backed settee—was empty. Lucy's first thought was the back yard, but when she crossed to the tall windows and pulled back the plum-colored drapes to peer out, there was no sign of Marcia there, either. No answer when Lucy called again. No light in the kitchen. Ah, but the door to the basement stairs was open, and to Lucy that meant a crisis. Troubles sprouted like mushrooms in the basement. All those pipes. Hot water heater. Fuse box. Furnace. Something forever going wrong. Poor Marcia, she thought, and could not quite suppress a pang of relief at its being, for once, poor Marcia instead of poor Lucy.

She hesitated at the top of the stairs. Surely Marcia had heard her come in? And why hadn't she turned on the light down there? Even in broad daylight the place was gloomy, swarming with shadows. Now it seemed to Lucy dark as a well, and as silent. Scaredy-cat. She found the light switch and flicked it on.

Instantly Marcia hissed at her from below. "Ssh!" The next moment her figure materialized out of the gloom, and Lucy felt the familiar tremble of forbidden laughter in her throat. So that was it. Marcia was standing against the far wall, listening.

She had always been shameless about it, and intense. Lucy was the one who got the giggles. They had discovered the potentialities of the far wall years ago, when they were children. And how almost like a child Marcia looked right now, in her dungarees and sweater, with the same rapt frown on her face, her head lifted in a gesture that was at once beckoning and threatening. "Come on," she used to say, "let's go down in the basement and listen. Only don't you *dare* laugh, or I won't let you stay." What strange, fascinating, garbled facts of life they had absorbed from their listening sessions! For the far wall had an acoustical quirk; it served as a sounding board for whatever was said in Daddy's office. When you considered how much time they had spent down there listening to clinical details, it was amazing that they had never been caught. Of course Mama, poor dear, had been far too innocent to suspect her little girls of such misbehavior. And Lucy—who, left to herself, would have spilled the secret to some of her school friends—had been terrorized into silence by Marcia. "If you ever tell a soul, I'll kill you. I will. I'll cut off your head, and then I'll put you through the meat grinder." Lucy had never doubted her sincerity.

But that was years ago. They were grown women now. They had left the days of listening far behind them, along with dolls and Santa Claus.

"What in the world," began Lucy. In a whisper; the old habit still had its grip on her. And the old excitement. She felt herself being pulled down the steps, as irresistibly now as then.

"Ssh!" Again the beckoning, threatening gesture.

Shivering slightly, she crept the rest of the way down and across to the wall. How well she remembered the chilly feel of it, the smell of dank cement, the hollow boom of Daddy's voice...

"Pam. Pam Sweetie, you're being silly. I keep telling you, there's nothing to worry about."

The other voice was high-pitched and synthetically sweet. "But darling, how can I help it? You know as well as I do how the girls are going to feel about it when they find out. They're not going to like it one little bit. They're going to say I'm just after your money—"

"I don't care whether they like it or not. Let them say it. I don't even care if it's the truth. So help me, I don't. Just so you marry me. Never mind why."

The laugh, too, was synthetically sweet. "Darling, what a thing to say! You know that's not why. It wouldn't matter to me if you hadn't a cent to your name ..."

Lucy closed her eyes. Darling. Pam Sweetie. (Neither she nor Marcia had paid much attention to Daddy's new nurse. Cheap-looking, with her bird's nest of blonde hair, her greenish eye shadow, her bosom which Marcia classified as chicken croquette formation, large economy size.) The girls. That's us, Lucy thought numbly. Marcia and me.

The false little voice was purling on. "Seriously though—Edwin, now stop it, I mean it!—seriously though, about the girls. Of course they'll always be welcome here, as long as they want to stay. I mean, I wouldn't think of turning them out of their home, poor things. It's just that you need the whole first floor for your office, you really do, and then if we decide to do the second floor over, and of course we'll need more living space because I have this thing, I simply can't stand being cramped up ..."

"Anything you say, sweetie, I told you, I'm signing the house over to you as soon as we're married. If the girls don't like it they can lump it. It's none of their business what I do with my property. None of their business who I marry, either. I've got a right to live my own life the way I want to, and the way I want to is with you."

"Well, me too. Naturally. Only I just don't want any trouble, is all."

"Leave it to me. There won't be any trouble, I'll see to that. I know how to handle the girls. We'll send them a telegram after we're married, and that will be that. They won't have a chance to make any trouble. Pam, Pam, a month from today we'll be on our honeymoon, taking off for Paris ..."

A muffled squeal. Sighs. Feet scuffling. And after a short silence Daddy's voice again, no longer through the sounding board; he was in the sitting room now. "Marcia! Lucy! Where are you?"

"Down here," Marcia called back. How could she sound so natural? "Putting my garden tools away."

"Oh. Well. I'm off. Bridge night, you know."

"I know. Have fun. See you later." Still so natural-sounding. But even in the dim light Lucy saw the furious, pinched-up look on her sister's face. She herself felt blank with shock. When Marcia started for the stairs she trotted along automatically. Follow the leader.

Upstairs all was quiet. But before she said anything, Marcia checked to make sure they were both gone. Darling. And Pam Sweetie. Then, in the sitting room, she turned and faced Lucy, who shrank back a little, as if she were somehow to blame.

"He's going to marry her. You heard him. He's going to *marry* her!"

"I can't believe it," Lucy quavered. "It's too—she's so much younger than he is, young enough to be his daughter. What will people say?"

"Nothing that isn't true." Marcia's eyes flashed. (She was the "handsome" one, Lucy the "pretty" one. Most people, meeting them for the first time, were surprised to learn they were sisters. Not at all the same type.) "It's perfectly obvious what she's after. The house. He knows it himself. If it didn't make me so mad I could even feel sorry for him. Signing the house over to her. *Bribing* her to marry him. And if we don't like being dispossessed we can lump it."

"But she said—"

"Poor things. That's what she said. That's what we are to her. A couple of poor relations taking up space in her house. Well, she needn't worry about me. No, thanks. I'm not having any."

"You mean you'd move out? Leave the house?" Lucy stopped there; she would not let herself ask the other, abject question. And me? You'd leave me? But it trembled inside her. She sat down on the love seat, sick with fear.

"Rather than share it with her, yes." Marcia's voice started out crisp, but there was an odd catch at the end. Her eyes made a lingering tour of the room. She blinked twice, very hard, and ran her fingers through her springy, wavy dark hair. "Seems funny, to think of living anywhere else. I used to envy the other kids, the ones that were always moving around from one apartment to another. We never moved, not even once ... Well. I shudder to think of what it'll be like when she gets through with it. She'll do it all over, of course. Glass bricks, I bet. Zebra striped upholstery. And my garden. She'll slap on a layer of cement and make a patio out of it. So they can have cook-outs. She'll chop down the ailanthus tree and put up a beach umbrella. Green and orange stripes." Her voice, which had taken on an edge of bitter zest, caught again. "I know how you feel about the house, Lucy, just one headache after another, but I—"

"No, no," whispered Lucy. True, she was always complaining about the constant domestic crises that plagued her, the responsibilities that so often seemed too much for her. But it wasn't the crises that wore her out; it was the dread of their annoying Daddy. The house itself was as dear to her as to Marcia. To think of this room, so steeped in memories of Mama and the special, happy days of childhood—to think of its being wiped out, turned, with one wave of Pam's unfeeling hand, into an enlargement of Daddy's office! And her own room upstairs! Her precious, private room that had belonged to her all her life, "done over"—Pam had said so—into God knows what kind of flashy abomination. To be uprooted from her room would be to lose a part of her identity. And to be abandoned by Marcia ... What would be left of Lucy? What would be left of her life?

"I can't stand it!" she cried. "It's too much, it's not *right*—"

"All the same, there it is," said Marcia rather absently. She groped for a cigarette in the pocket of her dungarees. Found one, and forgot to light it. "In a way, I suppose, we asked for it."

"*Asked* for it!"

"In a way. It was easy to stay here, instead of getting out on our own, the way we should have years ago—"

"But Marsh, we couldn't! How could we? With Mama sick for so long, and then my breakdown. We couldn't possibly!"

"Well, we didn't. We stayed right here in our soft little berth, letting His Nibs run our lives for us, figuring at least we were safe ... That's how I figured it, anyway. Like sticking with some job you can't stand, only they'll never fire you, so you settle for security and the pension you'll get when you retire. It worked both ways, of course. Nice and comfortable for His Nibs too. Convenient for him to have us around. Where else could he find a housekeeper that would keep everything running smoothly without his having to lift a finger, and cook his meals for him—when he felt like eating at home, that is—and put up with his moods? And all for no salary, just room and board."

"Oh, Marsh, no!" Lucy protested in anguish. "Daddy's always been so generous with us!"

"I know. But don't you see, that suited him, too, to make like Lord Bountiful with his charge accounts and his handouts. 'There you are, dear, run along and buy yourself something pretty.' Feeding his ego. At cut-rate prices. Only along comes Pam and pulls the rug out from under us ..."

"She's so vulgar!" Lucy wailed. "How *can* he!"

Marcia shrugged. "She's not my type either. But I'm sure Pam couldn't care less. She's strictly For-Men-Only."

"It's just an infatuation. He'll get over it."

"I wouldn't count on it. If he does, it'll be too late to do us any good."

"Maybe if we were to tell him how we feel about it, if we could make him see—"

Marcia laughed scornfully. "Tell him. Make him see. In the first place, we're not supposed to know anything about this thrilling romance of his. It's a secret. Remember? He's going to send us a telegram after the wedding. If he found out we've been eavesdropping, he'd blow his top and send us packing. In the second place, what's the use of trying to make him see something that doesn't make any difference to him? He doesn't care how we feel. We don't matter to him. He just simply doesn't care."

There was no answer to that. It couldn't be. But it was. It was the terrible truth: Daddy didn't care. The impact stunned Lucy; she felt nothing, only a queer weight in her chest, heavy and at the same time hollow.

But Marcia was still not through. She lit her cigarette and blew out a furious puff of smoke. "Actually," she said, "the amazing part of it is that he waited so long. If he was going to do something like this—and of course he was bound to, sooner or later, I see it now—why couldn't he have done it years ago? We might have had a chance, then. I had some ambition, when I was a kid. Who knows, I might have gotten into decorating, maybe even designing ... At least I wouldn't have let myself bog down, the way I have, into a nothing of a job."

A nothing of a job. Marcia's familiar cry of frustration and discontent. But a nothing of a job was more than Lucy had. She said desolately, "I don't know about me, though. Even when I was—younger."

"You'd have married somebody. The way you should have. The way you would have, without His Nibs to put the hex on anybody that looked at you twice."

"Don't," said Lucy. She couldn't bear it if Marcia mentioned Bernie in that flip way of hers, almost contemptuous, as if it had been no more than an adolescent crush. She added, "After all, you did marry somebody. Al. Or doesn't he count?"

"Not really," said Marcia, without rancor. "Oh, Al was a nice enough boy. If memory serves. I don't mean that. But he was just part of the mutiny I was staging, in my half-baked way. I knew when I ran off with him that we were never going to get away with it. I mean, we were under age. Of course His Nibs was going to come roaring after us and drag me back home by the scruff of my neck. Still, I had to stage it, my poor little half-baked mutiny. I had to make the gesture." She paused briefly. "Well. As I say, I only wish some smart little apple had trapped him into marrying her sooner instead of later. It beats me why one of them didn't."

"One of them?" Lucy asked in a strangled voice. "You mean he—"

Marcia stared at her. "Honestly, Lucy, didn't you know? Don't tell me you believed in all his medical conventions and bridge clubs and week end fishing trips. Why, I've been on to him and his girl friends ever since I can remember. Even before Mama died."

"No! I don't believe it!" She did, though; it was another terrible piece of truth, like his not caring. The pressure in her chest tightened. So heavy, so hollow. "How do you know?"

"How do I know? Look, Lucy, when I was twelve years old I saw him kissing that maid we had, the one with the pink hair. And remember the lady drama coach who used to live on the top floor? You don't think she ever paid any rent, do you? No, and she never had any pupils, either. Everybody knew about it, even Mama. He didn't make any bones about it. How you could have missed it ... After that it was the nurse he hired to take care of Mama. Nurses are kind of a specialty with him. For years it's been his faithful Miss Simmons, Simmy. She's not a bad sort. Why couldn't he have married her? She didn't play her cards right, I suppose. Like us. Along comes Pam Sweetie, and it's goodbye Simmy, nice to have known you."

"You've known all along—" Lucy's voice faltered—"and you never told me?"

"I took it for granted you knew. After all, Mama's been dead nearly twenty years, and she was practically an invalid for long before that. So it's only natural. A good-looking man like His Nibs ... He still is, you know, doesn't look anywhere near as old as he is. It's not just looks, either. Catch him in the right humor, and he can charm the birds out of the trees. You couldn't expect him to live on memories all this time."

No. Of course not. But Lucy had clung, like an obstinate child, to the image of Daddy-and-Mama. A fixed entity. In her little dream world Daddy had been capricious, awesome, unassailable. Rather like God. And, of course, free of ordinary man's appetites (what Lucy thought of as "all that"). When in reality ...

Woman chaser, she thought. Carrying on his cheap little affairs while poor Mama lay dying, while Lucy herself was renouncing Bernie because he (he!) had so decreed it. And now, after all the wasted years of devotion and self-effacement, she was to be cast aside with nothing of her own. No home, no job, no identity. Because he wanted Pam. Because he didn't care. He didn't care.

It was no use clenching her hands. They went right on shaking. Her chest could no longer contain the pressure; it rayed out, ominous as lightning, making her ears ring, blurring Marcia's crisp voice.

"... the age where men are apt to do these crazy things. And don't think our Pam doesn't know it. She's just the type to hold out for marriage. She'll take him not only for the house but every cent he's got besides." She brought both her fists down on the marble-topped table in a burst of impotent rage. "Oh, I could *kill* her!"

It was as if Lucy had been waiting for the word. She sprang up. Kill. The violent, exciting word. I could kill her! Oh, I could kill ...

There on the chair where she had dropped it when she came in (a lifetime ago) was the package wrapped in brown paper. The coffee mug she had bought for Daddy. She snatched it up. With all her strength she flung it to the floor.

The crash was glorious. Lucy burst into sobbing laughter.

II

When had it stopped being—not a joke, it was never quite that—but a manner of speaking? One of those jazzed-up expressions that you heard, and used, all the time. "How ghastly!" "It's adorable!" "I could kill her ..."

Marcia closed her eyes against the morning light that knifed in through the venetian blinds of her bedroom window. She lay on her back, flat as a mummy, with the sheet twisted around her, tight as a mummy's wrappings. She had a premonition about her head. Sure enough, it was a mistake to turn it. The ache twanged instantly into life. Another hangover. Disgusting ...

Because somewhere along the line it *had* stopped being a manner of speaking. They had actually discussed, she and Lucy—with the glassy logic of innumerable drinks and no dinner—they had actually discussed ways and means! A fake robbery, with Pam, courageous defender of the narcotics cabinet, struck down, her blonde birds-nest head bashed in, ostensibly by a crazed addict. A fatal fall down the stairs, an overdose of sleeping pills, a slug of some undetermined poison, all ostensibly accidental.

In Marcia's head there vibrated, along with the ache, the memory of another permutation in last night's discussion. Still a different method? Never mind, let it go, it was all alcoholic nonsense, anyway. They weren't going to kill anybody. Except the bottle. They had killed that, all right.

It was Marcia who had triggered both the discussion and the drinking. "I could kill her!" And right away, zing, there was Lucy, with blood in her eye, smashing the coffee mug and laughing like crazy. She calmed down after a while, and Marcia couldn't leave well enough alone, she had to speak up again: "I don't know about you, but I'm going to have a drink."

A drink. What an understatement that turned out to be! And Lucy—who was ordinarily such a ladylike drinker—Lucy had been with her all the way. She must be in really sad shape today. At least Marcia was used to it. Too damn used to it; quite often lately the vision of herself as a lush rose up like some grisly, chilling ghost. (Surely not, oh, surely not. Look at the way she had gone on the wagon right after New Years, for practically a week. That showed you. She could take it or leave it, any time she chose.)

Cautiously, so as not to jar her head, she worked one arm free of the twisted sheet, fumbled on the bedside table for her little clock, and maneuvered it into her line of vision. Almost nine-thirty. Another quarter of an hour and His Nibs would be champing for breakfast. He was taking his shower now; from his bathroom across the hall she could hear the rush of water. No matter how late his "bridge nights" might be, he was up by nine on Sundays. Seven-thirty on weekdays. Everybody else ought to be, too, in his opinion. He had no use for slug-abeds. And he believed in a good hearty breakfast, including two eggs, sunny side up.

At the thought of cooking those two eggs Marcia moaned. But they must be faced. Breakfast was her responsibility on week ends. There would be no peace in the house if she tried to duck it. She struggled out of her cocoon and heaved herself into a sitting position. A pause, while she waited for the rocking to subside. Then, holding her head firmly in place with both hands, she made her way to the bathroom which separated her room from Lucy's. The door was open, and she could see Lucy curled up in her bed like a fetus. The part of her face that showed looked swollen and blotchy.

You don't look so hot yourself, Marcia told her bleary reflection in the mirror. It was a habit of hers, on mornings like this, to inspect her own face thoroughly and pitilessly. Morbid curiosity. She got a kind of satisfaction out of viewing the ruins. There were new areas of erosion today, sure enough. Nothing much left intact except her teeth, and they felt fuzzy. She bent down—gently, gently!—and gave them a fierce brushing. Good old water. Good for swabbing up the ruins, good for smoothing the hair, best of all when taken internally. She drank long and deep, got into a housecoat, and transported her jangling head downstairs to the kitchen.

At least there were no left-over dirty dishes. That was one thing about no dinner. No dirty dishes, either. It must follow as the night the day. Oh my, thought Marcia, I am not the wellest woman in town. I must focus my mind. Start the coffee. Carve the grapefruit. Don't think about those eggs. Not yet. When the time comes God will provide the strength. Maybe. Meanwhile set the table.

The sitting room doubled as dining room, at least for any meals involving His Nibs. Eating in the kitchen was beneath him. Usually Marcia herself rather liked Sunday breakfast in the sitting room. But this morning she felt an aversion to the place; its atmosphere was still thick, not only with the smoke of last night's cigarettes, but with the heady, stored-up flavor of last night's conversation. That fantastic conversation which at the time had seemed so eminently reasonable.

She shoved back the drapes, opened the windows to the candid morning air, emptied the ashtrays into the fireplace. So much for the stale cigarette smoke. The other might be more of a problem. If it was really there at all. Marcia knew how unreliable her own perceptions were, on a day like this. Sharp in some directions, unbearably sharp; blurred in others. They produced all kinds of trivial distortions, oversights, misjudgments of distance, wayward fancies ...

The bottle, for instance. She nearly knocked it over while she was opening out the drop-leaf table, and what a pity that would have been because—unless her eyes were playing another one of their sly little tricks—it didn't seem to be quite empty, after all. Nonsense. Of course it was empty; they had killed it last night.

And what if they hadn't? Well, there was that old saying. The old joke. Ha ha. About a hair of the dog.

That would be enough of that. It would be different if she were a lush. Thank God she was not; she could still take it or leave it, any time she chose. So it was of absolutely no interest to her whether the bottle was quite empty or not. She couldn't care less. She was not even bothering to check her first, fleeting impression—which was almost certainly false, anyway. See how she was ignoring the bottle, going about her business of setting the table without giving it so much as a second glance.

Naturally, when she went back to the kitchen she took it with her. Empty or not, it wasn't a suitable centerpiece for Sunday morning breakfast. (Not that *he* didn't hoist a few himself, from time to time. But in a civilized way. Like Marcia. He was no lush, either.) And naturally she had to check when she got it to the kitchen, because—decisions, decisions!—there was the question of whether to throw it away or put it back in the cupboard. For a more suitable, civilized moment.

She took a firm grip on its neck and lifted it to the light. Her heart thumped, unpleasantly hard. Well, how about that? No trick, after all. There really was something left, an inch at least. She heard it slosh and chuckle; she saw it wink its lovely, evil eye at her.

Her interest, of course, was strictly practical. Throw away or put in cupboard, that was the question. And here was the answer. Put in cupboard. For later. A more suitable moment ...

Like the one—fast approaching, almost upon her—when she would have to face those eggs? Or maybe like now. Right now. Why not?

Because I'm not a lush, that's why not. Certainly you're not, whoever said you were? It's just that you need it, dear ... *Like a hole in the head. It's the last thing I need.* Well, you need something. Your nerves, look at the way you're shaking, and your poor head, and your heart thumping away, and this ravenous thirst. Why torture yourself? ... *I like it, I'm a masochist. Besides, what if he walked in and caught me?* Don't be such a baby! He's not going to catch you. Not if you're quick about it. There's so little left, anyway. Hardly worth saving. One little nip like that, why, it's just as if you were taking a spoonful of medicine. Of course you wouldn't do it under ordinary circumstances. But this is a crisis. He's going to marry that little tramp, remember, you're going to be dispossessed, and what's more Lucy, you can't abandon Lucy, you know you can't ...

All right, all right! I give up!

She unscrewed the cap and drank from the bottle, tilting back her head, opening her throat to the fiery path it made going down. There was more than she had thought. She paused for breath, gulped, paused, gulped again.

"Good morning," he said behind her, and her head jerked around convulsively. There he was, smiling his furious smile. Spare and distinguished in his dressing gown. His handsome, bad-tempered face glowed from shower and shave; the part in his hair—pewter-colored but still thick—was straight as a knife edge; beneath his clipped moustache his teeth showed white, intact as Marcia's own.

So. Had he purposely sneaked up on her? Or had her ears betrayed her, as they were perfectly capable of doing? No matter. There was nothing to do but look him in the eye and give him back his furious smile. "Good morning," she said. "I didn't hear you come down."

"So I gathered. Is this the way you usually start the day?"

"Why not?" She couldn't help it; he always had this effect on her. She wiped her mouth and deposited the bottle on the cabinet top. "I mean, doesn't everybody?"

"Possibly everybody does, in your circle." That was a crack at Joe. He wasn't supposed to know about Joe—nobody was, on account of Joe's wife—but trust His Nibs to figure it out. He wasn't gullible like Lucy, who swallowed it whole, the business about Marcia's having to work late some nights. And then, once, months ago, Joe had gotten looped and called here at the house, while she was out ... Don't worry, he knew about Joe. What little there was to know, and that little none too soul-stirring. "In your circle," he repeated. "Not in mine."

"Do I congratulate you? Or commiserate with you? I'm all confused."

"You certainly are." (She had asked for that one. Laid herself wide open. But then she invariably did. The whole thing was so stupid, so futile—her flippancies that stung no one but herself, her half-baked little rebellions. Why did she have this compulsion to start them in the first place?) "And if you think this sort of thing is going to make you any less confused—"

"Are you calling me a lush?" Her voice cracked on the word. But she would not give him the satisfaction of staring her down. Which was another mistake, another bit of costly futility. Her own eyes burned, hot as the fiery path in her throat. His were cold and clear and inhumanly accurate. Like a camera, they recorded an image of the subject on which they were focused. All right. Only they didn't stop there; they imposed this recorded image on the subject, on Marcia herself, so that she saw it too. And if looking in the mirror was bad—

That poet, that fellow with his "wad some power the giftie gie us" bit. He must have been out of his mind. Together she and her father inspected her raddled face. It was naked. No stylish make-up tricks to soften the ravages of defeat and discontent. Every line was exposed, every sag and pucker and tremor. (Yes. Her chin was trembling. She not only felt it; she saw it.) The bags under the eyes. The eyes themselves, bloodshot, and desolate. The haggard neck and tense body that could look so chic in the right clothes and that now—the housecoat had shrunk, and something had been spilled down the front—looked merely hungry. She shrank back against the cabinet, her hands clutching the edge of it, her eyes still locked in his. His cold contempt was hers, his exasperation and anger: How could you have let this happen to you? You were always the spirited one, not like Lucy, and now look at what you've turned into, look at what your life is. Miserable little job that you're not even sure of. Miserable little hole-and-corner affair with Joe that doesn't mean anything to either of you. Where's your pride, your self-respect? The high hopes you used to have? How dare you let it all go, and wind up like this, sneaking drinks before breakfast ...

"Stop it!" she cried. "It's not my fault! Leave me alone!"

"With pleasure. I can get my own breakfast if you—"

"I'll cook your damn eggs for you! I'm perfectly capable. Just don't call me *names!*"

For once it did not set him off on one of his tirades. He did not even point out that if anybody had been calling names it was Marcia herself. A shrug. A slight lifting of his eyebrows. Then the door to the sitting room closed behind him.

Of course the tirade would come later. He was sitting in there now, composing it while he ate his grapefruit. Well, let him. She had a few remarks to make to him, too. Who was he to go around despising other people? He wasn't such a model of virtue himself. Far from it. She might not be any prize as a daughter, but she was as good as he deserved. Better. Look at the kind of father he was and always had been. Selfish. Tyrannical. Nobody else would have put up with him all this time. They had been fools to do it, she and Lucy. But so was he a fool, marrying his Pam Sweetie, when anybody with a brain cell working could see what she was after. She would fix him but good, and if it weren't for the house Marcia would say more power to her. He had it coming to him.

So let him compose his tirade. Marcia was ready with one of her own. She would tell him. She would say...

It was seething inside her, all that she would say, when she entered the sitting room carrying the tray. (She had no recollection of cooking the eggs. That was what rage could do for you.) In silence—for she had decided that the first move must be his—she put the food on the table and poured the coffee.

"Thank you," he said, without looking up from the *Times*, which was an essential part of breakfast. He was very neat and firm with newspapers; in his hands they behaved. He folded them lengthwise, flipping from column to column and page to page with a minimum of fuss.

Marcia sat down opposite him. Sipped her coffee. Smoked a cigarette. And waited. The jangling in her head had receded for the moment. She had a grip on herself, now. There would be no more shrieking, no more of the panic that had almost put her over the edge, back there in the kitchen. She was all right, she was going to be perfectly all right. He could start now, any time.

But the silence held. Not utter silence, of course; the clock chimed, genteel and sprightly, the voice of a faded gentlewoman; there were little newspaper rustlings; little clickings of cup against saucer. No words. Outside the tall windows sunlight danced through the ailanthus branches onto the crocuses pushing up, the flagstones and patch of tender green grass. Her doomed garden. Doomed. Some of the sunlight spilled inside, but not enough. In the corners of the room the shadows still hung, dense, impervious to daylight. The indelible shadows of last night, what she and Lucy had said, what they had planned.

"Now remember, Lucy, the first thing is to keep our mouths shut." It was her own voice, disembodied, echoing there in the shadows. "We mustn't let on to him or anybody else that we know one thing about what he's planning to do. Pam. The house. Any of it. We don't know from nothing. Otherwise we're sunk. He'll never in the world believe it's an accident if we let it slip that we know ..."

Oh, but of course it had just been drunken yakking. She hadn't meant it seriously.

As she would prove any minute now, as soon as he started in on her. The lid would be off. She would tell him—among other things—just exactly what kind of a fool he was making of himself over Pam, and never mind that it wouldn't do any good as far as stopping him was concerned. It would do her good. And the plot that they had hatched would be blown sky high. Once and for all. (Not that there was the slightest possibility of their carrying it out, anyway. Talk. Just talk.)

Only he had to start first. That was the rule. So what was he waiting for? Why didn't he start?

"Let's be realistic about this, Lucy." What a feat, enunciation-wise!

What a triumph of tongue over alcohol! "Let's not kid ourselves. Even if we get all the breaks, it's not going to be easy. He's awfully sharp, you know. There's not much that gets past him." Lucy, she had thought at the time, was the weak spot. Had she ever in her life stood up to him? Never. Not once. Could she do it, even if her life—and Marcia's—depended on it? She was such a scaredy-cat. So ready to buckle under pressure. So hopelessly under his thumb.

And yet Lucy was the one, it was Lucy who had said ...

Marcia's mind shied like a terror-stricken horse. She sat bolt upright, staring at him, willing him to loose the tirade that would dispel the eerie echo of Lucy's voice and set her free. It must be an act; he couldn't possibly be unaware of her eyes fastened on him.

He remained haughtily silent. Another deft flick of the *Times*. Without looking up, he groped for his coffee cup.

Lucy was the one. With blood-curdling calm she had produced that other permutation, the one that had eluded Marcia's memory until now. "You know what would make more sense, Marsh? If we were to get rid of him instead of Pam. Really. It would be ever so much simpler ..." To Lucy it was no permutation; it was what she had been talking about all along. From the moment she smashed the coffee mug and burst out laughing, he and he alone had been Lucy's target. It was only Marcia who had needed the gradual, indirect approach. Well, and what of it? Since he had become Marcia's target, too, what of it?

There he sat, ignoring his own mortal danger. And hers, and hers.

"Why don't you *say* something?" she screamed. She slammed her fists down on the table. The dishes shuddered; the silverware jumped. He lowered his paper, elaborately patient, and she hated him for that too, along with all the rest—his silence, his arrogance, his refusal to save himself or her. "*Say* something! Don't just—"

Sobs choked her; the final indignity. She headed blindly for the door, found it somehow, and rushed out into the hall. She could not stop the sobs. They forced their way out in thin, ignominious bleats. They shook her like a rag in the wind. Halfway up the stairs she heard him behind her. "Marcia! Now wait a minute! Stop!"

Stop? Wait so he could see her reduced to this abject whimpering animal? She hurried even faster, stumbled, almost fell; and he had her, his hand closed on her shoulder, pinning her against the stair rail. She mustered all her strength to face him with a show of defiance.

"Marcia," he said. Quite softly. She saw his face through a blur of tears. But they were the last of her tears. She was through weeping.

Censure she could endure from him. Bullying. Anger. Even contempt.

But not pity. Not pity.

For this she would never forgive him.

III

"Afternoon, Mrs. Travers. Nice day, isn't it? Now, Cherie. Behave yourself."

"Lovely, simply lovely. How charming you look, dear. Chrys. Mum. Say hello to Cherie, like good boys."

The Pekinese—Chrysanthemum I and Chrysanthemum II—stopped waddling and gave the poodle an affronted stare. All that bouncing around! Insufferable. Cherie, who was used to their snubs, made a series of dancing lunges at them and threw in a Woof. Just for fun.

Their owners watched fondly and then turned their attention to each other. Mrs. Travers was large and stately; she went in for turbans and voluminous, tent-like garments. Little "Mrs." Sully (the quotation marks were Mrs. Travers'; she had an instinct for such things) wore plaid slacks and a kerchief tied under her chin. Like Cherie, she had an exuberant air.

The Sullys referred to Mrs. Travers privately as La Traviata.

"Where's Mr. Sully? Don't tell me he has to work, a lovely afternoon like this." Mr. Sully claimed to be a commercial artist. Free lance. He certainly worked at peculiar hours.

"He's still asleep, the lug." Mrs. Sully yawned. Also, to oblige La Traviata, she let her jacket blow open. See? Flat as a board. Not pregnant yet, praise be. "God knows what time we got in last night."

Mrs. Travers could have told her, to the minute. They were an uninhibited pair, and they had the fourth-floor apartment, right above hers. Not that she was complaining, mind you. Live and let live, that was her philosophy. "Merry nights make dull days," she said archly. "By the way, did you happen to hear the ruckus downstairs this morning?"

"No. Who? Marcia and the doctor have another fight?"

"It didn't sound like a fight exactly. But there was something peculiar going on. The way I happened to get in on it, I was taking Chrys and Mum out for their morning walk. Well. And I was also going to attempt to impress upon Marcia—if possible, which I'm beginning to doubt—that something has to be done about my kitchen sink. I mean, really! I don't think I've been unreasonable. You know how Lucy is. I make allowances. She tries, I suppose. And I must say, I don't envy her, having to cope with that handy man, that Hansen. Of all the surly—

Anyway, I thought I'd make one final appeal to Marcia. Well, I can assure you, I changed my mind on that score. In a hurry. I could hear her, all the way up on my floor. Screaming at him. The peculiar part was that he didn't seem to be saying anything. For once. The next thing I knew, here she came pelting up the stairs, the bottom flight, with the doctor after her, and believe it or don't, Mrs. Sully, but she was crying her head off."

"Marcia? Crying? You're kidding."

"Crying," repeated Mrs. Travers firmly, "as if her heart would break. I was flabbergasted. And poor Chrys and Mum, it upset them so, Chrys made a puddle right there in the hall ... Yes, we were a bad boy, weren't we, Chrys? Only it wasn't our fault ... As I say, the doctor after her. He grabbed hold of her. Whether or not he actually struck her I'm not prepared to say, though the temper that man has, I wouldn't put it past him."

Mrs. Sully didn't believe a word of it. Well, maybe every other word. But La Traviata wasn't a bad old girl; why spoil her fun? She produced an appropriate gasp.

"And still not a peep out of him, as far as I could tell. After a minute he went back downstairs, and she came on up. I met her in the hall, so I got a good look at her, but I'll bet you anything you like she didn't even see me, didn't even know I was there. Not that she was crying anymore. She'd stopped, just like that. But she had this funny look in her eye, Mrs. Sully. I can't describe it. It made my flesh creep. It literally made my flesh creep."

Mrs. Sully shivered companionably. She had always been suggestible.

"She reeked of liquor," Mrs. Travers finished. "Can you imagine? At that hour of the day!"

It struck Mrs. Sully as a letdown. After all those goose bumps. She said mildly, "Well, I expect Marcia does drink more than she ought to at times. Not that she's an alcoholic." For some reason she felt called upon to stress the point. "Of course she's not an alcoholic. I like Marcia, you know. She's got a lot of snap to her."

"So do I like Marcia. That's the reason I got so upset over it. To see her like that, that look in her eye. It wasn't just the liquor. You mark my words, Mrs. Sully, there's something very peculiar going on in that family. I can sense it, it's a gift I have, kind of a psychic gift. I've had it all my life. And I have very seldom been wrong." She gestured histrionically, and her voice sank to a whisper. "I have this bad feeling, something that's going to happen, violence, something terrible ..."

It was really rather impressive. What with the turban and all. Mrs. Sully couldn't quite suppress another shiver. For a block after they had parted—La Traviata to make one more turn around the park with Chrys and Mum waddling behind, she and Cherie to prance home—it seemed to her that the air was not so balmy, the sunshine not so bright.

But then she met Dr. Knapp, coming out the door as she went in, and looking like anything but a figure of dark, violent melodrama. He was jingling his car keys and whistling. Well set-up, well turned-out, and obviously in an affable mood. Sometimes he gave Mrs. Sully no more than a distant nod. But today it was a real smile, a tip of his hat, quite a gallant flourish as he held the door open for her. She couldn't help feeling flattered. He was that kind of man.

And inside, the door to the Knapps' sitting room was open, and she caught a glimpse of Marcia, in dungarees and sweater—as always on week ends—with a trowel in her hand. All set for a go at her garden. "Hi!" she called, in her clear, crisp voice. She sounded neither drunken nor distraught. Not in the least.

La Traviata and her forebodings. What nonsense!

Her spirits restored to their normal state of effervescence, Mrs. Sully let Cherie off the leash and raced her to the fourth floor.

"No," said Marcia with decision. "It won't work."

"I don't see why not," said Lucy.

It was evening, and they were settled cozily in her bedroom—Lucy on the chaise lounge with a cup of tea, Marcia cross-legged on the floor, with a highball beside her. (Though how she possibly *could*, after last night ... But there it was. A highball.) They had a little fire going in the fireplace; it made a pleasant flicker in the room, which held all the accumulated belongings of Lucy's lifetime: her brushes and paints, her favorite books and pictures, the dainty cream-colored furniture that had been her fourteenth birthday present. Just like old times, she thought, when Marcia used to come in for a bedtime chat. Only they weren't exchanging girlish confidences tonight.

"Why not?" she insisted. "You hear about things like that all the time. Hold-ups. Burglaries. I don't see why it won't—"

"Because it simply won't. To begin with, it's too complicated. Too many chances for us to slip up on something, some little thing that will tip the police off to the truth, that it's an inside job. Don't forget, this wouldn't be just another run-of-the-mill burglary, the kind they get a dozen times a day. They'd do some real digging on this one. They'd put us through the wringer, and not just once, either. Anything the least bit fishy, and we'd be the prize suspects."

"But if we keep our mouths shut, don't let them know we have a motive—"

"Oh Lucy, use your head! Good *night!* Once they catch on it's an inside job, who else is there for them to suspect? Mrs. Travers? The Sullys? I ask you! Even if we manage to keep our mouths shut, other people won't. Travers, for instance. I suppose she's heard some of the rows. Not you, you never fought with him. But me. I never bothered to keep my voice down." She grinned ironically. "Too bad I didn't have the foresight. Oh, Travers would have herself a ball. Then there's Miss Simmons. All the years she worked for him, don't tell me she doesn't know it wasn't always sweetness and light."

"But Simmy likes you!"

"She likes him better," said Marcia. "No. It's just too risky. Not to mention—Well, I couldn't bash his head in. Much as I hate him. Could you?"

Lucy looked off into space. Would it be like smashing the coffee mug? That marvelous moment of release?

"Of course you couldn't," Marcia told her. "It's out of the question."

"If we had a gun," Lucy offered feebly.

"We haven't. Neither has he. And even if we had, we wouldn't know how to use it. Certainly not in a way that would make it look accidental. That's what it's got to look like. A plain case of accident, so the police won't do too much digging."

"What about Pam? She's apt to stir up a fuss. On account of losing out on the house."

"She'll probably try. But I don't see how she can get very far. In the first place, there'll be only her word for it that he had any intention of marrying her. It'll be all news to us. Pretty incredible news, at that. What? A level-headed man like Daddy, planning to marry a little birdbrain like Pam? Preposterous! Which God knows it is. The important thing with Pam is not to let her get wise ahead of time. Just go along as usual, not paying any special attention to her, one way or the other."

They would have to go along as usual with Daddy, too. Not letting him get wise. Pretending that nothing was changed. And it might be that for Marcia nothing much was changed. She had always kicked against the traces. Now she was kicking harder. That was all. She doesn't know, thought Lucy, she doesn't know what it's like to have *everything* change—not just the degree, but the essence, the very essence...

"Why are you looking at me like that?" Suddenly Marcia jumped up. "Do you think I don't know how impossible it is, for us to be saying these things, planning these plans? Only we're doing it! It's happening! Don't look at me like that!"

"All right," said Lucy calmly. "I know we're doing it. I'm just trying to think. Something accidental. An accident ..."

It rained on Monday, a monotonous, glum drizzle. Lucy woke up tired. Which was not extraordinary. Sunday nights she was inclined to work in her sleep, anticipating the crises that might lie ahead, meeting them over and over again, wearing herself out in advance. The extraordinary thing was that this particular night had been so much like the others: a harassed and ineffectual grappling with domestic emergencies. How was it possible that Mrs. Travers' kitchen sink would have crowded from her mind the question of Daddy, some kind of an accident ...

Mrs. Travers, majestic in a plastic raincoat, trapped her on the stairs. Chrys and Mum were also in plastic raincoats, and all three fixed upon Lucy a stare of outraged reproach. They did not think they were being unreasonable, Miss Knapp. But there was a limit to their patience. They had a right to expect, Miss Knapp. A certain amount of delay was perhaps understandable. However. Furthermore, Miss Knapp, the Board of Health. They would have no choice in the matter.

Lucy cringed and stammered. "I don't understand it, Mrs. Travers. Hansen promised me faithfully. I'll remind him again. Right away. At once." (Her heart sank at the prospect.) "I'll see that it's taken care of, first thing."

You'd better. Mrs. Travers disdained to say it in words. Her expression spoke for her. A sniff. A wheeze from Chrys and Mum. An indignant, plastic rustle from all three as they swept on down the stairs.

It was just possible that Daddy had not heard. But one look at his face as he settled himself at the breakfast table, and Lucy knew that he had. "My God, can't we have *any* peace around here? What was all that yammering on the stairs? Enough to drive a man out of his mind!"

"Nothing, Daddy, really. It's just that Mrs. Travers kitchen sink—"

"I'm not interested in that woman's kitchen sink. Please. Spare me. Don't tell me about it. I've told you a thousand times, I don't want to be bothered with these matters. God knows I don't expect much of you, but it does seem to me you could handle a few simple, routine housekeeping details without getting the whole place in an uproar. Tell me, is that asking too much?"

She tried, abjectly, to shift her eyes, but his accusing glare paralyzed her. "Is it?" he repeated.

"Of course not, Daddy."

"Then why don't you do it?"

She was trembling like a rabbit when she escaped to the kitchen.

Where Marcia stood, coffee cup in one hand, cigarette in the other; weekday mornings she took breakfast on the fly. She was ready to leave for the office. Very smart-looking in her black suit and severe little hat. Silver hoop earrings. Just enough make-up: discreet touch of mascara, dramatic red mouth. Lucy felt the familiar surge of envy.

"What a lovely humor we're in this morning," Marcia said, with a dip of her head toward the sitting room. "Though I must say, when I heard Travers holding forth—Couldn't you shut her up? You know how he is."

On the verge of tears, Lucy burst out, "No, I couldn't shut her up! I can't do anything right around here! Twice now I've asked Hansen to fix her kitchen sink, and—"

"You don't ask Hansen. You tell him." Marcia's bracelets jangled irritably. "Oh, well. If you're going to get in a *state* about it. I'll pop across and get him on my way to work. How's that?" And she smiled, suddenly, lovingly; it was as if she had hugged Lucy.

But not Daddy. Far from it. Back in the sitting room Lucy met the same accusing scowl. He was not through with her yet. "I don't know why the temperature can't be regulated properly in this house. My room was like an icebox again this morning. I was given to understand, when I had the new furnace installed, that it was a simple matter of setting the thermostat. Possibly I misunderstood. Possibly, for some obscure reason, I was misinformed. But that was my impression. What was yours?"

How many times had she heard it before? How many, many times had she watched Mama cower, as Lucy herself was cowering now, under just such a punishing verbal barrage? It was a peculiarity of the old house that Daddy's room (of course his) should be difficult to heat, and that his fireplace should be the one that smoked. Incorrigibly. Persistently. Not that he could be bothered using it, anyway. The new furnace made no difference. Turn the thermostat up, and everybody else in the house broiled—quite apart from Daddy's roars of outrage when the fuel bills came in.

"A fine state of affairs when a man can't be comfortable in his own house." This was the wind-up; she recognized it with relief. Only today he gave it a new twist. "My God, I was better off with that old gas heater I used to have!" He slammed out of the sitting room and into his office.

Lucy sat on at the breakfast table, for once unmindful of dishes to be washed, marketing and cleaning to be done. The coffee in her cup stopped steaming, turned lukewarm and finally cold. The front door opened and shut several times. To let Pam in: "Good morning, Dr.

Knapp. Though what's good about it. Such weather!" Oh, so proper. To let Daddy out. Equally proper: "You can reach me at the hospital, Miss Caldwell. I'll be there till noon." To let Hansen in. Heavy and deliberate, his footsteps ascended the stairs to Mrs. Travers' kitchen sink. (Trust Marcia. Mission accomplished.) And still Lucy sat, aware of all these goings-on, but in an abstracted way.

She was busy thinking. About the old gas heater Daddy used to have.

Used to have? But it was almost certainly still down in the basement. It had been consigned there years ago on account of Mama, who in the last month or so of her life developed a terror of it. Nothing, not even Daddy, could persuade her that it was not an instrument of death. His death. On that one historic occasion he had given in and discarded the gas heater.

Supposing Lucy were to resurrect it now and have it reinstalled in his bedroom. He would not object. On the contrary. It might even be like his good old gauntlets that Lucy gave him. His good old gas heater that Lucy resurrected for him. And supposing, after a week or so, something were to go wrong, an accident, or a defect ... He used to light it in the evenings, before he went to sleep, and leave it on all night. That was what worried Mama. It might go out, she said, the flame might go out, while the gas stayed on and asphyxiated him in his bed. Impossible, Daddy used to argue, the heater was designed in such a way that the flame couldn't possibly go out unless you turned off the gas.

Unless you turned off the gas.

And if, after that, you turned it on again—neglecting, however, to light it—well, then Mama's dire prediction would very likely come true.

So simple. Yet not so simple, after all. Daddy's bedroom was off by itself, across the hall from hers and Marcia's, and they all three locked their hall doors on account of the tenants. If would be an act of sheer lunacy, to attempt getting past Daddy's locked door, inside and out again, all without waking him. No. The turning off and on of the gas must be managed from outside. From the basement.

All those pipes, Lucy thought with despair, and for a moment the sense of her own incompetence threatened to engulf her. Maybe if she waited to consult with Marcia ... It was the memory of Marcia's smile, oddly enough, that steeled her. Such a loving, warm smile. But—yes—tainted with condescension. The kind of smile one might give a child. As stinging, in its way, as Daddy's bullying. If only, just once, she could show Know-it-all Marcia, prove that she too was capable of effectual action!

She marched out of the sitting room, through the kitchen, and down the basement stairs, bracing herself against the dim dankness of the place. It did not take her long to find the heater; bundled into a gunny sack, it had been stowed away in the catch-all space under the stairs. Patiently waiting through all the years for this moment when someone, Lucy, would come and unwrap it. There it stood, bow-legged and top-heavy, like a quaint old servant called back into active duty. It had an air of great innocence; Lucy felt like patting it.

Now for the pipes. She faced them bravely, forbidding though they were, a monstrous gray jumble above her head, jutting out into inexplicable elbows, studded here and there with valves. How to find the right valve on the right pipe ... "Nowhere near as complicated as it looks." It was the voice of the repair man who had come last time, echoing cheerfully in her memory. Such a nice man, not like most of them. "Them pipes over there, they're for the two top floors. Separate meters, see. Yours is here." And he had whacked one set familiarly, before he got busy on the valve with his wrench. "Turn it this way, see, and it's off. This way and it's on. Nothing to it."

Lucy screwed her eyes shut, in a climax of concentration. She could see him, his blunt hand with the black-rimmed fingernails, the wrench, the valve, the pipe, the yellow light from the electric bulb gleaming just beyond his left shoulder.

Yes. She had it. She knew which valve on which pipe. Her heart swelled with triumph. She could even try it out—why not?—now, while she had the place to herself, so that tonight she could present the whole, workable, simple plan to Marcia.

She pawed through Hansen's box of tools for a wrench; by standing on the stool she could reach the valve comfortably. Though it seemed to resist her more than it had the repair man. She clambered down and found the hammer, up again and pounded firmly on the handle of the wrench.

"What in the hell do you think you're doing?"

Hansen. The hammer jumped out of her hand and clattered to the floor. Hansen. There he was at the foot of the stairs, staring at her out of his little, deep-set, bear's eyes. He was not tall, but muscular and broad. He wore a plaid windbreaker and a disreputable, painter's cap with the visor bent back. His face, round as a jack-o-lantern, was greedy with curiosity.

"Oh. Hansen. I didn't hear you. You scared me." Her own laugh appalled her, so false and nervous. "I was just—"

He stared. And waited.

"I was just—" Inspiration came to her. Or what seemed at first glance to be inspiration. "The water. It made the funniest noise in the pipes this morning, when I turned it on in the kitchen. I thought maybe if I tightened the valve—"

"That's the gas pipe you were beating on," said Hansen.

"No. Really? How stupid of me!" She got down off the stool and picked up the hammer. Her hands were slick with sweat. "I should have asked you, I guess, only I didn't like to bother you. I'm so stupid about these things."

He did not deny it. She watched, with relief, while the curiosity in his face gave way to sneering scorn. He would believe anything of her, anything whatever in the line of idiocy. Fine. Great. She was safe ...

Safe? She was lost. For his eyes, shifting from her, came to rest on the gas heater. He stiffened, peering at it. "Who hauled that old thing out? You're not planning to use it, are you, Miss Lucy?" (Marcia was "Miss Knapp to him. She was "Miss Lucy." And he begrudged her the "Miss.")

"Oh, of course not." Out came another of those awful laughs. "Daddy mentioned it this morning—he was complaining again about his room being cold—and I thought I'd just see if it was still down here. I wouldn't dream of using it."

She wouldn't dare. Not after her blundering inspiration of a moment ago. Which Hansen would remember, and with which, if she ever gave him the chance, he could destroy her. She knew exactly how he would make it sound to the police: "... claimed she was trying to fix the water pipe, but it was the gas pipe she was working on, and she'd already hauled out that old gas heater. Claimed she wasn't figuring on using it, just wanted to see if it was still there. It struck me kind of funny at the time ..."

Even now, it seemed to her, suspicion was crawling back into his face. The gas heater no longer looked innocent, but sinister, like a great poisonous toad squatting on the cement. She could not take her eyes off it. Worse still, she could not say what she ought to say, that Hansen was to get rid of it, she had dug it out for that purpose alone. For her plan was wrecked now. Nothing could be salvaged from it.

"Want me to throw it out for you, Miss Lucy?" He was smiling, slyly, almost as if they were conspirators.

"Yes. Please. I was just going to ask you to." Marcia's words came back to her. You don't ask Hansen. You tell him. "There's no sense in keeping it around if we're never going to use it, and of course we never will. I wouldn't dream of it. An old contraption like that. Why, it wouldn't be safe!"

"Okay, Miss Lucy." He picked it up and turned toward the stairs.

She thought she heard him chuckle.

On her way home from the super-market, Mrs. Sully bumped into Hansen. Almost literally; she had her hands full, what with Cherie, the shopping bag, and the umbrella, which kept obstructing her view. "Oops!" She righted the umbrella and smiled. Why not? Sometimes Hansen smiled back, sometimes he didn't. Like Dr. Knapp, he was entitled to his moods. Now that she had a good look at him, she added, "What in the world is that thing?"

He smirked. He wasn't really a very pleasant man; even Mrs. Sully had to admit it. "You want it? Miss Lucy said to throw it out."

"What—Oh. Some kind of a heater, I guess. Isn't it?" She wished she hadn't asked, somehow. His expression made her feel uncomfortable, as if the clumsy object he was lugging had some hidden, possibly obscene significance. "Of course I don't want it. Why should I?"

"Search me. Miss Lucy don't want it, either. She said. Throw it out, she told me. Wouldn't be safe to use it."

The smirk changed to a snicker. Mrs. Sully moved toward the door and clicked her umbrella shut with an air of finality. But she couldn't resist stealing one more glance. That was all it was, an antiquated gas heater. "Come on, Cherie. Hurry up. Before we get any wetter."

There was Lucy in the hall, just ready to start up the stairs. Had she been listening? The fantastic notion popped into Mrs. Sully's head for no reason whatever. Lucy looked pale and flustered. But then she usually did, poor creature; life was for her an endless procession of troubles. It showed in her face, of course: the lines of worry that creased her forehead, the fretful droop of her mouth. Yet she was still rather pretty, in a soft, washed-out blonde way.

"That Hansen," she said, with a self-conscious laugh. "I don't know why he has to keep you standing out in the rain listening to his complaints. Really, the man's impossible!"

"He wasn't complaining. He was just telling me about that heater he had, or whatever it was—"

"That's what I mean. Who cares about an old gas heater, for pity's sake? Why does he have to make a big deal out of it, just because I asked him to throw it away?"

Look who's making a big deal out of it, thought Mrs. Sully. She edged past Lucy, aware again of the uncomfortable feeling she had had with Hansen. "Oh, well," she said. "Nothing to get upset about."

"I can't help getting upset! If you only knew what I have to put up with—" Tears, always close to the surface with her, welled up in Lucy's eyes. She brushed at them, and left a streak of dust on her cheek. "I try," she wailed. "I try so hard, and it's no use, I just can't—I never do anything right around here!" She put her head down on the newel post.

"Oh, now, look." What Mrs. Sully really wanted to do, shame on her, was beat it up the stairs. Lucy occasionally had that effect on her, a tug of war between pity and aversion. So did sick people. She shifted her shopping bag and patted Lucy's shoulder; it felt hot and tense.

At that moment the door to Dr. Knapp's office opened and out came his nurse. A dish, if Mrs. Sully ever saw one. "Has the mail come yet? I—Miss Knapp! Is something the matter?"

Lucy's head jerked up, and she gave Miss Caldwell such a look— A glare. That was the only word for it. A dangerous fanatic glare that transformed her face, clenching its soft sagging outlines into an unfamiliar, rigid mask. Mrs. Sully was too astonished to move. Her hand fell away from Lucy's shoulder of its own weight. With an inarticulate sound, a kind of snarling sob, Lucy tore past her and up the stairs.

"Well!" Miss Caldwell's white nylon uniform swished. Her mascara blinked. "What was all that about? Do you know? Because I certainly don't. Did I do something?"

"It wasn't you," Mrs. Sully said, without conviction. "I don't know what happened to upset her. Something about Hansen. I think."

"Crazy, if you ask me." Miss Caldwell hesitated; then, with a shrug, she headed for the mail box in the foyer.

Slowly Mrs. Sully started up the stairs. It did not comfort her to notice that Cherie was unusually subdued. Dogs were supposed to be psychic about such things, weren't they? Like La Traviata and her premonition of something very peculiar going on, something terrible about to happen. Easy enough to pooh-pooh it yesterday, with the sun shining and Dr. Knapp smiling at her and Marcia's clear voice calling out to her.

But she had not seen Lucy yesterday. And that was what made it so chilling, that Lucy, poor ineffectual Lucy, should be the one to fit into La Traviata's lurid little scene as if it were her native habitat.

On the second floor, going past the closed door to Lucy's room, Cherie let out an anxious whimper.

"Shut up," said Mrs. Sully sharply. "What's the matter with you, anyway?"

IV

It didn't look like such a situation at first. Marcia, coming in at five-thirty that Monday evening saw through the open office door His Nibs shaking hands with somebody, presumably a newly arrived patient, a woman whose back was turned to her. And there was Pam Sweetie at her little desk, batting her eyelashes as usual.

He caught sight of Marcia and called her. "Come in a minute. Here's someone you'll be glad to see."

She doubted it. But what are you going to do? Then the woman turned around, and she began to get the picture. At least she recognized the odd note in her father's voice for what it was, relief.

Because it was Miss Simmons, of all people. Simmy. Who (to hear her tell it) had just happened to be in the neighborhood and couldn't resist dropping in to say hello, just for old times sake, and anyway, there was this private case in the offing, she'd been wanting to discuss it with Doctor, if he had a few minutes to spare ...

"Of course," he said, only a shade too heartily. "A pleasure. I'll be through here in half an hour or so, if you don't mind waiting."

She didn't mind. Not in the least.

Marcia knew her cue when she saw it. "Come on back and have a drink with me and Lucy. We were talking about you the other day, wondering what you've been up to."

She was rewarded with a grateful smile from him. Pam smiled too, as they went past her desk on the way out. One of those sweet, knowing smiles that were her specialty.

Lucy had a little fire going in the sitting room. She was looking more woebegone than usual, Marcia noticed. The weather, probably; she was apt to go into a decline on dismal days. And this one was dismal, all right. It was still drizzling steadily. But trust Lucy to mind her manners. She perked up for Simmy's benefit. There was the pleased-surprise business, and everybody said how great everybody else was looking.

It wasn't really true of Simmy. Oh, she had done her best. Anyone could see that. But somehow the "soft" hairdo and skillfully draped neckline of her dress only intensified the sharpness of her face. When you got right down to it, Simmy didn't have a great deal to work with, except for her flashing dark eyes. Today they seemed a bit on the feverish side. And Marcia didn't remember her as having so many nervous mannerisms. When she wasn't talking herself—chattering, really—she was working overtime at responding. All those exaggerated nods, smiles and frowns. All those gestures with the hands, which were tense and bone-thin. Odd-looking hands.

Well, of course Simmy wasn't any kid, and she'd had some tough breaks. Like everybody else that got mixed up with His Nibs. Everybody except Pam.

"I see she's still here," Simmy was saying, with a twitch of her head toward the office. "I suppose that means she's working out all right."

Marcia's eyes darted to Lucy, in swift warning. Careful. Remember, Simmy mustn't suspect. "Miss Caldwell?" she said. "Why, I guess so. To tell you the truth, I haven't paid too much attention. Lucy sees more of her than I do."

And Lucy did it up brown. "Oh, I'm sure she's okay. You know what a fuss Daddy would be making if she weren't. Naturally he can't depend on her the way he did on you. She hasn't your experience."

"Young," murmured Simmy bleakly. For a moment the jittering stopped. Her hands lay, hungry and empty, in her lap. "Who needs my experience?"

"Oh now, Simmy," Marcia began.

"He fired me, you know. Or maybe you didn't know." Simmy cocked her head, all animation again, her eyes recklessly bright. "Maybe you swallowed the bit about how I was resigning to go into private cases. That was just to save my face. Big of him, wasn't it? Oh yes, he fired me. You want to know why? Because he'd fallen in love with her, that's why."

Marcia was too overcome with embarrassed pity to speak. It was Lucy who produced the appropriate gasp: "What? I don't believe it! Daddy wouldn't—"

"Oh, wouldn't he! You've got a lot to learn about Daddy." She turned her bitter smile on Marcia. "More than Marcia has, I bet. Don't tell me you didn't know what the score was, as far as I was concerned."

That was when Marcia saw exactly how much of a situation it was. Simmy was here to make a scene, and nothing was going to stop her. The question for Marcia was, how much honesty could she afford? Not too much, she decided. But some. "If you mean I knew you were having an affair with him," she said, "I suppose I did. After all, you'd worked for him a long time, and ... Not that I figured it was any of my business. But frankly, Simmy, I think you must be way off the beam about Caldwell. I'm not blaming you, you understand. It was rough on you, for him to fire you like that. But why jump to the conclusion that things went sour for you and him on account of Caldwell? Or anybody else for that matter? It could just be—"

"I don't believe it for a minute!" cried Lucy. No doubt about it, she was displaying unsuspected talent for this sort of thing. "None of it. Simmy or Caldwell, either one. Daddy isn't like that! I don't know about you, Marsh, but I'm not going to listen to any more such talk. It's not— It's not decent!" She got up and ran out of the room.

Marcia's first impulse was to follow her. But at the door she paused.

"Don't let me keep you," Simmy said in a strangled voice. Her face had turned white. "I always thought you knew the facts of life. More than Lucy, anyway. But if you think I've been talking out of turn, too, why go ahead. I'll go back to the office and wait there. He's the one I want to see, anyway."

"Don't be ridiculous, Simmy. It was a jolt to Lucy, that's all. You know how she is about Daddy. He can do no wrong. She has always gotten along with him better than I have."

"Oh, well. Those scraps you used to have with him. I never took them seriously. You're too much like him to ..." Simmy's voice quavered up, high and thin. Suddenly she put her head in her hands. "What am I going to do, Marcia? I love him so, I love him so. I know I shouldn't be talking to you like this, but I can't help it, you don't know what it's been like for me, these last couple of months, not seeing him, not even talking to him. I can't stand it anymore!"

She rocked back and forth in Marcia's arms. No pride left. Given over to suffering so acute that Marcia seemed to feel it in her own breast. For all the good that did Simmy. But she had nothing else to offer—no comfort, no hope, not even the candid anger that she would ordinarily have put into words. She could not say them, of course: Look, you shouldn't waste time or tears on a first-class heel like him. He's not worth it, he's treated you shamefully, and you're quite right, he's not only in love with Pam but planning to marry her ...

She stared past Simmy's head, into the cheerful fire. She would have to get used to thinking of honesty as a luxury. Naturally, it would take a little time.

Meanwhile, Simmy was still pulling out the stops. "I can't quit thinking about him. Worrying. I wake up in the night, worrying about all the things that could go wrong without me here to run the office for him. Silly of me, isn't it? As if I were indispensable or something. Not just the office. He might get sick and I wouldn't know. He might—"

"That's pretty silly," Marcia said. "He's a horse. Hasn't been sick in years."

"But he might have an accident with the car. You know how fast he drives. Or he might get run over. That can happen to anybody. Or a plane crash. Besides, he was sick that once, remember. When he had the flu and they gave him penicillin. It could have killed him. Don't you realize that?"

"I'd forgotten," said Marcia. She became aware of an odd sensation, a kind of mental prickle. Sure enough, the penicillin episode had been a crisis. Back a few years, when they were giving it to everybody for everything. Turned out he was violently allergic. Yes. It could have killed him. "That won't happen again, now that he knows he's allergic. Be sensible, Simmy." You, too, Marcia. Don't go chasing bubbles.

"Sensible!" Simmy blew her nose fiercely. "How can I be sensible? It's no use, you don't even know what I'm talking about, you've never been in love."

Miserable and proud of it, thought Marcia. "Maybe not," she said, and sighed. "But I still think you're wrong about him and Caldwell. Unless, of course, he came right out and told you."

"He doesn't have to tell me! Do you think I can't see for myself? I knew the minute I laid eyes on her, sitting in there at my desk. Licking the cream off her whiskers. It was written all over her. Him too. Written all over both of them—"

"Well, Simmy," he said, from the doorway behind them, and they whipped around to face him. His expression struck Marcia as tentative, as if—though it was perfectly obvious that he had been there long enough to get the message—he would be ready and willing to pretend otherwise. He avoided her eye. Such fatherly delicacy, she thought. Touching.

But Simmy had put aside delicacy some time ago. Not to mention the fact that, in turning, she caught sight of herself in the oval mirror; her hand flew to her straggling hair, her tear-ravaged face. So there could be no pretending for her.

"Yes. 'Well, Simmy,'" she hissed at him. "It's true. Don't bother to deny it. I knew there was someone else, of course, when you picked that fight with me so you could fire me. I'm not all that naive. It's her. That floozey in there. She's the one. Naturally you had to get rid of me when she came along."

"Now, Simmy, let's try to calm down." He spoke gently enough. But his eyes measuring her were cold as a hawk's. "How can I do anything for you when you're all worked up like this, and not making sense? This business about Miss Caldwell and me—you're imagining something that simply isn't so, building it up in your own mind until it's clear out of control. You've got to stop it, Simmy. You've got to get hold of yourself before it's too late."

"Too late! That's a laugh. Before it's too late." She put her hands up to her mouth to hold back whatever it was, a sob or a laugh. "So you do deny it. You're calling me a psycho, a paranoiac—"

"I said that? My dear girl, you know I didn't. I said you're overwrought, and you obviously are. I'll be frank with you, I've been aware for some time that you weren't exactly stable. That's why I let you go, for your own good, because I felt you needed a change. But I didn't realize it had gone this far. If I had, believe me, I would have seen to it that you got the kind of help you need."

"But you're not calling me a psycho. Oh no. You wouldn't dream of it." Simmy's eyes glittered. She swallowed convulsively. "Edwin, Edwin!" she cried out. "How can you treat me like this? Can't you see what it's doing to me? I know it never meant to you what it did to me, but I thought—I thought you loved me a little ..."

"Why, I've always been fond of you, Simmy," he said smoothly. He gave her a perfunctory smile. "Still am, in fact." She made a rush toward him, and he caught her thin wrists easily in one of his powerful hands. "Where do you think you're going?"

"In there. To tell her all about you. We've got so much in common, Miss Caldwell and I. Oh, there's plenty I can tell her, and don't think I'm not going to. She'll have plenty to tell me, too. We can compare notes. Because don't worry, I'll get the truth out of her. You've given me all the lies I'm going to take. She'll tell me the truth if I have to choke it out of her. Let go of me!"

He did let go, so suddenly that she shot out into the hall and staggered against the wall. "Go ahead," he said. "You won't find anybody there. Miss Caldwell's gone home." (Of course, thought Marcia. He would have seen to that before he tangled with Simmy. One step ahead of her, all the way.) "Listen to me, Simmy. I have no intentions toward Miss Caldwell, honorable or dishonorable, except to keep her on here as my office nurse. I can assure you that her intentions toward me are equally businesslike. Thank God, if you'll pardon my saying so. Whether or not she's a floozey is a matter of absolutely no interest to me, as long as she does her job efficiently. Do I make myself clear?"

Simmy remained flattened against the wall, her arms outstretched as if in crucifixion, her great dark eyes fastened on him. He had the grace to flush slightly. "Yes, Edwin," she murmured. "Quite clear. I'm sorry I bothered you. It won't happen again." She let her arms drop and began to move, at a listless shuffle, down the hall toward the office.

"Bother be damned. You know I'll do anything in my power to help you—"

"Please. No more lies. Please."

He glanced at Marcia, lifted his hands in rueful resignation, shrugged. Then, with a brisk, "Here. Let me get your coat for you," he started down the hall after Simmy.

"Never mind. I'll get it," she said, so sharply that he paused.

Marcia turned away. Her head throbbed. Please. No more lies. They had not been all his; Marcia had contributed her share. Her shameful little share. And this was only the beginning. It was going to be lies, and more lies, from here on in. A log in the fire shifted, sending up a miniature fountain of sparks. The rain tapped stealthily at the window. I'll get used to it, she thought. I'd better. Meanwhile—

Meanwhile, damn it, there was Simmy's purse beside the chair. She would have to trot into the office with it, and face those eyes again. Unless he was still in the hall; if he was, she could pass the buck to him. It was no more than he deserved.

She reached the hall just in time to hear him sing out, "Simmy! What are you doing?" and see him gallop into the office. She broke into a gallop of her own. Simmy was at his desk, scrabbling feverishly in the drawer where he dumped the drug samples that came every day through the mail. Little boxes and bottles spewed out of her hands as he grabbed her. "Get out of there! What in the *hell* do you think you're doing?" He slapped her across the face, hard enough to leave a dusky red streak.

Marcia cringed. But Simmy hardly seemed to have felt that blow. "I can't even have that?" she said dully. "It's not much to ask, just to go to sleep, go to sleep and never wake up..."

"Oh, stop it. I might have known you'd pull something like this. It's right up your alley. The final touch of phoney melodrama. You didn't get anywhere with your big lost love scene, so now it's the suicide threat. Well, let me tell you, it's not going to get you anywhere either. You can go to sleep and never wake up any time, as far as I'm concerned, but not on pills you steal from me. Put your coat on and come along."

"No." She tried to draw back. "Where are you taking me?"

"I ought to take you to Bellevue. It's where you belong. But I won't. I'll drive you up to your brother's. Let him deal with you. Personally, I've had it. Get my coat for me, will you, Marcia? And here, you can straighten up the mess she's made of my desk while I'm gone. I won't be long."

"Here's your purse, Simmy," Marcia said. She was careful to avoid Simmy's eyes. It was bad enough to watch the thin, old-woman hands with their bravely painted nails closing automatically on the purse strap.

When they were gone she set about the chore of putting the desk drawer to rights. You name it, we have it, she thought as she bent to retrieve the packages that had wound up on the floor. Something for everybody. Certainly plenty for Simmy's long sleep. If she had only been quicker about it, what she took would never have been missed. Tranquilizers. Laxatives. Energy boosters. Vitamin supplements— His Nibs was partial to those; he carried a supply in his pocket and tossed off a couple after meals. Ointments for hemorrhoids, acne. Powders for the relief of menstrual pain. A couple of the little boxes had come open; Marcia swept up a handful of assorted capsules and tossed them in the waste basket. Pills for travel-sickness. Cough lozenges. Penicillin ...

The word jumped up at her. She stood still, feeling again the old mental prickle, hearing again Simmy's anxious voice: "It could have killed him. Don't you realize that?" Penicillin. Yes. It could have killed him. Could have. Could.

Footsteps in the hall. There was Lucy, peering in at the door. Three guesses where she had spent the last half hour or so. Down in the basement, listening.

"They're gone, aren't they?" she whispered. "Was it all right, what I did? I mean, the way I ran out when she—"

"Fine. Great. You were terrific."

"You too, Marsh. Marsh. You look so funny."

Well. She felt funny. She ran her fingers through the crisp waves of her hair. "Listen, Lucy," she said. "I know how we can do it."

U

They settled on the following Friday for the time. As Marcia said, the sooner the quicker, and what was that quotation about 'twere well it were done quickly ... She was always coming out with things like that, it seemed to Lucy, instead of concentrating on the practical details. Coming out with them, and then breaking into nervous laughter. Though in this case she happened to have a point. If they waited till after Daddy signed the house over to Pam, they would be providing themselves with a motive that would take a good deal of talking away.

And give Marcia credit, it was she who contrived to find out that he had not yet taken this drastic step. On the pretext of needing some advice about income tax, she called Mr. O'Conner, who had been their family lawyer for at least twenty years. Dear old Mr. O'Conner, always so helpful! The first thing he said was, "How's your old man? Haven't seen him in months. Though come to think of it—yes, here it is, I've got a note on my calendar, he's coming in the end of next week. Phoned the other day while I was out of the office. Sheriff's caught up with him again, I suppose."

The end of next week. That meant he was allowing a couple of weeks before he and Pam took off on their honeymoon trip to Paris. So far he had not said a word about going anywhere. But that was often his way; to spring his trips on them out of a clear blue sky. Even Lucy had gotten used to it. Oh, by the way (he was no doubt planning to say) I'm off for Paris day after tomorrow. Medical meeting. Be gone a couple of weeks.

Would he add that Miss Caldwell was going along, to take notes? Or would he pretend that he was giving her the time off?

With a jolt, Lucy realized that they would never know. Whatever he was planning to say, he would not be here to say it. After Friday, Daddy would simply not be here. She remembered a secret daydream she used to have when, as a child, she had read such old-fashioned books as *Little Women* and *Five Little Peppers*. Those fatherless story book children had enchanted her. Their cold boiled potatoes, their hand-me-down clothes, their gallant widowed mothers who took in sewing to keep the brood together ... She saw it all happening to her and Mama and Marcia. How pathetic they were, without Daddy! (Who had always died, vaguely and painlessly, some time before.) But also how free! Even in the realm of purest fantasy, Lucy had found it hard to imagine that kind of freedom. No longer to be ruled by Daddy's moods, which might switch from outbursts of temper to withering silence to spells of gaiety, all in one day. No longer to live under the constant, terrible threat of his disapproval.

She could not quite believe it now, when fantasy was turning into reality, and there was only a void where the yearning for his approval used to be. The old habit was still strong. She spent these final days harried by the same worries that had pecked away so much of her life. Don't overcook the roast. Remember to send Daddy's gray suit to the cleaners. Don't let him hear Mrs. Travers complaining about Hansen. Call the painters and tell them they weren't going to get paid until they fixed that corner in the office and fixed it right. Get the electrician in to check the switch in the foyer ...

Friday seemed a good choice, because he almost always had dinner at home on Fridays. When he reached for his bottle of vitamin pills, as usual after meals, it would not be there. Because Lucy would have carried out her assignment, which was to take it out of his jacket pocket at some point during the afternoon. At any point that suited her convenience: during office hours he wore a white coat and left his suit jacket hanging in the hall closet. The little bottle would be discovered, after a plausible amount of flurry, on the mantel piece, where Lucy would now remember having put it after lunch. "You forgot and left it out on the table. I found it when I was clearing away the lunch dishes. Here you are." And she would shake out the two capsules (which had been set aside, in readiness since Monday evening) and hand them to him.

She was the logical one, as Marcia pointed out. He was used to having Lucy wait on him hand and foot; such gestures from Marcia were rare. Besides, she had done her share by working out the plan. Lucy's gas heater fiasco she dismissed with a hoot of laughter. "You don't mean to tell me you were serious! There, I've hurt your feelings. I'm sorry ... Hansen? Don't worry, of course he didn't guess what you were really up to. It would never in the wide world occur to him or anybody else."

So Lucy would hand him the pills. The seizure would be prompt and violent; by the time Dr. Berman arrived—he might not be at home, and if he were would take at least half an hour to get downtown—it would all be over. After that it was simply a matter of telling their story with the proper nuances of shock and grief. Marcia called it the how-could-it-was bit. Until the eventual realization: "Remember the night Simmy was here, and the drug samples got all mixed up? That must have been how it happened—when he was straightening out the drawer he must have made a mistake and put some of the wrong pills in the vitamin bottle ..."

Their old friend Dr. Berman wasn't going to doubt them. He had been telling Daddy for years how lucky he was, to have two such charming, devoted daughters. They had nothing to worry about from him. Or from anyone else. Once Simmy was mentioned, they could explain, with some embarrassment, about her delusion that Daddy was carrying on a romance—imagine!—with his new little nurse. Poor Simmy, even Daddy hadn't realized until the other night how emotionally disturbed she was. Thus, neatly and convincingly, they would be getting in their licks ahead of Pam. Even if she could prove that Daddy had intended to marry her, she would not be able to make anyone believe that they knew about it. Let alone that they had murdered him to prevent it.

All at once it was Friday, the last morning, only so much like other mornings that Lucy had to keep reminding herself. In the sitting room Daddy ate his eggs, drank his coffee, read his *Times*. In the kitchen Marcia, ready to leave for the office, leaned against the sink with her cup and cigarette. Her face was haggard, and her hands shook. It might have been one of her hangover mornings. Except that Lucy knew she hadn't had a drink since Monday.

"This damn wind," Marcia said. "I could scream, it gets on my nerves so."

The day was bright but gusty. Whipped-cream clouds raced across the sky; the windows shuddered in their frames; the wind whooped and racketed.

"It doesn't seem to bother you," Marcia said. "The wind. I don't know, I must be allergic—" She choked off the word and stared at Lucy; there was something imploring in her eyes.

Who was the scaredy-cat now?

"More coffee, Daddy?" Lucy called into the sitting room. Her own hand, lifting the coffee pot, was steady as a rock. "See you tonight, Marsh." And she added, "Don't forget, you're on the wagon."

There he sat, the condemned man eating his last breakfast. He looked spruce and fairly genial. He did not glance up from his paper when Lucy came in. She was not even a source of irritation to him this morning. Just a pair of hands supplying more coffee. Of course he still had two more chances, at lunch and later at dinner, to stage a final tantrum. It would be fitting, she thought. Not that she was going out of her way to stir one up.

Things went along with remarkable smoothness all morning. She should have known it was too good to be true. But she was unprepared for the blow, which fell shortly after noon, when she had just returned from doing the marketing. She heard him come in the front door while she was in the kitchen unloading the groceries. He was back earlier than usual, she thought; did that mean he would want lunch ahead of time? Probably, because after a few minutes in the office he came on down the hall in search of her. He was still wearing his topcoat, and his face was ruddy from the wind.

"There you are," he said. "I forgot to tell you, I won't be here for lunch. Dinner either, for that matter. I'm going to play hookey and drive up to Connecticut for the week end."

"But you can't!" It burst out of Lucy. "I mean, what about—"

"We've cancelled my appointments for today and tomorrow. I'm giving Miss Caldwell the week end off, too. Answering service can handle the calls, and Berman will take over if there are any emergencies."

She felt as if she was going to tip over. She hung on to the sink and closed her eyes. There was a buzzing in her ears: Caldwell's going with him, of course, maybe they're getting married, why not, it figures, but they can't, not after we've got everything all planned ...

He said sharply, "Well. What's wrong with that?"

She clutched at the only straw in sight. "Nothing. Only I feel so queer. Giddy. And I've got this awful headache."

"You haven't been wearing your glasses. That's why. The vanity of women!"

"But what if it isn't my eyes, Daddy? What if it's—"

"Put on your glasses and take a couple of aspirin." He gave her a careless pat on the shoulder before he turned away. "I don't know what time I'll be back Sunday. So don't worry about meals on my account. You deserve the week end off too. Relax and enjoy it."

He set off jauntily. She heard him saying—for her benefit —"Come along, Miss Caldwell. Time to close up shop. I'll drop you off, wherever you want to go."

Don't go. Please, Daddy. Please don't go.

But the protest remained pent up, boiling inside her. And. by the time she reached the front door—at a slow stumble, instead of the run she intended—it was too late. He had already handed Pam Sweetie-Miss Caldwell into the car, and was sliding in behind the wheel. She had an instant's view of their profiles, vivid and curiously permanent, like heads stamped on a coin. His straight, arrogant nose and cold eye, set rather shallowly, so that it looked larger than it was. Her full mouth curved in its sweet half-smile that could not quite hide the sharpness of her chin. The emperor and his mistress.

The car shot forward, and they were gone. The wind, churning up a miniature tornado in the street, plastered a sheet of newspaper around the lamp post. The little tree flattened its leaves and lurched. The glass in the door rattled. Sound and fury, Lucy thought. Signifying nothing.

It was the kind of thing Marcia had been saying, these last few days. Marcia and her marvelous plan. As much a fiasco as Lucy's gas heater. But she would find a way, somehow or other, to blame Lucy, who never did anything right. Why didn't you stop him? she would say. All you had to do was...

Yes, what? Had anyone ever stopped Daddy from doing as he pleased? Of course not. They had been out of their minds to imagine it was possible. Lost in the stars. Two children, daydreaming, too bemused with their soap-bubble fantasy to notice that it had no relation whatever to reality.

A leaden apathy settled on Lucy. After a while she turned away from the door and moved, with dragging feet, down the hall to the sitting room. She sat on the sofa and listened to the senseless commotion of the wind. Now and then her gaze would wander to the telephone and she would tell herself that she should call Marcia. It seemed like such an effort. And Marcia would blame her. She would blame her even more, though, for failing to call.

There was a long silence after she asked for Marcia's extension. Finally a breezy voice said, "Miss Knapp's wire ... Sorry, she's not at her desk. Take a message?"

"Ask her to call her sister, please," said Lucy. She felt relieved, even though the postponement was only temporary. There was another angle, too—keyed up as she was, Marcia might go to pieces when she heard what had happened to her marvelous plan. At the very least, she would head for the nearest bar. She might desert Lucy, not come home tonight at all! Might already have done so ...

No. Lucy's hands made a sudden movement on their own, thrusting away the idea as if it were an actual physical threat. No, no. Granted that Marcia had been jittery this morning, maybe even on the point of cracking. But she would never run out on Lucy and leave her holding the bag. Never. It was unthinkable. Somehow or other she would have hung on to her nerve long enough to see their plan through.

It would be different, once she knew that the plan had blown up. No need to hang on to her nerve any longer, or stay on the wagon, or rush home after work.

But Lucy couldn't *bear* being left alone tonight. Let Marcia light into her for all she was worth, let her call her all kinds of stupid, let her get as drunk as she wanted to. Only don't let her stay away and leave Lucy alone, buried alive in solitude.

That was why she did not answer the phone. (Tell Marcia she had gone out, had been in the basement or on one of the upper-floors and hadn't heard it ring. Or—why pretend to be self-sufficient when she wasn't?—tell her the truth.)

Once started, it rang like crazy every ten minutes. The impulse to answer was so strong that she sat on her hands, tensely counting the demanding jangles. Marcia must be worried, she thought. She hoped. Maybe even worried enough to leave the office ahead of time.

Sure enough, it was only a little after five when she heard the front door open and Marcia's rapid footsteps in the hall. She rushed to meet her. "Marsh! Oh Marsh, thank God you're here! It's been so awful, waiting, and then—"

"Sh. Do you want him to hear you? What's the matter with you, anyway?" Bless Marcia, oh, bless her. Her snapping eyes; her voice, bossy, irritable, the way it ought to be; her none too gentle hand, hustling Lucy back into the sitting room and slamming the door shut.

"He won't hear. That's just it, he's gone away for the week end." She poured it all out, and Marcia stood, still as a stone, listening. Even her eyes seemed to be listening, wide and very bright.

At the end she said, "You should have called me."

"But I did! Only they said you weren't at your desk. That's why I left word for you to call me back. Didn't you get the message?"

"Naturally not. You ought to know that office by now. Nobody up there ever gets messages. Didn't you realize, when I didn't call you back?"

"Well, of course I wondered ..." Somebody else had made all those calls, then. But at least she wouldn't have to explain to Marcia why they had gone unanswered.

"I suppose you thought I'd chickened out." Marcia gave a short laugh. "Here you were, jittering, and there I was, likewise I'm sure. That's why I left early, I simply couldn't stand it another minute. And all for nothing. Or maybe not. Look at it one way and it's good practice. Kind of a dress rehearsal."

Lucy stared at her. "You mean we can still do it. But we can't? How can we? It's too late, especially if he's marrying her this week end."

"If. We don't know that's why they've gone to Connecticut. We don't even know she went with him. Not for sure. Though I agree with you, I think she did. But nobody told us so. We still don't know from nothing, as far as he's concerned. So what's to stop us from going ahead? He hasn't signed the house over to her yet. She'll get something, all right, if he's marrying her this week end, but we'll get the house. It's in his will." Marcia took off her hat and sailed it across to the sofa. It was a commanding gesture, somehow. "Good Lord, Lucy, don't tell me you're ready to back out, the first little hitch!"

"Of course not. I'm not backing out at all." And now that she thought about it, the way Marcia put it, so forcefully ... It was as if Marcia were pumping confidence into her. What a spineless alarmist she had been, jumping to the conclusion that all was lost simply because one small detail had gone awry! Their plan remained, undamaged, as workable on Monday as on Friday.

"We can't back out now, you know," Marcia was saying with quiet intensity. "Neither of us. We've gone too far ever to—"

The doorbell rang and kept ringing, a series of peals hysterical and importunate as the clanging of a fire engine. It had the same effect on both of them; they were out in the hall in a flash, knocking against each other in their frantic haste to answer it.

Dr. Berman stood there in the vestibule. Somewhat anti-climactically—or so it seemed to Lucy at first glance. He was a kewpie-shaped man, cozy and mildly comical. He took off his hat and there was his innocent head with only a few ruffled wisps of hair left.

"I tried to get you on the phone," he stammered. "Then I thought no, it's better if I come down, somebody's bound to be here, maybe the tenants will know where to reach you." He peered at them earnestly through his bifocals and tried again. "They got me, you see, through the answering service, I mean, the answering service put them through to me when they said it was an emergency ..."

"Okay, go on." Marcia's voice was crisp with impatience. "What's the emergency?"

"Daddy?" whispered Lucy, and Dr. Berman started as if she had pinched him.

Then he said, with the rapidity of a child reciting from memory: "You must prepare yourselves for a shock. There's been an accident, I'm afraid your father met with an accident. According to the police—"

"The police!" Which of them gasped it aloud, Marcia or Lucy herself?

"I was notified by the police." Dr. Berman ceremoniously placed an arm about each of them. "Apparently he lost control of the car on a curve and slammed into the culvert. He was killed instantly. Miss Caldwell too. She was with him. Both of them, killed instantly."

After the first stunning impact—fantasy colliding with reality—Lucy knew exactly what to do and did it as if she had been in training for this moment all her life. The buckling knees. The broken, sobbing outcry. Then, just as she was about to bury her head on Dr. Berman's kindly sustaining shoulder, she caught sight of Marcia's face.

"Marsh!" she said sharply.

But Marcia was already giving way to gulps of wild laughter. They rocked her. They burst out, even when she put both hands up to her mouth to hold them back. Words burst out too, in a gasping rush: "Dead? Both of them dead? Lucy, Lucy, did you hear what he said? Dead ... Not just him, both of them—"

Lucy dealt her a smart slap across the face. To Dr. Berman, who stood there blinking between them, she said, "Do something for her. Can't you see she's hysterical?"

At once he set up a professional bustle, though Marcia had shut up, she was shaking like a leaf but no longer making a sound, and she let him start steering her down the hall. Lucy, sobbing again, was the last to leave the open doorway where they had been standing. As she pulled the door shut, she saw out of the corner of her eye the little group on the sidewalk in front of the stoop.

They were standing there in the wind, their faces blank with curiosity. All three of them. Six if you counted the dogs. Mrs. Travers. Mrs. Sully. And Hansen. Yes, of course. And Hansen.

VI

"I told you so," said La Traviata with somber majesty. "Didn't I? I had a premonition of disaster. All my life I've been able to sense these things, and I am very seldom mistaken. Something terrible is going to happen to the doctor, I said. If you remember, Mrs. Sully, those were my very words."

What had stuck in Mrs. Sully's mind was more of a generalization, but why quibble? Certainly La Traviata had predicted violence, and certainly violence had befallen Dr. Knapp. Not to mention his nurse. If—as La Traviata put it—that was how you chose to identify Miss Caldwell. Nurse or whatever, it didn't matter now; it was all one to the worms. Mrs. Sully shifted from one foot to the other. She wished she wouldn't think such thoughts. Miss Caldwell had been just her age. Too young for the doctor. Much too young for death.

"They're not going to sell the house," she said, to change the subject. "Or so Hansen was telling me. I thought they might. Lucy's always grousing about how much trouble it is to keep it running, and somehow I thought Marcia would pull out if she ever got the chance—"

"Oh, but I don't think they'd seriously consider selling. After all, it's their home. Besides, what better investment could they make? It's not as if the doctor was *rich*, you know. He may have made plenty, but if you ask me, he spent it all and then some. I doubt if he left them anything except the house. No indeed, Mrs. Sully. As long as they keep the house they've got a nice comfortable income from the rent and no rent of their own to worry about. It's security for them, and they're not so young they can afford to sneer at security. I don't suppose Marcia makes much out of that job of hers, and Lucy couldn't get a job, let alone keep one, to save her life."

Yes. It made sense. They were standing in front of the house, where they had met—Mrs. Sully and Cherie on their way out, La Traviata and her darlings on their way in—and Mrs. Sully surveyed, with affection, the mellow brown facade with its trim white door and window boxes where geraniums blazed and ivy trailed. How pretty it was, especially in the springtime! Beyond the staid little gate the square of grass was like clipped, bright green fur, and the tree seemed to dance in the breeze. She had known when she first laid eyes on it a year ago that they would be happy here, and they were, they were.

Now there was a small oblong place, lighter in color than the rest of the house, where the plaque used to be—E.S. Knapp, M.D. Hansen had ripped it off, just the other day. And the venetian blinds at the office window were shut tight.

"I suppose they'll rent out his office," she said. "What used to be his office. I still can't believe it, somehow. He was so—alive. Only a couple of weeks ago ..."

Only a couple of weeks ago they had been standing here in the roistering wind, passing the time of day with Hansen, while up there in the doorway Lucy and Marcia were being told that something terrible had happened to their father. That wild burst of laughter from Marcia, her voice ringing out on a freakish gust of wind: "Dead? Both of them dead? Lucy, Lucy ... Not just him—" And then Lucy smacking her across the face. Well, of course. Standard treatment for hysteria.

The hysteria itself was what you might expect, too. Though naturally Dr. Berman hadn't used the graphic term Hansen used—and with what relish!—when he filled Mrs. Sully in on the details the next day. "Never knew what hit him. The way I heard it, his head was split open like when you drop a ripe melon and smash it. Hers too. One hell of a job for the undertaker."

"It's so strange," La Traviata was saying, in the voice she reserved for out-of-this-world commentary, "so strange, the way they're taking it. I mean, Lucy's the one you'd expect to go to pieces. She was so close to her father, so completely devoted to him. While Marcia—"

"Okay. All he had to do was snap his fingers and Lucy jumped. Just the same, I bet Marcia really liked him better, even if she did fight with him. He was a person to her, a human being. Not God Almighty, the way Lucy seemed to think."

"Mercy, dear, I'm not *criticizing* Marcia. You don't have to defend her to me."

"I'm not." But she was; she didn't know quite why. Except that she hadn't felt the same toward Lucy, since that day in the hall. The way she had carried on about Hansen and the gas heater. The look she had given Caldwell.

"You must admit," La Traviata was going on, "she's taking it harder than Lucy. She looks like her own ghost. Don't quote me on this, but I have the impression she's drinking more than ever, poor girl. I said to her the other day, I said, 'Marcia dear, it's none of my business, but why don't you try getting away from it all for a while? Just go off somewhere and commune with your own soul?' Well! 'Commune with my own soul!' she said, and you should have heard her laugh. Then she pulled herself together and said No, going off somewhere wasn't the answer and anyway, she couldn't leave Lucy—"

"Sh. Here she comes."

"Lucy dear, how pretty you look," La Traviata burbled, hardly missing a beat. And the smile she turned on Lucy was shiny and bland as mayonnaise. "Lovely afternoon, isn't it? Simply lovely ..."

Mrs. Sully left them to it. It seemed to her that Lucy was being pretty short with her answers. As if she suspected them of gossiping about her. Well, they had been. Not spiteful gossip, but still—You couldn't expect Lucy to like it. Mrs. Sully didn't like it herself.

"They were standing out there gossiping again," Lucy said, as soon as she shut the sitting room door behind her. "It was perfectly obvious. Travers started gushing all over me, the way she always does, and Sully couldn't get out of there fast enough. At least she had the grace to look ashamed of herself. More than I can say for Travers. Oh, so sweet! I knew right away she'd been at it for all she was worth."

"At what, for Lord's sake?" Marcia started to straighten up, thought better of it, and slumped back wearily in the big chair. "I swear, Lucy, you're getting a thing, a persecution complex. You suspect everybody of talking about you behind your back."

"Not everybody. Just certain ones. And don't forget, they're talking about you as much as me. With as much reason. More, in fact."

The only safe answer was silence. Marcia ought to know; she had tried them all. The honest remorse bit: Look, I'm sorry I blew up and laughed at the wrong moment. I'm sorry if they heard me. I'm sorry if they're yakking about it. I'm sorry. How many times do I have to say it? The attempt at reason: All right, supposing they are talking. The worst they can say is that I got hysterical and laughed when I heard he was dead. That's no crime. There *wasn't* any crime. So it doesn't matter if they talk their heads off. Can't you get that through your head? The refusal to be serious: Don't look now, but there's a sinister type in a black cape lurking outside the window. Skullduggery afoot. No doubt about it. You have the dagger? Yes. And I too am prepared. Ha! He will live to rue the day—Okay, so I'm being silly. Not a bit sillier than you. All this business about people spying and listening and whispering. Don't you see how absolutely ridiculous it is?

The trouble was that no matter what line she took at the beginning, she invariably wound up yelling. Which gave Lucy the chance to say, "Sh. They'll hear you." Which brought them right back to where they started, another loop around the same old circle.

Well, not today. No, thank you. Marcia wasn't having any. For once she was going to play it safe. Keep her mouth shut. Sip her therapeutic drink ...

That was part of what was eating on Lucy, of course. She had made such sad little attempts to keep Marcia from going out with Joe last night. Why didn't Joe come here for dinner? (For an excellent reason, but unfortunately one not fit for Lucy's maidenly ears.) Well, then, why couldn't they make it another time, some evening next week, when Lucy could plan something for herself and not be left all alone? (Here again it wouldn't do to explain that Joe's witch-wife didn't let him off the leash if she could help it.) All right, sad. But irritating, too. After all, Marcia was entitled to a whee if she could get it; how she had gotten through the last few weeks she would never know. And Lucy was a grown woman, it wasn't going to hurt her to spend a Saturday evening by herself. Did she expect Marcia to devote the rest of her life to baby-sitting?

Just the memory of that scene with Lucy last night sent her into a slow boil. The truth was that it had scared her; in its quiet way, it had been more disturbing than the fights she used to have with His Nibs. At least he never gave her this feeling of something clinging to her, softly, stubbornly searching out another place to grasp each time she managed to free herself ...

But Lucy couldn't help it. She had no one else. Literally no one; not even a lug like Joe to get drunk and go to bed with. At least Marcia had gotten away from His Nibs to that extent. For what it was worth. She stole a glance at Lucy, who was standing at the window, her profile silhouetted against the brightness outside. Childishly round forehead, narrow nose, lower lip caught between her teeth to keep it from trembling. Pity pierced her: an awareness of Lucy's inadequacy (which was *his* doing, he had kept her pressed into the vacuum of permanent childhood) and of her own responsibility. Not that she was always so adequate herself. But she was all Lucy had, the one person in the world.

"Marsh? Please don't be mad at me, Marsh."

"I'm not mad at you. Why on earth should I be?"

"Well, then, say something." Lucy turned toward her, imploringly. "You don't talk to me anymore. We used to have such good times together, evenings when Daddy was away. I thought—I thought it would be like that all the time ..."

"Sure. So did I. All we had to do was get rid of Daddy, I thought, and everything would be great. Only it isn't working out that way. You want to know why?" For some reason Marcia stood up, and realized at once that her therapeutic drink had done its work; her thoughts suddenly had the sparkle and ring of crystal. "Because he's foxed us again, that's why. Cheated us out of doing what we were primed to do, and so here we are with a left-over murder on our hands—"

"Sh!"

"Don't Sh me. It's the truth. We're stuck with our wonderful, terrible plan that we didn't get a chance to pull off. It's like something hanging around our necks, an albatross or something, and we can't get rid of it. So you suspect everybody of suspecting you, you're scared to be by yourself, and I'm the same as I was before, only more so. Because we're guilty of murder, without having murdered anybody."

"Are you crazy? Of course we're not guilty!"

"Oh yes we are. We meant to do it. We planned to do it. That makes us guilty. We're worse off than if we were murderers in fact, because it's still there, bottled up inside us, and how can it ever get out? If we'd actually done it, we could confess and be done with it. But they don't electrocute you, or even put you in prison, for thinking murder. It's got to be with your hands or it doesn't count. Don't you see what I mean, Lucy? As long as we live we'll never—"

"I see that you're drunk," said Lucy curtly. "Drunk again. Or maybe yet. Maybe you never sobered up from last night. I saw you when you came in, I know the state you were in. That's what I'm scared of. Not of being by myself."

Marcia steadied herself against the back of the chair. "What do you mean?"

"I mean I'm scared of what you may be saying when I'm not around to shut you up. How do I know you're not filling Joe up with all this stuff about guilt and confession?"

"You don't know. You'll simply have to take my word for it that Joe and I don't spend our time searching each other's souls. His interests lie elsewhere." But behind her bold front Marcia was aware of a distant whir of alarm. There seemed to be several blank spots in the sequence of last night's events. Like all at once they were in that bar with the cartoons instead of in the hotel room, and then all at once not that bar but another one, with pictures of horses. And what had she been talking about when Joe said, "You're all wound up, baby. Stop yakking and kiss me." Those words stuck in her memory, but not one of her own. "Anyway," she added, for Lucy looked as if she expected something more, "you say we're not guilty of anything. So what's the difference how much I talk? If I do."

"None, I suppose, if you don't mind having people think you're crazy. I do mind. I don't want you to wind up in an institution—"

"Oh, stop it! Don't be ridiculous. Nobody's going to put me in an institution."

"Not if I can help it," Lucy said, and why should it sound ominous to Marcia, why should it make her shiver? "But you've got to help too, Marsh. You've got to pull yourself together. Stop drinking so much. Stop talking out of turn, laughing out of turn—"

"Still harping on that. My lord, are you going to hold it against me the rest of my life? Can't I ever live it down?" Her voice must have risen; Lucy's eyes darted anxiously from door to window. But she did not speak, and Marcia's crystal-precise mind supplied the answers to her own questions: No I can never live it down. Yes she is going to hold it against me the rest of my life. She is never going to let me go, either. We are stuck with each other and with our left-over murder till death do us part. Not his, but somebody else's. Because we set death in motion, we geared ourselves for it, and we can't stop it now, we've got to ...

"No!" she cried violently. "I won't stand for it!" She rushed to the door and wrenched it open. There was Hansen, padding down the hall toward the front door, on his way out from some chore (perhaps) in the basement. Seen from the rear like this, he might have been a bear rigged out in a man's khaki work pants and shirt, carrying in his paw a tool kit. He was that thick and stolid and neckless. He must have heard the door open, but he did not turn around. In silence they watched his deliberate shambling progress past the office door and out into the foyer.

When he was gone, Lucy whispered in triumph. "There! Now will you believe me? He was listening, of course. He does it all the time. They all do. All the time."

Next day was Monday, Marcia's first day back at the office. Which, low be it spoken, was a relief to Lucy. Probably to Marcia, too; she complained about her job, but she missed it. Hanging around the house all day, with nothing to do but drink and putter in the garden, got on her nerves. That was all it was yesterday, Lucy decided hopefully. Boredom. And of course, hangover. The combination was enough to give anybody notions. Left-over murder, indeed! How could she be serious about such nonsense, and at the same time ignore the watching and listening and prying that were so obvious to Lucy? Well, the little episode with Hansen must have convinced even Marcia.

She seemed a bit subdued, but not in a bad humor, when she came down stairs in the morning. Late, as usual. No time for anything but a quick cup of coffee and a cigarette, though Lucy would have been all too happy to cook an egg for her. Or even just a slice of toast. It seemed so strange, with no one to get breakfast for.

"You'll be home for dinner?" she asked timidly, though she had meant not to ask; Marcia might feel she was pushing, and be annoyed.

"Don't worry. I'll be home." Yes. There was an edge there, all right. But Marcia cancelled it with one of her sudden smiles. And for further comfort, she added the routine goodbye phrases as she went out: "Well. Back to the salt mines. See you later."

I'll get a steak for dinner, Lucy planned happily. An extra nice one. She's going to be all right now. Everything's going to be all right now. We'll have one of our nice cozy evenings, just the two of us. A nice steak. And maybe an artichoke; Marcia's so fond of artichokes ...

She was halfway through the swinging door, with the coffee pot in her hand, before she remembered that the sitting room was empty. Daddy was not in there at the table, with his *Times* and his coffee cup, which by this time always needed refilling.

Really, she had to laugh at herself. How habit-ridden could you get!

The young man was standing on the stoop, waiting for her, when she came back from the market. At first glance she took him for a salesman, maybe one of those college boys selling magazine subscriptions. He had that kind of breezy, crew-cut look about him. "Hi! Miss Knapp?" he sang out when she turned in at the gate. "Lady with the dogs told me you ought to be along pretty soon. Here, let me give you a hand." And there he was, down the steps and in charge of her shopping bag before she had time to open her mouth.

He wasn't all that young, she saw, now that he was close at hand. The crew-cut was sprinkled with gray, and it receded from his forehead into two bays. There were fans of fine little lines around his eyes, and two deeper ones running from nose to mouth. Somehow she knew his tan came from a sunlamp, and now she thought—no longer of a real youth—but of a jaunty, beginning-to-age actor cast in a youthful role.

"I don't think I know you," she said stiffly.

"Don't apologize. No reason why you should." With his free hand he whipped out a card, which looked engraved but wasn't: C. Gordon Llewellyn. Photographic Portrait Studies. "The C. stands for Charles. So go ahead and call me Chuck. Everybody else does."

"I'm sorry, but I'm not interested in any photographs. Now if you'll let me have my shopping bag—"

"Wa-a-a-it a minute. You've got me wrong, Miss Knapp. Let's take it from the beginning again. I'm not making a pitch for your business. Not that I couldn't use it. And not that you wouldn't be a terrific subject." He let his eyes linger, in professional appreciation. "But business can wait. I've got something entirely different on my mind. It's about—" For once his glib tongue seemed to be failing him. His face was suddenly grave, and he gave Lucy a curious, sidelong glance. "It's about Pam Caldwell," he finished, in a hushed voice.

"Who?" she said sharply. And then, "Oh."

"Do you have a few minutes? It shouldn't take long. I'd appreciate it."

"All right. Yes. We'd better go inside," she added, from some animal instinct to take cover. Not that there was any chance of escaping the danger—if that was what C. Gordon Llewellyn represented. But she felt so exposed out here on the stoop. In the sitting room she would at least be sheltered from the public eye. She led the way down the hall and opened the door. Yes, it was much better inside. "Won't you sit down?" she said. She herself chose the little settee; its firm-cushioned back was like the arm of an old friend supporting her,

"Some lay-out you've got here." Mr. Llewellyn's eyes, as they took in the charming room, were openly admiring. "Terrific. Real stage-set stuff. And a garden yet! You and your sister, you've really got it made. Haven't you?"

"We like it," said Lucy. "You wanted to talk to me about Miss Caldwell?"

"Yeah, Pam. No kidding, Miss Knapp, I can't get over it. This layout. Terrific. You don't know how lucky you are. This day and age. A whole house to yourselves."

"We rent out the two top floors."

"I know, but even so." He leaned back in the big chair and crossed his legs. Very much at home. "Care for a cigarette?"

"No thank you. I don't smoke."

"No bad habits, huh? Me, I've got 'em all." He struck a match, then apparently sensed a chill in the atmosphere, for he stopped short of lighting up. "Excuse me. Maybe you'd rather I didn't—"

"It won't bother me in the least."

"Okay, then, if you're sure. To get back to Pam. I don't know how well you knew her, but I've been a friend of hers, friend of the family, you might say, for five six years now, and I don't mind telling you, it broke me up, what happened to her. A beautiful kid like Pam. A beautiful, sweet kid. They don't come any sweeter."

"I didn't know her very well. She'd only worked for Daddy a few months. She seemed—very nice."

"I still can't believe it. A beautiful kid like that, full of life one minute, and the next minute—" He snapped his fingers. "Just like that. Whammo. I just can't believe it."

All right, he couldn't believe it. Was that all he had come for, to give her his views on the suddenness of sudden death? Of course not. She must be very careful.

Before she could decide on the right words, he was going on. "Well, I don't have to tell you. Same way with your father. Only he wasn't a kid like her, he'd had a good whack at life, if you know what I mean."

"Still, it was a terrible shock," she said.

"Sure it was. And I'm not helping any, bringing it all back for you like this. I can tell from your face. You've got one of those expressive faces, Miss Knapp, I noticed it first thing. That's my business, noticing faces. Now don't get scared, I told you I'm not here on business."

"Why *are* you here, Mr. Llewellyn?"

"Call me Chuck. Everybody else does. Why I'm here is, Pam left some stuff at the office—or so her mother thinks—and she asked me if I'd drop around and pick it up. Nothing important, just a few personal belongings that her mother would like to have, if it's not too much bother."

"No bother at all." Her heart leaped with relief. And yet ... He had rolled it off so glibly. He was giving her another of those sidelong looks. "I didn't notice anything of Miss Caldwell's in the office, but then we haven't given it a thorough turning out yet. Naturally if there are any of her belongings here, her mother should have them. She could have just called and asked us to look—"

"That's what I said. But the fact is, the old girl's not entirely herself these days. It's been rough on her. So I thought okay, humor her, do it her way, what does it cost me? The worst that can happen is for Miss Knapp to throw me out on my ear, and I had a hunch, even before I saw you, that you weren't that kind."

"Oh, you did, did you?"

"Yes, I did, did I." He grinned companionably. "Because I saw the letter you and your sister wrote Pam's mother. You didn't have to do it, nobody was twisting your arm, you just did it out of the goodness of your heart."

She felt her face turning red with embarrassment. The note had been Marcia's idea; the situation, she said, called for some such corny gesture. "If you'd like to go into the office now," she said, standing up, "we can look for Miss Caldwell's things."

What else could she do? It did not matter whether Mr. Llewellyn was making his visit in all innocence, as he claimed, or whether he was playing some devious, dangerous game. She had no choice, at least at this stage, but to co-operate.

Mr. Llewellyn was as impressed with the office as he had been with the sitting room. "Terrific," he said, several times. "Boy, could I use this setup in my business! Real class. Not that I've got the kind of money a place like this will rent for—Or maybe you're not even planning to rent it, maybe you've got something else in mind."

"We haven't decided yet," said Lucy. "This is the desk Miss Caldwell used. I suppose it's the most likely place, if she left anything here."

Her thoughts swung, like a pendulum, between two hopes, two fears: there would be nothing, he was fabricating an excuse for snooping; there would be something significant, some proof perhaps of Daddy's honorable intentions toward Pam, some appalling, incriminating bit of evidence ...

But there couldn't be. They were not guilty. They had committed no crime.

He waited, deferentially, for her to begin the search. The bottom drawer yielded a bottle of silver nail polish and a shell-pink cashmere sweater.

"That's hers!" exclaimed Mr. Llewellyn. "I mean, that's her perfume."

It certainly was, and the sultry scent conjured up, as nothing else could have, the image of its vulgar, sex-flaunting wearer. Daddy's Pam Sweetie. Mr. Llewellyn's beautiful, sweet kid. Lucy could hardly bring herself to touch it.

The top drawer was a jumble of God knows what all—prescription pads, index cards, a cheap soiled cosmetic case crammed with little bottles of glop, several disintegrating cigarettes, bill forms, a cellophane rain hood, paper clips, bobby pins, a sticky bottle of hand lotion

And the diary.

Lucy's hand closed on it in an uncontrollable spasm. Hide it. Shove it back out of sight. Slip it into her pocket. Pretend to recognize it as her own. But she had already, in the first agonizing moment, spotted the gold-stamped name on its cover: Pamela Caldwell. Well, but that didn't mean he had spotted the name, or even the diary. Only she must be quick. Do something. Quick.

"What's that? A diary?"

"Where? I don't see any—"

"You've got your hand right on it," he pointed out. In spite of all she could do, another spasm overtook her; she watched with horror the furtive effort of her own fingers to push the drawer shut. Mr. Llewellyn's hand, toast-brown, golden-haired, intervened neatly. "See? I thought it looked like a diary."

As he lifted it out, a photograph that had been tucked between its pages slid to the floor. One of those night club photos: Daddy and Pam clicking their champagne glasses. She had her eye on the camera, naturally, drooping the eyelashes, projecting the bosom for all she was worth. But Daddy's eyes were fixed on her, and there was no mistaking his look of adoration. It made an ache in Lucy's chest.

"Who's the guy?" Mr. Llewellyn asked, and she could not speak. She did not have to; she had one of those expressive faces, and that was Mr. Llewellyn's business, noticing faces. "Oh," he said softly. "Look, maybe you'd like to keep this. I mean, it's as much yours as anybody's."

"Of course not. Why should I want it?" But that was a mistake, too, she thought despairingly. Whatever she said was a mistake. She had an impulse to get back at him somehow, find a sore point and press. "I'm sure it means a great deal more to you than it does to me. You were such an old friend of Miss Caldwell's. Such an old family friend."

Bull's-eye. But he was quick to recover. "You don't miss much, do you? Okay, I had a yen for Pam. At one time a terrific yen. Only you know how it is when malnutrition sets in, and what I mean, this was acute malnutrition. Pal-wise I was great. But romance-wise? Huh uh. First of all, I was too old for her."

"Too old? You were too old for her?"

"That's what she said." His smile was knowing. His eyes made the barest flick toward the photograph of Pam and Daddy. "And she had a point, you know. Oh, I admit I'm well preserved, get me in candle light and I don't look a day over eighty—Don't laugh, I mean it."

"I'm not laughing." But another gulp escaped her. This must have been how Marcia felt, when Dr. Berman brought them the news. If only she could slap herself!

"Well, life's like that." He added, as he tucked the photograph back into the diary, "He must have been quite a guy, from the looks of him. You're sure you don't want this? No? I'll take it along, then. The rest of this stuff I *know* you don't want." He made a tidy stack of it.

"The diary," she said faintly. "Shouldn't we just destroy it? I don't—I wouldn't want anyone reading my diary without my permission. Not even my mother."

He cocked his head, alert, thoughtful. "Yeah. I see what you mean. Still ... Seems to me it's for her mother to decide. Don't you think so? I do. Definitely. They were very close, Pam and her mother. Almost like sisters. She ought to have the say-so."

He would undoubtedly read it, the minute he was out of Lucy's sight. Well, and what if he did? What could Pam's diary reveal that he did not already know? Lucy herself had removed any doubts he might have had about Daddy and Pam. The diary would dot the i's, and cross the t's. The details of their wedding plans. Possibly a few little digs at "the girls," poor things. That was all. Because that was all Pam knew to tell.

Wasn't it?

She stood helplessly by while he stowed Pam's belongings away in the paper bag she found for him. He left the diary till last. Then he thrust out his hand, all engaging frankness, and there was nothing to do but shake hands with him.

"You've been awfully nice about everything, Miss Knapp. I can't tell you how much I appreciate it. No kidding. It's been a real pleasure meeting you. Who knows, maybe we'll meet again some day. Remember, any time you need a photographer, you know who to call."

"I'll remember. Goodbye."

"So long. Be seeing you. I hope."

She watched his wiry figure sprinting across the street to his car, a rather battered model that made a lot of noise on the take-off. He stuck his head out the window and waved. Taking it for granted that she was there, watching. *If he finds anything else in the diary, she thought, he'll be back. I'll know soon enough. He'll be back again. That's how I'll know.*

VII

"Hello? Marsh?" the telephone quavered into Marcia's ear. Lucy. In a twitter. She went on, her voice hollow with disaster, "He just called. He's coming back, Marsh. I knew it. I told you he'd be back."

"I know you did," Marcia said impatiently. That was all she had heard last night. Mr. Llewellyn. She was sick of the man without ever having laid eyes on him. "What does he want now?"

"He's got some kind of a proposition. Something he'd like to discuss in person, if it's all the same to me. A business proposition, he said."

It did have a sinister sound. But Marcia wasn't going to admit it. Not after the way she pooh-poohed the whole business: of course they had nothing to fear from Pam's diary. Lucy was up to her old tricks, imagining dangers that simply did not exist. Did not because they could not. The real danger—only Lucy couldn't see the woods for the trees—would come from inside themselves, not outside. If it came at all. For Marcia too might be borrowing trouble, in her own quaint way.

Into the phone she said, "Did you tell him to drop dead with his business proposition?"

"I couldn't! How could I? I said Mr. O'Conner is our lawyer and handles all our business matters, and he said—" Lucy choked. "He said, 'Oh, I don't think it's got to that stage. Not quite yet, anyway.'"

"Pull yourself together, Lucy. We went all through this last night. There's nothing to worry about. Can't be." She put down the paper clip she had been fidgeting with. Straightened the edge of her desk blotter. "So then what?"

"He'll be here this afternoon. Four-thirty or so, he said. Unless I'd rather he made it earlier—Oh Marsh, you'll come straight home from the office, won't you? Please. I simply can't face him alone. I'm scared I'll do everything wrong."

Great. Just great. Wouldn't you know? Joe had called. The one night he was free. "All right, I'll be there," Marcia said. "Stop dithering, will you? I'll make it as early as I can, and we'll get the damn thing settled, once and for all."

All right, she thought when she had hung up, it smacked of blackmail. Those slick, vague phrases: a business proposition. Oh, I don't think it's got to that stage. Not quite yet, anyway. But don't forget, it was hearsay, all of it, filtered through Lucy's eyes and ears, and in her present state of mind, Lucy was capable of distorting How-do-you-do into a deep, dark threat. Don't forget, either, that even the most enterprising blackmailer had to have something to go on. A crime. And there had been no crime. No matter what revelations Pam might have made in her diary, no matter what indiscretions Lucy might have let slip yesterday, the fact remained that Daddy and Pam had died accidentally. You couldn't get away from that.

So let Mr. Llewellyn try any game he wanted to. Marcia was ready for him.

She ducked out of the office fifteen minutes early and took a cab downtown. Funny, how sharp she felt; as if she were actually looking forward to this little skirmish. Mr. Llewellyn should have put in an appearance by now. Unless he had decided that a certain amount of waiting would act as a softening-up agent. So far he had shown no inclination to let any grass grow under his feet.

He was there, all right, and Marcia liked him on sight. Which was not only disconcerting—this particular possibility had not occurred to her—but puzzling: for she spotted him at once as a phoney. Photographic Portrait Studies, indeed. Feelthy postcards was more like it. The raffishness, the shadiness, shone through undimmed, though he was obviously working hard to palm himself off as the perfect gentleman, oozing respect and respectability from every pore. Debonair in his slightly seedy clothes, he sprang up when she walked in the door; remained ostentatiously on his feet until she and Lucy sat down; then sprang to produce cigarettes and a light. He performed these antics conscientiously, but light-heartedly too, as if, given the right opening, he might burst out laughing at himself. A bouncy, phoney little guy, trying to seem younger than he was, better-bred than he was, more successful than he was; still game, in spite of how often or hard life clobbered him, still expecting at any moment the stroke of luck that would turn him into a rich millionaire...

Let's not get carried away, Marcia reminded herself drily. That's all very well, but what's he up to? He's not here for his health, or yours either, you can depend on that.

She gave him a straight look and said briskly, "I understand you mentioned a business proposition, Mr. Llewellyn?"

Good. She had caught him a bit off balance, he had counted on a more gradual approach, more time to take her measure. Well. He might as well realize right now that she wasn't another Lucy. (Who sat on the edge of her chair, a scared rabbit poised for flight.)

"Well, yes. I did." He tapped the ash from his cigarette. Nonchalant as all get out. He hoped. "I got this idea, see, after I talked to your sister. It hit me just like that. Whammo. This terrific idea. Of course I don't know how it's going to sound to you. But I figured, what have I got to lose, nothing ventured nothing gained. That's me all over." They each got a big smile. Especially Lucy. "And incidentally, may I say again how much I appreciate your kindness yesterday. No kidding. It means a lot to Pam's mother to have those few little things of hers."

"I'm sure it does. Especially the diary." Marcia said boldly, and was surprised to see a flicker of something like embarrassment in Mr. Llewellyn's face. A blackmailer would have gloated. Wouldn't he?

"Yeah. Especially the diary." He grinned. Possibly he admired her nerve. "Anyway, thanks. And thanks for letting me come back today, too. Even if nothing come of it—well, it's still a pleasure making your acquaintance. I mean, I know class when I see it, and you've got it. You don't often see two such expressive faces. That's my business, you know, noticing faces. Not that you're anything alike. Never know you were sisters. Except that you've both got that special quality, I don't know if it's bone structure or what—"

Lucy looked flustered. Compliments affected her that way. "To get back to the business proposition," Marcia said. "We won't know how it sounds to us until we hear it. Will we?"

"Okay. Here goes. If it don't click with you, then I get A for Effort and that's that. Ever since I was here yesterday I've been thinking about this place you've got here, this layout. It really got me. You know? I kept thinking that's what I need, a place with some class to it. Where I am now—well, let's face it, it's a dump. Way uptown. Neighborhood's going down hill but fast. Not that I'm not doing okay. Don't get me wrong. But who wants to settle for okay when all they need is give them a break and maybe they'd be terrific? So here's the deal—I just want you to give me a chance at your father's office when and if you decide to rent it."

That was all? An aspiring tenant? It was as plausible, really, as Lucy's blackmailer. To Marcia. Not to Lucy; her frozen look made it clear that Mr. Llewellyn's business proposition confirmed what she had suspected from the beginning. As far as Lucy was concerned, they were stuck with Mr. Llewellyn. He could move in and never pay a cent of rent, and she would not dare utter a word of protest. She exuded fear, guilty fear; and Mr. Llewellyn—who, whatever else he might be, was no dope—must sense it. If he hadn't gotten ideas from Pam's diary, he was getting them now, from Lucy's face.

"Nothing's been decided, or even discussed, so far," said Marcia. She was both shocked and amused, she found, at the thought of turning Daddy's office over to a fifth-rate photographer. Tinted wedding pictures in the window. Or those arty productions, all suggestive shadows and curves. His Nibs would spin in his grave. "If we do rent it, I should think it would be simpler just to find another doctor, maybe someone who'd want to buy some of the equipment. After all, that's what it's set up for, a doctor's office. I'm not sure it would be suitable for your business."

Mr. Llewellyn assured her, passionately, that it would be. More than suitable. Perfect. Ideal. Leave the outer and inner offices as they were. Use the examining room as a dark room. "As far as your father's equipment goes, that's not going to be any problem. I can think of least three guys, just offhand, that I bet would snap it up tomorrow. Pay you a good price, too. I've got contacts on account of Pam being a nurse, you know."

"Yes. Lucy told me you were a great friend of Pam's."

"There!" he cried in triumph. "You have first names, after all. At least Lucy has. Lucy Knapp. Nice. Just right. I didn't like to ask—you might take it wrong, figure I was trying to get fresh or something—but you've got to admit, it's kind of complicated, calling you both Miss Knapp. So this is Lucy. And this is ..." He cocked his head at Marcia expectantly.

"Marcia," she supplied. "Didn't Pam ever mention us?"

"Not by name," he said easily. "Marcia. Hey, that's good too. Goes with your personality. So now you know what's on my mind, business-wise. I'm not trying to rush you into anything. Naturally you'll want to bat it around, talk it over with your lawyer, get his advice. I just wanted to get my bid in, that's all."

"You haven't really given us a bid," said Marcia, and out of the corner of her eye saw Lucy wince. But why stall around? They might as well know where they stood.

"Don't worry, we'll get around to that. All in good time. Of course you're not going to let it go for peanuts, the location alone is worth plenty, and then it's in good shape, well kept up. One thing I did think of, in case you'd be interested. I'm kind of a jack of all trades, you might say. Painting, gardening, carpentering, plumbing, electricity—you name it and I can do it. So maybe there's an angle there. Maybe I could pay off part of the rent taking care of the odd jobs around the house for you. There must be plenty of them. And you must pay somebody to do them as it is. So why not me?"

A disarming proposal, if Marcia ever heard one. And he seemed completely sincere; he flushed slightly at revealing, thus obliquely, the state of his finances. Even Lucy relaxed. She would probably be for any arrangement that involved getting rid of Hansen.

"The superintendent we have now lives just across the street," said Marcia. "That way we can call on him, if we have to, any time, day or night." Even as she spoke, she realized what Mr. Llewellyn's answer was going to be: he could use Daddy's office for both business and living quarters. No doubt had intended to, all along.

As he pointed out, there was no reason why it wouldn't work. "There's the bathroom. And plenty of room in the inner office for a studio couch. Who needs a stove or any of that jazz? Not me. Wouldn't know how to boil water. It's the one thing I'm not handy at—cooking. If there weren't any restaurants I'd have starved to death years ago."

He leaned forward eagerly, bright-eyed, aware that he was making headway. But smart enough not to push his luck. Marcia couldn't help smiling back at him, and he switched his gaze to Lucy. Who bent her head in confusion, and finally got out a few smothered-sounding words. "I don't know what to say ... We'll have to think it over ..."

"Sure you will," he assured her heartily. "That's all I'm asking you to do. Just think it over. Talk it over. Only don't forget to keep me in mind." He stood up—give him credit, he had a sense of timing—and held out his hand. "Will you shake on it, Miss Lucy Knapp and Miss Marcia Knapp?"

They would and did—Marcia with good-humored briskness, Lucy hesitantly. Mr. Llewellyn made quite a lingering business of that handshake with Lucy; so much so that it set her to blushing. And it set Marcia to thinking. Was it possible that their phoney friend here had his eye on more than Daddy's office? Of course it was; count on him to play all the angles. From his point of view, Lucy would be quite a promising angle. She owned a house, didn't she? Well, half a house. No telling how much besides. While she might not win any beauty contests, on the other hand she wasn't a witch, and anyway you couldn't have everything. She scared easy, probably didn't know what the score was, but if a guy played his cards right he might ...

Good Lord, thought Marcia, he certainly might. Lucy was a real babe in the woods when it came to men, a fortune hunter's dream. A little judicious flattery, and that would be it for her, the love of her life, all the more soul-shaking for being a little behind schedule.

"Okay if I call you in a day or two?" he was asking. He made it sound just intimate enough. Lucy obliged with another blush, and he turned to Marcia with his pleasure-to-have-met-you bit. She had the feeling that, with the minimum of encouragement, he would have winked at her.

She ought to warn Lucy. She intended to. Only she didn't seem to find the right opening. Lucy wouldn't give up on her blackmailing theory; she insisted on still another rehash. The diary, she kept coming back to the diary. How did they know Pam hadn't overheard them plotting? That might be the very reason Daddy had decided on the trip to Connecticut: because he knew about their conspiracy and was determined to nip it in the bud. It might all be there in the diary, plot and counterplot, right there in black and white. "What if it is?" Marcia burst out in exasperation. "How can Mr. Llewellyn or anybody else blackmail us for something we didn't do?"

But Lucy had an answer for that, too. It explained, she said, the modesty of Mr. Llewellyn's demands. He was feeling his way, testing to see how much the traffic would bear.

"Then let's make it clear right now that the traffic won't bear anything. Thumbs down on him and his business proposition. We're just not interested. Period."

"Oh, but we don't dare!" cried Lucy. "No telling what he might try next, out of spite. He might even go to the police with a story about how the car accident could have been rigged. I know they'd find out it wasn't; but think how ghastly it would be, just having them investigate. I couldn't stand it, Marsh! And besides—"

Whatever she might have gone on to say (and afterwards Marcia spent quite a time speculating) it was cut off by the telephone. Turned out to be Joe, checking to see if maybe she couldn't make it tonight after all.

"Go ahead," Lucy surprised her by saying. "Why not, if you want to? I'm too tired to be any company for you tonight. All I want to do is have a bite of dinner and fold up early. So don't stay in on my account."

It made a nice change from the pathetic scene she had staged at being left alone the other night. If Mr. Llewellyn could accomplish this with just a couple of visits, then more power to him. Let him come every day. Let him ...

The direction of her own thoughts shocked Marcia. Was she so lost to decency that she was willing to throw her sister to a fortune-hunting wolf (if that was what Mr. Llewellyn was) just so she herself would be free to carry on her shabby little affair with Joe? Of course not. It was all the sheerest supposition, anyway; Mr. Llewellyn most likely had nothing whatever to do with Lucy's attitude. She might, really and simply, be tired enough to welcome an evening alone.

I'll warn her tomorrow, Marcia thought as she ran upstairs to get dressed for her evening out. There's no rush. It will keep till tomorrow.

But again she didn't seem to find the right opening. Which was perhaps no wonder, considering the magnitude of her hangover. She crept through the day's work with the aid of three Bloody Marys at lunch time and tottered home at night to find Lucy chirpy as a sparrow.

"He called up again today. Mr. Llewellyn. Excuse me. Chuck. Just call him Chuck, everybody else does." In her debilitated state, Marcia could not tell whether Lucy's laugh was derisive or pleased. "He claims he's found a customer for Daddy's equipment. Wanted to bring him right down to look it over and make us an offer. I put him off, of course."

"I should hope so," said Marcia. "We haven't any idea of what it's worth. If you ask me, neither has he or this buddy of his. It's probably just something he cooked up, an excuse for calling you."

"Maybe," Lucy laughed again. Then, catching Marcia's eye on her, she added sharply. "That's not the way you sounded yesterday. He couldn't possibly be a blackmailer according to you. You even said you liked him."

"That doesn't mean I'd trust him any farther than I could throw him. If I ever saw a man with his eye out for the main chance, it's our boy Chuck."

"But that's exactly the point! I said from the start he was on to something, maybe even before he read Pam's diary—"

"Please, Lucy. Not again. Not tonight. If you want to rent Daddy's office to him, it's all right with me. Fine. Let's do it and be done with it. Only please let's not go into another depth analysis of Mr. Llewellyn. I'm not that interested in him."

"Well, if you think I brought up the subject because I'm *interested* in him! Because, let me assure you, I'm not any more interested in him than you are ..." Lucy flounced out to the kitchen to see about dinner.

In very high dudgeon indeed. Marcia poured herself a therapeutic drink. This was not the moment. No. This was definitely not the moment to warn Lucy.

As the week went by Mr. Llewellyn—or Chuck; for somewhere along the line Lucy lost her inhibitions about calling him what everybody else did—stepped up his campaign. He called at least once every day. Several times he dropped in on some pretext or other, if it was only to repeat that he was not trying to rush the Misses Knapp into anything.

He certainly was an eager beaver, Lucy said, with her little laugh, hall-derisive, half-pleased. One thing about it, Lucy said, it would give them as good an excuse as they would ever have for getting rid of Hansen.

"Well, my dear," said La Traviata, "how do you feel about the new tenant?"

Mrs. Sully felt kindly disposed, as she did toward most of the human race. "He seems nice and friendly. Wants to take some pictures of

Cherie. Free of charge. Just for fun and practice, because he's never tried photographing dogs."

"He mentioned something of the sort to me too. I'd be tempted, except that Chrys is so high-strung, poor darling. Yes, he does seem friendly, doesn't he? But you could have knocked me over with a feather. It never crossed my mind the girls would dream of renting to anybody except another doctor. Can't you just imagine what their father would have to say on the subject? A photographer, trespassing on his territory!"

Mrs. Sully giggled. "He can't be first-class, either, or he wouldn't be taking on the superintendent job. And oh brother, is Hansen's nose out of joint! He always acted as if he hated the job, but now that they've fired him he's mad as a wet hen. They'll be sorry, he was telling me the other day, they'll find out they can't treat him like that and get away with it. Of course it's just talk. You know Hansen. Never a pleasant word."

"Indeed I do know Hansen, and I must say, good riddance. I couldn't help thinking yesterday, when Mr. Llewellyn was helping me hang my curtains, I couldn't help thinking what a difference. He was so obliging and cheerful about everything. It must be a great relief to Lucy." She gave Mrs. Sully one of her portentous looks. "I declare, she seems like a different person. Already. I got the impression at first that they had known each other for some time, but apparently not. Apparently he was a friend of Miss Caldwell's. Did you know that?"

"Yes, he told me too." Mrs. Sully became very busy with Cherie's leash. She didn't want to gossip. Only it was so hard not to, once La Traviata got started.

"That's what makes it so peculiar. The idea of Lucy making friends with a friend of Miss Caldwell's. Doesn't it strike you as peculiar?"

"Not particularly," said Mrs. Sully. Offhand beyond belief.

"Well, it does me. You might not have been aware of it, but I've always had an instinct, I can sense these things. Take my word for it, my dear, there was no love lost between those two, at least not on Lucy's side."

"Maybe so," said Mrs. Sully, who did not have to take La Traviata's word for it. Not while she remembered—and she did remember, all too vividly—Lucy's face, fixed in that frightening, fanatic glare.

"And yet here she is, just like this with a friend of Miss Caldwell's. Why, she's positively blossomed out in the past couple of weeks! You'd almost think—"

"Cherie, behave yourself!" Mrs. Sully recognized her limitations: it was either gossip or turn tail. "Oh dear, look at the time, I simply must run."

And run she did, from La Traviata and her instincts for the peculiar, from what she would rather not hear put into words, because ...

She didn't know why. Just because.

VIII

Fear. How strange to live with it, get used to it, even thrive on it. For Mrs. Travers was right: Lucy could see in the mirror her own shining eyes and heightened color. It was like a fever running in her, sharpening her perceptions and quickening her to an abnormal animation. How strange, how different from the other fears ...

She had always been a scaredy-cat, afraid of so many things. The dark, Marcia, thunderstorms, fire engines, the blind man who used to live across the street, bugs, and snakes, her music teacher. And, of course, Daddy. But those other fears had paralyzed her. This was an exhilarating fear. To her Chuck's presence was a challenge, it was the bright eye of danger trained on her, daring her to make a wrong move. And here was the thrilling difference; instead of the old abject helplessness, she had a feeling of zest, sometimes even of power.

Life—which before Chuck moved in had been a series of dull defeats—now had a fine edge of drama. Defeat was possible, but so was victory. It was as if she and Chuck were playing an exciting game in which his aim was to trick her into revealing more than he already knew and hers was to keep that perilous unknown quantity—whatever he knew—within its present limitations. For no matter what Marcia said, he did know something, enough so that they did not dare risk calling his bluff. As Marcia had advocated: don't rent the office to him, she had said; let him try any funny business and see where it gets him. That was the trouble with Marcia. She had a streak of fatal recklessness, a willful blindness to danger.

The game that Lucy and Chuck played was in many ways a friendly one. When she came downstairs in the morning there he would be in his dungarees, cleaning the hall or polishing the brass or sweeping down the outside steps. He seemed to enjoy his job as super, and he was a whiz at it. The house had never gotten such good care from Hansen. "Morning, Lucy," he would call out. Breezy without being impertinent; Hansen's "Miss Lucy" was offensive, Chuck's "Lucy" was not.

Often they had a cup of coffee together, after Marcia left for the office. (That morning dash of Marcia's delighted him. "They're off!" he would cry, as she shot out the door, late as usual. They were on teasing, comradely terms.) With Lucy he was inclined to be more serious. The cup of coffee together habit started during the first week, while he was painting Daddy's office with one hand and moving in with the other. Busy as he was getting settled, he never once skimped on his super's chores. Never took the coffee invitation for granted either. Each time it seemed to come as an unexpected treat.

Whether or not she asked him for coffee—and sometimes she didn't, just to show him, and herself too, that she didn't have to—she was still sure to run into him half a dozen times during the day. If she didn't need his help with something or other, it was the other way round. He turned to her for advice about the best way to arrange his studio, about drapes, carpeting, the kind of sign he ought to have. She had such good taste, he said; he didn't always trust his own judgment in these matters. And as long as she was here, maybe she'd like to see some samples of his work. He was especially proud of his weddings—not just single pictures of the bride, but a volume of color photos recording for posterity the whole occasion. Politely Lucy leafed through shots of the happy couple with and without attendants, both sets of parents, bride cutting cake, bride throwing bouquet, gifts on display, happy couple kissing after ceremony, happy couple leaving on their wedding trip, amid showers of rice thrown by laughing friends. He already had several such jobs lined up for this coming June, Chuck said. There was good money in them. And it was smart business to develop a specialty. Llewellyn for wedding pictures, the way you think of Jensen for silver. Or Nedick's for hot dogs.

He made quite a business, one morning a couple of weeks after he had moved in, of inviting Lucy and Marcia for a house-warming drink. "The studio's still a shambles," he said. "But I've got the living room squared away, and that's something to celebrate. So why don't we? How about tonight when Marcia gets home from the office?"

Lucy hesitated, but naturally Marcia wasn't going to turn down a drink. "Sure. See you tonight. So long now. I've got to fly ..." And Marcia sprinted down the hall.

Lucy couldn't very well say no after that. The trouble was that at the last minute it turned out to be one of those days when Marcia had to work late—no telling when she'd be through, she said when she called—so there was Lucy holding the bag. Unless Chuck would decide to postpone the festivities.

Nothing of the sort. "Don't be silly," he told her when she suggested it. "Come on in. Marcia can help warm the house some other time. I've already mixed the cocktails. We can't let them go to waste."

It would have been too rude to refuse. He was so obviously set for his little party: all slicked up in white shirt and bow tie—well, Lucy herself had changed her dress and taken special pains with her hair—and she could see into the inner office, where he had set out glasses and little plates of canapés. She couldn't help feeling touched at the thought of his going to so much fuss.

But that was no doubt what he was counting on—to disarm her with this innocent-seeming social gesture. She must be more than ever on her guard.

She sat down warily on the edge of the studio couch, the principal piece of furniture in Chuck's "living room." It had seen better days. So had the bridge table, the two folding chairs, the chest of drawers and the little bookshelf which made up the rest of his household possessions. Lucy and Marcia had contributed a small Oriental-type rug and a couple of lamps. He was spending his money where it mattered—on the studio. Personal comfort could wait. Still, there were some cozy touches: bright-colored pillows on the couch and several of his photographs, the ones he called "art shots," on the wall.

"Happy days," she said as she lifted her glass for the first sip. "Best of luck." Oh dear, she was thinking, it's going to be awful, I won't be able to think of anything to say, it's different from just having a cup of coffee with him, if only Marcia were here ...

But he seemed completely unaware of her self-consciousness. He leaned back in his folding chair, stretched his legs, and beamed at her. "I'll drink to that myself. Happy days. Best of luck. To both of us. You know, I've got a feeling that's the way it's going to be from here on in. It goes in cycles, a person's luck. Just when you figure the going's too tough, you might as well cut your throat, whammo, that's when you start getting the breaks. Like me, the day I first turned up here. I don't mind telling you, I was dragging my tail. Not just on account of Pam. Everything. And look at what happened. All at once this idea hits me, it clicks with you, and here I am, all set for the big time, I hope."

"I'm sure I do too," said Lucy primly. "I didn't realize you were so depressed that day."

"Maybe I didn't show it, but oh brother, I was. You want to know something? So were you. Who knows, maybe we brought each other luck. Because I can tell, I know it hasn't been all beer and skittles for you, either."

She was startled. "What makes you say that?"

"Stands to reason. With your looks, you must have had plenty of chances to marry. Either the right guy hasn't come along, or the right guy did come along and something happened to louse it up." His eyes met hers gravely, warm with understanding. "If I'm talking out of turn, just tell me to shut up. But that's how it was, wasn't it? Something happened to louse it up?"

She nodded mutely. Bernie, oh Bernie, grieved the familiar inner voice. And to think that Chuck, of all people, should have the perception to recognize in her the marks of star-crossed love! To think that he should be the one to break down the wall of silent misery that had imprisoned her all these years! For that was what was happening. She heard herself saying, "It was so long ago. I don't know why I can't seem to get over it. The way other people do ..."

"You take things harder than other people. I saw that right away."

The words came haltingly at first, then faster and faster, a long-pent-up flood released at last. She hadn't realized there was so much to tell about Bernie. After all, it was just the one winter when she met him at art class. One wonderful winter of Bernie seeing her home, Bernie taking her to museums and concerts, Bernie's soulful Jewish eyes gazing into hers, his hand clasping hers while they wandered through the frozen park talking, endlessly talking. Art, Music, Life, Love. But of course Daddy was right. It wouldn't ever have worked, mixed marriage or not. How could it? How could they have lived, with Bernie's heart set on art school instead of something that had what Daddy called a future? No, it was doomed from the beginning, their immortal, star-crossed love.

She was trembling with exaltation and relief when she finished. For a moment Chuck's eyes remained fixed on hers, his listening eyes that, while she talked, had reflected like mirrors her remembered joy and sorrow. Then he refilled her glass and drew a long sigh. "Poor kids," he murmured. "Poor Lucy. So that's why you didn't finish art school."

"I had kind of a breakdown. Daddy sent me to this place in Connecticut for a month. Not exactly a sanitarium. More of a rest home. Anyway, they straightened me out. But I couldn't bear the thought of going back to school. It was a year before I even wanted to look at a picture, let alone paint one myself."

"If you could have gotten away, I mean, gone somewhere else to live—"

"I wasn't really well enough. Besides, Marcia had a job by then, so Daddy needed me here at home."

"Still, it wasn't much of a life for you, just staying home, running the house."

No. Not much of a life. "I didn't care what I did," she said. "Nothing seemed to matter." Daddy had mattered. She had loved him in those days, had believed that he loved her. When all he had ever given her was a few stray crumbs left over from his own full life, which she had known nothing about. She took quite a long drink of her cocktail. And there was Chuck again, with the shaker poised above her glass. "Oh, I shouldn't," she said. "I might get drunk."

"Why not, if you feel like it? You're among friends."

"Am I?" she asked. She felt such a longing for it to be true. But of course it wasn't. He was using that tired old gambit, plying her with liquor in the hope of catching her off guard, and she could not afford to let it happen. She must not forget that the only real bond between them was her fear.

"Sure you are." He cocked his head at her, smiling with every appearance of sincerity. "You've been talking to me as if you thought I was a friend. Believe me, Lucy, that's what I want to be, if you'll let me, if you'll stop shying away from me ..." He put his hand over hers, in a gesture that was as spontaneous as an affectionate child's. But she stiffened under it. It sent little tingling rays, like electricity, running up the inside of her arm. Fear? Of course, fear. He gave no sign of noticing. A final pat, and then he sprang up. "I'm going to fix us a little dividend. All we've got here is ice water. Okay?"

"A very small dividend," she said, and while he was in the bathroom getting more ice she crossed the room to peer at the books on his bookshelf. She was glad of the chance to compose herself. Not that she felt in the least drunk. But somehow rattled. I must change the subject, she thought; something impersonal; lightweight cocktail chit-chat, only I've never been much good at that sort of thing, maybe I can get him to talking about his work ...

She pulled out a thick volume on photography—and there it was, stuck back of the row of books. Pam's diary. Her hand jerked forward and closed on it, and at the same moment she heard Chuck's voice behind her. "Here we are—What's the matter? What are you doing?"

The photography book thumped to the floor as she whirled to face him. She still clutched the diary. No hopes of hiding it. His eyes, fastening on it, seemed to narrow with suspicion. All right, let him think she had been snooping; it was no worse than what he had done. "You lied to me," she said sharply. "You told me you gave this to Pam's mother."

"What? Oh. The diary." Back came his easy smile. "I did give it to her. And she gave it back to me. For a keepsake. Something to remember Pam by. She knew of course how I felt about Pam." Still holding the cocktail shaker, he came over and plucked the diary out of her hand. A casual gesture. But there was something reverent, almost caressing, about the way he held the book itself. "Don't look at me like that, Lucy. Why should I lie to you about Pam's diary, of all things? Why should it matter, who has it? After all, there's nothing important in it, nothing of any interest except to somebody like me—"

He stopped, staring at her, curiously at first, then with dawning comprehension. And she could only stare back, too panicky to utter a word. "So that's it," he said softly. "I just took it for granted you knew. Sure, it was supposed to be a secret, but those things always get around. I figured of course you knew all about it. You didn't, though. At least not for sure. That's it. Isn't it?"

"I don't know what you mean," she quavered.

"Come on now, baby, no need to be cagey with me." He tucked the diary under his cocktail shaker arm; his free hand closed on Lucy's shoulder, gently steering her back to the couch. "You're no dope. You had a damn good idea there was something cooking with Pam and your father. You saw that picture of them. That night club shot. It must have tipped you off, even if you didn't know before."

"No. I—It could have been just some special doctors' meeting or social affair, quite often Daddy took his nurse along—"

"Yeah. Sure. But what about the accident itself, where it happened? You think there was some special doctors' meeting up in Connecticut they were headed for? You must have gotten the message then. Only you didn't know how much was cooking. And that's where the diary comes in. I couldn't figure it out before. I knew it. I just took it for granted you did too."

"Knew what?" Because he obviously expected her to say something.

"Why, that they were planning to get married."

"What?" She tried to laugh. "You can't be serious! It's too fantastic, the idea that Daddy—"

"Okay, fantastic to you. But not to them. I wouldn't kid you, Lucy. It was all set. Honeymoon in Paris. The works." He tapped the diary. "It's all here. Just as you suspected. You don't have to read it now. I've told you. If I'd realized you didn't already know, I'd have told you at the start. Hell, I don't blame you for being curious. Only natural. Not that it makes any difference now what they were planning. Still and all, he was your father, you're entitled ..."

If only she could be sure that was all the diary contained! He had dreamed up such an unexpectedly plausible excuse for her interest in it. But could she trust him? He might only be baiting her, leading her to believe she was safe so that he could put the real pressure on her at some future time that suited him better. There it was, the poison-green volume, fat with its secrets, and here in her lap were her hands, clenched against the impulse to snatch it. To think that she had actually had it in her grasp for a moment, might have—if she had been quicker and brighter—managed to smuggle it out somehow or other! Or if she had even kept him from knowing she had seen it, so that she could come back for it later, when he was out of the house. Now he had the chance, in case he wanted it, of hiding it where she might never find it.

"I still can't believe it," she brought out finally. She looked up into his face, seemingly so open and sympathetic, and felt again the treacherous longing to trust him. "Surely Daddy would have told us. Maybe she just made it up? Kind of a daydream—"

"Not Pam. She wasn't the type. Both feet on the ground, that was Pam. Don't get me wrong. Chances are she really flipped over your father, even if he was quite a bit older. Sure she did, she wouldn't have been planning to marry him otherwise. I don't care what anybody says, it wasn't just the money." He floundered to a stop. His eyes shifted away from Lucy's.

"I didn't say it was."

"No, but it crossed your mind. Bound to. If I thought it would convince you to read the diary—" Her heart leaped with hope. But then he shook his head. "Nope. It wouldn't be fair to you or Pam, either one. You'd take some of it the wrong way. After all, you're only human, you've got feelings. Can't expect you to see Pam's side of it. I know how I'd feel if it was my old man. All it would do, it would put Pam in a poor light, and upset you, and what's the sense of that? You've had just about all you can take as it is." He crossed to the chest of drawers and thrust the diary out of sight. "There. That's the end of the whole business. I'm going to forget it. How about you?"

"I'll try." She put her hands up to her temples, conscious of her own pathos. "It's just that it's been a shock—"

"Poor Lucy." Again it was so spontaneous: suddenly he was beside her on the couch, one warm hand clasping both of hers, his arm around her, while the tingling rays blazed through her. She felt his breath against her ear, the male scrape of his cheek, and then yes, his mouth pressing against hers tenderly, fiercely, masterfully. She had forgotten what a kiss was, she had never known ...

She drew away, shivering.

"I've been wanting to do that ever since I first saw you," he whispered. "You knew it. Didn't you? Sure you did. Don't shy away from me, Lucy. You know I'll never do anything to hurt you. Don't be scared of me."

"I'm not scared of you." She wanted it to be true, for a moment it was true. Fear was what she had called it because she had forgotten what a kiss was. Fear was what she had fabricated out of her guilty imagination.

"That's all you can say, you're not scared of me? You don't like me or anything crazy like that?"

"Well, of course I like you, I just—"

"Now don't go spoiling it. I'll settle for that, for tonight anyway. Matter of fact, I'll drink to it." As he clicked his glass against hers, he added in a different tone, soft and humble, "Because I love you, Lucy. You're not like anybody I ever knew. You're the most wonderful thing that ever happened to me. Ever. In all my life. Let's drink to us."

"To us," she echoed. Her head lifted proudly. She felt radiant and powerful.

"Oops," Marcia said when she banged her head getting out of the cab. "Ceiling's low tonight, isn't it?"

"Watch yourself, Miss. Don't squash them watchacallems on your hat. Them poppies."

"Amenomes. I mean anemones. Poppies, the man says!" She and the cab driver had argued the subject companionably all the way downtown. He was a nice guy, the cab driver.

"So I'm not a gardener. Thanks, Miss. Take it easy now."

A very nice guy. He waited to see that she was safely up the steps and had the door unlocked before he drove off. As Joe had instructed him to do; Joe was apt to get very protective and punctilious on occasions, like tonight, when he couldn't see her home in person. They had cut it so fine that there was just time for him to make the last train. What with one more for the road, et cetera. So he had instructed the cab driver because get right down to it, Marcia thought expansively, Joe was a pretty nice guy himself, and here she was, safe home, never mind the time ...

Quiet. Do not disturb the household. Funny, how she still thought of His Nibs as being part of the household; in fact, the part that must especially not be disturbed. No danger now, of course. She paused, steadying herself for the climb up the stairway. How still it was, ghostly still, and her face looking back at her from the hall mirror was ghostly too, under the conversation-piece hat. She straightened it gravely. Amenomes. No. Anyway, not poppies.

It startled her absurdly to see, beyond the extravagance of hat, the office door opening. A man was standing there, silhouetted against the dim light. She knew perfectly well it must be Chuck. But she froze. She could not have turned around to save her life.

"Who—Oh, it's you, Marcia." Chuck, of course. Who else? "Hey, you scared me. I thought we had burglars or something."

"Small world. You scared me too." What made it an even smaller world was her impression that Chuck had had a drink or two himself. Not that he was looped, or anywhere near it. Lots of people wouldn't have noticed. Marcia happened to be in just the right mood to recognize the signs: a touch of grandeur in the way he handled his cigarette, a slight extra precision in his speech. Her heart warmed to him.

"Get a load of the hat. Terrific!" he said. And then, "So you had to work late tonight, eh? Nice work if you can get it."

Oh dear. His house-warming party. It had slipped her mind. "That's the trouble with lying," she said. "It's so embarrassing when you get caught. But it seemed like a good idea at the time. You've got to admit, 'I can't come to your party because I have to work late' sounds better than 'I can't come to your party because I'—well, because—"

"Yeah. You got a better offer. How you going to make that sound polite?" He grinned at her. He wasn't a bad guy, Chuck. Just out to work all the angles. "You don't deserve another chance. But I'm a good kid. How about a nightcap?"

"Why not?" She was going to feel like death warmed over tomorrow, anyway. Right now she felt great. What a shame to waste this fine, rare edge. Besides, she was curious. "Did you and Lucy get the house nicely warmed?"

It would seem so, from the looks of the living room. He hadn't gotten around to clearing away the plate of shrivelled canapés, the cocktail shaker and the rings it had made on the card table, or the ashtrays, which were all heaped with dead cigarettes.

"We missed you." He gave her a sidelong glance, rather like a wink. "After you called, Lucy showed signs of running out on me too. I had to do some fast talking to persuade her."

"You're the boy to do it. Never at a loss for words."

"Well, hardly ever. Straight shot okay with you? Say when."

"That's the thing about you. When. You may be a phoney, but you're honest about it. A genuine phoney, if you know what I mean."

"Gee, thanks. So tell me something, as long as we're on this frank and earnest kick. What's with Lucy? Why should she be scared of me?"

"For one thing, you're a man. Lucy's leery of all men. She's not used to them. She's led a sheltered life, if you know what I mean."

There was a moment of silence, as if they—or at least Chuck—were paying homage to this awesome phenomenon, a virgin in her thirties.

"You shouldn't take it personally," Marcia added. Really, she thought, she was being pretty adroit about the whole business. Pretty clever. Of course it was halfway the truth. "And another thing, you're a stranger, somebody she never heard of till all at once you dropped in out of the blue."

"Well, but I said right at the start I was a friend of Pam's."

"Anybody could have said that. Besides—"

"I know. She hardly knew Pam." Lucy must have protested a bit too much on that point. "The funny part of it is, she isn't scared of me all the time. Just sometimes. Then again she'll open up and talk up a storm, you'd think she'd known me all her life. Like tonight."

"Oh?" Marcia had a sudden hollow feeling. "You mean she got on a talking jag?"

"I guess you'd call it that. Anyway, she told me the whole story."

"Oh no," Marcia said involuntarily. She stared into his slightly battered face, topped by the rakish, graying crew cut. He stared back, all bright inquiry, like a fox terrier waiting for the ball to be thrown. The whole story. Lucy had told him the whole story. And she was the one who had worried about what Marcia might let slip, with a few drinks inside her and no Lucy around to shut her up. She was the one who—Never mind that. Set to and find a way—how? how?—to repair the damage. "No look, Chuck, you didn't take it seriously, everything she said. Did you?"

"Why not?"

"Well, it's a little hard to explain, without making Lucy sound like a liar. She isn't exactly. It's more—fabrication. You know. Fantasies. She's always been like that."

"Sure. Aren't we all?" He was still waiting—head cocked, ears pricked, eyes bright.

"And then she's not used to drinking much. So when she does have a couple, she's apt to get carried away. I said before, she's led a sheltered life, and she has. She's like a child in a way, she doesn't always distinguish between reality and imagination. It's partly the way she was raised. Too much father. She's not like me, she never got away from him at all. Not that I did entirely, but still—Actually, Lucy was devoted to him."

Chuck nodded wisely. "That's why she took it so hard, about him and Pam."

Marcia closed her eyes. Oh gawd, the whole story. "It gave me quite a turn, too. I admit it. And then the shock of his death. Their deaths. But really, Chuck, you see what I mean about fantasies. This blackmail notion of hers, for instance. Pure nonsense, how could anybody blackmail us? But try and convince Lucy. She'll get back on the beam in time. She always does. Oh dear, I'm making her sound like an absolute psycho, and she isn't at all, she just ..."

She could not have said what warned her. His expression did not change, his attitude remained the same. Too much the same, maybe. There was something unnatural about such complete stillness, such intentness. What had become of her heart-warming first impression, that he had a slight flicker on? For that matter, what had become of her own expansive glow? In its place there was this chilling sense of peril. One more word—and God help her, how did she know she hadn't already said it?—and over the brink she would plunge.

"So Lucy fabricates," he said thoughtfully. "You mean she made Bernie up out of whole cloth?"

In the nick of time she swallowed her gasp of astonished relief. *Bernie!* The whole story, she had thought, and all the time it was only Bernie, Lucy's forlorn little skirmish with romance. So long ago, so far away. Typical of Lucy in her cups, to trot him out for Chuck's benefit. And without even knowing why, poor soul; she was still unaware of the fact that she had a crush on Chuck, she thought all the shivers and flutters were fear.

"Oh, I wouldn't go that far." She took a sip of nightcap to settle her nerves. The thought of how close she had come to giving the show away made her hair stand on end. Well, she hadn't done it. Maybe an indiscreet word or two—she wasn't too clear, at the moment, as to just what she had said—but nothing irrevocable. She was pretty sure. "There was a real live Bernie, all right. I doubt very much if they ever got beyond the hand holding stage. But Lucy's blown it up in her mind until it's a big deal. Romeo and Juliet. Eternal love. All like that. It's kind of a perennial daydream. No particular harm in it, I suppose. Only ..."

"Only it's a hell of a way for Lucy to spend her life. Daydreaming over some shmo that didn't work out instead of finding herself one that would. I ask you, what kind of a life is that?"

"Not very peppy," said Marcia. "But at least she still believes in love." She gave him a stern look. "And don't you forget it, Mr. C. Gordon Llewellyn."

"All right," he said peaceably. "I believe in love myself. Don't you? Sure you do. It happens all the time. To the most unlikely people. I mean, people that at first glance you wouldn't think they'd have anything in common. All at once whammo, it hits them and—"

"You can skip the sales talk. It's wasted on me. Because I know what you're up to, Chuck, I'm on to your little game." She straightened her hat and stood up.

"Well, bully for you." Quite unabashed. There it was again: she couldn't help liking him. "So you know there's nothing to worry about. On the contrary. My intentions, Madame, are strictly honorable."

IX

"I'm exhausted," La Traviata announced vigorously. "Absolutely exhausted, my dear. Didn't get any good sound sleep until past three o'-clock. I declare, I don't understand what Marcia and Lucy could have been discussing at that hour of the night, but they went on, and on, and on."

"I didn't hear anything," said Mrs. Sully.

"You wouldn't, being on the top floor. And then I've always been such a light sleeper. Mr. Travers used to say if there was nothing else to keep me awake I'd imagine I heard the house plants growing. It's awful, being so highstrung."

Mrs. Sully produced the commiserating sound that was expected of her. But that was all. I will not ask, she repeated to herself. I am not going to gossip.

"I wouldn't dream of mentioning it to either Marcia or Lucy, of course. It's not as if they were quarreling. At least I don't think they were quarreling." She paused, but Mrs. Sully's resolve held firm. "Certainly nothing like what used to go on with Marcia and the doctor. And yet I had this strange feeling of—well, antagonism. As if they were on the *verge* of quarreling, if you know what I mean."

"Cherie," said Mrs. Sully. "Behave yourself."

"As I say, I simply can't understand why they should be discussing Chuck—Mr. Llewellyn—so exhaustively, at that hour of the night. Can you?"

"Chuck?" It slipped out. "I mean, are you sure you—"

"Oh, I heard that much of it. It was something to do with Chuck, all right. His name came up time after time."

"Then I don't think they could have been quarreling. They both like Chuck."

"I know, dear. I couldn't help wondering last night if that might not be the point. It might be, you know, if they both like Chuck enough."

"Ridiculous," said Mrs. Sully firmly. Poor silly Lucy was capable of getting romantic ideas about Chuck. But Marcia? Ridiculous.

"I expect you're right," La Traviata conceded. "I got the impression Marcia had had a nightcap with him before she came upstairs. Not that she needed it, from the sound of her. Lucy kept trying to shush her. I found it extremely upsetting, I suppose because they've always seemed so close."

Or because you couldn't hear as much as you'd like to, Mrs. Sully thought snappishly. All her good intentions, and yet she had let La Traviata trap her into another gossip session. No will power. She turned, intending to escape, and here came Hansen from across the street. Great. Just great. He was all they needed. And to make it perfect he was hauling something, a cumbersome contraption that rang an obscure, unpleasant bell in Mrs. Sully's memory. Something connected with a rainy day, and Lucy, Lucy crying and Hansen smirking ...

As he was smirking now. "Evening ladies." He padded toward them, thick, slow-moving, and unpredictable in an animal way: harmless as long as nobody interfered with him, possibly dangerous if roused. "Happen to know if Miss Lucy's home?"

"I don't know, I'm sure," said La Traviata grandly. Chrys and Mum went off into one of their fits of shrill yapping; Hansen was apt to affect them that way. On the other hand, Cherie seemed delighted to see him. To Mrs. Sully's embarrassment; she tightened her grip on the leash and waited for him to pass on.

Instead, he set down his burden, hitched up his pants, and shifted his after-dinner toothpick from one corner of his mouth to the other. His mean little eyes glinted at them. "That's some classy super they got now, ain't he? No wonder they fired me. I was okay till he came along. Then they couldn't get rid of me fast enough."

"It's their business. They've got a right to make a change if they want to," said Mrs. Sully. Gas heater, she thought, just an antiquated gas heater. Why should Lucy get upset? Why should Hansen be returning the thing, if that was what he was doing?

"Sure. It's their business. Oh, sure. Funny business, if you ask me. I see he's moved in bag and baggage. Making himself right at home. Wonder which one he's got his eye on? Hard to choose between them. Miss Lucy's crazy, and the other one's a drunk—"

"How dare you!" cried La Traviata. (Mrs. Sully was shocked into temporary speechlessness.) "This is absolutely outrageous. I refuse to listen to another word. You—you lout! You ought to be reported to the authorities. They could have you arrested for slander."

"Yes, and don't think Marcia won't do it, too, when she finds out what you've been saying." Mrs. Sully had her voice back, shaky but fierce.

"You want to bet on that?" He gave a gurgling laugh and picked up the heater. "If anybody gets arrested it ain't going to be me."

"You'll see! I'm going to tell Marcia—"

"Save your breath," Hansen said over his shoulder, as he padded on toward the stoop. The setting sun struck gleams from the heater, and outlined his hulking shape in a golden dazzle. "I'll tell her myself. Both of them. And lemme tell you something, too. If you know what's good for you you'll move out of there while you're still able to. You couldn't pay me to live in the same house with them two. I'd be scared I'd wake up dead."

They watched in fascinated silence while he shambled up the steps and into the vestibule. The whir of the door bell reached them, insolent and demanding.

La Traviata's plump hand reached for Mrs. Sully's. "I don't understand," she whispered. Her chins were quivering.

"Spite," croaked Mrs. Sully. "That's all it is. Sheer spite." But even when she closed her eyes she could still see the image of Lucy's face fixed forever in the fanatic glare of hatred.

From the sitting room, where she was stretched out in the big chair with her feet up, Marcia heard the departure of Mrs. Sully and Cherie, Mrs. Travers and the Pekes. There. Now she was all alone in the house. For she had come home from work to find Lucy and Chuck gone—"out to dinner, home early," according to Lucy's note. That would show Marcia, in case she didn't already know, just how far she had gotten with last night's attempt to explain the facts of life to Lucy. Well, she should have known better, than to try when she was half-lit. She had known better, only when she came up the stairs there was Lucy, frantic with suspicion, waiting to pounce. What had Marcia and Chuck been doing down there for the last half hour? Talking about Lucy. Hadn't they? Hadn't they? What had he told her? What had she told him? Everything no doubt. And a lot of lies about Lucy besides. Because Marcia wanted him for herself, she couldn't bear seeing Lucy happy even for a moment ...

What a shambles!

And there was more. One other zany touch. Lucy still clung to the notion that Chuck was bent on blackmail. Something about that damn diary again. Marcia couldn't sort it out. For that matter, after the hassle with Lucy she would probably never get the details of her conversation with Chuck sorted out, either. Only the word blackmail sent a twang along her nerves. Never mind, let it go, blackmail was not Chuck's little game.

That was how last night had wound up, with Marcia maneuvered into defending Chuck against the charge of blackmail instead of exposing him as a fortune hunter. So much for sisterly responsibility.

She was too beat to care. Let them marry—Chuck for money, Lucy for what she called love. They might live happily ever after, at that.

Happily. Happiness. Lucy still believed in those words; happiness was still a possibility to her. She too had planned murder, but it did not have the same reality for her, she did not see what was so calamitously clear to Marcia—that there was no difference between planning and doing. She had always had a talent for self-delusion, lucky Lucy. Give her enough time, and she would transmute their terrible plan into a harmless fantasy; shrug off the weight of guilt that hung around her neck; live happily ever after.

But not me, thought Marcia. Time won't help me. Nothing will. I am a terminal case. Incurable.

And she was all alone in the house. Why should she be so aware of it? Surely it was not the first time in her life? But she had a trembly feeling, as if she had reached some secret goal that she would recognize in just a moment, any second now ...

The room seemed to hold its breath. So still, so still. So shut off from the commonplace bustle outside: muffled rush of traffic, someone whistling, someone laughing, a remote television voice. The last of the sun's rays slanted out there, gilding the ailanthus leaves in her little garden. But here, with none of the lights turned on, she was marooned in dusk and spreading shadows. Darkness stealing in on her, and she was alone in the house, there was no one to stop her ...

From what?

I ought to turn on the lights, she thought. But she made no move to do so. Darkness was where she belonged, she welcomed it, she yearned to be engulfed, to be dissolved in it. The little makeshift respites of sleep and drink—what use were they? They did not last. But there was another darkness that at this very moment was moving toward her, closer, almost close enough to touch. The thrill of recognition leaped in her. Yes. Here was her goal: the final darkness.

She felt suddenly light and free, as if already she were rid of the weight she had hung around her neck with her own hands. Her own hands. She stretched them out in front of her; they were like his, strong, quick hands, clever-looking. Capable of so much, and yet they had accomplished so little. (It has to be with your hands or it doesn't count. They don't arrest you for thinking murder.) One more service, that was all she required of them. Then the darkness could dissolve them too. A very small service, one they had performed hundreds of times before. A simple twist of the gas jet. Well. And a few equally simple preparatory measures. She sprang up, light as a bird. Close the window; wedge the door shut, towels or newspapers would do it, that way Lucy would realize—

Lucy. She had a glimpse of how it would seem to Lucy, who all her life had been the timid one; Lucy the leaner, the clinger, the follower-of-the-leader. How lost she would feel, utterly abandoned—and for no reason that she could comprehend. It was not as if Marcia had anything to lose, while Lucy—Lucy was not incurable. She could be saved. So easily; it would take only a slight tinkering with the truth to set Lucy on the path of comforting self-delusion. She would take Marcia's word for it, partly from habit, partly because it was what she wanted to believe.

So why not? thought Marcia. She sat down at Mama's little writing desk—irritated, as always by its useless daintiness, it shuddered with every stroke of the pen—found a sheet of paper, and began. "Lucy dear, I started it, and now I'm ending it. You are not to blame. Remember that." She underlined boldly; that made it even bossier. "It doesn't matter that you talked about it. You would never have killed him." More underlining. "I would have. So the guilt is mine. That's why—"

The door bell pealed. She resolved to pay no attention. "—I can't go on living," she wrote. (Corny. But what were you going to do?) "Because I'm stuck with my left-over murder, and this is the only way I can get rid of it."

Persistent, whoever it was at the door bell. The peals continued, shrill and demanding and tireless. It was impossible to ignore them. Besides, the damage was already done; the first one had ripped through the fabric of her aloneness.

She got up and went quickly down the dim twilit hall. The feeling of bird-lightness was gone; she was trembling with tension. "Stop that noise," she said, when she opened the door and saw Hansen. She might have known. Typical of his thick-headedness, his insolence, to keep on ringing like that, long after a person with any decency would have given up and gone away. "What do you want?"

He was smiling slyly. "Miss Lucy home?"

"No, she isn't." She started to close the door, but he thrust his foot out—clumsily but effectively—and shoved with his shoulder. He was inside, close enough so she could smell him.

"You'll do then," he said.

"Well, you won't. You've got no business pushing in here. Get out." He stood immovable, and now she saw that he was lugging something. "What's that?" she asked sharply. But she already knew.

"Belongs to Miss Lucy. I thought I'd return it, now that I ain't working for you anymore."

"We don't want it. Lucy told you that. She told you to throw it away."

"Maybe she changed her mind." His smile grew even slyer. "Nothing wrong with it that I can see. Can't tell when it might come in handy. I wouldn't want it myself, but—"

"Then get rid of it."

"Oh, I wouldn't want to do that," he said sanctimoniously. "Not without Miss Lucy's say so. I'll bring it back some time when she's here."

"That won't be necessary. You can leave it now. We'll dispose of it ourselves and save you the bother."

"Bother? What bother? Glad to take care of it for you." His face creased in an oily parody of amiability. "No sense cluttering up your place with it if Miss Lucy don't want it. Meantime, long as I'm here, maybe you've got a minute to spare? For a little private visit?"

It was a mistake to hesitate—the glint of malicious triumph in his eyes told her that he had been sounding her out, hoping for some sign of uncertainty—and yet how could she help it? Her frayed nerves vibrated between the impulse to order him off the premises and the need to find out what he had come for. (If, indeed, he knew himself; he might be acting from blind spite. Probably was.)

"I'm busy just now," she began, but she had waited too long. He was already moving toward her, unhurried and unswerving as a tank. There was not room to get past him and the gas heater and make for the front door. If she stood still he would run her down. She was forced into a series of humiliating backward steps that brought her at last to the sitting room door. No chance to slam it in his face; he pressed in, practically on her toes.

She switched on the lamp and steadied herself against the big chair. She was not afraid; only tired. Hansen must not know how tired. To Hansen she must seem as cool and assured as ever. In haughty silence she waited for him to explain.

He set the gas heater down on the floor and stood lumpishly, his hostile little eyes fixed on her. "You think you're somebody, don't you? Think you can fire me, just like that, any time you feel like it, and I'll take it laying down. Well, I won't. I don't have to take nothing off of you. Nothing. Understand?"

"I'm not sure I do. If we had any kind of a contract I wasn't aware of it. I paid you two weeks wages when I gave you notice, and you seemed satisfied at the time. Have you decided you're entitled to more money?" There, she thought. If he was aiming at blackmail, he couldn't ask for a better opening.

But he did not take it. "It ain't the money," he said. He removed the toothpick from his mouth and stashed it thriftily behind his ear. "I got plenty to do without your lousy little job. I wouldn't work for you now no matter how much you offered to pay me."

"Fine. Because I have no intention of ever offering you a penny. So just what is your complaint?"

She watched contemptuously while his slow mind fumbled for an answer. Unfocused spite, just as she had thought. Him and his little private visit! It was getting him nowhere, and they both knew it. Only a lug like Hansen would have tried it. But of course he had been counting on Lucy. She turned her back on him. Went over to the desk and picked up the letter she had started to Lucy. I can't go on living ... Not only corny. Fantastic.

"No, you wouldn't offer me a penny." Hansen's voice, always guttural, thickened even more with rage. "I'm not good enough for you. But *he* moves right in and makes himself at home. Office space, living space—you can't offer him enough, can you? You think you're so much. Ordering me around. Putting on airs. Well, you're not fooling me any. I know a drunk when I see one. And that's not all—"

"It's enough, though." Strange, how little it bothered her. The truth was supposed to hurt. But he was such a stupid, clumsy, neckless brute—Yes, and cowardly, too, he was backing away as she advanced on him; comically scared of her and of what he had dared to say. "Now get out. I'm not interested in anything you know or don't know. Get out of here and stay out."

"You'll be sorry for this. You'll see. There's plenty I can tell if I want to. I know what you were up to, the both of you." He paused, and when he saw that he had still not dented her composure, he lost his head and blurted it out. "Murder, that's what."

Again the look of comic alarm. It saved Marcia; she laughed in genuine amusement. "Murder, did you say? Don't tell me, let me guess. Who, Hansen? Who did we murder?"

His mean little eyes shifted. So did his mean little mind, groping for a way to get at her, and not finding it. He muttered darkly. "Go ahead. Laugh. But I know what the score is. I could tell plenty—"

"You do that. You go right ahead and tell anybody you want to. Murder! Let me know if anybody believes you. Go on, don't let me keep you. Beat it." She marched across to the door and flung it open imperiously.

Lucy was there, bright-eyed, smiling a little, her hand reaching for the knob. "Hi, Marsh—" she began. Then she saw Hansen, and the pink glow faded, leaving her face pinched and gray. She cast a fearful glance over her shoulder. "I'll be with you in a minute, Chuck," she called, and Marcia caught a glimpse of him coming in the front door before Lucy whisked inside the sitting room and slammed the door behind her. She shrank against it, staring in terror at the gas heater.

Marcia's heart sank. But she made a stab at salvaging the situation. "Hansen's just leaving," she said, with false assurance.

It was hopeless; Hansen had no intention of leaving now that Lucy was here. He had what he wanted: somebody he could bully. The malicious, triumphant gleam was back in his eyes. He put on a falsetto imitation of Lucy's voice. "Oh yes, Chuck, I'll be with you in a minute, Chuck. So don't you go away, Loverboy Chuck ..." He chortled, transported by his own wit.

"Very funny," said Marcia. "Goodbye now."

"I told you I knew what the score was. Didn't I?"

"And I told you I wasn't interested."

"Yeah. But I bet Miss Lucy is." He leered. "Right, Miss Lucy? What's the matter? Scared it'll bite you?" He gave the heater a companionable kick. "I remember now, you said it wouldn't be safe. But I thought maybe you'd changed your mind. That's why I brought it back. You've got Chuck now, he can show you how to tell the water from the gas pipes."

Lucy's lips moved stilly. But no sound came out.

"What? You mean he don't know about the gas heater?" He gave a fat, gurgling laugh. "Well, now. It ain't right, to hold out on Loverboy Chuck like that. Why, he's practically one of the family. You just leave it to me. I'll tell him, if you're too bashful. Be glad to. I know he'll be interested. Couple of other things I can tell him, too. Things I heard before your sister got smart and fired me. Like the day I heard the two of you talking about murder—" He stooped to pick up the heater.

So he did not see Lucy dart across the room to the fireplace and snatch up the poker. He did not see her face as she went for him. Marcia did; it was she who alerted him by shrieking Lucy's name, she who saved him by grabbing Lucy's wrists, upraised for the savage blow.

"I'll kill you! Don't you dare tell him. I'll kill you! Marsh, let go of me, damn you, damn you, let me go ..." What fanatic strength there was in those slender arms, in that soft-looking body! It was all Marcia could do to hold her. And the ugly, fanatic face, nothing like Lucy's ...

Over her shoulder Marcia caught a glimpse of Hansen lumbering out the door in ludicrous, bear-like haste. Scared for sure this time; scared out of his few thick wits. A moment later, and the frantic struggle with Lucy was over. She went boneless in Marcia's arms, the poker thumped to the floor, her face was Lucy's again, weak and familiar, with quivering lips and eyes brimming tears.

"Is he gone?" she whispered.

"He's gone, all right." Marcia steered her over to the big chair and lowered her into it. She felt a sudden deep sadness. There was a sheet of paper on the rug—Oh yes, her letter to Lucy. Wouldn't do to leave it lying around loose. Automatically she bent and picked it up, tucked it into her purse, which she had tossed on the settee when she came in. Later. She would destroy it later, when Lucy wasn't around to notice and wonder.

Lucy slumped back in the chair, spineless as a rag doll. The easy tears still spilled out from under her half-closed eyelids. Yet she was smiling too, a queer mixture of shyness and pride. "I guess that will teach him. Won't it, Marsh? I guess I showed him ..."

"That's right," said Marcia absently. So right. So mortally right. And trust Hansen's cunning little animal brain to make the most of what Lucy had revealed—that murder in the Knapp household was by no means impossible, or even unlikely; and that the one sure way of evening the score was through Loverboy Chuck. Left to himself—and Marcia—he might not have thought of it. But thanks to Lucy, he knew exactly where to take his scraps of information, and what Chuck would make of them was anybody's guess.

Marcia sighed. "Let's have a drink," she said, and headed for the bottle.

X

After a while Lucy sat up, cautiously—for she had a not unpleasant, drained feeling, as if she were recovering from an illness—and took a sip of her drink. Out of politeness; because Marcia had poured it for her, and it seemed to her that Marcia was in a rather peculiar mood. Unusually quiet. Remote. But then everything seemed remote. There was a glaze between her and reality. Had Hansen actually been here, had she actually ...? Yes. The gas heater, squatting there on the rug, proved it. And the poker. She averted her eyes from both.

Well, she had settled Hansen's hash. Hadn't she? She would have liked to ask again, just to make sure. Only she was afraid of irritating Marcia. Besides, it was unnecessary. Of course she had settled Hansen's hash. He wouldn't dare show his face around here after this.

She could not, after all, resist: "We don't need to worry now, do we? I scared him out of telling Chuck—" Chuck. She stopped, remembering the precarious, incredulous excitement that had brought her flying down the hall, bursting to tell Marcia. Joy? Fear? It was neither. It was both. "Marsh," she said tremulously. "I've got something to tell you, Marsh." She did not know how to say it. And Marcia was no help; she was standing at the window, gazing out at the gathering darkness. "It's about Chuck."

"I know," said Marcia without turning around. "He asked you to marry him."

"You—How did you know?"

"I'm psychic."

She's jealous, she wants him for herself, Lucy thought. (As she had thought last night, waiting at the top of the stairs, boiling with suspicion, while Chuck and Marcia murmured down there.) She's always had beaus of her own, plenty of them. Yet she begrudges me even this one dubious little chance at romance ...

"I'm only teasing," Marcia turned, smiling the way she did when she was ashamed of herself. "But I'd have to be pretty dumb, not to guess after last night. He as good as told me what he had in mind."

"He did? What did he say?"

"Good Lord, Lucy, I don't remember his exact words! But I gathered his intentions were honorable. If you hadn't been in such a snit when I came upstairs, I'd have told you so."

"I'm sorry I was so impossible, Marsh. All those awful things I said to you! I don't know what possessed me."

"It's sometimes referred to as sex," said Marcia. "There are those who claim it makes the world go round."

"You think that's all it is with Chuck? Just—just physical attraction?"

Marcia gave a short laugh. "I rather doubt it. I never had a man ask me to marry him when all he wanted was to go to bed with me."

"Oh well, if you're going to take that attitude." Lucy's chin quivered. Marcia knew how she felt about such talk. Smarty. Vulgar. And to use it now, of all times, when she must realize how desperately Lucy needed a little sensible, sympathetic advice! Furthermore, when Lucy had just apologized for last night's outburst of suspicion. She wasn't so sure, now, that that apology had been called for.

"All right. Wrong attitude. Strike it from the record." She came over and sat down on the hassock at Lucy's feet. The light from the lamp struck one side of her face, picking out the drawn lines and giving her a sad, hollow-cheeked look. "I was just trying to show you how absurd—I'm sure it's more than physical attraction with Chuck. The point is, what is it with you?"

"With me?" Lucy felt the hot color rise in her neck. "Why, Marsh, you know I wouldn't—I'm not that kind. What a thing to say! It's just that I had such a funny feeling about Chuck at first, the way he came barging in with his story about Pam. If only he hadn't been connected with her!"

"You'd never have met him, except for Pam," Marcia pointed out.

"I know. But I can't quite get it out of my mind. I keep wondering if they're really true, the things he tells me, or if it's only because I *want* them to be true ..." She stared into Marcia's face hungrily. "Marsh, do you think he really loves me? I mean really?"

Marcia took a drag on her cigarette. "It's a possibility," she said drily. "Love. Don't ask me about love. It's out of my line."

"A possibility. But not the only possibility. That's what you mean, isn't it? He may be blackmailing me into marrying him because he knows about—"

"Oh, stop it, Lucy, I don't mean anything of the kind. You're being utterly ridiculous. If he really thought you were a murderer he'd be scared of you, he'd run like hell. Can't you see that?" Scared, thought Lucy. Like Hansen? He had been scared, he had run ... Relief welled up in her. Here was Marcia at her most comforting—brisk, bossy, impatient. "Marry him if you want to. What have you got to lose?"

There was a tap on the door, and Chuck's voice: "Lucy?" She jumped up and ran to the door; it was Marcia who thought to replace the poker in its stand beside the fireplace.

"You went off and left me," he said, and gave Lucy a special, private smile. "Hi, Marsh," he added, using Lucy's nickname for her for the first time. But in a nice, tentative way, as if he were proud to be trying out this added touch of familiarity. Marcia got the significance, all right; the glance she shot at him was sardonic.

He noticed the gas heater right away. "What's that thing?" And Lucy stood once more tongue-tied with terror.

Not Marcia. "Gas heater. Been in the family for years. Hansen was supposed to get rid of it weeks ago, but here he came hauling it back today. Just for kicks. He likes being a nuisance. How about a drink?"

"Sure. Fine. Listen, if he's giving you a hard time, that so-and-so, just say the word. I'll deal with him."

"Lucy already did. Scotch okay?"

"*Lucy?* Lucy dealt with him?"

"She did indeed." Lucy held her breath; surely, surely, Marcia was not going to be that reckless, that treacherous. "I've got news for you. She can be quite a spitfire, our Lucy, given the right circumstances. I must say, Hansen asked for it."

"What did you do, darling? Bite him?" It was all right; his eyes were dancing with amusement and admiration.

"I just—sent him on his way," Lucy said, with a spitfire toss of her head. "He'll think twice before he shows up around here again."

"And if he does, we all know what's eating on him. Pure, simple spite." Marcia handed Chuck his drink and lifted her own, with one of her unexpectedly radiant smiles. "Okay kids. What do I say? Bless you my children? Something along those lines? Not that I'm trying to rush you into anything—"

"So Lucy told you," said Chuck. Lucy blushed again, violently. I am happy, she thought. Marry him if you want to, what have you got to lose? "Sounds like she told you more than she did me. Because she left me sort of up in the air."

"Relax. You're all set for a happy landing. I hope."

For one bad moment it seemed to Lucy that she was being shut out of a secret. The look that passed between Marcia and Chuck was so knowing, so full of some meaning that escaped her. Then it came to her: he had been uncertain of Marcia's attitude, afraid she might weight the scales against him. She might have, too; they all three knew it. But she hadn't. That was all it was. What an innocent secret, after all!

"Lucy?" Chuck held out his hand to her, smiling tenderly, waiting for her answer. This was the way it ought to be, the way she had always dreamed it would be. I am making him the happiest of men, she thought as she floated toward him. It is really happening, I have found love at last.

"Excuse me if I choke up," said Marcia from the background. "It just gets me here."

"There's something I think you ought to know," Mrs. Sully blurted out. She was so obviously embarrassed that Marcia, whose patience was beginning to wear thin, couldn't help feeling sorry for her. "Or maybe La—Mrs. Travers has already spoken to you?"

"Haven't seen her all week," Marcia said crisply. Oh Lord, she thought, was she going to have to listen to another tenants' feud? Was that what Mrs. Sully had been leading up to for the past ten minutes? Then let her stop stammering and fidgeting and get *to* it! She had almost certainly been lying in wait for Marcia, watching from the hall, ready to pop out as soon as she saw Marcia turn the corner toward home. Never mind the fancy-meeting-you-here tone of her greeting. Cute as this kid was, she would never be an actress. An open-faced sandwich, if Marcia ever saw one.

"Oh. Well, then," said Mrs. Sully, and swallowed nervously.

"What's the trouble? You and Travers been having border incidents?"

"What? Oh no, it's nothing to do with us really." Another gulp, and Mrs. Sully took the plunge. "Only we both felt you ought to know, the tales he's been spreading. Hansen. The things he's saying about you."

It figured, of course. But Marcia's heart gave an extra beat. "Is that all it is? Hansen? He told me too. Called me a drunk. And maybe I am."

"Don't be silly. Of course you're not," said Mrs. Sully. A shade too quickly? "Anyway, that isn't the worst. Do you know what he's saying now? That—that Lucy tried to kill him! Can you imagine?"

Unfortunately, Marcia could. But she managed an incredulous laugh. "You're kidding! Me, maybe, but Lucy? She's such a scaredy-cat. It's too funny, to think of her threatening a lug like Hansen, attacking him with her bare hands—"

"A poker, he says." Mrs. Sully was giggling too. "Claims she went for him with the poker and he had to run for his life. It's all a pack of malicious lies, and I told him so. Mrs. Travers too. She said you could have him arrested for slander. You could, too."

"Why doesn't he call the police himself? Poor little defenseless Hansen, he needs protection. What a laugh!" She paused. Might as well shoot the works. "Did he say what set Lucy off? Or was it unprovoked, this attack of hers?"

"That's where it gets complicated." Some of the embarrassment came back to Mrs. Sully's pert little face. "It's something about an old gas heater. That was the first time he got going with his crazy talk, when he was lugging this heater back to you. To Lucy, rather. The second time was afterwards. Don't ask me what he meant, but he said—he talked as if he had something *on* you and Lucy, something terrible that he could tell if he wanted to—" She stopped. Her eyes skipped away from Marcia's. "He had said the word, then. Murder. And that's why Lucy went for him, he says, because she's afraid he'll tell Chuck. Mr. Llewellyn. You can guess what he's saying about her and Chuck."

"Yes," said Marcia. She knew what was called for: a softened version of the scene with Hansen, something plausible for Mrs. Sully to pass on to Travers. Not much of a trick, really. Mrs. Sully at least was already prejudiced against Hansen, she was anxious to believe, practically begging for reassurance ...

"It's just spite," she was saying sturdily. Putting the words in Marcia's mouth. "He's sore because you fired him. Anybody can see that."

"Yes," Marcia said again. She wet her lips, all set to go on. And then she saw Lucy down the block, coming home from one of her shopping expeditions. Lucy with the new lift to her head, the new spring to her step; trim and ladylike in her navy blue suit and white gloves and little veiled hat, "Sh. Here she comes. I mean—I'd rather you didn't mention any of this to Lucy. No point in upsetting her."

Mrs. Sully nodded and turned to watch Lucy too. Everybody waved.

After a moment she said, "Hey. What's the matter? What's she—"

A few yards away from them Lucy had stopped in her tracks, apparently transfixed by something across the street that had caught her attention. Her slender neck was thrust forward like a startled bird's; her whole attitude was so intent that with one accord Marcia and Mrs. Sully pivoted to see what it was she saw.

Well, thought Marcia. If it be now, 'tis not to come; if it be not to come, it will be now.

So it was now. Chuck and Hansen were emerging into the area-way of the house across the street, from the stairs that led down to Hansen's basement apartment. Only their heads were visible at first; they surfaced slowly, absorbed in conversation. Which wasn't surprising, either, considering what they were undoubtedly discussing. Hansen was pawing the air a bit. Chuck was making no unnecessary gestures. Too busy listening.

Until Lucy screeched at him. His name? Or just a wordless, savage protest? Anyway, it brought him bounding up the last few steps and across the street on the double. Mrs. Sully nearly jumped out of her skin, Cherie went off into a fit of shrill barking. Hansen, once he had located the source of the screech, scuttled back down the stairs, a groundhog scared by his own shadow and heading for the safety of his burrow,

Lucy stood on the curb and trembled. Marcia got to her first, for all the good it did her. Lucy neither saw nor heard her. Her eyes were so dilated that they looked almost black; once more her face was set in the strange, fierce glare; her hands in their white gloves were clenched and shaking uncontrollably. I've got to shut her up, Marcia thought in a panic, she's going to start screeching again in a minute, and this time they'll get the words: "I'll kill him! I'll kill him ..." But there was no holding her. She yanked herself free from Marcia.

Then she took one lunging step off the curb and collapsed—thank God, thank God—in a dead faint. Chuck got there just in time to catch her.

She had dropped her purse and packages. Automatically Marcia stooped to retrieve them. As she straightened up her glance fell on Mrs. Sully's face. It was white and blank as a sheet of paper. She had one hand up to her mouth, as if to hold back a scream. She looked like a child in the grip of a nightmare. Marcia had an impulse to comfort her.

It was better to say nothing. Better just to follow Chuck, who had started for the house, carrying his lady love, Scaredy-cat Lucy, so limp and helpless and harmless. So murderous. But she hadn't actually said the words. With luck, Marcia might still be able to save the situation.

Get Chuck off stage for that crucial moment when Lucy would come to. Shake some sanity back into her, explain away Hansen's story—crazy, spiteful—she had already laid the foundation for that the other night, the betrothal night, knowing as she did that nothing on earth was going to keep Hansen's mouth shut ...

Marcia squared her shoulders and clicked up the steps behind Chuck. "Into the sitting room," she told him, and her voice had not lost its ring of authority, even though she was so mortally tired. "Don't look so scared, I know what to do. She's had these fainting spells before. It's just nerves."

Once Lucy was laid out on the settee, she sent him upstairs for the smelling salts. "They're probably on her dressing table." Delaying action. "Or else the medicine cabinet in our bathroom." He was off like a shot. Damn it. But she couldn't very well tell him to take his time. She got a wet towel from the kitchen and slapped it hard against Lucy's face, which was clammy with sweat. Again. And again. At last the eyelids, delicate as tissue paper, began to quiver, the drooping lips tightened, the slim throat worked as Lucy sighed, swallowed, struggled back to consciousness. Her head rolled from side to side. Then suddenly her eyes were wide open and staring straight up at Marcia. They still had that glare. She heaved herself up onto her elbows.

"Hansen," she whispered hoarsely. "Where is he? I'll—"

Whack went the towel across her mouth. Tears sprang into her eyes, and she fell back with a piteous little moan. There. That was more like it.

"Shut up," said Marcia. From the upstairs hall came the hurrying thud of Chuck's footsteps: Now he was on the stairs. "You hear me, Lucy? Shut up. I'll do the talking. Understand?"

It had worked all their lives, and it worked now. Marcia would lead. Lucy would follow. She made a mewing sound of submission, perhaps of gratitude. When Chuck came tearing in with the smelling salts her eyes fluttered shut and her bosom heaved in the approved Victorian tradition.

"She's coming round," Marcia said. "A shot of brandy, and she'll be all right."

So Chuck rushed for the brandy and shot glass. "Does she do this often?" he whispered.

"Just now and then. When she gets upset. You know what it was this time, don't you? Hansen. I must say, I'm surprised at you myself, Chuck. I didn't think you'd give him the satisfaction of listening to a word of his garbage."

"Now wait a minute." His face got red. "You're making it sound as if I—The only reason I went over there was to tell him off. He kept calling me on the phone. Finally I got sore and told him if he didn't cut it out I was going to call the cops. Not that it would have gotten me anywhere, of course. He knew it. So did I. They're not going to get steamed up about nuisance phone calls. The only thing to do was go over there and straighten him out myself."

"I see." It was plausible enough, she supposed. And he was looking her in the eye. Earnest. Sincere. Manly. All those Boy Scout words. She wished her mental picture of him listening to Hansen, absorbed in listening, were not so sharp.

"My God, you don't think I *bought* any of the garbage he was trying to peddle, do you?"

"How was I to know? Or Lucy either? You looked pretty chummy from where I was standing."

"Chummy! With that son of a—Surely you know me better than that!"

"Do we?" She eyed him steadily. "What do we know about you, really? You turn up out of nowhere, a friend of Pam Caldwell's—"

"Okay, a friend of Pam's. And never going to live it down, apparently," he said with a disarming grin.

Which she ignored. "It works the other way too. Because what do you know about us? Precious little. It could all be true, what Hansen says. Don't you realize that?" (Lucy stirred, and Marcia tilted a little more brandy into her. Just to be on the safe side.)

"Sure. But I'll take a chance. That's me. A real sport." His eyes switched to Lucy, and he added softly, "Now I ask you. Does she look like a homicidal maniac?"

She looked, in fact, rather angelic. And she was keeping her mouth obediently shut. She chose this moment to open her eyes. They were clear and innocent, like a good child's. Chuck bent over her tenderly. "Lucy. Lucy darling ..."

An idyllic scene. Faith triumphant. Hansen or no Hansen, Chuck was hanging on to his honorable intentions. Marcia's own words came back to her: "If he really thought you were a murderer he'd be scared of you, he'd run like hell."

He wasn't scared. He wasn't running. He had had his chance and turned it down. Because he wanted the money, he wasn't a bad guy, just out to play the angles. And anyway, they were not murderers. No one had been murdered. So it couldn't be pity, the painful tightening Marcia felt in her chest. It was just the strain, the mortal tiredness, the letdown that came when a danger was past.

She turned away helplessly and poured herself a brandy.

XI

"I hope you'll be very happy, my dear," said Mrs. Travers majestically, and patted Lucy's hand.

Little Mrs. Sully murmured something no doubt seconding the motion. She did not pat Lucy's hand. Well, it wouldn't have been appropriate.

"Oh, I am," Lucy said. "So happy. So happy." She hurried on her way, wearing happiness like a magic halo. She hadn't meant to tell them; it simply spilled out. And, after all, why not? She was sure now. Hansen had done his worst last night, his very worst, and thank God he had, because otherwise she might never have been quite sure ... All his spiteful lies had served only to demonstrate the reality of Chuck's love and put an end forever to her doubts. Which had been more superstition than anything else, anyway: she had hesitated to believe because it seemed too good to be true. She knew now how true it was, how true Chuck was. So thank God for Hansen. He had accomplished through malice what Marcia had not been able to do through common sense.

So happy, so happy. And Daddy was not here to spoil it for her. Safe under her magic halo, she defied him. She deliberately stated to herself what he was not here to say: Fifth rate photographer. Upstart. A nobody. How long have you known him? A month? Well, well. Love at first sight, to coin a phrase. Know anything about his family? Prospects? Background? I thought not. As for the present state of his finances, I won't embarrass you with any inquiries. Not just a photographer, but a handy man as well. A plethora of talents. Dazzling. That's his car, that rattle-trap? What fun! Nothing wrong with his clothes that can't be remedied with a little womanly tact and guidance, a few well chosen Christmas or birthday gifts ... By the way, he's younger than you, isn't he? Not that it matters. I should have thought he was more Marcia's style than yours, she's always had a weakness for these diamond-in-the-rough types. Oh, they get along fine, do they? Uh-huh. I thought as much ...

She stopped there. No use carrying defiance too far. Daddy, of course, would not have stopped until there was nothing left of Chuck or romance or happiness to wither. After that he would have gotten out his checkbook. There you are, dear, run along, buy yourself something pretty. And after that he would have turned to Pam Sweetie and ...

Pam. It was queer, how the name could still evoke in Lucy a vague but powerful disquiet. The girl was dead. Nothing more to fear from her. Yet there remained this warning thrum, like a nervous reflex.

Habit, Lucy told herself. She went on up the staircase—how long had she paused there, defying Daddy?—and into her own beloved room. Pam would never get her clutches on it now. It was safe. As Lucy herself was safe.

And happy. So happy.

It came over her in the middle of the night. She woke up shuddering and sweating. Terrified. The wind, she thought at first; it had risen and the venetian blind was smacking against the window frame, the curtains sucked in and out like something gasping for breath. Just the wind. It always frightened her when it came up suddenly like this. She would be all right once she closed the window.

She peered out at the night. Swollen, ragged clouds scudded across the sky. The little trees across the street thrashed as if they were suffering. But there were a few lights in the houses. Comforting. And with the window shut the curtains gave up trying to breathe, and the blind stopped its racket.

She settled herself again in bed. But she was not all right. She lay rigid, her hands clenched outside the blanket, eyes straining up at the ceiling, heart hammering. Terrified. She waited for it to go away. It did not. The shuddering began again, and the sweating.

She sat up and wound her arms around her body, literally trying to pull herself together. It seemed to her that she was going to scream. Maybe she already had? But no one came to her help. Maybe they had all gone away and left her alone in the house, alone in the world ...

She could not bear it. She stumbled through the bathroom and into Marcia's room, sobbing.

"Now what?" Marcia said crossly, once she was awake and had switched on the bedside light.

"Marsh, I'm scared. The wind woke me up, and I can't help it. I'm so scared."

"Scared of what? The wind?"

"No. Yes. I don't know ..."

"Oh Lord," said Marcia. "Pre-marital vapors, I suppose." She reached for a cigarette. She was puffy-eyed, and one side of her face was creased from a wrinkle in the pillow slip. Propped on one elbow, with her nightgown strap falling down, she looked angular—she had never had any bosom to speak of—and uncompromising, like a good straight chair that could be counted on for support, never mind the soft cushions.

Lucy shook her head dumbly. She stood and trembled. Finally she blurted it out: "Pam's diary."

"Here we go again. Pam's diary. What about it?"

"He's still got it. Marsh. How can I ever be sure until I know what's in it?" Marcia stared, uncomprehending and scornful, and she floundered on. "Sure of Chuck, I mean. I have to be sure he really loves me—"

"You have to be sure. Look, Lucy, doesn't it count that he wants to marry you? That he refused to believe what Hansen told him? What's the guy got to do to convince you? Cut off his right arm? Come down to earth. Stop making like some kind of a half-baked romantic heroine. You're not. You're a woman that ought to have gotten married years ago, and now you've got a chance, and if you ask me you better grab it." She looked a little ashamed of her own bluntness. "Well. You do want to marry him, don't you?"

"Yes. Oh yes. More than anything in the world."

"So quit fussing about that damn diary and marry him."

"But don't you see, I *can't!* I have to be sure. I have to know. I'm not like you, you've always had beaus—"

"All right. I'm the voice of experience. Now hear this. You're never going to find anybody with no defects. The good-looking ones are dopes, or they're already married. The brains have lousy dispositions, or no money, or they're seventy-eight years old. Always something."

"I know that. I don't expect Chuck to be perfect. It isn't the same thing at all. I can't help it, I've got to see the diary." She went over and sat down, timidly, on the edge of the bed. "He must still have it down there, Marsh. We could find it if we tried. Sometime when he's out of the house—"

"What do you mean, we? You're not going to get me to help you rummage through his things. No, thank you. You'd be out of your mind to take such a chance. And for what? For nothing. Listen to me, Lucy. There can't be anything—incriminating, whatever you want to call it—in Pam's diary. How many times do I have to tell you? If Chuck thought you were capable of murder he wouldn't want to marry you."

"I know. That's what I'm scared of," said Lucy simply.

"But he *does* want to marry you! So that proves—"

"He could be just leading me on, pretending to be in love with me so he could trap me. Us. He could be a spy."

Marcia's answer to that was a hoot of laughter. "You're crazy," she said cheerfully. "You'll be yourself again in the morning. It's just one of those mad middle-of-the-night notions. Run along now. Back to bed. I'll fix you some hot milk and tuck you in."

It was an unusual gesture from Marcia; she wasn't the cozy type. She's humoring me, Lucy thought as she let herself be led back to her own bedroom, treating me as if I were a child. Maybe I am. Maybe she's right. But I have to know.

Before she turned out the light Marcia gave her a thoughtful look and said, "Promise me something, Lucy. Don't go rooting around for that diary. Promise?"

"Don't worry. I'm all right now." She hadn't promised, she thought gleefully as she snuggled into her pillow. So she wouldn't be breaking her word. Not that she would have let that stop her. But it wasn't very nice to lie, especially after Marcia had been such a comfort. In her way. Funny she couldn't see what it meant to Lucy, about the diary ... Funny she wouldn't help, she was always the ringleader ...

It didn't matter. Lucy was not a child. She could manage, if she had to, by herself.

It seemed to her an omen, that her chance came so quickly, only a couple of evenings later. Fate was on her side; she was meant to find the diary and learn the truth. And the truth would set her free. No more anxious seeking for hidden significances in whatever Chuck did or said. No more holding back for fear she was making a fool of herself. No more middle-of-the-night terrors.

There was this exhibit of photographic equipment uptown; Chuck would like to take a look at it. Tonight, maybe. When he suggested tentatively that Lucy might care to come along, she was quick to say No, oh no, she wouldn't know what it was all about, she would only be a nuisance with her stupid questions. Already she recognized the opportunity. Or rather, the half-opportunity, for she had to be able to count on Marcia's absence, too. There would be no search for the diary if Marcia got wind of it. And if she was in the house she would get wind of it. You could depend on that.

Here was where fate stepped in, right on cue: Marcia called in the afternoon to say she had to work late and wouldn't be home for dinner. Lucy's heart gave such a leap that for a moment she could not speak. "Lucy? Are you there?" Marcia said. "Oh. I thought we'd been cut off ... Not *really* late, I ought to be home by ten-thirty or so. All right?"

All right! It was perfect, a miracle of timing that would give Lucy more than the uninterrupted hour she wanted. It probably wouldn't take anywhere near that long; after all, there were only a limited number of hiding places in Chuck's quarters. If she failed to find the diary in an hour, she would know it simply wasn't there, he had chosen some other spot to keep his treasure safe. Which was a bridge she refused to cross until she came to it.

Getting in was no problem. She had keys to all the doors in the house. Her property, it was not really trespassing ... All the same, she felt like a burglar as she let herself in. It was eight-thirty. She had watched from the doorway, waving as Chuck drove off; her cheek still held the glow of his goodbye kiss. So tender, so loving. Surely so sincere? She paused, yearning to believe, achingly tempted to play the coward again—Scaredy-cat Lucy, now as always before—and accept without testing what he offered. Take him at his word. Forget her niggling little doubts. But that was it: their very smallness gave her the courage to test them. In a way, it was an act of faith, what she was doing.

She was doing it, all right, whatever it was. And whatever she was, cowardly or courageous. Her hand reached for the door and pulled it shut behind her noiselessly. No need to switch on the light; her feet knew the way and were already carrying her across the springy carpeting of the front studio. It would not be here, she thought. Except for drapes and carpet, the place was still practically unfurnished. One chair. And a tripod, looming out of the shadows like an angular ghost. There was no place to hide anything here—if indeed Chuck had anything to hide. An act of faith. She must remember that, and go straight to the chest of drawers where she had seen him put the diary. It would still be there. Or if not there, in the bookcase.

Her own noiselessness bothered her. She was glad to reach the inner office—no, it was Chuck's living-bedroom now—where her heels clicked on the parquet floor, and where at once she turned on the light. There. No burglar would have done that. What a forlorn little place it was, poor Chuck, and he was pleased with it, he had confided to her in a moment of candor that he had never had it so good. After they were married he could move upstairs to Daddy's bedroom. Or, better yet, Marcia might not mind taking Daddy's room and leaving hers for Chuck; she didn't have Lucy's deep-rooted feeling about her own precious room, where even Chuck would seem like an intruder, an invader ... She blushed at the thought. And get right down to it, who was invading whose room?

Act of faith, she reminded herself. She opened the top drawer. It was not there. The bookcase, then. There were only two shelves; she covered them both thoroughly. Then she went back to the chest and searched the other drawers. She had not been mistaken about which drawer. The diary was in none of them.

All right, it still didn't necessarily mean that he had hidden it on purpose. Plenty of other places where he might have left it, casually, absent-mindedly. Maybe he kept it always within reach, something to pick up whenever he thought of Pam. He admitted it himself, he had been in love with Pam. Might still be. Might see, in Lucy, a means of striking back at Daddy for winning what he had lost. That trollop. Both of them, panting after her. Daddy's Pam Sweetie. Chuck's beautiful, sweet kid.

Lucy-love was what he called her. His lady love. She was different, he said, not like anyone he had ever known. Not like Pam. As he was not like Bernie. Yet she had been in love with Bernie too. So it was possible, it could happen. Lucy-love.

Oh please, she whispered, oh please. But it was not in any of the plenty of other places either. How busy her hands were, shifting and lifting and replacing; and it was more than a search, it was as if they were stripping Lucy herself, peeling away layer after protective layer of hope, until nothing was left but a mindless, savage compulsion. Caution and shame left, along with hope; she got down on her hands and knees to look under the couch, under the radiator, under the chest. In the bathroom, she did not hesitate to scrabble through the dirty clothes hamper. Daddy's examining room—Chuck's dark room to be—offered as few possibilities as the front studio, but she explored them all.

And still she would not give up. It must be here, somewhere within the confines of these small rooms. Otherwise ... Maybe in his car? Beyond that she would not let her imagination go. Except for one grim and mental glimpse (she suppressed it instantly) of the rows and rows of lockers in Grand Central Station. It seemed to her, now, that Chuck's living room had taken on a gloating, sly look. I've-got-asecret-and-I-won't-tell. The mirror above the chest of drawers winked and darted at her a hateful reflection of her own face—her hair straggling, eyes bright with an animal sheen, mouth tight, like an old woman's. Lucy-love. His lady love.

She thought of another place. Under the mattress on the studio couch; she hoisted and heaved, reckless of disarranged cover and pillows. But afterwards she went through the motions of straightening them, listlessly, like a machine running down. And that was when she found it, while she was patting the cushions into a semblance of order. It was zipped inside the cover of the yellow corduroy pillow. Her fingers, encountering the bulge it made, jumped back as if they had been scorched. Then they recognized, and got busy. Her breath caught in an exultant sob.

The zipper resisted her, stuck, suddenly gave in. There. She had the diary. It sat in her hands, plump and green with its secret poison.

From the doorway Chuck said, "What the hell—?" and after a moment, "Oh."

She closed her eyes. He would be gone, of course, when she opened them again. He was a figment of her overwrought nerves. Scenes like this did not repeat themselves in real life. Only in dreams.

"Lucy," he said. Still there. Really there. A graceful ribbon of smoke curled up from the cigarette in his hand. The light was wrong: it made smudges of his eyes, expressionless. His voice had no expression, either. Just the flat statement of her name. Lucy.

It was she who accused: "You hid it."

"Yeah. But not well enough, from the looks of things." He took a step toward her. "Give it to me."

"Why did you hide it, if there's nothing important in it?" She tightened her clutch on it and scrambled to her feet. He stopped, after the one step forward. "That's what you said, the other time. Nothing important in it. Nothing of any particular interest. So why did you hide it?"

"Why do you want it so bad? You must figure there's something pretty damned important in it."

"No. I just—I've got a right to know. About her and Daddy. That's what you said, the other time, that it told about her and Daddy." But this was not like the other time. He was not supplying her with the plausible explanation for her own behavior she needed, as he had done then. He was not helping her, not offering her cocktails and sympathy and words of love. "I've got a right," she repeated.

"You've got no right to come barging in here behind my back, pawing through everything I own, ransacking the place. You might have asked me. But no, you couldn't take the chance, could you? I might not let you have it. You couldn't afford to take the chance." He was approaching again, watching her curiously. She could see the expression in his eyes now. Cold, stony-cold, and a flicker of something else. Unidentifiable. "You were so right. Okay. Hand it over. It's mine. Give it to me."

She shook her head wordlessly. The gesture of a stubborn child.

"Too bad I walked in on you so soon, before you could get it read." He paused, but she still did not speak. "Isn't it a shame, when you're so interested. But that's life for you, that's the way the Mercedes Benz ..." She had no warning; he was still talking when he pounced. The impact rocked her back onto the couch. One quick, strong wrench, and it was done: she was no longer clutching the diary.

"There," he said, patting the pocket of his jacket. "That's more like it." He was edging his way backward toward the door. She saw the film of sweat on his forehead, and it came to her what the puzzling flicker in his eyes might be. Fear. He might be afraid of her.

"Chuck!" She could not hold back the one entreating cry.

He hesitated for a breath or two, while it seemed to her that something, the design of their lives, was being decided. The wheel of fortune turned, the coin spiraled in the air.

And it came up disaster.

It showed in the impersonal way his eyes measured her, seeing—instead of his Lucy-love—a guilty woman who had been silly enough to put herself in his power. Calculating how much the traffic would bear. She knew, with dreadful certainty, what he was going to say: What's it worth to you? Make me an offer.

"Chuck," she begged him again, this time in a whisper.

"Yes? At your service. Now that we know where we stand, I don't see any reason why—"

The door bell rang. Two longs and a short: Marcia's signal when she couldn't find her key.

XII

The trouble with drinking your dinner, thought Marcia—and she ought to know, some people might even call her an authority on the subject—was that sometimes it was great, you fell into bed and conked out before the depression hit you, and sometimes it was gruesome and you didn't. Like tonight. Without the twenty minutes it took for the cab ride home she would have been all right; with it she was sunk. It was the time lag that did her in. Never blame the liquor.

All the way downtown she huddled in a corner and desolated, while the cab driver groused about traffic, the weather, and life in general. "Right?" he would say at the end of each morose paragraph. "Right," Marcia would echo. Kindred spirits. Her head had begun to ache. She decided that Joe was lying about where he had been all last week and why it had to be an early night tonight. Probably making time with some kid half Marcia's age. Bound to happen, sooner or later. And she didn't even have the gimp to make the break herself, she was going to hang around and let a lug like Joe toss her aside when it suited him ...

"Right?" demanded the cab driver as he pulled up in front of the house.

"Right," she said, and crept out, stiff with misery.

Naturally she couldn't find her key. It invariably chose moments like this to sink to the bottom of the compost heap in her purse. She grubbed for quite a while, propped against the iron railing beside the stoop, so as to get the benefit of the street light. It was interesting, some of the items that rose to the surface. Here was the pearl earring she thought she had lost, weeks ago; her favorite lipstick, also checked off as gone for good; the cigarette lighter that she still meant to get fixed some day; several bills that she really must pay, really; a letter she had written and forgotten to mail; slips of paper on which were scribbled cryptic notes to herself and orphan telephone numbers, something else in her own handwriting ... "Lucy dear, I started it and now I'm ending it." Oh gawd, her suicide note, what a piece of lunacy to have preserved *that* jolly little souvenir, she must remember to burn it. Never mind waste not want not. Write another one if she decided to cut her throat. Correction: Not if. When.

Meanwhile, no key. Oh well, it wasn't late. Lucy and Chuck were probably both still up. Holding hands, no doubt, or dreaming dreams about how to spend Lucy's money. She stuffed the mish-mash back into her purse, climbed the steps, and pressed the door bell two longs and a short.

"Hi, kids," she said when Lucy let her in. She could see Chuck in the studio doorway, silhouetted against the light behind him.

Lucy gave a kind of muted howl and fell on her neck. "Marsh! Oh, Marsh!" From there on it was incoherent. Only two points came through clearly: Lucy needed help, and she had been right from the beginning.

"What *is* all this? Lucy, shut up. Chuck. What's the matter with her? What did you do to her?"

"The diary!" wailed Lucy, and Marcia's heart sank. "It's what I said all along. I told you—"

"And I told you," Marcia said curtly. "I told you not to go looking for trouble. Why couldn't you leave well enough alone? All right. Where is the damn thing?"

"Here," said Chuck, and patted his pocket. "You want it as bad as Lucy does?"

"I don't want it at all. It couldn't interest me less." She met his eyes coolly. His shifted first. Good. She decided to take the only chance in sight. What did they have to lose? "I don't happen to be in love with you, like Lucy, so it's nothing to me what went on with you and Pam—"

"In love with him! I hate him!" Lucy pulled away from her violently. "If you think I could ever—After what happened tonight. No, let go of me. You're against me too. You're on his side. I always knew that too, I always knew ..." It wasn't an act. Her eyes glittered with hostility. Suddenly she put her hands to her face and fled down the hall to the sitting room.

Which was also good. She had done enough damage already. Anybody's guess, whether Marcia could pick up the pieces or not. We can try, she thought, and turned, with a baffled shrug, toward Chuck. One thing about it, her fit of despondency had passed. She felt sharp, like a knife whetted for action.

"Now," she said. "What's this all about?"

"As if you didn't know. You told her not to go looking for the diary. So you must have talked it over, the two of you. Don't try to play dumb now." He was cocky, all right. But still not quite insolent. So he couldn't be absolutely sure of himself. Besides, he liked her. They had always understood each other, Marcia and Chuck. Not on the same side, though; that was only Lucy's warped view.

"Why should I play dumb? Sure I told Lucy to stop stewing over Pam. After all, the poor girl's dead. What difference does it make whether you had an affair with her or not? But Lucy gets these notions. I told you before, she's led a sheltered life. She doesn't realize—"

"So that's your pitch, is it? She's jealous? Figures she'll get the real lowdown on Pam and me from the diary?"

"What else?" She gave him plenty of time to answer; he did not use it. Another point in her favor. "I'm not blaming you, Chuck, it would make me sore too to catch somebody going through my stuff behind my back. I'm assuming that's what happened with you and Lucy tonight. Nobody's told me for sure. I'm supposed to be psychic. My feet hurt," she added. "Could we maybe sit down, or is this a strictly formal session?"

He gave her a suspicious look, but he led the way into his living quarters. She sank down on the couch. He perched on a folding chair, alert and wary and a little seedy. Like a sparrow, she thought, and she grinned at him.

"It just goes to show," she said chattily. "I've always thought I was pretty good at sizing people up, but apparently I was way off on you. I had you pegged as—well, maybe shrewd operator's too strong. But I certainly didn't think you were the type to cut off your nose to spite your face."

"Who says that's what I'm doing?"

"Well, aren't you? Look, Chuck, I've got no illusions about you and Lucy." (It was just too bad, if Lucy had sneaked down to the basement to listen instead of staying in the sitting room where she belonged. The chance had to be taken.) "I knew what the score was from the start, and it was okay with me. After all, a guy can be decent and still out to play all the angles. I'd have stopped it long ago if I thought you weren't going to give Lucy her money's worth. The way I see it, it's a good deal for both of you. Too good to pass up just because you get into a squabble over Pam's silly old diary."

"I'm not so sure it's silly," said Chuck. "The way Lucy acted, I got the idea it was a matter of life and death."

"Stop hinting darkly and give me a cigarette. Please, can't seem to find mine ... Thanks. Now to get back to the way Lucy acted?"

"Listen, Marsh. That diary may not mean a damn thing to you, but it means plenty to Lucy, and has, from the minute she first laid eyes on it. Before she even thought of falling for me. I saw right off there was something fishy. First she tries to keep me from taking it with the rest of Pam's stuff. Then she gets into another sweat when she finds out I've still got it, I didn't give it to Pam's mother. And now she sneaks in and turns the place upside down till she finds where I hid it—"

"Hid it! What possessed you to hide it?"

"Because I'm like you say, I'm out to play all the angles. A shrewd operator. She started it herself, she gave me the idea. I see I've got something she's dying to get her hands on, naturally I decide it's valuable property, I better hang on to it just in case. No telling when it might come in handy. She don't trust me. Why should I trust her?"

"How childish can you get," said Marcia scornfully. "Shrewd operator! Adult infant's more like it. Of course Lucy wants a look at that diary. She's jealous of Pam. Double jealous. At first it was on account of His Nibs. Now it's on account of you. Can't you see that?"

"I can see it, all right. But that's not all I see." He got up and began to pace the floor moodily. Deciding how much he was going to say. She hoped he would say it all. Meanwhile, in case he glanced her way, she arranged on her face a bright, blank stare. He stopped in front of her and burst out: "No, by God, it isn't! What about Hansen?"

"Oh, please! Not Hansen again. We went all through that the other night. He said his piece, you didn't believe him, we were going to forget it ..."

"I know," he said helplessly. She saw, with that pang that was like pity, only why should she feel sorry for him, that he was on the brink of honesty, maneuvered there by her own show of candor and by their liking for each other. "But supposing Hansen's right about Lucy. Just for the sake of argument. Supposing the reason she blew up over the gas heater—and she did blow up, she admits it, so do you—was what Hansen says, because she actually had some hall-baked scheme of using it to murder Pam—"

"Is *that* what Hansen said! She planned to murder Pam!" Marcia's laugh rang out, genuinely astonished.

"Sure. Why not? Come to think about it, she had the best motive in the world." He leaned toward her, his eyes bright and intent. He made a rubbing motion with thumb and fingers. "The good old green stuff. I know. It was supposed to be a secret, that your old man was all set to marry Pam. Lucy claims she didn't know. But supposing she's lying. She could have found out somehow or other. Couldn't she?"

"Certainly. So could I. Did you ever think of writing for television? With your imagination you could go far."

"And if she did find out, she'd know damn well what it was going to mean money-wise. Sheltered life or no sheltered life. There's just one reason why gals like Pam marry guys like your old man. Right?"

"Right," said Marcia. "I take it back about writing for television. You ought to be driving a cab ... Never mind. So Lucy, having decided to give Pam the gas, not only confides in Hansen but also tells Pam all about it. Who naturally records it in her diary, just as any normal American girl would do—"

"She didn't confide in Hansen," Chuck pointed out stubbornly. "He got in on it by accident. And what worries her about the diary is that she doesn't know whether Pam was on to her or not. It scares her to think of what Pam might have guessed. Because Pam was nobody's fool. She knew how popular she was around here."

He must have gleaned that much at least from the diary. Yes, and (so much for the moment of honesty) he was using it as bait, tempting Marcia into showing that underneath she was as passionately curious as Lucy. "Then she knew more than anybody else," she said calmly. "We never paid much attention to her, one way or the other. Besides, nobody murdered her. Nobody murdered anybody."

"Yeah, but if Lucy planned it ... It must *do* something to you, to plan a thing like that. Whether you actually carry it out or not. You know what I mean? It's like you've crossed a line or something, and you can't ever get back to what you were before. I mean—"

"All right, all right, I *get* it!" Too shrill; he looked startled. And she had stiffened all over, she was probably staring at him. She bent her head. Another mistake; there in her lap were her hands which had done nothing but were nevertheless guilty. She forced a laugh. "Good Lord, Chuck, you sound like you'd been through it yourself. You have got an imagination!"

He laughed. But he was not through with Lucy. "No kidding, Marsh, the way she acted tonight, when I caught her. She'd just found the diary, see, hadn't had a chance to read it yet. She got this crazy look in her eye, I mean crazy. I don't blame Hansen for being scared of her. I was scared myself, for a minute. Then I thought what the hell, she thinks I'm a blackmailer, okay, I'll be one. See where it gets me."

"Oh, Chuck, you didn't! You didn't ask her for money!"

He turned a bit red. "Why not, if that's what she expects? Sure I would have. The only thing that stopped me was that you rang the bell just then."

"And thank God I did." Blackmail. She experimented with the word. The feel of it on her tongue was familiar; so was the way it made her nerves twang. As if she had used it herself, in some previous conversation with Chuck ... Was it possible? The night of his housewarming party, when she waltzed in half-lit and he made his honorable-intentions speech about Lucy. She had come within a hair's breadth of giving the whole show away that night, under the impression that Lucy had already done so. Blackmail. Was it possible to have committed such an indiscretion and not remember it for sure? Twang went her nerves again. Yes. Unfortunately. It was also possible that Chuck's mind was following a similar path down Memory Lane. He had a dawning look, somehow.

She did what she could to hold back the dawn. "Oops," she said, as her purse slid off her lap, with only a little encouragement from her. "Oh damn, everything's spilling *out!*" She hadn't really counted on the clasp springing open. However. The more diversion the better. They both got down on the floor for the retrieving job; it was companionable work. Chuck made the routine cracks about women, the junk they tote around in their handbags, and Marcia countered with the routine defense. Her keys turned up, flushed out of whatever cranny they had been hiding in. One lipstick and a perfume container had to be fished out from under the couch. Rolling stock, Chuck commented.

"There," Marcia said, cramming the purse shut on everything at last. "If we've missed anything, I just hope Lucy doesn't find it. She'd work up another fit of jealousy."

They sat side by side on the floor, looking into each other's eyes. After a moment Chuck said, "All right. I'll buy it. Lucy's jealous. What do I do now? You heard her. She hates me."

"Nonsense. Women in love always say that. Make with the sweet talk. Apologize. Prostrate yourself. You lost your temper, it drove you mad to think she didn't trust you. All like that."

"Give her the diary?" His face went crafty again. "She may insist—"

"I doubt it. She'll be too glad to have you back. No. I wouldn't give her the diary. I'd tell her I'd burned it up." She stood up and dusted off her skirt. "Good Lord, do I have to write the whole script for you? I've already done my share."

"Yes, you have," he said soberly. "You're a great little patcher-upper. I can't help wondering why. I'm no bargain, you know."

"I don't suppose you are. But if Lucy thinks so, and she does ... Somebody has to look out for her. She's never had a chance. I think she might have, with you. If you'll stop trying to play all the angles, that is. And you'd better. One more episode like tonight and brother, you've had it, you'll be out so fast you won't know what hit you. Do I make myself clear?"

"Any clearer, and the light would blind me." He held out his hand, smiling. "You can count on me, Marsh. Why not? I know when I've got a good deal. I'll see to it that Lucy gets her money's worth."

"Good. Now, look. Give me a couple of minutes with her first. That way she'll know she can stop hating you, and she'll have time to powder her nose ..."

She needed it, all right. Lucy had obviously not been down in the basement listening. She huddled on the sitting room couch, her face sodden with tears; Marcia heard the sounds of weeping before she opened the door.

"I've fixed it," she announced in an authoritative whisper. "I convinced him you're jealous of him and Pam, that's why you went after the diary. So for God's sake, Lucy, play it that way. Lay off the diary. There can't be anything in it that matters or I couldn't have convinced him. Have you got that?"

Sob. Sniff. But also a nod of the head.

"All right, then. Pull yourself together and blow your nose. He's coming in to apologize. He's still yours, if you want him."

She did not linger long. It was a relief to escape from Lucy's soppy gratitude, her clinging arms and flutters of hope renewed. Poor deluded Lucy—but she had her chance at happiness again, her little scrap of paradise was regained.

Courtesy of Marcia.

Something accomplished, something done, she thought as she climbed the stairs to her bedroom. Has earned a night's repose. But she was too keyed up for sleep. Even after a bath. She might take a sleeping pill, she supposed. Or. With an absent-minded air, as if it didn't matter one way or the other, she got out the emergency half-pint she kept tucked away, poured herself a shot, and curled up on the bed. Where she had tossed her handbag when she came in; she opened it and began idly to sort out its contents while she sipped. There was something she meant to do, oh yes, the suicide note ...

It was gone. She could not believe it at first. Now let's not panic, she told herself, it's got to be here, it's slipped down inside something, that's all. But after ten minutes of methodical search she faced the truth. It was gone. And there was only one place it could be: somewhere in Chuck's room. Under the couch, maybe under the rug, biding its time, waiting for a chance to tattle.

She must go after it now, before it exposed her as the liar she was. For there would be no talking her way out of this one; she had just squeaked by with Chuck tonight.

But once out in the hall, at the head of the stairs, she hesitated. Look at the fix Lucy had gotten into, with her search for the diary. This could be even worse. On the other hand, did she dare not take the risk? She might never have another chance.

Then she heard the door to the sitting room open, and the murmur of Lucy's and Chuck's voices as they came down the hall. It was already too late. No chance tonight; that was for sure. Probably no chance ever. They sounded definitely lover-like, down there. There was a soft, tremulous laugh from Lucy.

Marcia shivered. A great little patcher-upper. Oh, you bet. But as a smasher-upper she was more than great. She was the greatest.

XIII

"Trousseau shopping?" Mrs. Travers asked archly when Lucy met her at the corner on her way home. And when Lucy blushed: "I thought so. You have that look in your eye."

"Just a few little things. It's not going to be a fancy affair, you know. A quiet home wedding."

"Of course. That's the nicest. Have you set the date yet?"

Yes. They had settled everything last night, after the disaster that had not struck, after all. Thanks to Marcia's levelheadedness. Without her Lucy and Chuck might have let a stupid little misunderstanding wreck their happiness. For by now that was what it had become in Lucy's mind—a lover's quarrel over nothing, or nearly nothing, with Marcia appearing like their good angel in the nick of time to set them straight again. True love following its classic course; it never ran smooth. How sweet the making up had been: Forgive me, I was jealous. Forgive me, I couldn't bear to think of your not trusting me. Forgive, forgive. No more secrets. No more doubts. I love, you love, he loves, we love ...

Yes indeed, the date was set. Not June, as Chuck had urged, and as Lucy herself would have liked. But it seemed a little too soon, on account of Daddy. Early August would look better. All right, Chuck conceded, if by early August she meant August first. A week of honeymooning at the beach, or just possibly Bermuda, provided he got the breaks he was hoping for. Bermuda in any case, Lucy decided, only she would have to manage it tactfully; he was very touchy about spending her money. As he should be. She loved him for it.

It all sounded lovely to Mrs. Travers. "I was just saying to Marcia, you'll be next, I told her. Weddings come in pairs. She claims she's not the marrying type, but as I said, I've heard that one before. Mark my words, I told her, it will be your turn next. I can sense these things ... She doesn't look too well today. I hope she's not overdoing."

"She had to work late last night. And I don't think she slept very well." In spite of her own euphoric state, Lucy had noticed how shockingly pale Marcia was this morning, and how jittery. Usually on Saturdays she slept late. But not this Saturday. She was already up when Lucy came downstairs. Prowling around restlessly; chain smoking; possibly taking a few of her famous therapeutic nips. And so impatient that the gush of girlish confidences froze on Lucy's tongue. "Of course I'm glad you made up," she had snapped. "Good Lord, I engineered it, didn't I? And don't think it was easy, after the way you bollixed everything up!" It shut Lucy up. She had left early for her appointment with Pierre (a new hairdo this morning, which Mrs. Travers said was wonderfully becoming, and Lucy was inclined to think so herself) and her afternoon of shopping. She was used to Marcia's moods. They came and went. By this time her irritability had probably vanished without a trace. Whatever its cause: hangover, breakfast time trauma, or— Or jealousy.

It was a rather thrilling idea. For once, for the first time in their lives, Marcia might have cause to envy her. It gave an added fillip to her bliss.

"I suppose she's working in the garden," she said to Mrs. Travers. "A lovely day like this."

"I expect that's where she was heading. I ran into her and Chuck in the hall as I was leaving."

So Chuck was back. He had had one of his wedding jobs this morning. The door to his studio was closed; Lucy paused, tempted to tap with her keys or call his name. Better not, though. He was probably busy in his dark room. Which was deserted. And so was Marcia's little garden. How pretty it looked, now that the roses were beginning to bloom! The tree was in full leaf, the afternoon sunshine splashed down, there was a gay little breeze. The sitting room seemed almost sombre in contrast.

Funny, where Marcia could have got to. She wasn't upstairs, either. Lucy put her packages down on the bed. No one to show them to. And her new hairdo. She wasn't quite so sure about it now. A little too bouffant? A lighter shade, too; maybe Pierre had gotten carried away? If only Marsh were here to say Don't be silly, you look great ...

The basement, she thought. Of course that was where Marcia was, getting out her gardening tools. She went back downstairs very quietly, aware of something sly and chilling in her own mind, like a snake starting to uncoil. Yes. The basement too was empty. Its dampness made her shudder. She closed her eyes, trying to remember roses, dazzle of sunshine, bliss.

Then she crossed to the listening wall. "Something missing from your purse?" Chuck was saying affably. "You wouldn't mean this, by any chance? I wondered how soon you were going to miss it."

Well, it didn't come as any particular shock. Marcia had known he must have found it. A piece of note paper couldn't just dissolve. Unfortunately. She had had her chance and taken it, with him and Lucy both out of the house. But no amount of searching could turn up what simply wasn't there. So she had already known.

She swallowed and said casually, "I'd like to have it back, if you don't mind. Not that it's of any importance. Just a piece of nonsense, really."

"Fascinating nonsense, though. I probably ought to apologize for reading it. But you know how it is. You happen on something like this, figure it must be something of your own, and before you know it you've—"

"I know how it is. Don't bother to apologize. That doesn't make you a rat, just because you read it."

Big joke. He laughed appreciatively. "Thanks, dear. I thought you'd understand. It doesn't make me a rat, either, just because I'm out to play the angles. Or does it?"

She watched in silence while he folded the note and tucked it in his pocket. Thank God she had enough self-control not to grab. It would have been too humiliating. Futile, too. Finally she said, "I guess not. Only you're wasting your time. Because there aren't any angles to play."

"No? That remains to be seen. I've got nothing to lose by trying."

"You've got everything to lose. I think I mentioned last night, it's a good deal for both of you. Lucy gets a husband, you get money. And I gathered you agreed. Why throw a good deal away for nothing?"

"You're so right. I wouldn't think of throwing it away for nothing. But if I can make a good deal better, if I can get the money without marrying Lucy—Well, why not?"

> The basement wall was dank and cold as death. But it supported Lucy; she pressed her back against it, and felt the chill and slickness of its sweat, seeping in through her clothes, through her skin, her flesh, deep into the marrow of her bones. Her ears rang with listening.

"Get the money without marrying Lucy ..."

"You're not stupid, Marsh. You know what I mean. This goodbye note, this piece of nonsense. All right, if you say so. But expensive nonsense. It's going to cost you, to get it back. It's going to cost you the house."

"You're out of your mind," she said calmly. "I won't pay you a cent for it. Keep it and be damned."

"Who said keep it? You don't want it, I take it to the police."

"Go right ahead. See where it gets you. The police have enough real crimes to keep them busy. They're not going to bother with anything this flimsy. Good Lord, Chuck, use your head! A note I wrote, or started to write, one night when I was drunk and disorderly in my mind—"

"Disorderly? Not from where I stand. It fits right in with what I said last night. I had it all straight, didn't I? Except it wasn't Pam you were after, it was him. Your old man."

"What's the difference? It was just a fantasy, anyway. Nobody killed anybody. They died in an accident."

"Yeah. Or what looked like an accident. Of course nobody looked very hard at the time. The police might get kind of curious now. It's not just the note, you know. I've still got the diary. Remember? And then there's Hansen's story about how Lucy tried to kill him."

"His word against mine," said Marcia contemptuously. "I was there that night. I saw what happened."

"Right. And you've got a damn sight better reason to lie about it than he has." He paused, and their eyes met; she had a queer impression that he was suffering too. He flushed angrily. "Why can't you be reasonable? Don't you see what an ugly mess it's going to be if I go to the police? No matter what they find or don't find, believe or don't believe. They'll put you through the wringer, they'll crucify you—"

"I know. Your heart bleeds. Especially since you won't be getting a nickel out of it." She felt a surge of confidence, for the first time. "Don't try to bluff me, Chuck. I know you won't go to the police. You're overplaying your hand. You should have stopped when you were ahead of the game."

"You're the one that's trying to bluff!" he burst out. "And if you think it's going to work you're crazy. Maybe you won't listen to reason, but Lucy will. Don't forget, she's in this too. She's going to get her chance to pay up, and if I know Lucy she'll jump at it. And you'll jump right along with her, whether you like it or not."

Listen. Lucy still stood, rigid against the basement wall. Lucy will listen to reason. But not Marcia. Oh no, Marcia was like Daddy; nobody could ever tell them anything. She had insisted not only on going her own wrong-headed way, but on dragging Lucy with her. Had refused to believe in danger, refused to listen to reason. But Lucy will. Listen.

"Lucy," Marcia said. Her chest felt like an accordion, and somebody suddenly squeezing it. She had forgotten what this would do to Lucy. It would destroy her. Not just the loss of the house, money, whatever Chuck was demanding. The terrible, irreparable loss would be the intangible one. Total annihilation. Her dream of love exposed as the self-delusion of a lonely, foolish woman; her pride bludgeoned to death; her lifelong trust in Marcia shattered ... Yes, that too; there would be no way of keeping her from knowing that Marcia had been aware of Chuck's aim all along and had cynically furthered it.

"You can't do this to Lucy," she cried. "Chuck! You're not such a monster! You can't!"

"I don't want to," he began, and her ear, desperate for hope, caught a shamed note in his voice. Of course he was not such a monster, he wasn't a bad guy—hadn't she liked him on sight?—only a shrewd little operator who saw a chance to clean up and couldn't resist it. But he was bluffing himself as much as her. When push came to shove he wouldn't be able to go through with his ruthless blackmailer act. He had a heart, much as he would like to think he hadn't.

He cleared his throat. "I got nothing against Lucy. But that's not going to stop me. You get first crack at my proposition. Turn me down, and I take it to Lucy. It's up to you."

"What do you mean, it's up to me? It doesn't make any difference whether I turn you down or not. Either way, Lucy's going to know what you are, why you asked her to marry you, what a fool you've made of her—"

"With you backing me up, dear. You could have fixed my wagon, romance-wise, any time you wanted to."

Lucy pulled her hands free of the basement wall and pressed them against her ears. Don't listen, don't. Shut out the voices, the treachery that she had always known was there, the two of them sided against her, laughing at Lucy-love, Lucy-fool behind her back ... But hands were not enough. Nothing was enough. With mindless efficiency her ears went on about the business they had been built for. Listen.

"All right! I didn't do it! She fell in love with you. I wanted her to be happy ... This will kill her, Chuck. You know it will."

Again he went into an angry bluster. "Don't think that's going to stop me, that kind of talk. You're so worried about what it's going to do to Lucy, figure a way to swing it without telling her. It's okay by me. Just so I get what I'm after."

Figure a way. Was it possible? She could concoct a story for Lucy, of course, one that would make herself the villain. (No problem there; she *was* the villain.) But it was no good unless it also saved Lucy's face. She was going to have to suffer another disappointment in love. Which, bad as it was, was still not the worst. She might survive the loss of love, Chuck, her home. But not the loss of every last shred of self-esteem. She must somehow be able to believe that it was she who was rejecting Chuck, instead of the other way round. Somehow ... It was such a small thing, really, to salvage from the general disaster. Surely it could be managed?

"Take your time," said Chuck. "Think it over." He could afford to be magnanimous, now that he had pried her out of her original go-to-hell position. He must have known all along that he could do it, with Lucy as the lever.

She said bitterly, "You're playing with dynamite, you know. If we're the killers you think we are, what's to stop us from polishing you off? It's exactly what you're asking for."

"Maybe. Naturally it occurred to me." Oh, naturally! "I'll chance it. Like they say, nothing ventured nothing gained."

"But you already had it made! Once you and Lucy were married, you could—"

> At last Lucy remembered her legs. That was what they had been built for—to carry her ears out of torturing, listening range. They were stiff at first. She lurched like a stunned animal as she crossed the basement floor to the stairs. After that she was all right, quiet and quick and steady. Through kitchen, sitting room, hall. (Where the door to the studio was still shut.) Up the front stairs to the sanctuary of her bedroom. She saw, with astonishment, that she looked the same; she had expected her mirror to give back the image of an old, old woman. But the listening did not show. Neither did the coldness that had seeped into her bones and that nothing was ever going to dispel.

"Lucy," Chuck said thoughtfully. "Let's put it this way. I'd rather blackmail a murderer than marry one." He tapped the pocket where he had tucked her note. "No matter what it says here. Don't try to kid me. Lucy might have swallowed that bit about you being the guilty one, not her—That was the idea, I gather. You were getting Lucy off the hook, looking out for her the way you always do."

"That was not the idea. There was no idea. I told you before, it's just a piece of nonsense. I didn't know what I was doing." Her accordion of a heart. Somebody gave it another squeeze. And because Chuck knew it, he had her where he wanted her.

She swallowed. "You said I could take my time ..."

"Sure. Think it over. We ought to be able to work something out, between the two of us." There was warmth and eagerness in his voice. She realized the fantastic truth: he liked her; even now, he wanted her to like him and would do his best to help her figure some way of looking out for Lucy. They were still, in a sense, allies.

In a sense. Up to a point. "You're so good to me," she said. "How much time? Five whole minutes, maybe?" Gratifying response: his face reddened as if she had slapped him.

"I'll give you two days. Till Monday. That ought to do you. A smart babe like you. Take it or leave it."

There was nothing to do but take it. You could think a lot of thoughts in two days. Scheme a lot of schemes. Die a lot of deaths. No; not and be any use to Lucy. And that, after all, was the whole point; otherwise you wouldn't think of taking it, you would tell him to go to the police and the hell with it.

"Let's get it straight," she said wearily. "I have till Monday to think it over. After that, Lucy hears about it. One way or another."

"Right. It's up to you, how much of it she hears, and who she hears it from. You can play it to suit yourself. Tell her right now, if you want to—"

"No! Not until after I've talked to you again on Monday. You mustn't—"

"Don't worry about me. I won't be here to tell her. Not that I would, anyway. But I've been called out of town on this job, see. That leaves you to think in peace. I'll be back Monday, any time you say. We settle it then. No more stalling. And no funny business, either. Because I'm putting this—" Again he tapped his pocket—"in a nice safe place, along with a note of my own, just a few well chosen words in case anything should happen to me. I don't really think anything's going to. But you never know. A little insurance doesn't hurt. Oh yes, and the diary. So don't get any fancy ideas. They won't work. There. Does that cover everything?"

"It would seem so. You want the house signed over to you, you said?"

"That's all."

"There isn't much else, you know. Yes, of course you know. You must have checked."

"It's enough," he said. "I'm not greedy." The grin he flashed at her was, incredibly, the old engaging grin she remembered from their first meeting. When she had spotted him for a phoney and had liked him anyway.

She had a curious moment of seeing him as a small-time operator drawn, through chance and his own avarice, into a deal that was beyond his scope; he did not know how much beyond, and barged in blithely, trusting that luck would carry him through.

"Monday afternoon, then." It was almost as if she were warning him. "Here in the studio. Four o'clock." She would get Lucy out of the house on some pretext, while she and Chuck came to terms. And the office would have to limp along without her on Monday. She would be busy at home. Thinking.

XIV

"Like old times, isn't it," said Lucy. "Just the two of us, having Saturday night dinner together. The way we used to, B.C. You know. Before Chuck. That's how I think of it now. B.C. Before Chuck." She waited for the tiny spasm beside Marcia's mouth. Then she gave a tinkling laugh. "Silly, isn't it? But I guess everybody's a little silly when they're in love. Another roll, Marsh? While they're hot?"

"I haven't finished this one yet." Marcia crumbled another piece off her roll and raised it halfway to her mouth. Then she put it back on her plate. "They're very good."

"Delicious. Chuck should be here. He's so fond of them. But isn't it marvelous, this job that came through today? Even if it does take him out of town for a couple of days ... It's the one he's been hoping for, you know. We've both been keeping our fingers crossed. He probably told you, it means we can go to Bermuda for our honeymoon."

"No, he didn't tell me."

"I was so afraid it wouldn't come through. He's got his heart set on Bermuda, and I didn't see how I was going to wangle it without hurting his pride. Poor darling, he's terribly sensitive about money. We'd have had to call it a wedding present from you, or maybe Cousin Wilbur. Because he'd never touch a penny, if he knew it was my money ... You're so quiet, Marsh. Don't you feel well?"

"I'm all right. A little tired."

"Not enough sleep last night. Poor Marsh. And it's all my fault, for making such a fuss about that stupid diary. I declare, I don't know what possessed me! It could have been the end, for Chuck and me. Really. You were a lifesaver, Marsh. As usual. I can always count on you to straighten things out for me. The best sister anybody ever had." The spasm beside Marcia's mouth was more noticeable this time. Could she be pushed to the breaking point? Maybe. If she had enough drinks. But she was going very easy on the liquor, Lucy noticed, no doubt on guard against her own loosened tongue. And it was just as well: Lucy didn't want her to break down. At least not yet. Let them go on thinking she was a love-sick fool, completely taken in by their lies. Such sweet lies; Chuck's farewell this afternoon had been a masterpiece. Well, she was rather proud of her own performance. Just the right degree of diffidence when at last she had tapped on the studio door: Chuck darling, if you're busy I'll go away ... Oh Marsh, I wondered where you were, I thought you must have gone out. She had stood the test of that first searching glance from Marcia; had produced the right sounds of pride and joy at hearing Chuck's news about the job; had brushed aside the tear or two at parting ... How easy it was to lie. And how interesting to watch Marcia squirm.

She burbled on: "In a way I'm glad it happened. Last night, I mean. It taught me a lesson. I know now Chuck really loves me, I'll never doubt him again. And I got it all out of my system at last, about Pam and the diary. How I could ever have been jealous of Chuck and her! It was just one of those things, a passing infatuation. As for that crazy notion I had at first about Chuck trying to blackmail us—Well! You kept telling me it was crazy. Remember? Remember, Marsh?"

"I remember! Stop *chattering*, will you?" Marcia flung down her napkin and pushed back her chair.

The silence throbbed. Then Lucy said in a small voice, "I didn't realize I was boring you. Excuse me. I'll get the coffee."

When she came back Marcia was standing at the window. "Sorry," she said over her shoulder. "I didn't mean to blow up like that. Go ahead and chatter. You're entitled." No answer. She came back and sat down at the table. "Umm. Coffee smells good."

Still no answer. Lucy discovered that she could make her chin tremble at will.

"Oh, come on, Lucy. Forget it. I said I was sorry. You know how snappish I get when I'm tired."

Lucy gazed at her, large-eyed. Then she said gently, "It's all right. My fault. I should have seen it before."

"Seen what? What are you talking about?"

"I'm not blaming you, Marsh. It just never occurred to me, because always before it's been the other way round. I've been the one to be jealous of you."

"Jealous! You think I'm—Well, I'm not! I wouldn't have Chuck as a gift. Believe me."

"So that's what you think of him, is it! He's good enough for me, but not for you. I didn't get that impression at the beginning. You were the one that liked him. Long before I did. Now all at once you wouldn't have him as a gift."

Had she gone a little too far? Marcia's eyes were sparkling with genuine anger. "Listen, Lucy. This is absolutely ridiculous. You can like somebody without having *designs* on them, for gawd's sake! If I wanted Chuck for myself, would I have straightened things out for you last night? It's not the first time, either. Why, I've played Cupid practically from the start! And now you accuse me of—I've had it! I give up!" Again she flung down her napkin. This time she headed for the door.

"Marsh, please! Please, I take it back, I didn't mean it, apologize, I see now how silly—"

But Marcia saw her chance to escape and took it. She slammed off down the hall without answering.

This was what came of too much needling; the subject was likely to wriggle free. Temporarily free. So it didn't really matter. Lucy sat down again and sipped her coffee.

Jealousy. She thought of all the times she had envied Marcia, all the reasons. Marcia was afraid of so little; Lucy of so much. Scaredy-cat Lucy. Follow-the-leader Lucy, always trailing along just far enough behind to get caught ... But not blamed. No one ever mistook Lucy for the ringleader. That credit went to Marcia. Yet for all her trouble-making, she was Daddy's favorite; he took pride in her rebellious temper, even when—perhaps most of all when—it was directed against himself. Lucy he dismissed along with Mama. They were already subdued. No challenge there. Ah, how jealous she used to be of the fights Marcia had with Daddy! And then the beaus. Always a flock of them for Marcia; only Bernie for Lucy, who was supposed to be the pretty one. What good was pretty when she shrank back, abject and tongue-tied, at the sight of a boy? Except Bernie; and he, of course, had been promptly quashed. Well, Marcia's elopement with Al had been quashed too. But not Marcia herself. It was just an episode to her; she shrugged it off and went her merry way, staying out too late with this one, getting drunk with that one, slipping in and out of affairs as casually as she changed her shoes. Full-fledged affairs; Lucy, who for years had kept her eyes decorously closed to the fact, opened them now. The gentleman-caller level where Lucy still twittered and fluttered was to Marcia child's play. Literally. Since their early teens, long before she eloped with Al, there had been an aura of superior knowledge about Marcia. She hadn't been scared to explore the mystery; she knew about what Lucy thought of as "all that." So did practically everybody else. Except Lucy.

How they must have laughed at her behind her back, Marcia and Chuck; the two of them allied against her, just as she had always suspected. Always. Their easy way with each other, the jokes they shared, the suggestion of a secret understanding. It was there, all right, very likely in more ways than one. Marcia wouldn't have him as a gift. She said. Well, she probably wouldn't, now that he had gotten hold of her note and blossomed out into open blackmail. But before today ... Why not? She was shameless enough, they both were, to play a cynical love game of their own, even while they were conniving to marry Chuck off to Lucy. Yes, and to go on playing it if the marriage had gone through. What Lucy didn't know wouldn't hurt her.

But what they didn't know was going to hurt them. That she could guarantee, even though she hadn't yet worked out the details. This time the laugh was on them. Because their secret understanding was no longer secret, and they didn't know, they still thought of Lucy as the prize sucker, ready to believe anything they told her. Which was exactly the way she wanted things. It gave her—for once, for once—the upper hand, the chance to pay them back.

Elation flooded her. She could not sit still with such yeasty power working in her. It lifted her out of her chair and sent her skimming around the room. She began to laugh—silently at first, then out loud, in gusts that sounded like sobs.

Fortunately like sobs. Because suddenly the door opened and there was Marcia again: "What are you laughing about?"

Her hands flew to cover her face. "Laughing? I'm not, I'm ..." It was easy to fake a crying fit; Marcia had so often reduced her to tears. She sank down on the settee, head bent, shoulders heaving. "Please, Marsh, don't be mad at me. Of course you're not jealous of Chuck and me, I don't know why I said such a thing. Forgive me, Marsh ..."

After a minute Marcia said wearily, "Oh, skip it. Stop crying. I'm not mad at you." She administered one of her half-contemptuous little pats. "Come on, now, Lucy, it's not worth all this fuss. Forget it, and tell me what in the *hell* I did with my cigarettes, will you? They aren't upstairs, so they've got to be down here somewhere ..."

They were on the mantel. Lucy, still sniffling but helpful, found them. She was all right now, she said. And no, Marcia wasn't to help with the dishes. Lucy knew how tired she was, she was to go back upstairs and relax.

"So I'll be in a better humor tomorrow, you mean?" Marcia said, thus making her act of contrition. "Okay, dear. I'll try."

When she was gone, Lucy firmly suppressed the impulse to laugh again. It was too soon. The time for laughing would come later. Now she must think.

Think. Because there must be a way, a counter-proposal that would satisfy Chuck without completely demolishing Lucy. All she had to do was think of it. Marcia, her head ringing with the sleeping pills that hadn't worked, sat back on her heels and put down her trowel. The sun rested like a benediction on her shoulders. The roses smiled at her, the morning glory vine waved its tendrils, the ailanthus leaves danced. Help me, she implored her garden, for God's sake help me. But it was too much to ask. The pretty flower faces continued to nod, brainlessly cheerful. Her morning's work had kept her from going crazy. Period. She was as far as ever from the answer she had to find. Had to. Before tomorrow afternoon at four o'clock.

There it was again: old fever-and-chills time seizing her and tossing her from one hand to the other. She couldn't decide which was worse—the fever phase, when it wasn't enough time, four o'clock tomorrow was hurtling toward her with sickening speed; or the chills phase, when it was too much time, more than she could possibly endure.

Especially without a drink. Did she dare? It might help her to think. Since she wasn't doing any good the way she was—and let's face it, she wasn't—what did she have to lose? It would at least ease her misery for a few hours of the interminable hours that stretched between now and four o'clock tomorrow. That was the risk: it might ease her too much, she might disintegrate and spill the whole business to Lucy ahead of time, before she had sought out the answer, which must exist somewhere, in some hidden layer of her mind. But if she was very careful about how many drinks; after all, she didn't disintegrate quite that easily—

There was a caterpillar inching purposefully up the rose bush in front of her. A fuzzy fellow, like a miniature, mobile feather boa. But death on roses. She dislodged him and whacked him in two with her trowel.

Of course she didn't disintegrate that easily. It would take more liquor than there was in the house to make her tell Lucy before she absolutely had to. If she felt a talking jag coming on, she could simply turn and run, the way she had done last night. Better yet, she could avoid Lucy altogether, along with the rest of the human race. Hole up somewhere—His Nibs' room, Lucy seldom went in there—with a bottle for company and herself to talk to, if she had to talk. Talking was no use, anyway. What she had to do was think. Think.

Absently she scuffed some crumbs of dirt over the caterpillar. One of God's creatures. All right; but so were roses, and you had to make a choice. You had to accept the fact that some of God's creatures were no damn good. The law of rose-preservation, as basic as the law of self-preservation ...

She froze, like a dog pointing. Here it was, the way she had been hunting, the answer she had known must exist. Or at least a way, an answer. There was a difference. More than one way of skinning a cat. Many a question had more than just the one answer. Right?

Right. Because it wasn't the same thing, there was this world of difference. She had whacked the caterpillar automatically, without thinking. But a man, a fellow human being, even one who threatened to destroy your sister, root and branch ... Not to mention the practical considerations. The law of self-preservation wasn't the only one in operation. You didn't just scuff a few crumbs of dirt over a man and forget him.

She ought to know. She had been through this before. As she had pointed out to Chuck: "If we're the killers you think we are, what's to stop us from polishing you off?" Only this time it would be a solo performance. Count Lucy out. But completely out: she must have no hand in any of it, before, during or after. That was the whole point—to salvage something for Lucy out of the shambles that Marcia had made of their lives. If not love and marriage, then security and some remnant of her self-respect. Chuck was lost to her in any case. If you could call him a loss; and Lucy could. But not an unbearable loss, provided she did not know its true nature. She must somehow be left believing that he loved her to the end. As a matter of fact, such a loss would appeal to Lucy; it had the tragic-heroine touch.

But was it possible? There was Chuck's little bundle of insurance, put away in a nice safe place, just in case anything should happen to him. Marcia's note. (No problem there: it pointed to Marcia, not Lucy.) Pam's diary. (She still had a strong suspicion he was bluffing on that. The old opportunist making the most of Lucy's anxiety.) And a note of Chuck's own. (Which might very well point to her too, not to Lucy.)

It would be interesting to know exactly what well chosen words he had put into that note. She had a hunch that, dead or alive, Chuck would present himself in the best possible light. Blackmail wasn't precisely flattering, from any angle. It could be touched up, though. A few judicious strokes, and blackmail became a civic duty, the extortionist turned into an upright citizen bent on furthering the cause of justice. Yes, she would bet on it. There were no crass details like marrying for money or payment for silence in Chuck's note.

She had that much on her side, hers and Lucy's. Plus the fact that this time around there would be no nonsense about covering up either the murder or her own guilt. A plain, straightforward job: Get Lucy off the premises. Let him have it. Confess.

It was what she longed for, to confess, not only about Chuck—that would be obvious, anyway—but about the other left-over one, the murder-that-wasn't-a-murder except to her. Well, but it was she who counted. She was the one who had it hanging around her neck. She was the terminal case, with nothing to hope for but oblivion, the final darkness that would dissolve her, guilt and all. For her it was the only answer, as she had recognized the night she wrote the note.

If only she hadn't been stopped that night, or had at least had the sense to destroy the note, or ... Yes. If only she had seen yesterday what she saw now, and had whacked Chuck in automatic obedience to the law of self-preservation. It would have been the natural reaction. And look at the trouble it would have saved—no chance for Chuck to stash away his little bundle of insurance, no danger of Lucy's learning the whole crushing truth, no more tormenting problems for Marcia to work out. Why, once Chuck was out of the way, she could have sent herself rushing into the oblivion she yearned for, she could be dissolved by now!

But she had missed her chance. She didn't have the natural reactions; she had felt no impulse to whack Chuck. She felt none now. Which was her tough luck, because she was apparently going to have to do it anyway, and what was more, stick around afterwards to make sure Lucy didn't get tangled up in the loose ends.

Prison, she thought. They'll try me, they'll send me to the electric chair. Okay. Just so they don't *dawdle* about it.

Meanwhile, there were problems to work out. Oh brother, were there problems. In the first place—

"Hey there," called Mrs. Sully from the top floor window. "Okay if I borrow the step ladder? I'm cleaning the venetian blinds."

Well, that was life. Interruptions. Marcia went inside to open the basement door for her, and a couple of minutes later she came bouncing downstairs, pert as a robin in her shorts. And irritatingly sociable; Marcia's short, abstracted answers did not discourage her in the least. On the contrary, they seemed to spur her on to talk for two. Before Marcia knew what was happening, she had been chattered out into the garden again, and Mrs. Sully was rhapsodizing over the roses.

They were her favorite flowers, and Sunday was her favorite day of the week, and June was her favorite month of the year. Which made everything just great except for the venetian blinds, and probably they developed your character, like Latin, though if Chuck were around she'd be tempted to let her character stay stunted and get him to ...

In the first place—Marcia dropped Mrs. Sully's thread in favor of her own—there was the problem of method. It wasn't the same as picking up a trowel and whacking a caterpillar. It wasn't the same as His Nibs, either; there had been a lifetime of mutiny boiling in her then, and the pill, something impersonal about a pill. Especially with Lucy to hand it to him. But Marcia had thought of it, and that was what counted. Too squeamish to bash his head in. Not too squeamish to think of the pill. There wasn't any nice impersonal pill to think of for Chuck, so it would have to be—I can't, she thought frantically. Can't. Can't. I have to. There isn't any other way.

Mrs. Sully seemed to be asking her a question: "She's not back yet, is she?"

"Who?"

"Who? Well, Lucy, of course. I was just telling you, I met her earlier when she was on her way to church. That's how I know about Chuck being gone."

"Sorry, I'm in a fog today. No, she isn't back yet. Why?"

"Nothing," said Mrs. Sully, and blushed.

But Chuck himself might think of another way. We ought to be able to work something out, between the two of us, he had said. And, I got nothing against Lucy. It would be to his own advantage to think of a way, and he was bright enough to see it. Insurance or no insurance, he must be aware that if he pushed Marcia too far she might go berserk. What would she have to lose? Of course he was aware; he would be ready with a solution tomorrow, probably already had it figured out and was holding it in reserve.

"What?" she said, for Mrs. Sully looked as if she might have asked another question.

"I didn't say anything. It was just that Lucy—" Mrs. Sully swallowed, fidgeted, breathed deeply, and blurted: "It's too ridiculous, and I told her so. You like Chuck. Sure. For Pete's sake, so do I. Does that mean I'm jealous because he's going to marry Lucy? Of course not, and neither are you."

"Lucy told you I'm jealous?"

"Well. She hinted at it. Didn't I think you'd been acting funny lately, kind of on edge ... I didn't get it at first. But then she said she sometimes wondered if you could be upset about her and Chuck, and that's when I let her have it. After all! She shouldn't go around *talking* like that. Somebody might take her seriously. La Traviata, for instance. I mean Mrs. Travers. She'd eat it up."

"Yes, I suppose she would," Marcia said thoughtfully. Maybe the police would too? I did it out of jealousy, she might tell them. I wanted him for myself. I couldn't bear to have Lucy get him. But there was Chuck's little bundle of insurance, waiting to make a liar out of her. If she could somehow get her hands on it ...

"And what about Chuck?" Mrs. Sully's eyes flashed with indignation. "He wouldn't eat it up, of course. What he'd probably do, he'd probably decide Lucy was too sick in the head to bother with. And I wouldn't blame him!"

... or if she and Chuck together could concoct some story for Lucy, using this preconceived notion of hers as the basis ...

"I hope I convinced her," said Mrs. Sully, "but I'm not sure. That's why I'm telling you. Maybe she'll listen to you. Then again, maybe I'm just being a busybody." She paused. Poor child, she looked stricken. "But I like you, Marcia. Lucy too, of course. Believe me, I'm not trying to stir up trouble. Somebody ought to set Lucy straight for her own good."

"Yes. As you say, ridiculous. Absolutely ridiculous. Me jealous of Lucy and Chuck! Why, nothing could be farther from my thoughts. I wouldn't dream of trying to muscle in on her territory. Good Lord, she's my own sister! I've got some standards left, I hope. In a way, you know, it's funny." She produced, with no trouble at all, a tense, artificial laugh. "I mean, the idea that Chuck and I—It's terribly funny. Don't you think so? Don't you think it's a hilarious idea?"

"Well, I—" Mrs. Sully, bless her heart, was eyeing her doubtfully.

"Excuse me. I can't help laughing, it's so funny." She put her hands up to her face to stifle the laughter; through her fingers she observed Mrs. Sully observing her. More uneasily than before. "There. I'm all right now. I've stopped. Sorry, I'm really not myself today. I don't know what's the matter with me lately, I've been so on edge."

"Spring fever, or something," offered Mrs. Sully without much conviction. She remembered that she had come down for the ladder. That charming tell-tale face of hers! Marcia could read it like a book. Mrs. Sully was worried. She suspected they were both pretty sick in the head, Lucy and Marcia both. She was sorry she hadn't kept her mouth shut.

But Marcia was glad. Thanks to Mrs. Sully, she had the jealousy motif—it hadn't registered last night; trust Lucy, though, not to let go of a notion once she latched on to it—and surely there must be a way of using it. Surely, surely, it would give her another answer. All she had to do was think. Start again, with the jealousy business, and think. Think.

XV

"Yoo hoo," Lucy home from church, called cheerfully through the sitting room window. Marcia was out there in the garden. Not working. Not drinking. Not doing anything for once. Limp as a rag doll, she slumped in one of the canvas chairs, her legs in their faded dungarees stretched out, one motionless hand dangling almost to the flagstones. As if she were dead, thought Lucy, and she felt suddenly breathless.

But when she called again the long, elegant legs shifted and Marcia's head turned toward her. Her face was shockingly drawn, wrung dry of animation and color. Even her hair seemed to have lost its crisp vigor. Lucy stole a glance at her own face in the mirror, her astonishing face that still had not changed. The same soft, rather pretty effect, the same anxious-to-please expression.

"Are you all right, Marsh? You look kind of dragged out."

"Now that you mention it, that's how I feel. Do you suppose I'm coming down with something?"

Instantly Lucy went into a solicitous bustle. Temperature? Headache? Upset stomach? Sore throat? "I do hope it's not one of those mean summer colds." She pulled off her white gloves and stepped through the window to lay her hand against Marcia's forehead. She went to fetch the aspirin. Suggested hot soup and fruit juice. And rest. For of course that was the point; Marcia was laying the foundation for a day at home tomorrow, she wanted to be on hand when Chuck got back. What had they settled between themselves after Lucy stopped listening yesterday? Probably nothing definite. But Marcia must have succeeded in stalling him off till tomorrow. A couple of days grace to think it over and decide what she was going to do. As if she had any choice!

"Or look, Marsh, how about a drink? It might be just the thing. A drink and a good rest. Sleep it off, whatever it is."

After a brief mental struggle, Marcia gave in. "Oh well, why not? Please, Lucy, stop fussing! I'm not an invalid. I'm perfectly capable of pouring myself a drink." She looked better already; just the idea was enough to revive her.

So, on the surface, it was like many other Sunday afternoons they had spent together in the garden. Lucy made sandwiches, which she ate and Marcia didn't. But then she often drank her lunch on week ends.

There was the Sunday *Times* to glance through; as usual, Lucy couldn't resist reading bits out loud, though she knew it irritated Marcia.

"Listen to this, Marsh, they've got a new bird at the zoo, some rare kind of parrot from South America that—"

"Remember the way he used to handle the paper?" Marcia said dreamily. "So tidy. Even with one hand, while he was eating breakfast."

Lucy did not ask who. She sat still, staring at the cluster of newspaper at her feet and seeing Daddy, coffee cup in one band, *Times* firmly under control in the other. Super-imposed was that final mental image of his profile and Pam's, imperious, like heads stamped on a coin. The emperor and his mistress, setting off on their last trip.

"Crazy, isn't it?" said Marcia. "I miss him. I keep getting these little jolts. Expecting him to pop out of his office. Forgetting he won't be there for dinner. Do you?"

"Not very often. Not anymore."

"And you don't ever feel—guilty?" Marcia's eyes were shiny. The liquor, no doubt. But it wasn't like her to get maudlin.

"Of course not. For mercy's sake, Marsh, stop brooding about something that didn't happen."

"No. It didn't happen. Maybe it never would have. Maybe we never would have. Not really." Marcia leaned forward, as if she were snatching at the idea physically. But after a moment she sank back. "I would have. That must be the difference. You wouldn't have. But I would have. It was my idea, remember. Only fair that I should be stuck with it. God, am I stuck with it!"

"Nonsense," said Lucy. "The only thing you're stuck with is too many drinks on an empty stomach. And this cold or whatever it is coming on."

"That's right. I'm not well, am I? Not at all well. Matter of fact, I'm incurable. I've known it for some time. That's why I—" She caught her breath and darted a quick, scared look at Lucy.

"Why you what? What are you talking about?"

But Marcia had a grip on herself now. "It'll keep," she said lightly. "I'll tell you all about it some other time. I'll write you another letter. I mean, a letter." She gave an odd laugh.

"All right, if you want to be like that. If you won't tell me what's the matter ..."

"I don't have to tell you. According to Mrs. Sully, you've already got everything figured out."

"Mrs. Sully?" said Lucy. And then, hollowly, "Oh."

"That's right. Mrs. Sully. Oh. She told me all about your chat this morning. You ought to know better than to confide in a candid little camera like her."

"I ought to know better than to say such things to anybody!" Lucy cried. "I don't know why I did it, I didn't mean to, it just—Oh, Marsh, I don't blame you for hating me. It was awful of me."

"That's what Mrs. Sully said. Somebody might take you seriously, she said." But Marcia's tone was curiously detached. It wasn't like last night. She was only pretending to be angry. "And who knows, maybe somebody might."

"But I don't even believe it myself! Not really. And of course Mrs. Sully didn't believe it, she told me exactly how silly—"

"So did I, last night," Marcia pointed out. "But then I would. She's such a nice, normal creature, Mrs. Sully. A good one to try it out on. I suppose that's what you were looking for. Reassurance. Somebody besides me to tell you it was silly."

"What must she think of me!"

"She thinks we're both kind of crazy. A couple of maniacs, that's us." Marcia grinned and stood up. "Skip it, Lucy. What the hell, what difference does it make if I've got a secret yen for Chuck? My problem. Excuse me while I take to my bed. Remember, I'm a very sick woman."

She weaved a bit, going in through the window. More pretending, like the anger? It crossed Lucy's mind. And something else came to her, when she was alone. A clicking into place of stray facts: the goodbye note they had talked so much about yesterday, the expensive piece of nonsense that Chuck was threatening to take to the police, something Marcia had started to write one night when she was drunk and disorderly in her mind ... I'll write you another letter, she had said just now, and then the way she had laughed, so odd, and the scared look in her eye, as if she had realized, in the nick of time, how close she was to revealing more than she meant to ... The guilty feeling that she was stuck with, God, was she stuck with it ...

So that was it, thought Lucy. A suicide, confession note. Unfinished but damning. Trust Marcia to start such a note and stop in the middle, to tell the truth when it would be discreet to lie and vice versa, and then—oh, this was the typical Marcia touch—to let it fall into Chuck's hands, exactly where it would do the most damage. Out of carelessness or recklessness, it didn't matter which, Marcia had plenty of both. All her life she had insisted on courting disaster. Well, now it was hers, and she wasn't satisfied with throwing just herself over the precipice; she wanted to drag Lucy along with her. Only this time she wasn't going to get her way.

The long, long game of follow-the-leader was over. It had ended yesterday at the listening post in the basement where, now that Lucy thought of it, loving Daddy had also come to an end. They were both of a piece, Marcia and Daddy. She had wasted her life on them, blindly trusting, and they had played her false. Chuck, too. All of them.

The afternoon sun spilled down, warm on her cheek, but inside, in her bones, she was impervious; nothing could reach that core of coldness. Her mind, too, was cold, and very busy. Presently, when all the stray pieces were fitted into place and she could see the pattern they made, she gathered up the lunch dishes and went inside. She would have liked to laugh. But that was another lesson she had learned yesterday. The gusts of exultant laughter stayed inside, along with the coldness.

Monday morning. Marcia woke—yes, she had actually slept, and for hours, precious, irreplaceable hours when she should have been thinking—to the patter of rain against the window. A pleasant sound. So many pleasant things in the world, if you didn't count the people. Including yourself. Especially yourself.

Very softly, the door opened, and Lucy peeped in. "Marsh? You awake?"

Here we go again. People. "Time is it?" she croaked.

"It's nine. I let you sleep because—"

"Nine! I'm late, I'll be late to the office." She sat up. Her head jarred. "Oh my," she said feebly.

"—because it's out of the question for you to go to the office today." Illness, especially Marcia's, always brought out an officious streak in Lucy. Oh well, she didn't often get a chance to be the boss. And anyway, it suited Marcia's purpose. "Weather like this, pouring rain, and you with a cold coming on. You want to get pneumonia? I'll call the office."

She insisted on bringing Marcia's coffee to her in bed. Which would have been all right except that she settled down with a companionable cup of her own and a gush of cheerful bedside conversation. "Cozy, isn't it? I love the house on rainy days. Well, sunny days too, of course. I suppose I just love the house period. I can't imagine living anywhere else. Can you?"

Sure. A desert island would be great. Or a nice empty cave. Untouched by human hands. Marcia mumbled something that must have sounded like agreement, because Lucy prattled on.

"Isn't it lucky Chuck feels the same way? He does, you know. It's the kind of old-fashioned house he's always wanted to live in, as far back as he can remember. He was enchanted with it, the minute he saw it, and isn't it lucky? I mean, supposing I'd fallen in love with somebody that hated fireplaces and high ceilings, somebody that insisted on moving to one of these ultra-modern, mass-production apartments—Why, I'd be miserable. I simply don't think I could stand it." Her shallow blue eyes grew round with alarm. Was there a glint of something else, something like malice? Impossible; she couldn't know that she was needling Marcia. She was like a child, telling herself ghost stories for the fun of the fake shivers. "But there. I don't have to stand it, do I? I don't know why I'm going on like this ... Poor Marsh, you do look pale. Maybe I ought to call Dr. Berman."

"Now don't start that," snapped Marcia. "I've got you fussing over me, and that's enough. I can't take Dr. Berman too." Silence. Lucy's chin quivered. "I mean, he's such an old woman!"

"I am too, I suppose. Just because I worry about you—"

"Well, you shouldn't. A slight cold, for Lord's sake, and right away I'm on the critical list. As long as I've got the strength to be cranky you don't need to worry. You ought to know that."

Lucy obliged with a small laugh. Poor dear, so easily wounded, and—ordinarily—so quickly comforted. But it was no ordinary wound that threatened her now, and Marcia's power to comfort would be wiped out along with Lucy's trust in her. Marcia's throat closed up; in the middle of raising her coffee cup to her lips she suddenly set it down again.

"Not hot enough?" Lucy asked at once. "I can reheat it. Or maybe you'd like some fresh?"

"No, no, it's not that. I just—" She cleared her throat desperately. "I just now remembered. We're due at O'Conner's office this afternoon. You know, about the estate. Those little legal oddments he's been stewing over."

"Not today. Tomorrow. Tuesday."

"Didn't I tell you? I meant to. He called me at the office Friday and switched it to today. Something's come up, he can't make it tomorrow. He'll have a fit if we put it off again."

"But Marsh, you can't go paddling downtown in the rain, feeling the way you do! I'll call and—"

"Wait. Maybe by four-thirty it'll clear up and I'll be okay. That's when he said, four-thirty. I was going to nip out of the office early." She paused, seeming to consider, and went on glibly. "You could go, anyway, even if I don't."

"But Chuck's coming back this afternoon! Besides, Mr. O'Conner always mixes me up, all that legal language, I'm so stupid about it—"

"Sure, so am I. We don't have to be bright, that's what we have him for. He knows what he's doing, even if he doesn't speak English ... I forgot about Chuck. Oh, me. No telling when O'Conner can work us in if we don't show up today. He's out of town so much in the summer. But there, I'm sure I'll be all right by four-thirty. I'll go. I don't mind a bit, going by myself." Bravely she ignored the fit of coughing that seized her. "A little rain won't hurt me. I'm not really sick. I'll go, and get it over with."

It worked (thank God) like a charm: Lucy sprang to defend her title as chief martyr. Marcia was not budging out of the house today, and that was that; she, Lucy, would cope with Mr. O'Conner, and never mind Chuck. After all—she clinched the matter with a radiant smile—she was going to spend the rest of her life with him, so what did an hour or two matter? As a matter of fact, if she left a little early it would give her time to stop in at that shell shop right around the corner from Mr. O'Conner, a fascinating place ...

She suspected nothing, why should she? When she turned up at Mr. O'Conner's office and found it was all a mistake, the appointment for tomorrow had never been changed, she would be puzzled and annoyed. Later, perhaps, she might be grateful for the alibi Marcia was providing for her. Whatever happened with Chuck, Lucy would be in the clear. That was the first step: to get her out of the house so that Marcia could negotiate with Chuck. Or try to. And if negotiation failed, it was Marcia's problem, and hers alone. Lucy, safely off on her wild goose chase, could have no possible hand in its solution.

Which was as far off now as it had been yesterday. Face it, face it. You don't know what you're going to do, you still have no plan, the jealousy motif has led you nowhere, you're counting on him to solve it for you. He might. He won't. Why should he?

"You're shivering," Lucy said. She began twitching at the blanket. "There. Now you snuggle down and go back to sleep. I'll be downstairs if you need anything. Don't get out of bed, just bang on the floor and I'll hear you."

She bustled off. The rain tapped at the window, and from the street below came the hiss of traffic on wet pavement. Time sifted away.

A couple of hours later, when she crept downstairs in her robe and slippers, the house seemed hushed to her, like an empty church. Had Lucy gone out? She was not in the sitting room; Marcia paused briefly at the window to look out at the drenched roses and shrunken morning glories. The kitchen too was empty. Very tidy: breakfast dishes washed and drying in the rack, refrigerator purring, pilot light gleaming. Lucy must have gone out. A quick trip to the grocery, probably to get something for Marcia's lunch. Calves foot jelly or something.

So Marcia had chosen the right time. Very shrewd of her. Her hand was clenched on the set of keys in her pocket. That was another shrewd move, to bring her keys; Lucy was apt to carry her set around with her. Now it was a simple matter of choosing her weapon and planting it in the studio where it would be handy if she needed it. When she needed it. She might as well cut out this wishful thinking right now and be realistic; she was going to need it. And why should she boggle at Chuck, when she had already crossed the line (his phrase came back to her) three months ago? Yes. What she had plotted then and never carried out made what she was going to do today inevitable. Once you crossed the line you couldn't ever get back to where you were before. You were committed to murder. No use bucking it.

Premeditation, she thought in a detached way, and noiselessly opened the drawer of the cabinet. The choice of weapons was hers. She removed the short-handled carving knife; it fits nicely into the pocket of her robe. Then she went quickly down the hall to the studio. The key made no sound turning in the lock. The carpet muffled her footsteps as she crossed to what was now Chuck's living room. The door stood open. Inside the smell of stale cigarettes hung in the ghostly, rainy-day twilight. They would have their interview here this afternoon. And she would sit in this chair. She slipped the knife under the seat cushion and turned to go.

A sound came from the direction of the dark room. A clatter. Not loud, but magnified by the surrounding silence. It was not her imagination, it came again. More curious than alarmed—after all, the knife was safely out of sight—she went over and opened the door. Lucy whirled, her hand at her throat in classic startled pose.

"Marsh! What in the world—"

Yes. What in the world? The answer rolled out, glib and ready-made. "I was looking for you. I couldn't imagine where you were."

"But you're not supposed to be out of bed! You were going to pound if you wanted anything."

"I didn't want anything, really. I just felt like getting up ..." There was a chemical smell, a clinical kind of light from the one silver-coated bulb. It was reflected in the row of bottles on the shelf above the metal trays. Six bottles lined up, according to size, like stairsteps. Lucy's face was a pale blob against the shadows. "Don't look so scared. What are you doing in here, anyway?"

"Just tidying up a little. I usually do, you know, and Chuck's getting back this afternoon, I wanted to make sure the place wasn't a mess. I'm not scared. I didn't hear you till you opened the door, that's all."

"Lucy. You're not still on that diary-hunting kick."

"Well, I should hope not! How stupid do you think I am? I know, pretty stupid. But we got that all straightened out the other night. Besides, Chuck got rid of the diary, he burned it up. Really, Marsh!"

"Forget it. It was just a passing thought." And a mistaken one: of course Lucy was bright enough not to repeat a performance that had all but wrecked her dream of love. There was another of those accordion squeezes in Marcia's chest as she turned again to the living room. "You've finished tidying in here, haven't you?"

"All through." The light clicked off, and Lucy came out too. "I'll just open the window so it will air out. There ... Honestly, Marsh, are you sure you ought to be out of bed?"

"I'm tired of bed. And I feel quite a lot better. I'm even a little hungry."

Which was a lie, but it sent Lucy into a pleased flurry of suggestions: Soup? Toast? A poached egg? And food would help to pass the time.

There was nothing to do, now, but wait for Chuck to get back.

XVI

What a stroke of luck, thought Lucy, that her own departure for Mr. O'Conner's office should coincide with Mrs. Travers' dog-walking expedition! Perfect timing: here was a ready, and more than willing witness to the fact that Lucy had left the house at a little after three, when Chuck was not yet back. But then she had been lucky all the way, she had even managed to get through that appalling moment in the dark room with her mission accomplished and Marcia none the wiser. The tidying-up explanation had sprung to her lips with almost embarrassing ease. An accomplished liar, as the saying went, with only a couple of days' experience.

Mrs. Travers was walking not only Chrys and Mum, but the Sullys' Cherie as well. "They've gone to Jersey for the day," she reported. Another stroke of luck for Lucy; she wanted a witness for only a selected few, not all, of her comings and goings. "And poor Cherie suffers from car sickness—yes, we have a delicate tummy, haven't we?—so she's having her little outings with us today." The combination of snubs from the Pekinese and syrup from their mistress seemed too much, even for Cherie's effervescent spirit; she hardly bounced at all.

It was not actively raining at the moment. In the mild gray air the little tree in front of the house looked vividly green, and the puddles in the sidewalk shone like mirrors. On their way to the corner together, Lucy told all about Marcia's illness, Chuck's imminent return, the appointment with Mr. O'Conner that had to be kept, such a nuisance, she'd much rather stay home, especially with Chuck due back, but at least it gave her a chance to poke around in this enchanting shell shop ...

Mrs. Travers said archly, "Are you sure it's safe to trust Marcia and Chuck together? I've sometimes wondered if she might not like him pretty well herself."

"I wouldn't say this to everybody, but so have I. Just once in a while. And of course at first I took it for granted that she was the one he liked. It never entered my head it could be *me*."

"Modesty," put in Mrs. Travers. "You're very pretty, dear."

"Then when I found it was me, had been from the start—Well! No, I'm not worried." She let her laugh ring out, happy and confident. "I know I can trust Chuck. I think a woman can always tell, don't you? when it's the real thing."

"Indeed I do." Mrs. Travers exuded tender, female wisdom. "Like Mr. Travers and I. I never had a moment's doubt. Anyway, Lucy, I was only teasing. I didn't mean it *seriously*."

They parted, on a sustained note of gush, at the corner—Mrs. Travers and her charges for a waddle around the park, Lucy ostensibly for the subway. She did set off in that direction. Several times she looked back to check on Mrs. Travers' progress, which was even more impressive than usual, what with Cherie and all those plastic raincoats. Ridiculous old creature, thought Lucy. But useful. At the end of the next block, she doubled back, so as to approach the house from the rear. Ordinarily this could not be done; it was possible now—her luck again—because the buildings directly behind their house had been torn down and the new construction was not yet under way. It was not likely that Marcia or anyone else would notice her making her way through the rubble and nipping in by way of the basement door. She had an explanation in case she needed it. The same explanation she intended to use on Chuck and Marcia when—if she was not spotted now—she would burst in, breathless and exasperated: I forgot my *wallet!* Can you imagine! I got all the way to the subway and discovered I was penniless ... Chuck darling, you're back!

Naturally it would be a rapturous reunion. And naturally she would put off her second departure for Mr. O'Conner's office; why waste time in a shell shop when she could spend it with her beloved instead? Her two beloveds: Chuck and Marcia. It wouldn't take long, half an hour at the most. Once more she ran through the one-two-three routine that she had mapped out for herself and that she must be able to do automatically, whether her mind happened to be working or not. One tiny oversight could mean ruin. This time when she left she would take pains not to be seen by Mrs. Travers or anyone else who mattered. Since the switch in appointments was of course phoney—poor Marcia, such a transparent liar—she didn't have to make it by four-thirty. Fifteen minutes later would do just as well; no one was going to contradict her. Just so Mr. O'Conner or his secretary or someone was there to confirm her visit. They would all puzzle over how such a mix-up could have happened. Oh well, no great harm done, she could come back tomorrow. She and Marcia. (She must remember to put it that way.) Then the return trip home—where she would make her shocking discovery, report it, and collapse.

I can be a recluse, she thought exultantly. I can shut myself away from all of them. No more loving, no more trusting, no more being betrayed. I'll be safe. No more people. Just me, snug and invulnerable in my very own house where no one can get at me. I can shut them out forever. On account of my tragic love affair. It will get to be a kind of legend—how I once had a sweetheart, only my sister wanted him for herself and rather than let me have him she ...

The basement, which used to fill her with such childish dread, now seemed to her the heart of the house, the place where everything began. She felt at home in its chilly gloom. Her rubber-shod feet made only a whisper of sound as they carried her across the cement to her listening post. She had left Marcia upstairs, taking a therapeutic hot bath before she crawled back into bed. Which of course she had no intention of doing. Another one of her transparent lies for Lucy's benefit. She might already be dressed and downstairs, waiting for Chuck. Ready for him? Don't be ridiculous. Marcia never really planned things out in advance. She counted on her occasional flashes of inspiration to carry her through. This time even she must have a premonition that there might not be any miracle flash—yes, Lucy had seen the glaze of fear in her eyes—but she was still incapable of plotting a course of action and sticking to it. As Lucy was doing.

Oh, she was ready for any eventuality. If Marcia, having spotted her return, called down the stairs, she was prepared with her forgotten-wallet excuse. And after that she was prepared to stall till Chuck got back. A run in her stocking, a broken shoulder strap, something in her eye. Though it was obvious by now that Marcia had not seen her, she was not going to have to stall.

Good. She preferred it this way, waiting here for the sound of Chuck's arrival. He would be punctual, probably ahead of schedule, eager for his showdown with Marcia. Well, Lucy was eager too.

Presently she heard a door open and shut above her. Then foot-steps: Marcia taking up her stand in Chuck's living room. She had put on high heels for the occasion; a typical Marcia gesture. Maybe she had some fuzzy notion of charming him back into line. Ha! One thing sure, she wasn't easy in her mind. The heels tapped nervously, almost frantically, back and forth across the floor. Marcia was like Daddy, she hated waiting for anything. Even for disaster.

Patience, Lucy told those restless clicking heels. All in good time. There was just enough light for her to make out the hands of her watch; it was three-thirty. She checked to make sure she still had the little bottle. She too had dressed for the occasion, in her full skirt with the patch pockets. Yes. There. Ready. Everything under control.

She felt excited but poised. She leaned against the familiar dankness of the wall and waited for her cue.

Old Father Time, still up to his fever-and-chills tricks. The fever phase of hurry-hurry had seized Marcia while she was dressing (no need to look beaten, even if you were); now she was stuck with the slow, creeping chills. Twenty-five minutes yet. Unless the clock had stopped, which it had not, it was clicking its tongue at her, busy as a bird dog. She made another trip across Chuck's living room. And back.

He wouldn't be late? No, he wasn't cruel, just greedy. And shrewd, don't forget, shrewd enough to see that he'd better help save something out of this mess for Lucy if he wanted to save his own precious skin. Because that was what it amounted to, and there was the knife under the seat cushion to prove it.

The trouble was that right now there wasn't anything to do. It was all done, everything she could think of, at least: Lucy out of the way (she had thank God swallowed the O'Conner business), Marcia herself chic in her good old basic black, you could dress it up, dress it down, suitable for any occasion, including murder. Ready for action, spoiling for it, in fact. She had never been any good at waiting.

Across the room again. And back. His Nibs used to hold forth here, crisp in his white jacket, too crisp for some people's taste. If they wanted soothing bedside manners let them find another doctor. Odd, though, he had been good with children, surprisingly patient. And fun. Oh, when she was a little girl she had thought he was such fun, her handsome father who was so proud of her ... What would he have prescribed for her present condition? She knew, all too well. Nothing to be done, he would have said curtly. The disease has already advanced too far for treatment. A terminal case. Next patient.

I don't know what else you expected, he might have added as a parting shot, getting mixed up with riffraff, turning my offices over to a fifth-rate photographer. Lucy of course; but I thought you'd have better sense.

The door to the dark room stood ajar. She pushed it open, just to be doing something, and clicked the light on and off a few times. Acid smell, gleam of metal, glassy wink from the row of six bottles on the shelf—No, five, she must have counted wrong this morning. She closed the door and leaned against it, fighting a sudden, strong impulse to scream. She won. She always had, so far.

It was twenty-one minutes to four. Twenty-one and a half. All right, what was half a minute one way or the other? Just a middle-sized eternity, that was all. Not to be confused with olives, which came only in colossal and super-colossal, or with sugar, which came in fine, superfine, and extra super-fine ...

Now, now, that was enough of that. A drink would be nice, she thought wistfully, but it wasn't permitted. She had already had her quota. She lit a cigarette and inspected her mascara in Chuck's mirror. You're ravishing, Marcia. Too, too divine.

Was that the front door opening? She listened, transfixed. Sure it was. It was Mrs. Travers and company, making more than the usual hullabaloo. Yelps, admonitions and toenail clickings, all punctuated by the measured, majestic tread of Mrs. Travers' feet. The procession wended its way up the stairs. There. Silence again.

She made an unnecessary trip to the bathroom. Then she went into the front studio and looked out the window at the wet street. He had found a parking place right in front of the house and was just getting out of the car. Seeing her, he waved. The next moment he came bounding in, friendly as a puppy. How engaging his grin was, how candid his expression, how natural his greeting: "Hi, Marsh, you look great. I'm ahead of time, hope you don't mind. What a day! Nice weather for ducks."

She was shaking hands with him—actually!—before she could stop herself. When she pulled away violently, he looked a little hurt, as if he could not imagine why. But it didn't take him long to recover. "Well, here we are," he said cheerfully, when he had followed her into the living room and shrugged out of his raincoat. "Sit down, make yourself comfortable. I take it Lucy isn't around?"

"She's gone out for an hour or so. That ought to give us time."

"Sure. Fine. How about a drink?"

"No, thanks." He was standing in front of her chair; for a moment their two facades—hers cool and brittle, his jaunty—slipped, and their eyes locked in something curiously like commiseration.

He asked the question first. "You got something figured out?"

"Not completely. Call it a glimmer."

"That's the ticket. Me too. Looks like we're in business."

She could not help it, she felt comforted. And hope soared in her; he would back down on his demands, admit he had been bluffing, together they would find a way out of their crazy predicament. Because no matter how hard he tried, he was simply not a monster. He was only a sharp little guy who had stumbled into the big time and would be glad to get out while he was still ahead of the game.

All the same, she must be cautious. "That remains to be seen," she said. "It takes two to make a deal. Three if you count Lucy."

"I thought you were so anxious to keep her out of it. Did you change your mind and tell her, after all?"

"Certainly not. But she has to be considered. More than anyone, really."

"If you say so." He sat down on the couch and faced her with his alert terrier air. "This glimmer of yours. It's got something to do with Lucy?"

"Well, yes. It's an angle I didn't think to mention when we were having our little chat the other day." Oh, she must be very cautious, she must not let him know how flimsy an angle. "Matter of fact, you probably—"

The front door slammed. There was a rush of approaching footsteps, and Lucy's breathless voice: "Chuck! Chuck darling, you're back! I saw your car ..." She rushed in, starry-eyed; at sight of Marcia she stopped short. "Marsh? But you're supposed to be in bed!"

"I revived," said Marcia drily. "How about you? You're supposed to be on your way to O'Conner's."

"The stupidest thing, I forgot my *wallet!* Can you imagine? Got all the way to the subway before I realized, and there I was, without a cent ... Chuck darling, how are you?"

Marcia went over to the window and fiddled with the venetian blind till they got through their tender moment. Give Chuck credit, he was carrying it off with considerable style, though he had been caught as much off balance as Marcia. He had actually looked embarrassed for a split second. Give him credit for that too, she supposed. Typical of Lucy to come popping in like this; she had a gift for the inopportune. Though on second thought ... No, not so inopportune, after all. Here was fresh kindling to keep her suspicions going; Marcia, miraculously restored to health and decked out in time to greet Chuck; obviously making a play for him. Those suspicions might come in very handy, from Marcia's point of view.

Only she was in for another nerve-wracking spell of waiting. Lucy would stick around now until the last possible moment. And if Marcia was all this revived, why shouldn't she be expected to go along to

O'Conner's? Oh Lord, she might have to fake a relapse. She produced an experimental cough.

"There," Lucy cried at once, "you're still coughing, Marsh. Are you sure you're warm enough? She's such a difficult patient, Chuck. I gave her strict orders before I left, and she doesn't pay the slightest attention. The minute my back is turned here she is flashing around downstairs as if there wasn't a thing wrong with her. I just wish Daddy was here. He'd make her toe the line."

"Too bad he isn't." Chuck sent an impish glance in Marcia's direction. "No kidding, I've often wished I'd had the chance to meet him. I've got a feeling I would have liked him."

"Well, let me tell you, it wouldn't have been mutual," said Marcia shrewishly. "You ought to be damn glad he's not here. You'd be bounced out of here so fast you wouldn't know what hit you."

"Why, Marsh, what a thing to say!" Lucy protested. "Even if it were true—"

"It is. Out with him, honorable intentions and all." She got a bitter enjoyment out of seeing Chuck flush. All right, he had started this little game of darts; he was going to get as good as he gave. "Oh, I can just hear His Nibs! 'Who is this fellow, anyway? A nobody, a two-bit picture-taker moving into my house, taking over my office! He's got a feeling he'd like me, has he? Of all the unmitigated gall!' That would be just the beginning. He'd go on from there."

"Only he isn't here to say anything, is he?" said Chuck pleasantly. "As it happens. So that makes him even more of a nobody than me."

A moment of silence, while Lucy's eyes made worried little trips from one of them to the other. "Don't. Please. How did we get started on this? I mean—"

"Never mind," said Marcia. "I'll behave. I didn't realize Chuck's feelings could be hurt so easily."

"Who, me? I've got a hide like an elephant."

But she had gotten under it. Something else: she had found out that, if she had to, she could use the knife. Not automatically, not like the caterpillar; but in a flash of rage. Because he had gotten under her skin, too, the brash little punk, with his patronizing crack about liking His Nibs. If they had been alone, that would have been the moment. She needn't worry about her own faltering resolution. The knowledge brought a sudden, exhilarating lift to her heart. She and Chuck exchanged one of their comradely grins.

Reassured, Lucy was burbling along: "There now, why don't we go in the sitting room and have a drink or something? Chuck's back, we ought to celebrate." She tucked her arm in his and flickered her eyelashes. "Isn't it lucky, I allowed time for the shell shop, I won't have to leave for twenty minutes or so ..."

"I already offered Marcia a drink and she turned me down."

"A cup of coffee, then. I'd love one myself. Just the thing on a rainy afternoon, and it won't take me a minute to fix it. Come on, Marsh, good for your cold." She was already urging Chuck along toward the door; with a helpless shrug Marcia followed. After all, it shouldn't be too much of a trick to get Chuck back here for their postponed confab. She thought yearningly of a drink. No, it would have to be coffee. Maybe one small, quick shot after Lucy left, to keep her nerve at the right level.

How touchingly pleased Lucy was with her impromptu coffee party, bustling around like a happy child! "No, Marsh, I'll fix everything, you and Chuck sit down and be nice to each other while I'm in the kitchen. You might just switch on the table lamp, Chuck dear. Oh, I do love this room. Don't you? So cozy. My favorite room in my favorite house, and my two favorite people in it." She paused, slender and girlish in her full skirt, her eyes shining.

If she was posing a little (and she was; she couldn't resist stealing a glance at herself in the mirror) there was no real harm, only the sorry embarrassment of seeing a grown woman go through these charming-child antics. Into Marcia's mind there sprang the memory of a long-ago nursemaid, something she used to say: *What are you up to, Lucy? You're acting just too sweet to be true ...*

The clock chimed four, startling Chuck, who had been engrossed in the study of his own feet. His glance at Marcia was involuntary, his smile wan and short-lived. "Well. Four o'clock," he said.

"I can count too. But thanks, anyway."

They sat, once more becalmed. Fifteen minutes more, possibly twenty; Lucy wouldn't care if she was late for the O'Conner appointment. Her two favorite people came first. *What are you up to, Lucy?*

Here she was, pushing through the swinging door with a tray: cream and sugar, a plate of cookies, dainty embroidered napkins, the silver spoons engraved with her name. "Another five minutes for the coffee," she told them. "You're so quiet, you two! Is this your way of being nice to each other? We're having a party, not a funeral!"

Chuck mumbled something about companionable silence. Help, aid, succor, thought Marcia, and went over to the window. "It's stopped raining," she reported. Well. Inanity was infectious; a well-known scientific fact.

A party, not a funeral. That was what Lucy thought. It came to her that she was having her last look at her garden. The roses would go on blooming, without her to see; she would never know whether the nasturtiums did well or not, or what color the phlox turned out to be. She had nothing else to say goodbye to, only her garden, this little patch of prettiness that she had not only created but somehow managed not to destroy. The good deed in her naughty world. And she was entitled to her fancies: why shouldn't she imagine, if it pleased her, that her garden was weeping goodbye to her? The flagstones glistened with wetness, the grass was achingly, poignantly green, raindrops trembled like unshed tears among the rose petals.

She unlatched the window and started to step through. Behind her Chuck said, "Hey. Where you going?" They were alone again; Lucy had gone back to the kitchen.

"I want my yellow rose."

"Let me. I'll get it for you."

"Don't do me any favors," she said. And then, passionately, "It's my garden. You don't belong in it."

The air outside was moist, mild, sweet-smelling. A little shower of drops spattered down on her hair from the ailanthus tree as she bent to pick the rose. She tore off the stern between two ruddy-tinged thorns; it was a perfect rose, its inner petals still unfurled. She held its freshness against her cheek. Sweet. Sweet.

Too sweet to be true. What are you up to, Lucy?

She turned and looked into the kitchen window. Lucy was framed there in profile, between the sheer, looped-back curtains. She was busy setting out the cups and saucers. What absorption in the line of her bent head, with its gently curving forehead and over-refined nose! Her lower lip was caught between her teeth; a pathetic little second chin was creased in below the first one. When she had the cups arranged on the tray to suit her, she unplugged the percolator. Now she would pour ...

What she did instead had no meaning for Marcia at first. She watched in simple curiosity as Lucy fumbled in the pocket of her skirt, brought out a little bottle, opened it, and shook something into two of the cups. She was very quick about it. The bottle was recapped and back in her pocket before Marcia's mind began to interpret what her eyes had recorded. Once started, there was no stopping it. It was as if someone had pushed the plunger on a pinball machine; a precise, complicated pattern of one click setting off another until the final whirring bong.

Poison. Lucy means to poison Chuck and me.

She had no recollection of moving, but here she was in the sitting room, adding her farewell rose to the bouquet on the mantel piece, saying in an undertone to Chuck, "Don't tell Lucy I was out there. She'd fuss, on account of my cold."

It would have been a nice ironical twist, though: Lucy worrying over the state of Marcia's health while she served her that cup of coffee. But then the irony had been there all day, unseen by Marcia. Yesterday too. And Saturday night: Lucy had known then, she must have overheard their conversation, she really had been laughing when Marcia surprised her ... A great little actress. As Marcia should have remembered from her performance with Simmy that night months ago. And who had come close to cracking when Dr. Berman turned up with the news about His Nibs? Not Lucy, not Lucy. But Marcia had chosen to forget whatever did not fit her mental image of Lucy as a defenseless child, cry-baby, scaredy-cat Lucy forever following the leader. To forget or, even more cavalierly, to ignore: Lucy needling her; Lucy planting the jealousy-motif seeds in little Mrs. Sully's mind; Lucy in the dark room, caught in the very act of snitching the bottle of poison, yes, that was where it came from, didn't photographers use something-or-other, cyanide, for touching up? Irony again: Chuck providing the means for his own death.

So much surer and easier than the knife under the chair cushion, which was all Marcia had been able to think of, and which she might never have brought herself to use.

"Listen, Marsh," Chuck was whispering, "don't look at me like that. We can work something out. Believe me ..."

Believe him. There wasn't time, and even if there had been—Work something out, the man says. His innocently avaricious eyes saw nothing beyond the surface. Money. The good old green stuff. He didn't know what it was really about; he would die still not knowing.

Marcia, on the other hand, had known from the beginning, when she and Lucy first crossed the line. Oh, Lucy had crossed it too; the only difference was that, unlike Marcia, she refused to admit the fact of their guilt. We didn't do it, we only planned it ... Yes, and from then on they had been stuck with it (and with each other); they had committed themselves to murder—if not their father then someone else. Somebody, somebody must die.

Chuck must, it seemed. And Marcia. Well, but wasn't that more or less as she herself had planned it? A prompt death for Chuck; a postponed one for her, to make sure that Lucy stayed in the clear, with something, not much but something, salvaged from the ruins. So why should she object to Lucy's solution, which guaranteed a quick death for her as well as Chuck? She had resigned from life some time back, the night she started that note to Lucy. (And didn't finish. And forgot to destroy.) So why ...

"Here we are," Lucy said gaily, coming in with her tray. She set it down on the table beside the cream and sugar. Wisps of steam rose from the fragile cups. "I'm sorry, it took longer than I expected, but I know you both like it strong, so that's how I made it. What's a few minutes extra? Mr. O'Conner can just wait."

... Because, for one reason, it probably wouldn't work. There were too many loose ends for Lucy to get tangled up in. Even if Chuck's little bundle of insurance didn't trap her, there was Hansen waiting his chance ... And no Marcia to look out for her. She could never in the world pull it off by herself. Didn't she understand that she was stuck with Marcia no matter how much she might hate her? And she did. Oh, how Lucy must hate!

"Don't get up, Chuck darling," she was running on, in her bright, false voice. "I know what everyone takes. Cream and two sugars for you, cream and one sugar for me, nothing for Marsh. I'll bring it to you. Really. I want to."

Hate. The way she had hated Hansen when she went for him with the poker. And even then, Marcia had clung to her delusion that Lucy was somehow exempt from responsibility. In her way, she too had refused to admit the fact of *their* guilt. Hers, she had insisted. But it was theirs, not hers alone, Lucy's too, share and share alike. For the first time in her life she saw her sister as an equal. Lost as Marcia was lost. Beyond saving. No hope for either of them. That was the real reason Lucy's solution was no good. Somebody must die, yes. But not somebody irrelevant like Chuck.

"Thanks," she said as Lucy set her cup down on the little table at her elbow. "I think I'll let it cool a minute."

"Yes, do. Wait for Chuck and me. We'll drink a toast. Shall we?"

The right solution was so obvious, and surely not impossible, even with so little time left. At the prospect of action she felt the old irrepressible lifting of her heart. Of course not impossible.

She waited until Lucy was setting out the other two cups, hers and Chuck's, on the coffee table beside the settee. He was already there, waiting for Lucy to sit down beside him.

"Damn!" Marcia said, snapping her fingers in exasperation. She sprang out of her chair and started for the door. "I just remembered, I meant to shut the studio door behind me when we came in here, but you know, I don't think I did, and you may not have noticed, Lucy, but the front door was on the latch ... I'll just check, they shouldn't be left open, should they?"

She paused, and Chuck, good boy, leapt to his feet. "Let me. I'll check. Hold everything."

She was even luckier than she had hoped: Lucy followed him and watched from the door as he sprinted down the hall. Her back was to Marcia—overconfidence, it never paid—and Marcia was standing beside the coffee table, within easy reach of the two pretty little cups that looked the same but weren't.

It couldn't have been easier, the quick, silent switch. She went over and watched beside Lucy while Chuck tested the studio door which, what do you know, she really had forgotten to shut, and the front door, which was also on the latch. A final dividend of luck.

They were back in their places, smiling at each other. "A good thing you remembered," Chuck said.

"Yes, isn't it?" A better thing than he realized; he would never know what a favor she had just done him. To him it would seem like a lousy break, and just when he thought he had it made—the house his, or at least a nice little wad of dough, and then whammo! Every damn nickel down the drain, right back where he started. That was life for you. At least the cops couldn't pin anything on him; he had everything to lose, nothing to gain ... Oh well, pick up the pieces and start over again.

Lucy sighed blissfully. "A toast," she said. "To us."

"To us," Chuck echoed, and Marcia too, though she let her glance stray to the mantel and her farewell rose.

They lifted their cups and drank.

THE END

Jean Potts Bibliography (1910-1999)

Mystery Novels:

Go, Lovely Rose (1954; winner Best First Novel Edgar Award)
Death of a Stray Cat (1955; reprinted in omnibus as Dark Destination, 1955)
The Diehard (1956)
The Man With The Cane (1957)
Lightning Strikes Twice (1958; reprinted in the UK as Blood Will Tell, 1959)
Home Is the Prisoner (1960)
The Evil Wish (1962; finalist Best Novel Edgar Award)
The Only Good Secretary (1965)
The Footsteps on the Stairs (1966)
The Trash Stealer (1968)
The Little Lie (1968)
An Affair of the Heart (1970)
The Troublemaker (1972)
My Brother's Killer (1975)

Mainstream Novel:

Someone to Remember (1943)

Short Stories:

The Lady Afraid (*Woman's Home Companion*, Feb 1942)
The Other Woman (*Collier's*, Aug 24, 1946)
Restless Redhead (*Liberty*, Feb 1948)
The Box of Apples (*McCall's*, March 1949)
A Family Affair (*McCall's*, Nov 1949)
The Bracelet (*McCall's*, Dec 1951)
The Heart Must See (*McCall's*, Apr 1952)
The Engagement Ring (*Thrilling Love*, Oct 1952)
Let's Start All Over Again (*American Magazine*, Apr 1953)
The Girl He Didn't Marry (*Woman's Day*, Jan 1954)
A Long Day's Journey (*Cosmopolitan*, July 1954)
The Ideal Gift (*Family Circle*, Oct 1956)
The Withered Heart (*Ellery Queen's Mystery Magazine*, Feb 1957)
Murderer # 2 (*Alfred Hitchcock's Mystery Magazine*, Jan 1961)
Just Like Jessica (*Redbook*, Feb 1963)
The Only Good Secretary (*Cosmopolitan*, July 1965)
The Inner Voices (*Ellery Queen's Mystery Magazine*, Apr 1966)
In the Absence of Proof (*Ellery Queen's Mystery Magazine*, July 1985)
Two on the Isle (*Ellery Queen's Mystery Magazine*, Jan 1987)
The Lady Macbeth Case (*Ellery Queen's Mystery Magazine*, Nov 1990)